T0359869

Special EDITION

Believe in love. Overcome obstacles. Find happiness.

Dog Days Of Summer
Teri Wilson

A Small Town Fourth Of July
Janice Carter

MILLS & BOON

DOG DAYS OF SUMMER
© 2024 by Teri Wilson
Philippine Copyright 2024
Australian Copyright 2024
New Zealand Copyright 2024

First Published 2024
First Australian Paperback Edition 2024
ISBN 978 1 038 91070 7

A SMALL TOWN FOURTH OF JULY
© 2024 by Janice Hess
Philippine Copyright 2024
Australian Copyright 2024
New Zealand Copyright 2024

First Published 2024
First Australian Paperback Edition 2024
ISBN 978 1 038 91070 7

MIX
Paper | Supporting
responsible forestry
FSC® C001695

Published by
Harlequin Mills & Boon
An imprint of Harlequin Enterprises (Australia) Pty Limited
(ABN 47 001 180 918), a subsidiary of HarperCollins
Publishers Australia Pty Limited
(ABN 36 009 913 517)
Level 19, 201 Elizabeth Street
SYDNEY NSW 2000 AUSTRALIA

Cover art used by arrangement with Harlequin Books S.A.. All rights reserved.

Printed and bound in Australia by McPherson's Printing Group

Dog Days Of Summer
Teri Wilson

MILLS & BOON

USA TODAY bestselling author **Teri Wilson** writes heartwarming romance for Harlequin Heart. Three of Teri's books have been adapted into Hallmark Channel original movies, most notably *Unleashing Mr. Darcy*. She is also a recipient of the prestigious RITA® Award for excellence in romantic fiction and a recent inductee into the San Antonio Women's Hall of Fame.

Teri has a special fondness for cute dogs and pretty dresses, and she loves following the British royal family. Visit her at www.teriwilson.net.

Dear Reader,

Surprise, and welcome to Bluebonnet, Texas! Would you believe that I've lived in Texas my entire life, and this is the very first time I've written a miniseries set in my home state? *Dog Days of Summer* is officially my twenty-seventh book for Harlequin, so I figured it was time. Also, I had a ball writing my last book, *Fortune's Lone Star Twins*, which is part of the legendary Fortunes of Texas series and obviously set right here in the Lone Star State. So I decided to create my own town in the Texas Hill Country. Bluebonnet is full of small-town charm, swoony heroes and dogs.

Lots and *lots* of dogs.

Dog Days of Summer is the first book in my new Comfort Paws series, featuring stories about therapy dogs and the relationships that spring up around them. This series is really meaningful to me, personally, because I do volunteer pet therapy with my dog Charm. I've been involved with this sort of volunteer work for many years. In fact, my first therapy dog was a golden retriever named Nellie, and she was my inspiration for Lady Bird in *Dog Days of Summer*.

I hope you enjoy this romantic journey with Maple and Ford!

Happy reading,

Teri

DEDICATION

For our special friends
at Juniper Village Lincoln Heights
and Northwood Elementary School

xoxo Teri and Charm

Chapter One

So this was Texas.

Maple Leighton wobbled in her Kate Spade stilettos as she stood on a patch of gravel across the street from the Bluebonnet Pet Clinic and fought the urge to hotfoot it straight back to New York City. What was she even doing here?

You're here because you sold your soul to pay for veterinary school.

A doctor-of-veterinary-medicine degree from a top-rated university in Manhattan didn't come cheap, especially when it was accompanied by a board-certified specialty in veterinary cardiology. Maple's parents—who were both high-powered divorce attorneys at competing uptown law firms—had presented a rare, united front and refused to fund Maple's advanced degree unless she followed in their footsteps and enrolled in law school. Considering that her mom and dad were two of the most miserable humans she'd ever encountered, Maple would've rather died. Also, she loved animals. She loved them even more than she loathed the idea of law school. Case in point: Maple had never once heard of animals clawing each other's eyes out over visitation rights or who got to keep the good wedding china.

Especially dogs. Dogs were always faithful. Always loyal. And unlike people, dogs loved unconditionally.

Consequently, Maple had been all set to plunge herself into tens of thousands of dollars of student-loan debt to fulfill her dream of becoming a canine heart surgeon. But then, like a miracle, she'd been offered a full-ride grant from a tiny veterinary practice in Bluebonnet, Texas. Maple had never heard of the clinic. She'd never heard of Bluebonnet, either. A lifelong Manhattanite, she'd barely heard of Texas.

The only catch? Upon graduation, she'd have to work at the pet clinic for a term of twelve months before moving on to do whatever her little puppy-loving heart desired. That was it. No actual financial repayment required.

Accepting the grant had seemed like a no-brainer at the time. Now, it felt more like a prison sentence.

One year.

She inhaled a lungful of barbecue-scented air, which she assumed was coming from the silver, Airstream-style food truck parked on the town square—a *literal* square, just like the one in *Gilmore Girls*, complete with a gazebo right smack in its center. Although Bluebonnet's gazebo was in serious need of a paint job. And possibly a good scrubbing.

I can do anything for a year, right?

Maple didn't even *like* barbecue, but surely there were other things to eat around here. Everything was going to be fine.

She squared her shoulders, pulled her wheeled suitcase behind her and headed straight toward the pet clinic. The sooner she got this extended exercise in humiliation started, the sooner it would be over with.

Her new place of employment was located in an old house decorated with swirly gingerbread trim. It looked like a wedding cake. Cute, but definitely not the same vibe as the sleek glass-and-steel building that housed the prestigious veterinary cardiology practice where Maple was *supposed* to be working, on the Upper West Side.

She swung the door open, heaved her bag over the threshold and took a glance around. There wasn't a single person, dog, cat, or gerbil sitting in the waiting room. The seats lining the walls were all mismatched dining chairs, like the ones in Monica Geller's apartment on *Friends*, but somehow a lot less cute without the lilac walls and quirky knickknacks, and Joey Tribbiani shoveling lasagna into his mouth nearby. The celebrity gossip magazines littering the oversize coffee table in the center of the room were so old that Maple was certain the couple on the cover of one of them had been divorced for almost a year. Her mother had represented the wife in the high-profile split.

I turned down my dream job to come here. A knot lodged in Maple's throat. *Could this* be *any more of a disaster?*

"Howdy, there."

Maple glanced up with a start. A woman with gray corkscrew curls piled on her head and a pair of reading glasses hanging from a long pearl chain around her neck eyed Maple from behind the half door of the receptionist area.

"Can I help you, sweetheart?" the woman said, gaze snagging on Maple's shoes. A furrow formed in her brow, as if the sight of a patron in patent-leather stilettos was somehow more out of place than the woefully outdated copies of *People*.

Maple charged ahead, offering her hand for a shake. "I'm Dr. Maple Leighton."

A golden retriever's tawny head popped up on the other side of the half door, tongue lolling out of the side of its mouth.

"Down, Lady Bird," the woman said, and the dog reluctantly dropped back down to all fours. "Don't mind her. She thinks she's the welcome committee."

The golden panted and wagged her thick tail until it beat a happy rhythm against the reception desk on the other side of the counter. She gazed up at Maple with melting brown eyes. Her coat was a deep, rich gold, as shiny as a copper penny, with the feathering on her legs and underside of her body that goldens were so famous for.

Maple relaxed ever so slightly. She could do this. Dogs were dogs, everywhere.

"I'm June. What can I do for you, Maple?" the receptionist asked, smiling as benignly as if she'd never heard Maple's name before.

It threw Maple for a moment. She hadn't exactly expected a welcome parade, but she'd assumed the staff would at least be aware of her existence.

"Dr. Leighton," she corrected and pasted on a polite smile. "I'm here for my first day of work."

"I don't understand." June looked her up and down again, and the furrow in her brow deepened.

Lady Bird's gold head swiveled back and forth between them.

"Just one second." Maple held up a finger and then dug through the vast confines of her favorite leather tote— a novelty bag designed to look like the outside of a New York pizza parlor, complete with pigeons pecking at the sidewalk—for her cell phone. While June and Lady Bird cocked their heads in unison to study the purse, Maple scrolled quickly through her email app until she found the most recent communication from the grant committee.

"See?" She thrust the phone toward the older woman. The message was dated just over a week ago and, like every other bit of paperwork she'd received about her grant, it had been signed by Dr. Percy Walker, DVM. "Right here. Technically, my start date is tomorrow. But I'd love to start seeing patients right away."

What else was she going to do in this one-horse town?

June squinted at Maple's cell phone until she slid her reading glasses in place. Then her eyes went wide. "Oh, my."

This was getting weird. Then again, what wasn't? She'd been in Bluebonnet for all of ten minutes, and already Maple felt like she'd landed on a distant planet. A wave of homesickness washed over her in the form of a sudden craving for a street pretzel with extra mustard.

She sighed and slid her phone back into her bag. "Perhaps I should speak with Dr. Walker. Is he here?"

June went pale. "No, actually. I'm afraid Dr. Walker is…unavailable."

"What about the other veterinarian?" Maple asked, gaze shifting to the old-fashioned felt letter board hanging on the wall to her right. Two veterinarians were listed, names situated side by side—the familiar Dr. Percy Walker and someone named Dr. Grover Hayes. "Dr. Hayes? Is he here?"

"Grover?" June shook her head. "He's not in yet. He should be here right shortly, but he's already got a patient waiting in one of the exam rooms. And I really think you need to talk to—"

Maple cut her off. "Wait a minute. We've got a client and their pet just sitting in an exam room, and there's no one here to see them. How long have they been waiting?"

June glanced at an ancient-looking clock that hung next to the letter board.

"You know what. Never mind," Maple said. If June had to look at the clock, the patient had already been waiting too long. Besides, there was a vet in the building now. No need to extend the delay. "I'll do it."

"Oh, I don't think—" June began, but then just stood slack-jawed as Maple swung open the half door and wheeled her luggage behind the counter.

Lady Bird reacted with far more enthusiasm, wagging her tail so hard that her entire back end swung from side to side. She hip-checked June and nearly wiped the older woman out.

Someone needs to train this dog, Maple thought. But, hey, at least that wasn't her problem, was it? Goldens were sweet as pie, but they typically acted like puppies until they were fully grown adult dogs.

"Where's the exam room?" Maple glanced around.

June remained mum, but her gaze flitted to a door at the far end of the hall.

Aha!

Maple strode toward the door, stilettos clicking on the tile floor as Lady Bird followed hot on her heels.

June sidestepped the rolling suitcase and chased after them. "Maple, this really isn't such a good idea."

"Dr. Leighton," Maple corrected. Again. She grabbed a manila folder from the file rack hanging on the back of the exam-room door.

Paper files? Really? Maybe she really could make a difference here. There were loads of digital office-management systems specifically designed for veterinary medicine. Maybe by the time her year was up, she could successfully drag this practice into the current century.

She glanced at the note written beside today's date on the chart. *Dog seems tired.* Well, that really narrowed things down, didn't it?

There were countless reasons why a dog might be lethargic. Some serious, some not so worrisome at all. She'd need more information to know where to begin, but she wasn't going to stand there in the hall and read the entire file folder when she could simply go inside, look at the dog in question and talk to the client face-to-face.

A ripple of anxiety skittered through her. She had zero

problem with the dog part of the equation. The part about talking to the human pet owner, on the other hand…

"Dr. Leighton, it would really be best if we wait until Grover gets here. This particular patient is—" June lowered her voice to a near whisper "—rather unusual."

During her surgical course at her veterinary college in Manhattan, Maple had once operated on a two-headed diamondback terrapin turtle. She truly doubted that whatever lay behind the exam-room door was something that could shock her. How "unusual" could the dog possibly be? At minimum, she could get the appointment started until one of the other vets decided to roll in to work.

"Trust me, June. I've got this." Maple tucked the file folder under her arm and grabbed hold of the doorknob. "In the meantime, would you mind looking into my accommodations? Dr. Walker said they'd be taken care of, but I didn't see a hotel on my way in from the airport."

She hadn't seen much of anything from the back seat of her hired car during the ride to Bluebonnet from the airport in Austin, other than wide-open spaces dotted with bales of hay.

And cows.

Lots and *lots* of cows.

"Dr. Walker…" June echoed, looking slightly green around the gills. She opened her mouth, as if to say more, but it was too late.

Maple was already swinging the door open and barreling into the exam room. Lady Bird strutted alongside her like a four-legged veterinary assistant.

"Hi there, I'm Dr. Leighton," Maple said, gaze shifting from an elderly woman sitting in one of the exam-room chairs with an aluminum walker parked in front of her to a much younger, shockingly handsome man wearing a faded denim work shirt with the sleeves rolled up to his elbows. Her attention snagged on his forearms for a beat.

So muscular. How did that even happen? Swinging a lasso around? Roping cattle?

Maple's stomach gave an annoying flutter.

She forced her gaze away from the forearms and focused on his eyes instead. So blue. So *intense*. She swallowed hard. "I hear your dog isn't feeling well this morning."

There. Human introductions out of the way, Maple could do what she did best and turn her attention to her doggy patient. She breathed a little easier and glanced down at the animal, lying as still as stone on the exam table and, thus far, visible only in Maple's periphery.

She blinked.

And blinked again.

Even Lady Bird, who'd muscled her way into the exam room behind Maple, cocked her head and knit her furry brow.

"I, um, don't understand," Maple said.

Was this a joke? Had her entire interaction at this hole-in-the-wall practice been some sort of weird initiation prank? Is this how they welcomed outsiders in a small town?

Maybe she should've listened to June. How had she put it, exactly?

This particular patient is rather unusual.

A giant, Texas-size understatement, if Maple had ever heard one. The dog on the exam table wasn't just a little odd. It wasn't even a dog. It was a stuffed animal—a child's plush toy.

And Cowboy Blue Eyes was looming over it, arms crossed and expression dead-serious while he waited for Maple to examine it as if it was real.

Don't say it.

Ford Bishop glared at the new veterinarian and did his

best to send her a telepathic message, even though telepathy wasn't exactly his specialty. Nor did it rank anywhere on his list of abilities.

Do not *say it.*

Dr. Maple Leighton—she'd been sure to throw that *doctor* title around—was definitely going to say it. Ford could practically see the words forming on her bow-shaped, cherry-red lips.

"I don't understand," she repeated. "This is a—"

And there it was.

Ford held up a hand to stop her from uttering the words *stuffed animal.* "My grandmother and I prefer to see Grover. Is he here?"

"No." She lifted her chin a fraction, and her cheeks went as pink as the blossoms on the dogwood trees that surrounded the gazebo in Bluebonnet's town square. "Unfortunately for both of us, Grover is out of the office at the moment."

"That's okay. We'll wait," Ford said through gritted teeth and tipped his head toward the door, indicating she should leave, whoever she was.

Instead, she narrowed her eyes at him and didn't budge. "I'm the new veterinarian here. I'm happy to help." She cleared her throat. "*If* there's an actual animal that needs—"

"Coco isn't eating," Ford's grandmother blurted from the chair situated behind where he stood at the exam table. "And she sleeps all day long."

As if on cue, the battery-operated stuffed animal opened its mouth and then froze, exposing a lone green bean sitting on its fluffy pink tongue. There was zero doubt in Ford's mind that the bean had come straight off his grandmother's plate during lunch at her retirement home.

Dr. Maple Leighton's eyes widened at the sight of the vegetable.

Lady Bird rose up onto her back legs and planted her paws on the exam table, clearly angling to snatch the green bean for herself.

"Down, Lady Bird," Ford and Maple both said in unison.

The corners of Maple's mouth twitched, almost like she wanted to smile…until she thought better of it and pursed her lips again, as if Ford was something she wanted to scrape off the bottom of one of those ridiculous high-heeled shoes she was wearing. She'd best not try walking across the cobblestone town square in those things.

Her forehead crinkled. "You know Lady Bird?"

"Everyone in town knows Lady Bird," Ford countered.

Delighted to be the topic of conversation, the golden retriever opened her mouth in a wide doggy grin. This time, Maple genuinely relaxed for a beat. The tension in her shoulders appeared to loosen as she rested her hand on top of Lady Bird's head.

She was clearly a dog lover, which made perfect sense. She was a vet. Still, Ford couldn't help but wonder what it would take for a human being to get her to light up like that.

Not that he cared, he reminded himself. Ford was just curious, that's all. Newcomers were somewhat of a rarity in Bluebonnet.

"Can I speak to you in private?" he said quietly.

Maple lifted her gaze to meet his and her flush immediately intensified. She stiffened. Yeah, Maple Leighton definitely preferred the company of dogs to people. For a second, Ford thought she was going to say no.

"Fine," she answered flatly.

Where on earth had Grover found this woman? She had the bedside manner of a serial killer.

Ford scooped Coco in his arms and laid the toy dog into his grandmother's lap. She cradled it as gently as if it was a newborn baby, and Ford's chest went tight.

"I'm going to go talk to the vet for just a minute, Gram.

I'll be right back. You take good care of Coco while I'm gone," he said.

"I will." Gram stroked the top of the dog's head with shaky fingertips.

"This will only take a second." Ford's jaw clenched. *Just long enough to tell the new vet to either get on board or get lost.*

He turned, and Maple had already vacated the exam room. Lady Bird, on the other hand, was still waiting politely for him.

"Thanks, girl," Ford muttered and gave the dog a scratch behind the ears. "Keep an eye on Gram for me, okay?"

Lady Bird woofed. Then the dog shuffled over to Ford's grandmother and collapsed into a huge pile of golden fur at her feet.

"Good girl." Ford shot the dog a wink and then stepped out into the hall, where Maple stood waiting for him, looking as tense as a cat in a roomful of rocking chairs.

It was almost cute—her odd combination of confidence mixed with an aching vulnerability that Ford could somehow feel deep inside his chest. A ripple of…something wound its way through him. If Ford hadn't known better, he might have mistaken it for attraction.

He crossed his arms. "You okay, Doc?"

"What?" She blinked again, as if someone asking after her was even more shocking than finding a fake dog in one of her exam rooms. Her eyes met his and then she gave her head a little shake. "I'm perfectly fine, Mr.…."

"Ford."

She nodded. "Mr. Ford, your dog—"

"Just Ford," he corrected.

Her gaze strayed to his faded denim work shirt, a stark contrast to the prim black dress she was wearing, complete with a matching black bow that held her dark hair in a thick ponytail. "As in the truck?"

He arched an eyebrow. "Dr. *Maple* Leighton, as in the syrup?"

Her nose crinkled, as if being named after something sweet left a bad taste in her mouth. "Back to your 'dog'..."

Ford took a step closer to her and lowered his voice so Gram wouldn't hear. "The dog isn't real. Obviously, I'm aware of that fact. Coco belongs to my grandmother. She's a robotic companion animal."

Maple took a few steps backward, teetering on her fancy shoes in her haste to maintain the invisible barrier between them. "You brought a robot dog to the vet because it seems tired. Got it."

"No." Ford's temples ached. She didn't get it, because of course she didn't. That hint of vulnerability he'd spied in her soulful eyes didn't mean squat. "I brought my grandmother's robotic companion animal here because my gram asked me to make the dog an appointment."

"So you're saying your gram thinks Coco is real?"

"I'm not one-hundred-percent sure whether she truly believes or if she just *wants* to believe. Either way, I'm going with it. Pets reduce feelings of isolation and loneliness in older adults. You're a vet. Surely you know all about that." Ford raked a hand through his hair, tugging at the ends. He couldn't believe he had to explain all of this to a medical professional.

"But Coco isn't a pet." Maple's gaze darted to the exam-room door. "She's battery-operated."

At least she'd had the decency to speak in a hushed tone this time.

"Right, which is why Grover usually tells Gram he needs to take Coco to the back room for a quick exam and a blood test and then he brings the dog back with fresh batteries." He threw up his hands. "And we all live happily ever after."

"Until the batteries run out of juice again." Maple rolled her eyes.

Ford just stared at her, incredulous. "Tell me—does this pass as compassion wherever you're from?"

"I'm from New York City," she said, enunciating each syllable as if the place was a foreign land Ford had never heard of before. "But I live here now. *Temporarily.*"

Ford's annoyance flared. He wasn't in the mood to play country mouse to her city mouse. "As much as I'd love to take a deep dive into your backstory, I need to get back to Gram. Can you just play along, or do we need to wait for Grover?"

"Why can't you just replace the batteries when she's not looking? Like, say, sometime before the dog gets its mouth stuck open with a green bean inside of it?"

"Because Gram has been a big dog lover her entire life and it makes her feel good to bring her pet into the vet. She wants to take good care of Coco, and I'm not going to deny her that." He let out a harsh breath. "No one is."

Maple just looked at him as if he was some sort of puzzle she was trying to assemble in her head.

"Are you going to help us or not?" he finally asked.

"I'll do it, but you should know that I'm really not great at this sort of thing." She pulled a face, and Ford had to stop himself from asking what she meant. Batteries weren't all that complicated. "I'm not what you would call a people person."

He bit back a smile. Her brutal honesty was refreshing, he'd give her that. "Could've fooled me."

"There are generally two types of doctors in this world—general practice physicians, who are driven by their innate need to help people, and specialists, who relate more to the scientific part of medicine," Maple said, again sounding an awful lot like she was talking to someone who'd just fallen off a turnip truck.

If she only knew.

"Let me guess. You're the latter," Ford said.

Maple nodded. "I have a specialty in veterinary cardiology."

"Got it. You love dogs." It was a statement, not a question. "People, not so much."

She tilted her head. "Are we talking about actual dogs or the robot kind?"

Ford ignored her question. He suspected it was rhetorical, and anyway, he was done with this conversation. "June can show you where Grover keeps the batteries. I'll go get Coco."

"Fine," Maple said.

"I think the words you're looking for are *thank* and *you*." He flashed her a fake smile, and there it was again—that flush that reminded Ford of pink dogwood blossoms swirling against a clear, blue Texas sky.

"Thank you." She swallowed, and something about the look in her big, brown doe eyes made Ford think she actually meant it.

Maple and her big-city attitude may have gotten themselves clear across the country from New York to Texas, but when she looked at him, *really* looked, he could see the truth. She was lost. And he suspected it didn't have much to do with geography.

She turned and click-clacked toward the lobby on her high heels.

"One more thing, Doc," Ford called after her.

Maple swiveled back toward him. "Yes? Is there a teeny tiny robotic mouse in your pocket that also needs new batteries?"

Cute. Aggravating as hell, but cute.

"Welcome to Bluebonnet."

Chapter Two

If Maple had been the type to get teary-eyed, the way Ford's Gram reacted once Coco was back up and running might've made her crack. The older woman was as thrilled as if Maple had breathed literal life into her ailing little dog, and she promptly ordered Ford to get Maple a pie from someplace called Cherry on Top as a thank-you gift.

But Maple wasn't the type to cry at work, not even when his gram called her "an angel sent straight from heaven." So she averted her gaze and focused on the jar of dog treats sitting on the counter in the exam room until her eyes stopped stinging. All the while, Lady Bird nudged her big head under Maple's right hand, insisting on a pat. The dog was relentless.

As for the pie, Maple wasn't holding her breath.

"So long, Doc." Ford held the door open for his grandmother and escorted her out of the clinic without so much as a backward glance.

Maple sagged with relief once they were gone. She wasn't sure why the pang in her chest felt so much like disappointment.

She rubbed the heel of her hand against her breastbone, ignoring the way Lady Bird's soft gaze bore into her as if the dog could hear Maple's thoughts. Still, it was unsettling.

She turned her back on the dog to home in on June, still

stationed behind the reception desk. "Do we have any more patients waiting to be seen? *Live* ones, that is?"

"I tried to warn you," June insisted as she replaced a jumbo-size pack of size C batteries in one of the overhead cabinets above her desk. "And no, we don't have any more patients waiting. But it looks like someone is here to see you."

June's gaze darted over Maple's left shoulder, toward the tempered glass window in the front door. Maple's heart thumped in her chest as visions of pie danced in her head. *Stop it*, she told herself. *What is wrong with you?*

Bluebonnet was small, but not small enough for Ford to have already procured a baked good and made his way back to the clinic. Also, she didn't want to see him again. Ever, if she could help it.

She followed June's gaze and caught sight of a red-faced man marching up the front step of the building's quaint covered porch. Again, no animal in sight—just a middle-aged human with salt-and-pepper hair and an angry frown that Maple felt all the way down to her toes.

Before she could ask June who the man was, he burst through the door and stalked toward Maple. He looked her up and down, jammed his hands on his hips and glanced at June. "Is this her?"

"Yes, sir," June said.

Lady Bird, clearly unable to read the room, wagged her tail and panted as she danced circles around the cranky visitor.

Actually, he wasn't technically a visitor, as Maple realized when she spotted the monogrammed initials stitched onto his shirt collar—*GH*, as in Grover Hayes. Oh, joy.

"You must be Dr. Hayes." Maple stuck her hand out for a shake. "I'm Dr. Leighton."

"So I gathered." He narrowed his gaze at her. "Unfortunately, the first I'd heard of you was when June called me a little while ago to tell me that a complete and total stranger had insisted on treating Coco in my absence."

In Maple's defense, the only reason she'd taken over the appointment was because he'd been late. Still, this didn't seem like the time to point out his breach in professional etiquette.

She'd come all this way. Today had been *years* in the making. How was it possible that Percy Walker, DVM, hadn't informed a single other person at this practice that she was starting work this week? It just didn't make sense. The practice had paid tens of thousands of dollars for her education, and not a single other person here knew who she was?

"I don't understand." Maple shook her head.

"That makes two of us," Grover huffed.

"I have years' worth of emails, some as recent as a week ago. If we could just talk to Dr. Walker, I'm sure we can clear all of this up." Maple took a deep breath. The sooner Percy Walker materialized, the better. "Do you know when he's going to be in? Technically, my start date isn't until tomorrow. I came by the office because I just got to town, and I was ready to hit the ground running."

She glanced toward her suitcase, still sitting behind the reception desk like a fly floating belly-up in someone's soup. "Plus, I'm not sure where I'm staying. Dr. Walker said my accommodations in Bluebonnet would be taken care of by my grant."

Now that Maple was saying all of this out loud, she realized it sounded a little off. She'd just flown across the country to a strange town in a strange state with no idea where she might be staying. For all she knew, Percy Walker was an internet catfish.

Except catfish didn't ordinarily fund someone's higher

education, did they? Didn't catfishing usually work the other way around? Even so, either of Maple's lawyer parents probably would've been delighted to point out a dozen red flags after looking over the simple one-page contract she'd signed when she'd accepted the grant.

Which was precisely why she'd never shown it to them.

"I'm afraid Dr. Walker won't be coming in." Grover went even stonier faced, a feat that Maple wouldn't have thought possible if she hadn't witnessed his near transformation into an actual gargoyle with her own two eyes. "Ever."

Maple blinked, even more alarmed than when she'd walked into the exam room to find a fake dog on the table. "Ever?"

"Ever," Grover repeated.

What was going on? Had her one and only contact at Bluebonnet Pet Clinic gotten fired? Resigned?

In either case, did this she mean she could go back to New York now? Could she really be that lucky? Maple felt a smile tugging at the corners of her lips.

"Dr. Percy Walker passed away eight days ago. The funeral was yesterday morning," Grover said.

And just like that, the smile wobbled off Maple's face. "What?"

Passed away, as in *dead*. Now what? Was she free to grab her suitcase and get on the next plane back to New York? As heavenly as that sounded, it just didn't seem right.

Of course. June chose that moment to oh-so-helpfully chime in, "For the record, I tried to tell you that too, Maple."

Dr. Leighton. Maple swallowed. She didn't bother correcting the receptionist this time. What was the point?

"Wait a minute." Every last drop of color drained from

Grover's face as he regarded her with a new wariness. "Your first name is Maple?"

She nodded. "Yes. Maple Leighton, DVM."

"Why didn't you tell me this?" Grover's gaze flitted toward June. Lady Bird's followed, as if the golden was trying to keep up with the conversation.

Good luck, Maple thought. She could barely keep up with it herself.

"She *really* prefers to be called Dr. Leighton," June said, peering at Maple over the top of her reading glasses.

Maple had worked long and hard for that degree. Of course, she wanted to be called "Doctor," although perhaps she shouldn't have been so eager to correct June. Clearly, no one here cared a whit about her veterinary degree. Inexplicably, all Grover seemed interested in was her first name.

"Does my first name really matter all that much?" Maple asked. This day was getting more bizarre by the minute. Had she traveled to Texas, or fallen down a rabbit hole, Alice in Wonderland-style?

"In this case, it just might," Grover said, looking distinctly unhappy about it. "We need to talk. Follow me."

He swept past her without waiting for a response.

Maple glanced at June, who simply shrugged. Clearly, she didn't know what was going on any more than Maple did.

Lady Bird trotted gleefully after Grover, which frankly, felt like an enormous betrayal. Completely unreasonable, since Maple had known the dog for all of twenty minutes. Still, it was nice having someone on her side in the middle of all this chaos. Even if that someone was a dog.

Then, just as Maple's heart began to sink to new depths, Lady Bird stopped in her tracks and turned around. The golden fixed her soft brown eyes on Maple and cocked her head, as if to say, "What are you waiting for?"

Hope fluttered inside Maple, like a butterfly searching for a safe place to land.

"I'm coming."

Dr. Grover Hayes's office was located just off the reception area, behind the very first door on the right. By the time Lady Bird led Maple there, Grover was already seated at his desk and shuffling through a pile of papers.

"It's around here somewhere. Just give me a second," he said. Then he nodded toward a chair on the other side of his desk, piled high with file folders. "Sit."

Maple assumed he was talking to her rather than Lady Bird, although in all honesty, it was difficult to tell. She had a feeling if he'd been addressing the dog, he would've been more polite. So she scooped the stack of patient files into her arms, deposited them on a nearby end table and sat down. Once Maple was settled, Lady Bird plopped on the ground and planted her chin on the tip of one of her stilettos.

Perhaps it was that tiny show of affection that gave Maple the confidence to assume she was actually employed at the clinic, despite all current evidence to the contrary.

"I was thinking that while I'm here, I could help us get started on a digital office system. Having patient files on a cloud-based platform would save loads of time."

Grover glanced up from the stack of papers in front of him and snorted. "Our system works just fine."

Maple's gaze swiveled from the mountain of files she'd just removed from her chair to the mishmash of documents on Grover's desk. "I can see that. Efficiency at its finest."

"And let's not forget that you don't even work here, missy," Grover added, although he seemed to have lost a fair bit of his bluster.

What *was* the man looking for, anyway? Had the mention of her first name somehow reminded him that he did, indeed, have a copy of her grant paperwork lying around somewhere?

"Ah, here it is." He grabbed hold of a slim manila envelope and frowned at the words written neatly across the front of it before shoving it toward Maple.

Last Will and Testament of Percy Walker

"Take it." Grover shook the envelope until Maple begrudgingly accepted it.

She placed it in her lap, unopened, where it sat like a bomb waiting to detonate. Her mouth went dry. *Something about this feels woefully inappropriate.* Maple didn't really know Percy Walker. They'd exchanged little more than a handful of emails over the past four years. Why would his business partner just hand her his last will and testament?

Maple shook her head. "I'm sorry? Why do you want me to have this?"

"Go on." Grover waved a hand at her. First impressions were rarely one-hundred-percent accurate, but he didn't seem at all like the type of person who'd have the patience to deal with an elderly woman and her beloved robotic companion animal. Wonders never ceased, apparently. "Open it."

She lifted the flap of the envelope and slid the legal document from inside.

The pages of the will were slightly yellowed with age. Maple's eyes scanned the legalese, and familiar words popped out at her—phrases that had been part of her parents' vocabulary for as long as she could remember. She still had no idea what any of it had to do with her.

"Would you care to give me a hint as to what I'm looking…for?" she asked, but her voice drifted off as her gaze snagged on the first paragraph of the second page.

I have never been married. As of the date of this will, the following child has been born to me:
    Maple Maribelle Walker

Maple's heart immediately began to pound so hard and fast that Lady Bird lifted her head and whined in alarm.

"This isn't me." Maple shook her head. If she shook it any harder, it probably would've snapped right off and tumbled to the floor. "It can't be. My last name is Leighton."

But her first name was obviously Maple, and her middle name, which she'd hadn't mentioned to anyone in Bluebonnet, was indeed Maribelle.

What were the odds this was all some crazy coincidence? Maple had never met another living soul who shared her first name. In Manhattan, she'd grown up among a sea of Blairs, Serenas, and Waverlys, acutely aware that she hadn't fit in. Maybe it was a more common name down here in Texas?

"My parents are both divorce lawyers," she said, as if that fact was relevant in any way. "In *Manhattan*. I'm not even from here."

"Clearly." Grover let out a laugh.

Finally, they agreed on something.

"What's your middle name?" he asked, frowning like he already knew the answer.

Maple reached down to rest a hand on Lady Bird's head. The dog licked her with a swipe of her warm pink tongue. Maple took a deep breath. "It's Maribelle."

If the furrow in Grover's forehead grew any deeper, Maple could've crawled inside of it and disappeared.

"Surely there's another Maple Maribelle who lives right

here in Bluebonnet," she said, but she was grasping at straws, and she knew it. If there'd been anyone else who remotely fit the bill, Grover wouldn't have gone pale the moment he'd heard her first name.

"I'm afraid not," Grover said. "I think it might be time for you to call your lawyer parents up in New York to try and get to the bottom of this. In the meantime, I'll give Percy's attorney a call and see if he can come right over."

"But why?" The last thing Maple wanted to do was call her mother and father. When she'd told them she was starting a new job this week, she'd conveniently left out the part about the practice being located in Texas. They didn't know about the grant, either. For all they knew, she was still living in her little studio apartment in the city, ready to launch her new career as a veterinary cardiologist.

As she *should* be.

In hindsight, Maple clearly should've gotten their advice before signing on the dotted line.

"With all due respect, Percy Walker is dead. Why would I need to get my family involved?" She picked up the last will and testament by the very tip of the corner of its stapled pages. Maple hadn't wanted to rid herself of an item so badly since the last time she'd played a game of hot potato. She would've thrown the document across the desk if she hadn't suspected that Grover would toss it right back at her. "What difference does any of this make?"

Couldn't they simply pretend none of this had happened? No one else needed to know that her first and middle name matched the one listed on Percy's will. Maple wasn't his daughter, full stop. She knew it, and now Grover knew it. Case closed.

Maple didn't know why there was a voice screaming in the back of her head that things couldn't possibly be that simple. She almost wanted to clamp her hands over her ears to try and drown it out. Even the comforting weight of Lady Bird's warm body as the dog heaved herself into a sit position and leaned against Maple's legs failed to calm the frantic beating of her heart.

"I'm afraid it makes a very big difference, young lady." Grover sighed, and Maple was so thrown by this entire conversation that she forgot to get offended at being referred to in such a condescending manner. "If you're the Maple Maribelle listed in that document, that means you're Percy's sole beneficiary and you've inherited everything—his house, his half of this veterinary practice…"

Lady Bird let out a sharp bark.

Grover's gaze drifted toward the golden retriever. "*And* his dog."

Chapter Three

Maple tried her mother first, but the call rolled straight to voice mail, so she left a message that was as vague and chipper as possible. Other than a brief mention of Texas, she in no way hinted at her current existential crisis. No need to panic anyone. This was all just some huge misunderstanding. As soon as she met with Percy's attorney—the only one in town, apparently—Maple could get on with her new life in Bluebonnet.

She was assuming Grover would let her stay, of course. Whether or not Percy left behind any paperwork documenting her grant didn't really matter. Maple owed the clinic a year of work and, as unpleasant as it seemed, she intended to fulfill that obligation. If Grover wouldn't let her stay...

Well, she'd simply deal with that later. Right after she managed to convince Grover she was in no way related to his recently deceased business partner.

"It's not true," she said aloud, as if the crammed bookshelves and clutter scattered atop Percy Walker's desk could hear her. Grover had banished her to Percy's office to make her phone calls, against Maple's fervent protests.

Lady Bird, who'd sauntered into the office on Maple's heels and promptly arranged herself on a faded flannel dog bed in a corner by the window, lifted her head from her paws. She cocked her head and eyed Maple with obvious skepticism. Or maybe Maple was just anthropomorphizing. She had a tendency to do that on occasion.

"I'm not his daughter." Maple fixed her gaze on the dog. "Seriously, I'm not. I don't belong here."

Lady Bird's tail *thump-thumped* against her dog bed. The golden clearly wasn't listening.

"A simple phone call will prove it." Maple turned her cell phone over in her palm and scrolled through her contacts for her dad's information. If her mom wasn't answering, maybe he could help. She couldn't keep sitting here in a strange man's office in a strange town, trying to convince a strange dog that she really was who she said she was— Maple Maribelle Leighton of New York City.

Before she could tap her father's number, her phone rang with an incoming call and Maple jumped. She really needed to get a grip.

It's Mom. She pressed a hand to her abdomen as her mother's name scrolled across the top of the phone's small screen. *Thank goodness.*

"Hi, Mom," she said as she answered, going for bright and confident, but managing to sound slightly manic instead.

"Hi, honey."

Wait. That wasn't her mother's voice. It almost sounded like her father.

Maple frowned down at her phone. "Dad?"

"It's both of us, Maple," her mother said.

"*Both* of you?" Maple glanced at Lady Bird in a panic. The last time her parents had joined forces, it had been to try and talk her into going to law school. If they were willing to put aside their many, *many* differences to join forces, things must be far more dire than Maple imagined.

But wait—Maple hadn't even mentioned Percy or his

will in her voice mail. How could they possibly know she'd been calling about something as delicate as her parentage?

"You mother said you're calling from Texas," Dad said.

And there it was.

Maple's heart sank all the way to her stilettos, which seemed to be covered in a layer of barbecue-scented dust. One brief mention of Texas had been enough to get her parents back on speaking terms?

This couldn't be good.

"I'm here for work. Remember when I told you about my vet school scholarship?" Maple swallowed. Lady Bird, sensing her distress, came to stand and lean against her legs, and Maple felt a sudden swell of affection for Percy Walker. Whoever he'd really been, he'd raised a lovely, lovely dog, and that alone spoke volumes about his character. "There was a small technicality I might not have mentioned."

"What kind of technicality?" her dad asked. Maple could hear the frown in his voice clear across the country.

"In exchange for a full ride, I agreed to spend a year working at a pet clinic here in Texas." Maple took a deep breath. "I guess you could say I live here now. *Temporarily.* Something strange has come up, though, so I wanted to call and—"

"Where in Texas?" Mom asked in a voice so high and thin that Maple barely recognized it.

"It's just a small town. You've probably never heard of it." Maple bit down so hard on her bottom lip that she tasted blood.

Maybe if she didn't say it, she could stop this conversation before it really started. She could keep on believing that she knew exactly who she was and where she'd come from. She could swallow the name of this crazy place and pretend she'd never set eyes on Percy Walker's last will and testament.

In the end, it was her dad who broke the silence. And the moment he did, Maple couldn't pretend anymore. There was more to her educational grant than she'd thought. Had there ever even *been* a grant? Or had it simply been Percy's way of getting Maple to Texas? To *home*?

Maple shook her head. She'd never felt farther from home in her entire life.

Dad cleared his throat. "Tell us the truth. You're in Bluebonnet, aren't you?"

An hour later, Maple stared in disbelief at a version of her birth certificate she'd never set eyes on before.

It had been sent via fax from her mother's office in Manhattan, straight to the dinosaur of a fax machine at June's workstation in the pet clinic's reception area. Maple wouldn't have believed it if she hadn't seen it herself—not even after her mom and dad had calmly explained they weren't actually her birth parents. Maple had been adopted at only two days old. Charles and Meredith Leighton had flown down to Bluebonnet and collected her themselves.

It had been an open adoption, arranged by one of their attorney friends. Maple's birth mother had only been seventeen years old, and she'd died in childbirth. The grief-stricken father had been so overwhelmed that he'd agreed to give the baby up, under one condition: the adoptive parents had to promise to keep the baby's first and middle names. Maple Maribelle. Once Maple held the faxed birth certificate in her trembling hands, she understood why.

Mother's Name: Maple Maribelle Walker

The words went blurry as Maple's eyes swam with tears. She'd been named after her birth mother. Everything she'd read in Percy's last will and testament had been true. The man who'd paid for her education and brought her to Bluebonnet had been her *father*.

And now he was gone.

They both were.

"Let's see that, missy." Grover snatched the birth certificate from her hands.

At some point, Maple was going to have to school this man on how to speak to his female colleagues. But, alas, that moment wasn't now. She was far too tired to argue with the likes of Grover Hayes. All she wanted to do right now was crawl into bed and pull the covers over her head. Too bad she still had no idea where she was staying.

"Believe me, no one is as surprised by this crazy turn of events as I am," Maple said as Grover studied the document.

Grover made a noise somewhere between a huff and a growl. Lady Bird's ears pricked forward and she cocked her head.

"We need to talk," Maple said, even though she had no idea what she was going to say. Up was down, down was up and nothing make sense anymore.

"Just come home," her mother had said.

"I've booked you on the first flight out of Austin tomorrow morning," her dad had added. "First class."

It had been decided. Maple had never belonged in Bluebonnet. As far as her parents were concerned, she should just come back to New York and forget her ill-fated trip to Texas had ever taken place. They'd fallen all over themselves apologizing for never telling her the truth about her birth. Maple couldn't remember either of her parents ever uttering the word *sorry* before. It was almost as disorienting as learning she'd been born right here in Bluebonnet.

"Indeed, we do." Grover stalked toward his office, fully expecting Maple to follow.

What choice did she have?

At least June shot her a sympathetic glance this time. Maple gave the receptionist a wan smile and fell in step behind Grover as Lady Bird nudged her gold head beneath Maple's hand.

The dog was growing on Maple. Technically, the golden was hers now, right? She could pack the dog up and sweep her off to New York if she wanted to. Not that Maple would do such a thing. New York City was made for purse dogs. Life in Manhattan would be a major adjustment for a dog accustomed to living in the wide-open spaces of Texas. It wouldn't be fair.

But that didn't stop Maple from dreaming about it.

"I've been thinking things over, and I've decided to let you off the hook," Grover said as soon as the office door shut behind them.

Maple heaved another pile of file folders out of the office chair she'd occupied earlier and plopped down on the worn leather. "I'm not following."

"For the grant. You and Percy had an agreement, did you not? A fully funded veterinary education in exchange for one year of employment here at Bluebonnet Pet Clinic?" Grover leaned back in his chair.

Maple nodded. "Yes, but…"

"But I'm letting you off the hook. Percy's gone now. I think we both know the real reason he wanted you to come here." Grover shrugged. "I see no reason to make you fulfill your obligation. I think this morning proved you're not a good fit here. Wouldn't you agree?"

Ooof. He was one-hundred-percent right. There was no reason why his words should've felt like a blow to the chest, but they did.

"Agreed." Maple gave a curt nod and tried her best not to think about the way she'd spoken to Ford Bishop earlier. The appointment had been a total disaster. Yet another reason to put this town in her rearview mirror as quickly as possible.

Lady Bird sighed and dropped her chin onto Maple's knee.

"So." Grover shrugged. "You're free to go."

Maple gripped the arms of her chair so hard that her knuckles turned white. The effort it took not to sprint out of the building, roadrunner-style, was almost too much to bear. "I'm leaving on the six a.m. flight out of Austin tomorrow morning. My ticket is already booked."

Her dad had even managed to pull some strings and gotten Maple another shot at her dream job. The veterinary cardiology practice that had made her such a generous offer after graduation still wanted her to come to work for them. When Maple had asked how that was possible, since she knew for a fact that the position had been filled after she'd turned it down, her father had simply said that veterinary cardiologists got divorced, just like everyone else did. He'd apparently represented Maple's new boss in a nasty split and was now calling in a favor.

"Good." Grover nodded. *"Excellent."*

Maple knew she should ask about Percy's estate. Didn't she need to sign some papers or something? There was the veterinary practice to think about… Percy's personal effects…and his dog.

She could deal with all of that from New York, though. Her parents were lawyers. Maple probably wouldn't have to lift a finger. They could make it all disappear, just like they'd promised on the phone.

None of this is really your responsibility. You can walk

away. Grover just said so himself. Maple buried her hand in the warm scruff of Lady Bird's neck.

Charles and Meredith Leighton had been divorced since Maple was in first grade. The separation had been monumentally ugly—ugly enough that she could remember hiding in her closet with her stuffed dog, Rover, clamping her hands over her ears to try and muffle the sound of dishes smashing against the marble floors. They were two of the city's highest paid divorce attorneys, after all. Fighting dirty practically came naturally to them.

The fact that they seemed to have to put aside their many, *many* differences to help Maple deal with Percy's estate and get her back to New York was nothing short of surreal. In the ultimate irony of ironies, she'd managed to fulfill her childhood dream of stitching her broken family back together. All it had taken was the accidental discovery of a whole *other* family that she never knew existed.

"Where am I supposed to stay tonight?" Maple said, willing her voice not to crack.

Grover opened the top drawer of his desk and pulled out an old-fashioned skeleton key, tied with a red string. He set it down and slid it toward Maple.

She eyed it dubiously. "What is that for?"

"It's the key to Percy's place." Grover paused, and the lines on his face seemed to grow deeper. "Although technically it's your house now."

Not for long.

She reached for the strange key and balled it into her fist. Percy's house was the absolute last place she wanted to go for her few remaining hours in Bluebonnet. She longed for a sterile beige hotel room—somewhere she could hide herself away and feel absolutely nothing. Unfortunately, the closest place that fit the bill was nearly fifty miles away. Maple had already done a search on her cell phone.

She slapped the key back down on the desk.

"I'm not sure staying at Percy's house is the best idea. I don't even know how I'd get there. I don't have a car." With any luck, Uber hadn't made it all the way to rural Texas. "Didn't I see a sign for a bed-and-breakfast near the town square? I'm sure that's much closer."

"Closer than next door?" Grover stood, reached for his white vet coat and slid his arms into its sleeves. "I think not."

"Percy's house is right next door?" Maple squeaked.

Of course, it was. The population of this place was probably in the double digits.

"Yes, he lived in one of the Sunday houses. He owned this one, too, until he sold it to the practice." Grover cast a sentimental glance at their surroundings. Then his gaze landed on Maple and his expression hardened again.

"What's a Sunday house?" she asked before she could stop herself. Why spend any more time in Grover's presence than absolutely necessary? The wording made her curious, though. She'd never heard of such a thing in New York.

"A Sunday house is a small home that was once used by ranchers or farmers who lived in the outlying area when they came into town on the weekends for social events and church. Sunday houses date back to the 1800s. There are still quite a few standing in the Texas Hill Country. A lot of them are historical landmarks." He glowered. "You might want to brush up on some local history before you think about selling the place."

"I'll get right on that," she muttered under her breath.

"Percy's home is the pink house just to the right of this one." He fumbled around in the pocket of his white coat and pulled out a banged-up pocket watch that looked like something from an antique store. He squinted at it, nodded and slid it out of view again. "I'd walk you over there, but I've got an appointment with a turtle who has a head cold."

Sure he did.

Maple didn't believe him for a minute. Grover just wanted her gone. At least they'd finally agreed on something.

"You can leave the key under the front mat when you head out in the morning. Have a safe trip back home," Grover said, and then he strode out of his office with a tight smile.

Nice to meet you, too, Maple thought wryly.

Lady Bird peered up at her with a softness in her warm brown eyes that made Maple's heart feel like it was being squeezed in a vise. Was she moving too fast? Maybe she should slow down a take a breath.

She closed her eyes, leaned forward and rested her cheek against Lady Bird's head. A voice in the back of her head assured her she was doing the right thing.

This was never what you wanted. Now you have an out. You'd be a fool not to take it.

Maple sat up and blew out a breath. Lady Bird's tail beat against the hard wood floor. *Thump, thump, thump.*

"Come on." Maple said, and the dog's big pink tongue lolled out of the side of her mouth. "Let's get out of here."

She sure as heck wasn't going to spend the night in Percy's house alone, and Lady Bird seemed more than willing to accompany her.

June was clearly more conflicted about Maple's decision to fly back to Manhattan. She at least had the decency to look somewhat sorry to see Maple go.

"You don't have to be in such a hurry, you know," the older woman said as Maple took hold of her wheeled suitcase. "Don't mind Grover. I know he seems madder than an old wet hen, but he's not that bad once you get to know him. He and Percy were really close. He's taking the loss hard."

So hard that he basically ordered his dead friend's long-lost daughter to leave town immediately. Do not pass GO. Do not collect 200 dollars.

Maple fought back an eye roll. "I'm going to have to take your word on that, June."

June nodded and fidgeted with her hands. "You let me know if you need anything tonight, Dr. Leighton. I'll be 'round to collect Lady Bird first thing in the morning. She's been staying with me since Percy's passing, but you take her tonight. That dog has a way with people who need a little TLC. She's actually sort of famous for it around these parts."

Maple suspected there might be more to that story, but before she could ask June to elaborate, a client walked into the clinic holding a cat carrier containing a fluffy black cat howling at the top of its lungs.

"I think that's my cue to go." Maple tightened her grip on the handle of her suitcase. "Thanks for everything. And June…?"

June regarded her over the top of her reading glasses. "Yes, Dr. Leighton?"

"You can call me Maple." Maple's throat went thick. She *really* needed to make herself scarce. It wasn't like her to get emotional around strangers. Then again, it wasn't every day that she learned something about herself that made her question her place in the world.

June's face split into a wide grin, and before Maple knew what was happening, the older woman threw her arms around Maple's shoulders and wrapped her in a tight hug.

It had been a long time since someone had embraced

Maple with that sort of enthusiasm. As much as she hated to admit it, it felt nice.

"I really should go now," she mumbled into June's shoulder.

June released her and gave her shoulders a gentle squeeze. "Goodbye now, Maple Maribelle Walker."

Leighton, Maple wanted to say. *My name is Maple Leighton.* But the words stuck in her throat.

She dipped her head and dragged her luggage toward the door, carefully sidestepping the cat who was now meowing loud enough to peel the paint off the walls. Lady Bird trotted alongside Maple as if the cat didn't exist. Golden retrievers were known for their unflappable temperament, but this really took the cake.

If Grover hadn't told Maple which house in the neat row of half-dozen homes with gingerbread trim had been Percy's, she still would've located it easily. Lady Bird led the way, trotting straight toward the little pink house with her tail wagging to and fro.

A nonsensical lump lodged in Maple's throat at the sight of it. It looked like a dollhouse and was painted a pale blush-pink that reminded her of ballet slippers. Everything about the structure oozed charm, from the twin rocking chairs on the porch to the white picket fence that surrounded the small front yard. Maple couldn't help but wonder what it might've been like growing up in this sort of home, tailor-made for a little girl.

Tears pricked the backs of her eyes. There must be something in the water in this town. Maple never cried, and this was the third time today that she'd found herself on the verge of weeping.

She took a deep inhale and pushed open the gabled gate in the white picket fence. Lady Bird zipped past her, bounding toward the tiny covered porch. The dog nudged at something sitting on the welcome mat while Maple hauled her bag up the front step.

"What have you got there, Lady Bird?" Maple muttered as she rummaged around her NYC pizza-parlor handbag for the ridiculous skeleton key Grover had given her earlier. Was there *anything* in Bluebonnet that didn't look like it had come straight out of a time capsule?

The key felt heavy in her hand, weighted down by yesteryear. Maple's fingers wrapped around it, and she held it tight as she bent down to see what had captured Lady Bird's attention.

Once she managed to nudge the golden out of the way, Maple saw it—a large pink bakery box with the words *Cherry on Top* printed across it in a whimsical font.

Her breath caught in her throat. Ford Bishop had really done it. He'd done as his grandmother had asked and brought her a pie. Maple had been so busy with her identity crisis that she hadn't eaten a bite all day. She hadn't even thought about food. But the heavenly smell drifting up from the bakery box made her mouth water.

She picked it up, closed her eyes and took a long inhale. The heady aroma of sugar, cinnamon and buttery pastry crust nearly caused her knees to buckle. Then her eyelashes fluttered open, and she spotted the brief note Ford had scrawled on the cardboard in thick strokes from a magic marker.

The man had terrible handwriting—nearly as indecipherable as that of a doctor. Maple had to read it a few times to make out what it said.

Doc,
I wasn't sure what kind of pie you liked, so I went with Texas peach. The peaches were homegrown here in Bluebonnet. There's more to love about this place

than just dogs, although our canines are admittedly
stellar. Just ask Lady Bird.
Regards,
Ford Bishop

Maple's heart gave a little twist. She couldn't even say
why, except that she'd spent the entire day trying to hold
herself together while her life—past, present, and future—
had been fracturing apart. She didn't belong here in Texas.
That much was clear.

But the secret truth that Maple kept buried deep down
inside was that she'd never fully felt like she'd belonged
anywhere. Not even New York. She'd always felt like she
was on the outside looking in, with her face pressed against
the tempered glass of her own life.

Maple had always blamed her social anxiety on her
parents' divorce and a lifetime of learning that love was
never permanent, and marriages were meant to be broken.
Her mom and dad had never said as much aloud, but they
didn't have to. It had happened in their very own family.
Then Maple had quietly watched as her parents battled on
behalf of other heartbroken husbands and wives.

She'd avoided dating all through high school, afraid to
lose her head and her heart to someone who might crush
it to pieces. Then in vet school, she'd decided to prove
her parents wrong. She'd thrown herself into love with all
the naivete of a girl who hadn't actually learned what the
words *prenuptial agreement* meant before her tenth birthday. When she fell, she fell hard.

Justin had been a student in her study group. He was
fiercely competitive, just like Maple. She'd foolishly believed that meant they had other things in common, too.
Two peas in the pressure cooker of a pod that was veterinary school.

For an entire semester they did everything together. Then, near the end of the term, on the night before they both had a final research project due in their animal pathology class, he disappeared...

Along with Maple's term paper.

At first, she'd thought it had to be some weird coincidence. He'd been in an accident or something, and she'd simply misplaced her research paper or left it at the copy place, where she'd had all one hundred pages of it bound like a book for a professional aesthetic. But Maple knew she'd never make a mistake like that. Instead, she'd made one far more heartbreaking. She'd trusted a boy who'd used her for months, biding his time until he could swoop in and steal her research project so he could turn it in as his own.

By the time Maple flew into her professor's office the following morning to report the theft, Justin had already switched out the cover page and presented the work as his own. The professor insisted there was no way to tell who'd copied whom, and Maple had been left with nothing to turn in. It had been the one and only time in her life she'd received an F on a report card.

Lesson learned. Her parents had been right all along.

But maybe there was more to the detached feeling inside of Maple than her messed up childhood and her ill-fated attempt at romance. Maybe the reason she'd never felt like she fit in was because she'd been in the wrong place. The wrong *life*.

If Maple hadn't known better, she would've thought the wistful feeling that tugged at her heart as she read and reread Ford's note might have been homesickness. Nostalgia for a place she'd never really been but longed for, all the same.

Homegrown here in Bluebonnet. Her gaze kept straying back to that phrase, over and over again, as she stood on the threshold of Percy Walker's home, clutching a pie that had been a reluctant thank-you gift from a perfect stranger. Somewhere in the distance, a horse whinnied. Lady Bird whimpered, angling for a bite of peach pie.

It wasn't until Maple felt the wetness on her face that she realized she'd finally given up the fight and let herself cry.

Chapter Four

Percy's landline rang in the dead of night, jolting Maple from a deep sleep.

At first, she thought she must be dreaming. It had been years since she'd even *heard* the shrill ring of a landline. She scarcely recognized the sound. Then, once she dragged her eyes open, she realized she was in a strange bed in a strange house with a strange dog sprawled next to her.

Yep. She plopped her head back down on her pillow and threw her arm over her face. *Definitely a dream.*

But then she caught a whiff of cinnamon on her forearm, and everything came flooding back to her at once. She was in Bluebonnet, Texas. Percy Walker, DVM, was her father, and Maple had found out the truth too late to do anything about it. No wonder she'd eaten an entire peach pie straight from the box for dinner while Lady Bird chowed down on a bowl of premium dog food.

That pie had also been *delicious.* Hands down, the best she'd ever tasted. Maybe Ford had been right about the virtues of homegrown produce. In any case, Maple had zero regrets about the pie.

She let her swollen eyes drift shut again. She'd wept throughout the entire peach-pie episode, and subsequently had the puffy face and blotchy skin to show for it. Lovely.

Her mother would no doubt book Maple a facial the second she deplaned at JFK.

At least the landline had stopped ringing. A quick glance at her cell phone told her it was after two in the morning. If she fell back asleep in the next fifteen minutes, she could still get a good three hours of shut-eye before her hired car showed up to take her to the airport in Austin. As she'd suspected, Uber wasn't a thing in Bluebonnet. It was going to cost her an arm and a leg to get to the airport on time because she'd had to book a service all the way from the city.

Worth every freaking penny, she told herself while Lady Bird snuffled and wheezed beside her. The dog snored louder than a freight train. Alas, not quite loud enough to drown out the landline as it began to ring again.

Maple sat up and tossed the covers aside. "Seriously?"

Who called a dead man's house at this hour?

She stumbled toward the kitchen, where the phone—a vintage rotary classic with a cord approximately ten thousand feet long—hung just to the left of the refrigerator.

Maple plucked the handset from its hook. "Whoever this is, you've got the wrong number."

"Oh." The woman on the other end sounded startled. Again, *seriously*? Couldn't people in Bluebonnet tell time? "I was looking for Lady Bird. Is she not there?"

Maple felt herself frown. "Lady Bird is a dog."

"Of course, she is. Is she available?"

Maybe Maple really *was* dreaming. "You want to speak to Lady Bird on the phone?"

She glanced around, but for once, the golden wasn't glued to her side. No doubt she was still splayed diagonally across the bed, belly-up.

"That's cute, but no. This is Pam Hudson. You can call me Nurse Pam. Everyone does. I work at County General

Hospital, and we were hoping Lady Bird could come in to visit with a patient."

Maple blinked as something June said in passing earlier came back to her.

That dog has a way with people who need a little TLC. She's actually sort of famous for it around these parts.

Lady Bird must be a therapy dog. Therapy dogs were specially trained to provide comfort, support, and affection to people in health-care settings. Why hadn't anyone said anything?

Probably because it was none of Maple's business, considering she already had one stylishly clad foot out the door and she hadn't planned on taking the golden with her.

"I apologize for the late hour, but we have a little boy here who's had quite a difficult night, and he's been asking for Lady Bird for the past half hour. It would mean the world to him if she could come visit, even for a few minutes," Nurse Pam said.

"Right now?" Maple asked in a panic.

No. Just…no.

Therapy dogs didn't visit patients all on their own. They worked as a team in conjunction with their owners. And as of today, Lady Bird's owner was Maple.

But Maple wasn't cut out for that type of work, as evidenced by the epic disaster at the pet clinic. She was the absolute last person who should be visiting someone sick and vulnerable. Therapy dog handlers were compassionate. They were active listeners and knew how to engage with people experiencing all sorts of challenges or trauma. They were confident in social situations.

Maple was none of those things.

"I know it's late. I'm so sorry for the interruption, but Oliver always lights up when Lady Bird is here. Percy was always so good about bringing the dog around whenever we called, no matter the hour. I know this is none of my business, but I heard you're his daughter." Pam's voice cracked. "We're really going to miss him around here."

Maple's throat clogged.

Not again. She was done with crying. She'd had her pie-fueled moment of weakness. There was no reason whatsoever to get emotional over a person she'd never met before.

"Do you think you'll be able to bring Lady Bird by?"

The nurse was relentless. Fortunately, Maple had the perfect excuse. "I'm sorry, but even if I wanted to—" *which I don't* "—I can't. I don't have any way to get there. I don't have a car. In fact, I'm leaving early in the morning, and—"

"That's an easy fix!" Pam gushed. "Don't you worry. Someone will be by Percy's house to pick you up shortly."

Maple froze, a deer in headlights. This couldn't be happening. "Wait, no. That's really not—"

Pam interjected, cutting her off. "No need to thank me. We help one another out here. It's the Bluebonnet way."

Of course, it was. Maple couldn't wait to get out of this place and back to New York, where she was hemmed in by people on every side and none of them knew her name or cared a whit about her.

She opened her mouth to protest again, but it was too late. There was a click on the other end of the line as Pam hung up the phone.

Maple gaped at the receiver. She tried pressing the silver hook where the handset usually rested, but no amount of jabbing at the ancient device would make Pam reappear.

"Nope," Maple said aloud. "Nope, nope, nope."

She wasn't going to do it. Pam couldn't make her. Maple would just call the hospital back and refuse.

But Maple had been half-asleep when she'd taken the call and couldn't remember the name of the hospital the nurse had mentioned. Nor did she know what floor or department Pam had been calling from. All she remembered was that the patient was a little boy named Oliver and that Oliver was having a tough night.

Join the club, Oliver.

Maple dropped her forehead to the phone and concentrated on taking deep breaths. As out of it as she'd been a few minutes ago, she was wide-awake now. Any minute, a stranger intent on dragging her to the hospital was going to knock on the door and they were going to find Maple on the verge of a panic attack, dressed in her favorite cupcake-themed pajamas with pie crumbs in her hair.

This town was the *worst*. How did introverts survive here?

The dreaded knock at the door came in just under twenty minutes. Maple had barely had time to pull on her softest pair of jeans and a J.Crew T-shirt with sketches of dogs of various breeds drinking cocktails from martini glasses. Comfort clothes. Clothes that said she was staying in for the night, no matter what Nurse Pam had to say about it.

She swung Percy's front door open, ready to dig in her heels.

"Look, I—" Maple's tongue tripped over itself as she took in the sight of the man standing on her porch dressed in hospital scrubs. She swallowed hard. "It's you."

Ford Bishop.

Just how small was the population of this town? The man was everywhere—bringing his grandmother into the pet clinic, buying pies, delivering therapy dogs to the hospital in the dead of night. Maple apparently couldn't swing a stick in Bluebonnet without it smacking into one of his nicely toned forearms.

Oh, no. She was staring at his forearms again, wasn't she?

She blinked hard and refocused on his face...on those

eyes of his that somehow made Maple want to close her eyes and fall backward onto a soft featherbed.

Something was very clearly wrong with her. She was suffering from some sort of pie-induced hysteria. Maybe even a full nervous breakdown.

Ford tilted his head, studied her for a beat and gave her a smile that almost seemed genuine.

"Hey there, Doc."

Ford squinted at Maple's T-shirt.

Were those dogs? Drinking *martinis*? Interesting choice for a late-night visit to the children's wing of a hospital, but Ford wasn't judging. He was honestly shocked that Pam had managed to twist Maple's arm into bringing Lady Bird to visit Oliver at all.

Shocked, but relieved—so relieved that he'd have happily chauffeured Maple to the hospital in her PJs, if necessary.

"What are you doing here?" Maple asked, blinking rapidly, and Ford's relief took a serious hit.

"I'm giving you and Lady Bird a ride to County General," Ford said. Why else would he be on her doorstep in the middle of the night, dressed in scrubs with his truck still running at the curb?

He wasn't sure why she couldn't drive herself. Percy's truck was newer than his, and as far as Ford knew, it remained parked right in the garage, where he'd left it. But Ford was happy to give Maple and the dog a ride, if needed. He just wanted to get Lady Bird to the hospital by any means necessary.

"There's been a misunderstanding." Maple shook her head. "Lady Bird isn't feeling up to it."

At the mention of her name, Lady Bird made herself visible by nudging the front door open wider with her snout.

The dog wiggled past Maple to offer Ford a proper golden-retriever greeting, complete with tail wags and copious amounts of drool.

Ford dropped to a knee to let Lady Bird plant her paws on his shoulders and lick the side of his face. The dog's wagging tail crashed into Maple's shins. When Ford looked up at her, a deep flush was making its way up her neck.

Liar, liar, pants on fire, he thought.

"I'm no vet, but it seems to me if this dog was feeling under the weather earlier, she's suddenly made a miraculous recovery." Ford stood, and Lady Bird added an exclamation point to his observation by continuing to prance around him like he was hiding bacon in the pockets of his scrubs.

For the record, he was not. The only thing in Ford's pocket was his cell phone, which pinged at least once an hour with a text from Gram. The last missive had been a photo of Coco lying at the foot of her bed watching *Jeopardy* on the small television in Gram's room at the senior center.

"Thank you for the pie. It was heavenly," Maple said, and Ford was pretty sure he spotted a crumb from the crust of said pie in her hair, but he thought it best not to mention it. "But this day has been a real doozie. Pam kind of strong-armed me into the whole pet-visit thing, and I just…can't."

Ford crossed his arms. After this morning, he shouldn't have been surprised. This was a kid they were talking about, though. Was she really saying no?

"Don't look at me like that." Maple scowled.

"How am I looking at you?"

"Like I'm evil incarnate." She gave her chin a jaunty upward tilt. "I told you I wasn't a people person."

Ford narrowed his gaze at her. "Is that what I should say to the eight-year-old little kid who's been puking all night after his most recent chemo treatment when he asks why he can't see Lady Bird?"

She recoiled as if she'd been hit.

"Sorry. That was probably too harsh." Ford held up his hands. He wasn't in the business of guilting people into doing good deeds, all evidence to the contrary.

And he certainly didn't think Maple was evil incarnate. Lost, maybe. Overwhelmed, certainly. Bluebonnet was a small town, and, of course, Ford had heard about Percy's last will and testament. As hard as it was to believe, Maple was Percy Walker's daughter.

The way she wrapped her arms around herself told Ford that no one found it more impossible to believe than she did.

Time to start over. "Look, Oliver is a sweet kid. His mom works nights. He's tired, and he's very sick, or else I wouldn't be standing here on your porch at two in the morning asking for this small favor."

It wasn't small to the average person—especially a person who seemed to have at least a dash of social anxiety. Ford knew this. He just really, *really* wanted Oliver to get a few minutes with Lady Bird. Once the kid set eyes on that dog, he'd sleep like a baby for the rest of the night. Happened every time.

"Lady Bird will do all the work. Oliver will hardly even look at you, I promise. The dog is the star of the show. I'd take her there myself, but I can't. I could get called away, and hospital rules say I can't leave a patient alone with a therapy dog." Ford shifted from one foot to the other. He needed to get back to work. "Please?"

"You can't leave a patient alone with a therapy dog, but you *can* leave them with someone you don't really know? Someone who isn't even the therapy dog's owner?" She chewed on her bottom lip.

"Aren't you, though?" Ford glanced down at Lady Bird, who'd planted herself directly between them with one big paw resting on Maple's toe. Her impractical stilettos had been replaced with an oversize pair of house slippers. Brown corduroy and large enough to look like they'd come from the men's department. Ford realized he hardly knew Maple, but the shoes definitely seemed out of character.

Then it hit him: the shoes belonged to Percy.

"I'm not staying," Maple said with a shake of her head. She gestured to the house, the dog, and the town in general. "I'll figure out what to do with all of this later, but I can't stay here. I'm going back to New York in the morning."

Ford bristled, even though he couldn't help but think the slippers told a different story. Maple Walker Leighton was more curious about her birth father than she wanted to admit.

But that wasn't any of Ford's business. As for why the sight of her in those slippers filled his chest with warmth, he really couldn't say.

"Please," Ford said again and then reached to pluck the crumb from her hair. He just couldn't help it. Maple's lips parted ever so slightly at his closeness, but she didn't move a muscle. He held up the crumb between his thumb and forefinger. "What if I promised you more pie?"

Her expression softened. Just a bit—just enough for the warmth in Ford's chest to bloom and expand into something that felt far too much like longing.

No, he told himself. *Don't even think about it.*

This was a business transaction, not a flirtation. He was offering pie in exchange for her dog-handling services. That was it. Come tomorrow, Ford would never set eyes on Maple again.

He swiveled his gaze toward Lady Bird. "Tell Maple there's nothing to be afraid of. She might even have fun."

"I'm not afraid," she sputtered.

"I beg your pardon, I'm not talking to you. This is a conversation between me and the dog." Ford flashed her a wink, and then fixed his gaze with Lady Bird's again. "Go on, tell her."

Lady Bird tossed back her head and let out a *woo-woo* noise somewhere between a howl and a whine.

Maple laughed, and the sound was as light and lovely as church bells. She should really let her guard down more often. "This is *craziness*. Have you two practiced this routine?"

No, but Lady Bird had a wide array of tricks in her repertoire. Percy had trained the dog well, and Ford had seen the golden in action enough times to have committed some of her commands to memory.

Ford didn't tell Maple that, though. He just waggled his eyebrows and shot her one last questioning glance.

"Okay, fine. I'll do it." She thrust two fingers in the air. "Under two conditions."

"Done." Ford nodded, turned toward his truck and whistled at Lady Bird to follow.

"Wait!" Maple shuffled after them in her too-big slippers. "You don't know what the conditions are."

Ford swung open the passenger-side door of his truck and Lady Bird hopped inside. "I'm guessing the first one is pie."

She crossed her arms, all business. "Accurate."

Ford wondered what, if anything, could make this woman relax. Not that it mattered since she was so dead set on leaving, but it might have been fun to try and find out. "And the second?"

"You've got to promise to get me home in plenty of time to meet my car service for my ride to the airport in the morning."

"No problem, Doc," he said and gave her a curious look, which Maple either didn't notice or chose to ignore.

"I'll be right back. I need to put on some shoes and grab my purse," she said.

"We'll be waiting right here." Ford banged his hand on the hood of his truck and felt his mouth hitch into a grin as she disappeared back into the house.

You've got to promise to get me home, she'd said. Not *back here* or *back to Percy's house*.

Whether or not she'd realized it, Maple had just called this place home.

Chapter Five

After they'd arrived at the hospital, Maple tried to hang back and linger in the doorway to Oliver's room so Ford could check and make sure the little boy wasn't asleep, but Lady Bird had other ideas. The golden hustled right inside, dragging Maple behind her as if they'd been issued a personal invitation. Which she supposed they had, basically.

If the child was disappointed to find Maple on the other end of Lady Bird's leash instead of Percy, he didn't show it. His entire face lit up the second he spotted the dog.

"Lady Bird. You're here!" Oliver scrambled to push himself up in his hospital bed for a better view.

"Hold up, there. I've got you," Ford said as he reached for the call-button remote and pressed the appropriate arrow to raise the head of Oliver's bed.

Maple wondered if the mechanical sounds or the moving piece of furniture might spook Lady Bird, but she handled it like a pro. She shimmied right up to the edge of the bed and gently planted her chin on the edge of the mattress, easily within Oliver's reach.

The boy laid a hand on the golden retriever's head and moved his thumb in gentle circles over Lady Bird's soft, cold fur. "I knew you'd come."

If Maple had still been harboring any doubts about caving and letting Ford take her to County General, they melted away right then and there. A lump formed in her throat. *I knew you'd come.* Even at his young age, Oliver already knew what made dogs so special. They were loyalty and unconditional love, all wrapped up in a warm, furry package. The very idea of Lady Bird failing to show up to comfort him in the dead of night was inconceivable.

The ball of tension in Maple's chest loosened a bit. Even if Oliver ended up despising the sight of her, like everyone else in this town, at least she'd done one thing right. She'd gotten the dog here and managed to help preserve the child's belief in the goodness and loyalty of man's best friend. It felt good, despite the fact that she was still doing her best to blend into the beige hospital walls.

"Oliver, bud. I want you to meet a friend of mine." Ford smiled at her, and for reasons she really didn't want to think about, her heart went pitter-patter. "This is Maple. She's taking care of Lady Bird for now."

Maple held up a hand and took a step closer to Oliver's bed. "Hi."

"Hey," Oliver said without tearing his gaze away from the dog. Lady Bird had nudged her head so it fully rested in the boy's lap, and her eyes were trained on his pale face.

"I've got to go check on something, okay?" Ford glanced at the smart watch on his wrist. "I'll be back in about fifteen minutes. Twenty, max."

He was leaving? Already?

Ford shot her a reassuring wink. "Oliver, take it easy on Maple, okay? She's shy."

Maple's face went warm. "I'm sure we'll be fine."

She was sure of nothing of the sort. So far, the people she'd met in Bluebonnet weren't at all like the people she knew back home. She'd been in town for a day, and already everyone seemed to know more about her personal business than she typically shared with friends, much less strangers. There were no walls here. No barriers to hide behind. No *crowds*. She felt wholly exposed, which was especially nerve-racking considering she was trying to adjust to a whole new version of herself as a person.

You're still Maple Leighton. Absolutely nothing about your life has to change.

But what if she wanted it to?

She didn't, though. Of course not. Maple had a plan— a plan that she'd worked long and hard for. Grover had given her full permission to skip the first wasted year of that plan and move full steam ahead toward her dreams. Her dad had already paved the way for her to walk right into her perfectly planned future. Now wasn't the time to entertain change.

Something about the quiet intimacy of a hospital room in the middle of the night was making her question everything, though. Time seemed to stand still in places like this. The outside world felt very far away.

Maple took a deep breath and moved to sit in the chair that Ford had dragged too close to Oliver's bedside for her. This was crazy. She had no clue what to say or do, and panic was already blossoming in her chest as Ford sauntered out of the room in his blue hospital scrubs.

"You like dogs, huh?" she said quietly after Ford was gone.

Oliver nodded but didn't say anything. He just kept toying with Lady's Bird's ears, running them through his small fingers. The dog's eyes slowly drifted closed.

"She really likes that." Maple smiled. "I love dogs, too."

"My mom says when I'm better, I can get a dog of my own." Oliver's gaze finally swiveled in her direction. The dark circles under his eyes made her heart twist. *When I'm better...* She prayed that would happen and it would be soon. "When I do, I want one just like Lady Bird."

"She's quite special." Maple's throat went thick, and she wondered what would happen to the dog once she'd gone. She'd been staying with June since Percy's passing, but the older woman hadn't said anything about keeping Lady Bird and giving her a permanent home.

Why would she? This dog is supposed to be yours *now.* Maple's grip on the leash tightened.

"Do you want to see some pictures I drew of her?" Oliver asked with a yawn.

Maple nodded. "I'd love to."

Oliver pointed at his bedside table. "They're in the top drawer. You can get them out if you want to."

"Are you sure?" Maple hesitated. She wasn't sure rummaging through a patient's nightstand was proper protocol.

But Oliver seemed determined. He nodded. "There's a whole bunch of drawings in there, right on top of the chocolate bars I'm not supposed to know about. My mom keeps them for me. She's going to make a whole book out of my drawings for me when I leave the hospital."

"That's a great idea," Maple said, biting back a smile at the mention of secret chocolate. Something told her nothing got past Oliver.

She pulled open the drawer and sure enough, there was a neat stack of papers covered in bold strokes of crayon nestled inside.

"These are amazing, Oliver." Maple slowly flipped through the drawings, which seemed to chronicle Oliver's stay in the hospital.

In the first few, the little boy in the pictures had a mop of curly brown hair. Soon, the child in the drawings had a smooth, bald head, just like Oliver's.

"That's Ford," Oliver said when her gaze landed on a rendering of a man in familiar-looking blue scrubs with a stethoscope slung around his neck.

Maple grinned. "It looks just like him."

Except the kid had forgotten to add a yellow halo above Ford's head. Maple still wasn't sure what, exactly, Ford did around here, but she had a feeling that escorting therapy dogs and their handlers to the hospital wasn't part of his official job description.

He was almost too wholesome to be real—like the humble, flannel-wearing, small-town love interest in a Hallmark movie. Whereas Maple was the big-city villainess who always ended up getting dumped for a cupcake baker in those sticky-sweet movies. It happened every time. How many cupcake bakers did the world *actually* need, anyway?

"And here's Lady Bird." Maple held up the next drawing, which featured a big yellow dog sprawled across Oliver's hospital bed, definitely a case of art imitating life. "I'd know that big golden anywhere. I really love your artwork, Oliver."

The child gave her a sleepy grin. "There's lots more."

"There sure is." Maple sifted through page after page of colorful renderings of Lady Bird, and she felt herself going all gooey inside. Not full-on cupcake-baker-gooey, but definitely softer than she normally allowed herself to feel around people she'd only just met.

Then she flipped to the next page, and her entire body tensed.

"That's Lady Bird with Mr. Percy." Oliver lifted one hand from the dog's ear just long enough to point to a crayon-sketched figure with gray hair and an oversize pair of glasses perched on his round face.

Mr. Percy. Maple's *father*.

She wasn't sure why his likeness caught her so off guard. She knew good and well that Lady Bird was Percy's dog, and he'd been the one to take the dog on her pet-therapy visits. But something about seeing him drawn in

Oliver's young hand brought back the feeling she'd had just hours ago when she'd toed off her stilettos and slid her feet into his slippers.

She still wasn't quite sure why she'd done it. The shoes had been placed right next to the bed in the small home's master bedroom, as if Percy was expected to climb out of bed and slip them on just like any other day. Before she'd known what she was doing, she'd put them on and tried to imagine what it might be like to follow in her birth father's footsteps. Was it just a coincidence that she'd become a veterinarian, just like him, or was there a part of him still living inside her? Perhaps there had been, all along.

Maple wasn't sure what to believe anymore. All she knew was that somewhere deep down, she was beginning to feel a flicker of connection to a man she'd never met before.

And it scared the life out of her.

"Ford said Mr. Percy is in heaven now," Oliver said.

Maple's heart squeezed into a tight fist. She knew next to nothing about her birth father, but heaven seemed like just the right place for the kind man in Oliver's drawing.

"Ford's right," she heard herself say.

Oliver's eyes drifted shut, then he blinked hard, jolting himself awake.

"Oliver, it's okay if you fall asleep. Lady Bird and I will be here when you wake up. I promise," Maple said.

"Really?" the little boy asked, eyes wide as he buried a small hand in the ruff of fur around the dog's thick neck.

"Really." Maple nodded.

What was she saying? She had a plane to catch and a whole life waiting for her back in New York. Her *real* life, as opposed to the one here in Bluebonnet that was rapidly beginning to feel like some kind of alternate universe.

But try as she might, Maple couldn't think of a more

important place she needed to be at the moment than this hospital room. For once in her life, she was right where she belonged.

"You *do* realize what time it is, don't you?" Ford narrowed his gaze at Maple, still sitting at Oliver's bedside mere minutes before the deadline she'd given him when he'd picked her up earlier and all but dragged her to the hospital against her will.

"Not precisely, but I have a good idea," she said, gaze flitting toward the window, where the first rays of sun bathed the room in a soft golden glow.

Ford crossed his arms. "You made me promise to get you home in time for your rideshare to Austin. That means we need to go now, or all bets are off."

"I guess all bets are off, then." Maple reached over the guardrail of the hospital bed and rested a hand on Lady Bird's back. The big dog was stretched out alongside Oliver, paws twitching in her sleep.

Ford didn't know what to make of this unexpected turn of events. The dog's part in the impromptu sleepover was no surprise whatsoever. He'd seen Lady Bird sleep anywhere and everywhere, and the golden seemed especially fond of Oliver.

Maple, on the other hand…

Ford felt himself frown. Every time he thought he had this woman figured out, she threw him for a loop. It almost made her fun to be around.

"Why are you looking at me like that?" she asked.

"How am I looking at you?" Ford crossed the room to drag the other armchair closer to the recliner, where Maple had her feet tucked up under her legs. He raked a hand through his hair and sat down.

She gave him a sidelong glance. "Like you don't believe me when I say all bets are off."

"Probably because I don't. You seemed awfully sure about catching that rideshare."

She shrugged, but the way she averted her gaze told him her decision hadn't been as casual as she wanted him to believe. "I promised Oliver that Lady Bird would be here when he woke up."

Ford nudged her knee with his. "Careful there, Doc. You almost sound like a people person."

She turned to glare at him, but he could tell her heart wasn't in it. "I'm sure it's just a phase. I'll get it over it soon enough."

"If you say so." He bit back a smile.

"Can I ask you a question?" she asked, deftly changing the subject.

He leaned back in the chair and stretched his legs out in front of him. "Shoot. I'm an open book."

"What exactly do you do here?" She eyed his scrubs, and a cute little furrow formed in her brow. "Are you a nurse?"

"I'm a pediatrician. I have a solo practice in Bluebonnet, but I've got privileges here at County General. Oliver is one of my patients." Ford had, in fact, been Oliver's doctor since the day he'd been born. He loved that kid. Sometimes being a small-town doctor meant you got a little too close to your patients, although Ford usually didn't consider that a problem.

Oliver's case was different, though. *Special.* He would've moved heaven and earth to see that child healthy again.

The furrow in Maple's brow deepened, and Ford had the nonsensical urge to smooth it out with a brush of his fingertips. "Please tell me you're joking. You can't be a doctor."

"Not a joke. I assure you." A smile tugged at his lips. He

was enjoying her befuddlement a little too much. "What's wrong, Doc? Have you got a thing against physicians like you do against robotic animals?"

She regarded him with what could only be described as abject horror. "I do when said physician intentionally let me believe he wasn't a doctor."

Ford shook his head. "I never intentionally misled you. Name one time I did that."

"How about every single time you've called me Doc?" She was blushing again, and Ford wasn't sure if it was embarrassment or rage. Probably some combination of the two, if he had to guess.

"But you *are* a doctor—a doctor of veterinary medicine. As I recall, you seem especially proud of the title." Okay, so maybe the nickname had been somewhat of a taunt. Ford hadn't been able to resist.

She gasped as if she'd just remembered something, and then she covered her face with her hands. "Oh, my gosh. You let me go on and on about the two types of doctors, didn't you?"

"You mean general-practice physicians who are driven by their innate need to help people and specialists who relate more to the scientific part of medicine?" Ford said with his tongue firmly planted in his cheek as he parroted her own words back to her.

"I guess we know which one you are, Mr. Hometown Hero." She snorted.

She had him pegged, that was for sure. Ford had made it his mission to become a pediatrician back in the fifth grade when his best friend, Bobby Jackson, had died from acute myelogenous leukemia. Over the course of a single little league season, Bobby had gone from being the star pitcher for the Bluebonnet Bears to being bedridden with the disease. By Christmas, he was gone. Ford's small world had crumbled down around him, and in a way, he'd been trying to put it back together ever since.

So, yeah, he'd gone into medicine to help people. Was that really such a bad thing?

Lately, he'd begun to wonder. If he'd become a specialist instead of a pediatrician, he could've done more for Oliver and other children like him.

Children like Bobby, he thought as the memory of his best friend floated to the forefront of his mind. It had been years since Ford had spent the night at Bobby's ranch, tucked into their matching Spider-Man sleeping bags in the treehouse in Bobby's shady backyard. Two and a half decades, in fact. But he still remembered those nights like they'd happened yesterday—the shimmering stars overhead, the swishing of the horses' tails as they grazed in the pasture just beyond the barbed-wire fence, the feeling that Bluebonnet was the safest place in the world and nothing bad could ever happen there...

Ford knew better now, obviously. But that didn't stop him from doing his level best to make it true. He'd moved away once, and that had been a terrible mistake. Now, he was home for good and still trying to hold things together, as if it was possible to carry the entire town on his back. At least that's what his sister always said.

Maple resumed glaring at Ford, a welcome distraction from his spiraling thoughts. Why did things always seem so much more hopeless in the dead of night?

"You're impossible. I can't believe you didn't tell me," Maple said.

Ford arched an eyebrow. "You didn't ask."

She sure as heck hadn't. She'd barreled into town like a tornado, all too ready to flatten everything and everyone in her wake.

That had certainly backfired.

Ford had heard all about Percy's last will and testament. There were no secrets in Bluebonnet. By now, everyone in town knew that Maple Leighton was Percy Walker's long-lost daughter.

She'd had quite a day. Ford should probably go easy on her, but where was the fun in that? Besides, Maple didn't seem like the type who wanted to be treated with kid gloves. Everything Ford knew about her thus far screamed the opposite.

He slid his attention away from Oliver and Lady Bird, still sleeping soundly in the hospital bed, and found Maple watching him, eyes glittering in the darkened room. Their gazes met and held, until her bow-shaped lips curved into a knowing smile.

A delicious heat coursed through Ford, like wildflower honey warmed by the summer sun. "What's the grin for? I thought I was impossible."

"Oh, you definitely are." Her eyes narrowed, ever so slightly. "And that just made me realize something."

"What's that, Doc?"

She looked away, focusing on the boy and the dog. But Ford could still spy a ghost of a smile dancing on her lips. "You're not quite as nice as you seem, Ford Bishop."

Chapter Six

"What are we doing here?" Maple peered out the windshield of Ford's pickup as he pulled into one of the prime parking spots along Bluebonnet's town square.

He shifted the truck into Park and nodded at Cherry on Top Bakery, situated directly in front of them. "I promised you pie. Or have you decided to forgo that condition, too?"

Maple's heart thumped at the mention of her conditions. Missing her rideshare had seemed like a perfectly logical decision an hour ago, when she'd been sitting at Oliver's bedside with Lady Bird. Now, not so much.

She swallowed. Oliver had woken up shortly after she'd learned Ford was the boy's doctor. Maple had seen his eyes flutter open and then slam shut when he realized the adults were still there. Oliver made a valiant attempt at faking it, no doubt to prolong saying goodbye to Lady Bird. But as soon as Ford told Maple in a loud whisper that the hospital breakfast for the day would include sweet-potato, hash-brown egg nests—Oliver's favorite, apparently—the child sat up, bright-eyed and bushy-tailed.

Ford had escorted Maple and Lady Bird out of Oliver's room just as his breakfast arrived. Approximately two seconds later, panic settled in the pit of Maple's stomach.

What was she *doing*? She was supposed to be halfway to Austin right now, not sitting in close proximity to an actual gazebo beside Ford in his charming, vintage pickup truck. He had one of those classic turquoise Fords from the 1960s, and naturally, it was in perfect, shiny mint condition. What else would Dr. Small Town Charm drive?

·"The condition absolutely still stands." Maple was starving. She hadn't eaten a thing since diving head-first into the peach pie Ford had left on her front porch the night before. "But look, they're not open yet."

She waved toward the Sorry, We're Closed sign hanging in the bakery's front window. The rest of the town square was deserted, as well. Maple wasn't sure what time sleepy small towns like this typically woke up, but apparently it was sometime after 6:42 a.m.

Ford shrugged and flashed her a smile worthy of a toothpaste commercial. "I know the owner."

"Of course you do." Maple rolled her eyes.

Ford climbed down from the driver's seat and Lady Bird, who'd been nestled between them on the bench seat during the ride back to Bluebonnet from County General, bounded after him.

Maple paused, wondering how fast she could get to Austin if she went straight back to Percy's house to pack her things and summon another hired car. Why was this state so darn big?

Lady Bird gazed up at her with an expectant wag of her fluffy gold tail. *Are you coming or what?*

Maple's stomach growled, right on cue. There had to be other flights from Austin to New York today, right? They were both huge, metropolitan cities. Just because she'd missed the early morning flight didn't mean she was stuck here indefinitely. Surely, there was time for a tiny bite of pie.

She slid out of the passenger seat and headed toward the bakery, where Ford swung the door open like he owned the place. Lady Bird pranced straight inside while Maple lingered on the threshold.

She glanced at Ford as he held the door open for her. "Are dogs allowed in here?"

"What dog?" A woman with a high blond ponytail juggled pies in each hand and winked at them from behind the counter. "I don't see any dog, just my sweet nurse friend Lady Bird."

Lady Bird immediately got an extra spring in her step at the sound of her name. She trotted toward the counter, nose twitching in the general direction of the pies, which smelled like they'd just come straight from the oven.

"Hi, there. I'm Adaline." She slid the pies onto the counter and waved at Maple with an oven mitt decorated with the same whimsical cherry print as her ruffle-trimmed apron.

"I'm Maple."

"Maple is new in town," Ford said as he lowered himself onto one of the barstools at the counter. He gave the stool next to him a pat. "Come on, scaredy cat."

Adaline lifted an eyebrow.

"Maple is a tad shy," Ford said. "Right, Lady Bird?"

Maple *really* wished he'd stop staying that, although she supposed it was preferable to Ford broadcasting the fact that she'd told him she wasn't a people person. Did he have to say anything at all, though? Why did it feel like the entire town was populated by oversharers?

Lady Bird woofed her agreement before collapsing in a heap at Ford's feet. Great. Even the dog had an opinion about her social skills.

"Oh, wait." Adaline's eyes lit up. "You must be the peach pie from yesterday."

"That was me." Maple took the seat next to Ford. "It was delicious, by the way."

"So delicious that she insisted I bring her in for more." Ford pointed at one of the pies in front of Adaline. "Do I smell cherries?"

Adaline jammed her hands on her hips. "Ford Bishop, are you seriously waltzing in here less than an hour before we open, expecting to eat my inventory?"

"Yes." He nodded. "Yes, I am."

Maple glanced back and forth between them, wondering how they knew each other. The vibe between them was playful, but it didn't have a flirtatious edge.

Maple breathed a senseless sigh of relief. Lady Bird lifted her face from her paws and gave Maple a little head tilt, as if the dog could read her mind. Intuition was a valuable quality in a therapy dog, but in this case, it just seemed nosy.

And way off base. Maple didn't have a jealous bone in her body where Ford was concerned. In fact, a small-town baker was exactly the sort of person he should be with. Maple should be rooting for these two crazy kids.

Then why aren't you?

"Fine," Adaline said, relenting, then she reached for a silver cake server. "But only because Maple is new in town, like you said. She deserves a proper welcome."

"I'm not really, though—new in town, I mean." Maple protested as Adaline served up an enormous slice of cherry pie and slid the plate toward her. Her mouth was already watering. "I'm not staying in Bluebonnet. I'm leaving today, actually."

Probably, anyway. She still needed to get that figured out.

"Oh." Adaline shot Ford a loaded glance, which Maple had no idea how to interpret. "What did my brother do to scare you off so quickly?"

Maple's fork paused halfway to her mouth. "You two are brother and sister?"

That made sense. No wonder they seemed so comfortable around each other.

"We are." Adaline pulled a face, as if being related to Ford was something to be ashamed of.

Maple decided right there and then that she liked Adaline Bishop. She liked her a lot. Too bad she'd never see her again—or eat any more of her delicious baked goods—after today.

Maple swallowed a forkful of pie, and it suddenly felt like a rock in the pit of her stomach.

"I didn't do anything to scare her off. This big-city wariness you're observing is Maple's natural state. I've been nothing but welcoming." Ford cut his eyes toward her. When he looked at her like that—as if his dreamy blue eyes could see straight into her soul—she sometimes forgot how to breathe. It was beyond annoying.

Maple focused intently on the rich red cherries on her plate. "Except for the part where you tricked me into examining a fake dog. And then dragged me to the hospital in the middle of the night. And then lied about being a doctor."

A bark of laughter burst out of Adaline. "Oh, this is getting good. She's got your number, Ford."

"She also has quite a flair for exaggeration," Ford countered. "Where's *my* pie, by the way? You just gave her a supersized slice, and I'm still sitting here empty-handed."

"Hold your horses. I was just getting to know my new bestie." Adaline shot Maple a wink as she cut a significantly smaller piece of pie for her brother. "Too bad you're not staying, Maple. I have a feeling we'd be great friends."

"Yeah," Maple said quietly. "I think we would, too."

A heaviness came over Maple that she wanted to attribute to lack of sleep, but it felt more like regret. Aside from her study group in vet school, she didn't have many friends in New York.

"Are you sure you have to go so soon?" Adaline picked up a mixing bowl and began measuring cups of flour to dump into it.

"I actually just missed my flight. I need to try and get another one later this afternoon. Everything right now is a little—" she swallowed and didn't dare venture a glance in Ford's direction "—complicated."

Adaline nodded as if she understood, but a flicker of confusion passed through her gaze. How could she possibly understand when Maple still hadn't managed to get a handle on her current circumstances herself?

"I need—" she began, ready to rattle off a list of perfectly rational reasons why she needed to get back to Manhattan, starting with her highly coveted position at the veterinary cardiology practice. But before she could utter another syllable, her cell phone rang, piercing the awkward silence that had descended at the mention of Maple's missed flight.

She dug the phone out of her purse and nearly dropped it when she spied her mother's name flashing across the top of the display screen. Lady Bird let out a long, drawnout sigh.

Maple's gaze darted toward the dog, but the golden's sweet, melting expression only sharpened the dull ache of regret into something much more painful. What was going to happen to Lady Bird once she was gone?

Maple gripped her phone tight. "I should probably take this."

Lady Bird was practically the mayor of this town. The dog would have no trouble whatsoever finding a good home. Maple wouldn't be surprised if there ended up being a contest of some sort. She just needed to keep her eye on the prize long enough to get out of here.

The front door had barely closed behind Maple when Adaline abandoned her baking to give Ford a sisterly third degree.

"What do you think you're doing?" she said, pointing a wooden spoon at him for added emphasis.

Ford should've known this was coming. But truly, his sister was barking up the wrong tree.

"I'm eating my pie." He aimed his fork over his plate for another bite.

"Nice try." She slid the plate away from him, and his fork stabbed nothing but air. "You know what I'm talking about. What's going on between you two?"

Adaline cast a purposeful glance over his shoulder toward the town square, where Maple was now pacing back and forth as she talked on the phone. Lady Bird scrambled to her feet, trotted toward the door and proceeded to stare out the window at Maple while emitting a mournful whine.

"Nothing whatsoever is going on. Like I said, I'm just here for the pie. I'm perfectly content to mind my own business." Ford waved his fork\between his sister and Lady Bird. "Unlike you two."

"Oh, please. From what Maple said, it sounds like you've spent an awful lot of time together in the past twenty-four hours." Adaline pointed her wooden spoon at him again.

Ford just wanted his pie back. Was that really too much to ask?

"For the record, Maple hasn't even been here twenty-four hours yet." He snagged his plate back while Adaline processed what he'd just said. "And she's already got one foot out the door, so I repeat—nothing whatsoever is going on."

His sister eyed him with thinly veiled skepticism. "You bought her a pie yesterday, and from the looks of things, you just spent the night together."

Ford loved his sister. He really did. He loved Bluebonnet too, with all his heart and soul…despite the fact that the general population of his hometown—Adaline, included—had never believed in the concept of privacy. Every place on earth had its downside.

"We spent the night at County General. *Working.* I had patients to attend to, and Maple brought Lady Bird for a therapy-dog visit. That's all. I promised to bring her here in exchange for coming to the hospital in the middle of the night."

Adaline's expression turned serious. "Was this for the little boy who has leukemia?"

Ford's teeth ground together. He'd already told his sister too much about Oliver. He'd never disclosed the child's name, but even talking about one of his patients in vague terms went against his ethics as a physician.

The similarities between Oliver's case and his memories of Bobby were too much, though. Same diagnosis, same age, same sickening feeling in Ford's gut. Every time he ran Oliver's blood count or checked the results of his most recent bone-marrow aspiration, Ford was plunged straight back to that awful summer when Bobby stopped showing up at the baseball diamond and his parents couldn't look him in the eye when they tried to explain what was wrong. In a moment of weakness, he'd shared only the bare basics of Oliver's story with Adaline. She'd known Bobby, too, and she'd been there when Ford's safe little world had been rocked straight off its axis. Telling her had felt right at the time, and for a moment, a bit of the weight had lifted off Ford's shoulders. He'd been able to breathe again.

It had been a mistake. He knew that much now. Things

had been easier when Ford could compartmentalize his feelings and pretend everything was fine. He couldn't do that anymore now that Adaline knew the truth. It seemed Ford's sister had as much interest in his favorite patient as she did his romantic pursuits, and Ford had zero desire to discuss either.

"You know I can't talk about that," he said.

She held up her hands. "I know, I know. I just hope he's doing okay. It's sweet that Maple came up there so late, whatever the reason. Staying all night is a pretty big deal. That's all I'm saying."

Ford shot her a sardonic look. "Is it really *all* you're saying?"

That would be a first.

Adaline crossed her arms and huffed. "Fine. You bought Maple an entire pie yesterday. That seems significant, wouldn't you agree?"

Granted, Ford wasn't generally in the business of feeding women baked goods. Until recently, apparently.

"The peach pie was Gram's doing, not mine. I was simply following orders." He gave his dessert an aggressive jab with this fork. Why did he feel the need to defend himself when he was telling the truth? Nothing had happened between him and Maple, and nothing ever would. Period. "I took Gram and Coco to the vet yesterday, and Maple works there. Or she did... Clearly, that's changed."

He was getting whiplash trying to keep up with Maple's plans. Not that where she lived or worked was any of his business. He just needed to know how to get ahold of Lady Bird, that's all.

Ford choked down the last bite of his pie and pushed away his plate. He'd lost his appetite all of a sudden.

Adaline took the plate and placed it in the sink behind the counter. Then she planted her hands on the smooth Formica and fixed her gaze with his, eyes wary. Obviously, she wasn't buying what he was selling. "Do I need to remind you what happened the last time you got involved with a woman who wasn't suited for small-town life?"

She absolutely did not. Ford couldn't have forgotten that particular disaster if he'd tried. And, oh, how he'd tried— many, many times. Certain heartbreaks had a way of burrowing deep, though.

"No need," Ford said.

"Are you sure? Because Maple seems really great. I was serious when I said I thought we'd be great friends. But she's obviously not cut out for Bluebonnet."

Ford knew better than to ask his sister to elaborate, because that would mean he was taking Adaline's warning seriously. Which he wasn't. He had no interest whatsoever in history repeating itself, and Maple had been trying to escape Bluebonnet since the moment they'd first met. How could he forget?

I'm from New York City. But I live here now...temporarily.

They'd practically been Maple's first words to him, and Ford had heard them loud and clear. It wasn't possible to place a bigger emphasis on *temporarily.*

"She'll be gone by tomorrow morning, and it can't come soon enough. You can stop worrying about me." Ford jerked his head toward Lady Bird, still pining at the door while she kept track of Maple's every move. Adaline's pristine, polished glass was rapidly becoming smudged with golden-retriever nose prints. "Lady Bird over there might be a different story."

"That dog loves everyone," Adaline said.

Ford shook his head. "This is different."

Adaline's forehead scrunched. "How can you tell?"

"I just can." Ford's heart went out to the poor dog.

He wondered if the golden could tell that Maple was related to Percy. A while back, he'd read an article in a medical journal that speculated dogs could identify blood relatives purely by smell. If that was the case, Maple was now the closest thing Lady Bird had to Percy, whom she'd adored with unfettered devotion.

"Mark my words. If you're worried about anyone, it should be Lady Bird," Ford said. For once, the dog didn't respond to the sound of her name. She kept her gaze trained out the window, laser-focused on Maple's every move.

"Are you sure you're not just projecting?" Adaline cleared her throat. "From where I'm standing, you and Lady Bird have matching puppy-dog expressions. That's all I'm saying."

"That's *all* you're saying? Again?" Ford arched an eyebrow. "Is that a promise this time?"

It was too early in the morning for a deep dive into his love life. Not that he had any love life to speak of, which was purely intentional.

"For now. As for the future, I make no guarantees." Adaline wadded up her dish towel and threw it at his face.

"Duly noted," Ford said dryly.

Ever the perfect therapy dog, Lady Bird abandoned her post to shuffle back to the counter and press the bulk of her warm form against Ford's leg. Then she rested her chin on his knee with an audible sigh, leaving Ford to wonder which one of them was supposed be on the receiving end of the comfort being offered.

Man, dog…or, quite possibly, both.

Chapter Seven

The best Maple could do was get on standby for a two o'clock flight out of Austin. She'd checked all the major airlines, and there wasn't an empty seat to be found, much to the dismay of her mother. *And* her father.

Once again, the Leightons had joined forces as soon as they'd found out that Maple had missed her morning flight. She'd done her best to assure her mother she still had every intention of returning to New York as soon as humanly possible. But no sooner had she admitted to missing her rideshare than her father had jumped on the line.

What was happening? Who knew the only way to get her parents back on speaking terms was for her to go rogue, flee to Texas, and accidentally discover she'd been adopted.

Surely, Maple could get a standby seat on one of the five flights scheduled to leave between afternoon and midnight. What were the odds she'd get stuck here…*again*?

"Not going to happen," she said out loud as she folded her cupcake pajamas and placed them in her suitcase.

Lady Bird lifted her head from her paws, where she was resting on the dog bed in the corner of Percy's bedroom. She tilted her gold head in the irresistible way that dogs had been doing since the dawn of time, and a fresh wave of guilt washed over Maple. How was she going to leave this sweet dog behind? Lady Bird was the only remaining tie she had to the father she'd never known. Was she seriously going to get on a plane and let someone else take care of her when Percy had specifically left the dog in her care?

You never knew him, she reminded herself. Things would be different if she'd known she'd been adopted before Percy passed away. It was too late to get to know her birth father, and it was definitely too late to build a life in a place like Bluebonnet. She'd spent a full year as an intern for her cardiology specialty. Small towns didn't need veterinary cardiologists. Even if she wanted to stay and follow in Percy's footsteps at his charming little pet clinic—which she didn't—doing so would mean wasting a large chunk of her education.

And then there was the matter of Dr. Grover Hayes. If she stayed, he would be her *partner*. Maple didn't know which one of them would find that prospect more horrifying. It would be a disaster, full stop.

"Why am I even thinking about any of this? I'm not staying." She slammed her suitcase closed and zipped it shut. Then her gaze fell to Percy's bedroom slippers sitting neatly beside the bed, where Maple had returned them to their proper place.

Her eyes immediately filled with unshed tears, and she squeezed them closed tight, determined not to get weepy about a total stranger who just so happened to share her DNA. What was wrong with her? She never let her emotions get the best of her like this. No wonder her parents were concerned.

Maple sniffed and squared her shoulders. Then she opened her eyes and found Lady Bird sitting at her feet, holding Percy's slippers in her mouth.

You've got to be kidding me, dog.

Maple stared as her throat squeezed closed.

"Fine." She gently snatched the shoes from the retriever's jaws. "I'm taking these with me. Happy now?"

Lady Bird's mouth stretched into a wide doggy grin as her tail swished back and forth on the bedroom's smooth wood floor.

"You're really something, you know that?" Maple whispered. She shook her head, unzipped her bag, and carefully placed the slippers inside.

The vintage rotary phone in the kitchen trilled, causing her to jump. It was a good thing she wasn't staying, because she'd never grow accustomed to that sound.

"We're not answering that," she said, but before the words left her mouth, Lady Bird was already trotting toward the source of the noise.

Maple followed, keenly aware of which party seemed to be in charge in this relationship. Spoiler alert: it wasn't Maple. But that was fine for now. So long as the dog was bossing Maple around, she didn't have much time to think about a certain pediatrician who seemed to possess a warm and wonderful center that was as soft and gooey and perfect as a cinnamon roll fresh out of the oven.

He healed sick children. He frequented his sister's pie shop. He pretended his grandmother's robot dog was real. Was Ford even a real human being?

She eyed Lady Bird while the phone continued to ring. "I already told you we're not answering that."

But what if it was County General again? What if something had happened to sweet little Oliver?

Maple plucked the receiver from its hook, all the while telling herself that answering the call had nothing whatsoever to do with Ford Bishop, even though a teeny tiny part of her heart did a backflip at the thought of seeing him one more time before she left Bluebonnet for good. "Hello?"

"Oh, good morning! So happy you picked up. Is this Maple Walker?"

Maple's entire body gave a jolt. *Walker.* Percy's last name, not hers.

Was there a single soul in all of Bluebonnet who hadn't heard that Maple was his long-lost daughter? Apparently not—yet another reason to get back to Manhattan, where the details of her birth certificate weren't front-page news.

Maple "Um. Yes, but—"

"Thank heavens," the caller said before Maple could point out that her last name was actually Leighton, despite whatever she might have heard via the town rumor mill. "Technically, I'm calling for Lady Bird, but she's yours now, right?"

Once again, Maple had no idea what to say. This time, she didn't even try to come up with a response. She just kept her mouth shut and frowned down at Lady Bird.

I told you we shouldn't answer the phone.

The dog's plumed tail wagged even harder.

"This is Virginia Roberts over at Bluebonnet Senior Living. We were expecting Lady Bird fifteen minutes ago for her regular weekly visit. Can you let me know when she might arrive?"

"Oh." Maple's stomach churned. She couldn't allow herself to get roped into another pet-therapy visit. No way, no how. "Well…"

"We have about a dozen residents gathered in the lobby, ready and waiting. I'd hate to have to disappoint them." Virginia cleared her throat.

Maple gritted her teeth and counted to ten, steadying herself to say no. Granted, she technically had time to squeeze in a pet visit since her ride wasn't coming for another three hours.

But still…

No.

Just say it, she told herself. *Sorry, but no.*

Then she made the mistake of glancing back down at Lady Bird. She blinked up at Maple with such trust and devotion in her soft brown eyes that Maple's resistance crumbled on the spot.

"We'll be there as soon as we can."

Luckily, the senior center was located just off the town square, a short two-block walk from Percy's house. Maple followed the walking directions on her iPhone's GPS, but she could've simply allowed Lady Bird to guide her there, because the golden clearly knew where they were headed. She tugged gently at the end of her leash, making the left at the town square, followed by an immediate right, without any guidance whatsoever from Maple. The closer they came, the harder Lady Bird's tail wagged. When the sign for Bluebonnet Senior Living came into view, Maple could barely keep up.

It was a blessing, really. Maple's social anxiety didn't have time to kick in before Lady Bird dragged her through the door.

The young man who worked at the front desk lit up like a Christmas tree the instant they crossed the threshold. "Lady Bird! It's so good to see you! We've got a big crowd waiting for you, as usual."

The dog's tail swung back and forth, but her overall demeanor instantly changed. A steady calmness came over her, as if she knew she was here to work, just like it had at the hospital.

Maple couldn't help but swell with pride, even though she had nothing whatsoever to do with Lady Bird's training. That had been Percy's doing. Was it strange that she felt connected to them both, somehow?

"Hi, I'm Maple." She lifted a hand to wave at the young

man stationed at the reception desk while he pulled a box of dog biscuits out of his bottom desk drawer. "Sorry we're late. I didn't realize Lady Bird had a visit scheduled for today."

"No worries," he said as Lady Bird rose up onto her hind legs and planted her front paws on the desk to politely take the treat he offered her. "We're just glad you were able to make it. Her visit is every Tuesday morning at eleven, just so you know. We always have it listed on the social calendar."

He tipped his head toward a wall calendar covered with colorful stickers and handwritten activities like bingo and movie night listed in bright magic marker. A paw print featured prominently on every Tuesday square beside Lady Bird's name.

Now would be the time to mention that Lady Bird's future visits were up in the air, but when Maple glanced beyond the reception desk and saw a large group of residents sitting in wheelchairs and peering toward her and Lady Bird in anticipation, she just couldn't do it.

She took a deep breath as the first tingle of nerves skittered down her spine. This wasn't like the calm, quiet visit with Oliver. This was an entire group of people who would all be focused on Maple and the dog.

More the dog, she reminded herself.

They could do this. *She* could do this, so long as Lady Bird was on the other end of the leash.

Finished with her biscuit, the dog licked her chops and hopped back down to all fours. She dropped into a perfect sit position and gazed up at Maple expectantly.

Maple stared back, unsure what the dog was waiting for.

"Go visit," a deep voice rumbled from just beyond the reception desk.

"Excuse me?" Maple leaned to the left, and that's when she spotted him. *Again.*

Maple's heart did a rebellious little flutter.

She swallowed hard. "You."

"You," Ford echoed, narrowing his gaze at Maple.

He hadn't expected to see her again, well...*ever.* Once she'd ended her call earlier at Cherry on Top and come back inside the bakery, she'd been all business. She'd been in such a hurry to get back to Percy's house so she could pack and make new travel arrangements that, much to Adaline's consternation, she hadn't even finished her pie.

Their goodbye had been strained and awkward, and all the while, Ford had told himself it was for the best. Life could go back to normal around here.

Never mind that the prospect of normal suddenly felt a little dull. A little predictable.

A little lonely.

Ford gritted his teeth and reminded himself he didn't have any romantic interest in this woman. She was going to leave skid marks in her wake when she finally left town.

"What are you doing here? I thought you had a plane to catch," he said bluntly.

"I did." She blinked her wide doe eyes, a deer caught in headlights. "I mean I do. It's not until later this afternoon."

Ford dropped his gaze to the dog sitting at her feet, wagging her little gold heart out. A pang of...something hit him dead in the center of his chest. As much as he wanted to believe it was pity for the poor animal, it felt more like empathy. "If Lady Bird and I didn't know better, we might think you didn't really want to go."

"Good thing you both know better, then," Maple said, but she suddenly couldn't seem to meet his gaze. She seemed to be staring intently at his forearms, visible below the rolled-up sleeves of his denim shirt. Then she gave her head a little shake and aimed those wary eyes of hers back on his face. "What are *you* doing here? You're a pediatrician. Shouldn't you be passing out lollipops somewhere?"

Ah, there she was—the mouthy outsider that seemed to love nothing more than getting under his skin.

The joke was on Maple, though. Ford could see right through the arrogant little act of hers. It was simply a way of keeping people at arm's length, like the armored shell on an armadillo.

"I'm off today. Once a week I do an overnight at County General, and my office is always closed the following day. I was here to play bingo with my gram." He gave the pocket of his denim shirt a pat. "But if you have a hankering for a lollipop, I might have one on me."

"Thanks, but I'm good." She held up her hand to stop him, which was just as well since he was only teasing. "What did you say a minute ago, though? I'm not sure I caught it."

"The part about you having a plane to catch?"

"No." Her forehead puckered. "It was something about a visit."

"Ah. 'Go visit.'" Ford cast a glance at the dog. "That's what Lady Bird is waiting for you to say. Percy always gave her that command at the start of a therapy-dog visit."

Maple's gaze flitted toward the golden. "Go visit, Lady Bird."

The dog immediately stood and started trotting toward her senior fan club, already assembled in the living room area of the lobby.

Maple flashed Ford a grin over her shoulder. "It worked! Thank you."

"You've got this, Maple," he said with a wink.

"Wait." She stumbled to a halt. "You're not leaving, are you?"

He'd planned on it. Visiting Gram had provided him with a welcome distraction from work, but Ford had other things to do on his day off. Bingo had ended a good twenty minutes ago, yet here he stood.

"Why? Do you want me to stay?" Ford shifted his weight from one booted foot to the other. The words had fallen out of his mouth before he could stop them. Of course, that's not what Maple wanted.

"Yes." She nodded vigorously, eyes pleading with him. "I mean, if you don't mind, that would be great. I really don't know what I'm doing, and you've clearly been around Lady Bird and Percy on their visits."

"There's really not much to it. That dog is a natural." He had no business staying and spending more time with her. Hadn't he just promised his sister earlier that he wasn't getting emotionally involved?

Good luck with that. A bitter taste rose up the back of his throat. Ford's emotions had been running roughshod over him for months now. What he needed to do now was lock the horse back in the barn.

"You're right. Sorry, it was just a thought." Maple cast a panicked glance toward the senior citizens, and Ford did his best to pretend he wasn't intrigued.

The woman was a study in contradictions. Why was she here when she so clearly wanted to be anyplace else?

"I'll stay," he said, telling himself he was simply doing her a favor, just like he would anyone else in town.

Her pretty mouth curved into a smile. "You will?" Ford ignored the telltale thump of his heart as relief flooded her features. Tried to, anyway.

He tipped his head toward the common area. "Yep, but you should probably go ahead and get started. Gram and her friends don't like to be kept waiting. They're going to eat you two alive."

Maple's face fell.

"I'm kidding, Dóc." He leaned closer and gave her nose a playful tap. "Relax. Everyone's just happy you and Lady Bird are here. Trust me, you've got nothing to worry about."

"Except that I'm not certified to be doing this and everyone here has most likely been gossiping about me nonstop for the past twenty-four hours," she said with a wince.

She wasn't wrong, but dwelling on either of those things wasn't going to get her through the next half hour.

"Get through this visit, and I'll feed you more pie." Ford held up a finger. "Or better yet, barbecue. You can't leave Texas without a visit to Smokin' Joes."

Her nose wrinkled. "Why do I feel like now isn't the right time to admit that I don't like barbecue?"

That was downright blasphemous, but Ford had to cut her some slack. She'd obviously never had proper barbecue before. "That settles it. It would be a crime for you to leave Texas without giving our brisket a fair try. If you don't like it, fine. But you at least have to taste it."

She blew out a breath. "Okay, but only because you're saying."

"It's a d—" Ford swallowed the word *date* just in the nick of time "Deal."

"It's a deal," she repeated. Then she took a deep inhale and turned her attention toward Lady Bird. "Come on, Lady Bird. Let's go visit."

Chapter Eight

Maple really shouldn't have been so worried. Lady Bird knew exactly what to do, and as her handler, Maple was pretty much just along for the ride.

The dog moved deftly between wheelchairs, resting her head on the arm handles and allowing easy access for pats and scratches behind her ears. She didn't miss a beat, padding from one resident to the next, greeting everyone with happy tail wags and a wide doggy grin. Just a few minutes into the visit, Maple found herself relaxing into her role as Lady Bird's human sidekick.

Most of the seniors reminisced about dogs they'd known or shared stories about their childhood pets while Lady Bird worked her golden magic. A few residents even grew teary-eyed as they interacted with the dog, and Maple realized she shouldn't have worried so much about what to say. She didn't need to talk at all, really. Mostly, the retirees just wanted someone to listen.

Maple could do that. She liked hearing about the dogs that had meant so much to the seniors in years past, and it warmed her heart to see how simply petting Lady Bird for a few minutes could bring back such fond memories.

"Here you are again, you sweetheart," a woman with short salt-and-pepper hair and dressed in a colorful muumuu said as Maple and the dog approached her wheelchair.

"Oh, Lady Bird, I know I tell you this every week, but you remind me so much of my precious Toby."

The woman hugged Lady Bird's neck, closed her eyes and rocked back and forth for several long moments. Then she offered Maple a watery smile. "I had to give my dog up a few months ago. He lives with my granddaughter now."

"I'm so sorry to hear that." Maple pressed a hand to her heart.

"These visits help, you know. I never miss seeing Lady Bird. It's the highlight of my week." The woman cupped the dog's face with trembling hands. "Isn't that right, darling?"

Lady Bird made a snuffling sound and nodded her big gold head.

And so it went, from one bittersweet exchange to the next, until Maple's gaze landed on a familiar face.

"Hi, there," she said as they reached Ford's grandmother, sitting at the end of a floral sofa with her walker parked in front of her. The infamous Coco sat propped in a basket attached to the front of the mobility device. "It's good to see you again."

Lady Bird touched noses with the stuffed animal as if they were old friends.

"I remember you." Gram's face split into a wide grin as she gazed up at Maple. "You're the pretty new veterinarian."

"That's right." Maple kneeled beside Lady Bird so she and the older woman were on eye level with one another. "How is your little dog feeling today?"

"Much better, thanks to you." Gram reached shaky fingertips toward Lady Bird and rested her palm on the dog's smooth head.

"I'm glad to hear it. Treating her was my pleasure," Maple said, and the tug in her heart told her that she meant it. She ran her hand along Coco's synthetic fur and the dog's mechanical head swiveled toward her. It blinked a few times, and then its mouth dropped open and the toy dog made a few panting sounds, followed by a sharp yip.

"Coco likes you," Gram said.

"I'm glad. I like her too." Maple smiled. She could feel Ford's gaze on her, and when she snuck a glance at him, he was watching her with unmistakable warmth in his eyes.

Maple's heart leaped straight to her throat, and she forced herself to look away.

"Next time, we're bringing Coco to you instead of Grover." Gram leaned closer, like she wanted to tell Maple a secret. "He won't like that, but he'll get over it."

Maple couldn't help but laugh, and for a second, she let herself believe that there really would be a next time. Would that seriously be so bad?

Lady Bird nudged her way between Gram and her walker, plopped her head on the older woman's lap and peered up at her with melting eyes. Gram placed her hands on either side of the dog's face and told her she was a good girl, just like Coco.

"It's so nice that you brought Lady Bird here today. Your daddy would be so proud of you, you know," Gram said, eyes twinkling.

For a disorienting second, Charles Leighton's face flashed in Maple's mind. Her dad had never been much of a dog person. Neither of her parents really understood her affinity for animals, but she liked the thought of making her family proud.

When Maple had been a little girl, before her parents' marriage had broken down for good, she'd often thought if she could just be good enough, she could make things better for her family. Looking back, that was certainly when her anxiety had started. She'd foolishly thought that if she could behave perfectly, she could fix whatever had gone wrong between her mom and dad. She'd tried her best in school, but no amount of straight A's on her report card or gushing reviews from her teachers about her polite classroom demeanor changed things. Her parents' relationship kept spiraling out of control, and the only other thing Maple could do was try and make herself smaller so she wouldn't get caught in the crossfire.

That was all a very long time ago, obviously. But old habits died hard. Maple loved her parents, as imperfect as they were. She still wanted them to be proud of her—maybe even more so than if she'd followed in their footsteps and gone to law school. All during veterinary school, she'd waited for one of them to realize how wrong they'd been. Surely, they'd noticed how passionate she felt about helping pets…how *right* it seemed. She'd found her purpose. Shouldn't that make any parent proud?

Her mom and dad still didn't fully understand, but that was okay. Maple was a fully grown adult. Now she chose to believe that somewhere deep down, they really were proud of her, even if they didn't share her love for animals. And even if they didn't show it. Still, she couldn't help thinking that even the Leightons might appreciate the power of a dog's unconditional love if they could see Lady Bird in action.

But then, as Maple was reminding herself that the golden would be the absolute last thing Charles and Meredith Leighton would care about here in Bluebonnet, the true meaning of Gram's words sank in.

Your daddy would be so proud of you, you know.

Maple's smile felt wooden all of a sudden. "Oh, you mean Percy."

"Of course, I do." Gram nodded. "You're so much like him it's uncanny."

"I—" Maple shook her head, all too ready to disagree.

She was nothing like her biological father. Clearly, Percy had been deeply devoted to his community. Lady Bird had a busier volunteer schedule than any human she'd ever met, but the dog couldn't spread joy and happiness without a handler. Their therapy-dog work had been Percy's doing. He'd lived in a quaint town in a tiny pink house with fanciful gingerbread trim. He'd paid for her entire education, despite the fact that she didn't have the first clue who he was.

Percy Walker had left behind some very large shoes to fill, and those shoes had nothing to do with the slippers Maple had so hastily shoved into her bag.

"I think Lady Bird's hour is up."

Maple blinked and dragged her attention back to the present. Ford must've picked up on her sudden feeling of unease, because there he was, swooping in to save her from the conversation. She wasn't prepared to talk about Percy. It hurt, and she wasn't altogether sure why.

This, she thought. *This is why I asked Ford to stay.*

Thank goodness she had. She'd choke down an entire plate full of barbecue in gratitude, if necessary.

"Gram, isn't it just about time for arts-and-crafts hour?" he prompted with a glance toward the activities calendar.

"We're making crepe paper flowers today—dogwood blossoms, just like in the town square," Gram said.

"That sounds nice." Maple gave Lady Bird's leash a gentle tug to guide the dog out of the way while Ford helped his grandmother to a standing position behind her walker.

The woman in the muumuu who'd told her about Toby tugged on the sleeve of Maple's lemon-print Kate Spade dress. "You and Lady Bird are welcome to stay and make flowers with us."

"I'd love to, but I'm afraid Lady Bird and I already have plans this afternoon." Plans involving a food truck and a certain do-gooder who'd just rescued her right when she'd begun to feel out of her depth.

Oh, and catching a plane. She couldn't forget that crucial item on her agenda.

"Maybe another time," Gram said as she gripped the handles of her walker.

Maple didn't have the heart to admit that she and Lady Bird wouldn't be coming back. Instead, she simply smiled and said, "I'd like that very much."

Maple wasn't a thing like Percy Walker, but there was a certain type of magic about Lady Bird's therapy-dog sessions. Maple could feel it from the other end of the leash. She wasn't a patient, and these visits weren't about her, but accompanying the dog and seeing the effect she had on people filled her with hope. Joy. Peace...

And along with those precious feelings, the idea that perhaps it was okay that she wasn't just like her biological father. Maybe, just maybe, simply wanting to be like him was enough.

Ford cupped a hand around his ear and leaned closer to Maple, who sat opposite him at one of the picnic tables in Bluebonnet's town square. "I'm sorry, Doc. I'm going to need you to repeat what you just said. I'm not sure I heard correctly."

Maple's pupils flared. "You heard me the first time."

"Naw." Ford shook his head and offered Lady Bird a small bite of brisket, which she gobbled down with tail-wagging enthusiasm. "I don't think I did."

"Fine, you win." She pointed at the empty paper plate in front of her. "That was the most delicious meal I've ever eaten. Happy now?"

He winked. "Kinda."

"You're impossible." She reached to snag a Tater Tot from his plate.

He gave her hand a playful swat, but it didn't deter her in the slightest. "So I've heard."

After Lady Bird's visit to the senior center, Ford had made good on his promise to take her to Smokin' Joes. She'd hardly said a word during the short walk to the food truck, other than a quiet thank-you for intervening when Gram had brought up Percy. He'd swiftly changed the subject, poking fun of the fact that Maple continued to walk all over town in her fancy high heels, but she hadn't taken the bait. Not even when he promised her free medical services when she eventually twisted an ankle on the cobblestones in the town square.

It wasn't until she'd taken her first bite that she'd seemed to get out of her head. The second Joe's brisket passed her lips, she'd visibly relaxed. Within minutes, her eyes had drifted closed and the sigh she let out bordered on obscene. Ford had never been so jealous of a slab of beef, but there was a first time for everything, apparently.

"Seriously, where has real Texas barbecue been all my life?" Maple dabbed at the corners of her cherry-red mouth with her napkin.

"Right here in the Lone Star State, darlin'," Ford said.

Was he *flirting* with City Mouse?

It certainly appeared that way. Ford probably needed to reel that in. This wasn't a date, even though it sort of felt like one. It shouldn't, but it did. Or maybe Ford was just so rusty in the romance department that he'd forgotten what a real date felt like.

Probably that.

"Clearly, I should've made my way to Texas before now." Maple laughed, and then her forehead puckered like it always did when she was overthinking something. "Other than when I was a newborn, I guess."

She glanced around the town square, gaze softening ever so slightly as she took in the gazebo, the picnic tables surrounding Smokin' Joe's silver Airstream trailer and the dogwood blossoms swaying overhead. "I feel like I should remember this place. I know that's weird, but I can't help it. This could've been my home."

It still could.

He didn't dare say it. He shouldn't even be thinking it.

"There's so much I don't know about Bluebonnet... about my very own father." Maple swallowed, and then her voice went soft and breathy, as if she was telling him a deep, dark secret. "I wish I'd known him. Or, at the very least, that I knew a little bit more about him. Everyone in town seems to have known Percy, and I never got the chance to meet him."

"Maybe I can help. What do you want to know?" Ford didn't realize his fingertips had crept across the table toward Maple's until their hands were somehow fully intertwined. He told himself he was simply offering up moral support, pointedly ignoring the electricity that skittered over his skin at the softness of her touch.

"Everything." She shook her head and let out a laugh that was more than just a little bit sad around the edges. "Honestly, I don't even know where to start. He was a whole person with a whole life. It's easier to think of him as a stranger, but then someone will say something about him that resonates, and it catches me so off guard that I feel like the wind has just been knocked out of me."

Which is exactly what had happened at the senior center. He'd seen the pain wash over her face the second it happened, and in that fleeting moment, Maple's eyes had brimmed with a loneliness that had grabbed him by the throat.

He couldn't remember making a conscious decision to try and extricate her from the exchange with Gram. It had been pure instinct. He'd wanted to protect her, which was patently ridiculous. Maple was perfectly capable of taking care of herself. She'd made that much clear since day one.

But Ford knew there was more to Maple than the prickly image she seemed so hell-bent on showing to the world. She kept insisting she wasn't a people person, but last night when he'd seen her with her dainty feet swimming in Percy Walker's bedroom slippers, a hidden truth had shimmered between them. Maple wasn't a people person because she'd never had anyone in her life who she could fully trust with her innermost thoughts and feelings. She was hungry for connection, whether she wanted to admit it or not.

Against his better judgment, Ford wanted to help her find it. Adaline liked to say he was a fixer, and maybe she was right. He spent the better part of his time setting broken bones, mending scraped knees, and stitching childhood accidents back together. But bodies were like souls. No matter how tenderly they were cared for, they still bore the scars of yesteryear.

Just because he wanted to help her didn't mean he was in danger of developing feelings for her. And even if he was, he'd survive. Nothing would come of it. By this time tomorrow, she'd probably be busy examining a Park Avenue purse dog.

"What if we start small? That might feel less overwhelming. If you could ask me one thing about Percy, what would it be?" Ford gave Maple's hand an encouraging squeeze.

"Oh." Her bottom lip slipped between her teeth, and

Ford was momentarily spellbound. "Just one thing. Let me think for a second…"

She glanced around as if searching for inspiration until her gaze landed on Lady Bird. The big golden panted with glee, and Maple instantly brightened.

"Oh, I know." She sat up straighter on the picnic bench, and Ford could feel her excitement like little sparks dancing along the soft skin of her hand. "He was so into pet therapy. I'd love to hear how that started…how he first got involved with that kind of volunteer work. You don't happen to know, do you?"

"As a matter of fact, I do," Ford said.

"So…" Maple leaned closer, until Ford could see tiny flecks of gold in her warm brown irises. Hidden treasure. "Tell me."

"Okay." Ford nodded.

This was going to be rough at first, but if she could stick with him until the end, he had a feeling it was a story she'd like. It would definitely give her a bit of insight into the type of man her biological father had been.

"About five years ago, Percy's mother was diagnosed with an aggressive form of breast cancer," he said, only mildly aware that he'd begun to move his thumb in soothing circles over the back of Maple's hand.

"His mother." Her breath caught. "That would be my grandmother."

Ford nodded. She'd found a family and lost it, all in one fell swoop. Percy Walker had died without a single living heir besides Maple. "She taught first grade at Bluebonnet Elementary when I was a kid. I wasn't in her class, but Adaline was. She could probably tell you stories about her sometime if you were ever interested. Miss Walker was a big dog lover. Never met a stray she didn't love, if word around town was to be believed."

"That must be why Percy loved animals so much." Maple grinned and shook off a bit of her melancholy. "Maybe even why he wanted to be a veterinarian."

"No doubt," Ford said. And that love—that passion—had found its way to Maple, too. Against all odds. The good Lord really did work in mysterious ways sometimes.

"Go on. Tell me more," Maple prompted.

"Miss Walker entered hospice care within just a few weeks of her diagnosis. Bluebonnet Senior Living has a skilled nursing unit, in addition to assisted-living and memory-care wings. They made space for Miss Walker in a private room once it became clear she was in her final days and needed around-the-clock care. From what I remember about that time, Percy would work in the clinic all day then head straight to the senior center and sit by her bedside for hours, long into the night. Like most late-stage-cancer patients, she slept a lot and drifted in and out of consciousness." Ford cleared his throat.

Maple was gripping his hand fiercely now, bracing herself for whatever came next. A bittersweet smile tipped her lips when Lady Bird moved to lean against her leg. That dog was more intuitive than any human being Ford had ever met.

"While Percy's mom was in hospice care at the senior center, one of his patients gave birth to a litter of puppies. There were some mild complications, so the mama dog stayed at the pet clinic for a few weeks so Percy and Grover could keep an eye on her. One day, Percy piled all the puppies into a big wicker basket and took them with him on his visit to see his mom." Ford shrugged. "That probably wasn't technically allowed, but everyone knew how much Miss Walker loved dogs."

"So the staff at the senior center looked the other way?" Maple asked.

"Pretty much. She was dying. I'm guessing everyone just wanted her to have one last puppy cuddle, even if she might not have been lucid enough to realize it was happening," Ford said.

Maple shook her head, her brown doe eyes huge in her porcelain face. "That is both the saddest and sweetest thing I've ever heard. Please tell me she woke up long enough to see the puppies."

"She did. In the eulogy he gave at his mom's funeral, Percy said he placed the basket of puppies on her bed. Then he took her hand and ran her fingertips along one of the tiny dog's soft fur. He called what happened next a miracle." Ford had been at the funeral and heard Percy tell the story himself. When he spoke, the look on his face had been so full of wonder that there hadn't been a dry eye in the church.

"A miracle?" Maple tilted her head, and Lady Bird did the same in a perfect mirror image. Ford hadn't seen anything so cute in, well…ever.

Don't get attached to either of these two. Alarm bells clanged in the back of his head. *Ding, ding, ding.* Too late.

He swallowed. "Yeah. A bona fide miracle. Miss Walker opened her eyes, and as soon as her gaze landed on the basket, she broke into a glorious smile. Percy said for the first time in days, he had his mom back. She was herself again. She spent hours cradling those pups, cooing at them and laughing as tears ran down Percy's cheeks."

"Oh…" Maple's fingertips slipped out Ford's grasp and fluttered to her throat. "Wow."

"Yeah, wow." Ford's hands suddenly felt as if they had no purpose. He slid them into his lap. "Miss Walker passed away the following morning."

"Seeing her so happy with those puppies was Percy's last memory of his mom, and that's why he got involved with pet therapy. That's just...*incredible*." Maple's eyes went liquid.

"'There's no better medicine than a basketful of puppies,' your dad used to say. You want to hear something even more incredible?" Ford tipped his head toward Lady Bird. "This goofy dog who seems to have fallen head over heels in love with you was one of those puppies."

Maple gasped. "Lady Bird? Seriously?"

"Seriously." Ford's eyes flashed back to Maple, and he felt the corners of his mouth curl. He'd underestimated how good it would feel to help her put a piece of her family puzzle in place. He could've sat at that picnic table and kept talking and talking until he ran out of words.

If only she didn't have a plane to catch.

"Good girl, Lady Bird," Maple whispered against the soft gold fur of Lady Bird's ear.

The dog swiped Maple's cheek with her pink tongue, tail thumping happily against the square's emerald-green grass. Maple gave her a fierce hug, and for reasons Ford really didn't want to contemplate, an ache burrowed its way deep into his chest...all the way down to the place where he held his greatest hopes.

And his greatest hurts.

Ford shifted on the picnic bench. He needed space... just a little breathing room. But then Maple sat up and met his gaze, and he couldn't seem to move a muscle. She was looking at him in a way she'd never beheld him before— with eyes and heart open wide. Then her focus moved slowly, *purposefully*, toward his mouth.

Ford's breath grew shallow as Maple stood and leaned all the way across the picnic table. She came to a stop mere millimeters away from his face, lips curving into an uncharacteristically bashful grin.

"Yes?" she whispered.

"Yes," Ford said quietly. He couldn't get the word out fast enough.

Then she gave him what was undoubtedly the most tender, reverent kiss of his life. Just a gentle brush of her perfect lips, and Ford was consumed with a kind of yearning he'd never known before.

More. The blood in his veins pumped hard and fast. *More. More. More.*

She pulled back just far enough to smile into his eyes. "Thank you."

"For?" he asked, incapable of forming more than a single, strangled syllable.

"For telling me that story about Percy and the puppies. It might be the best gift anyone has ever given me."

Ford really hoped that wasn't true. Maple deserved better than that. She deserved a lifetime of birthdays with cake piled high with pink frosting and blazing candles, Easters with baskets full of chocolate bunnies and painted eggs, a puppy with a red satin ribbon tied in a bow around its furry little neck on Christmas morning. She deserved the perfect kind of love she seemed so hungry for. Yesterday, today…always.

He reached and tucked a lock of dark hair behind her ear. "There are more stories where that one came from."

But to hear them all, you'd have to stay.

Maple's gaze bore into his, and neither of them said another word. Bluebonnet could've burned to the ground around them, and Ford would've scarcely noticed. Then she kissed him one last time, and her lips tasted of honey and barbecue. Of soft Texas sunshine. Of the slow, sweet dog days of summer.

And only just a little bit of goodbye.

Chapter Nine

"Good morning, Maple." June looked up from the receptionist desk as Maple walked into the pet clinic the following morning with Lady Bird prancing at her heels. "Good morning to you, too, Lady Bird."

Lady Bird's tail swung back and forth. Maple shifted the bakery box and coffee carrier she held in her arms and breathed a little easier. She thought she'd braced herself for anything. Not this, though. The last thing she'd expected was a friendly morning greeting delivered with a smile.

"Good morning, June." She handed the older woman a steaming cup of coffee in a paper cup with the Cherry on Top logo printed on its side. A peace offering, since Maple hadn't exactly been the easiest person to get along with the last time she'd breezed through the door.

"Oh, my. Thank you." June accepted the coffee and took a small sip. "Is this Cherry on Top's famous Texas pecan blend?"

"It sure is," Maple said. Points to Adaline for suggesting her house signature blend.

Maple had been nervous about showing up here again today, especially since everyone in town thought she'd gone back to New York yesterday, as planned. She'd walked to the bakery as soon as they'd opened and picked up treats for the office, figuring they couldn't try and turn her away again if she came bearing pie and coffee. Mission accomplished.

The funny thing was, Adaline hadn't been surprised to see her, either. She'd even invited Maple to a book-club meeting later tonight, and despite the fact that spending an evening with a new group of total strangers would ordinarily be an automatic no-go, Maple had found herself saying yes. If she was going to stay in town for a while, she might as well try and make some friends. Get a little involved.

It's what Percy would have done.

"You know we have one of those fancy K-Cup machines here, right?" June nodded toward the area behind the reception counter. "You don't have to walk all the way to the town square just for coffee."

"I figured. I just wanted to do something nice for you and Dr. Hayes." Maple felt her determined smile wobble a bit.

A fresh wave of dread washed over her at the thought of facing that man again, even though he was technically her partner. They were *equals*. There was no reason for her to be intimidated by him...

Except for his overall grumpy demeanor, along with the fact that this was his home turf and he clearly considered Maple an unwelcome interloper. Other than that, things between them should be just peachy.

June's face creased into a sympathetic smile. "Do you want to hear a little secret, sweetheart?"

"Um, okay."

"Grover's bark is a lot worse than his bite," June said in a mock whisper. Then she winked and shifted her gaze over Maple's shoulder as the bells on the front door chimed. "Good morning, Grover. Maple is here for work, and she's brought us coffee and pie. Isn't that sweet?"

Great. He was already in the office. Any second now, he'd be standing right behind her.

Maple had hoped for a few minutes to get her bearings before her grump of a partner showed up. At the very least, she'd wanted to put her things down and slip a white lab coat over her flippy black-and-white polka-dot dress. No such luck.

She straightened her shoulders, pasted a smile on her face and turned around to face her partner.

"Hi there, Grover." She shoved one of the coffees at him and pretended she belonged there. Because she *did* belong. This practice was half hers now, whether he liked it or not.

Maple really needed Grover to get on board, though. The ink on her veterinary school diploma was barely dry. Last night, she'd made the decision to stay in Bluebonnet and work at the clinic...at least for a while. She just couldn't go back yet, and she certainly couldn't leave Lady Bird. *Ever.* Now that she knew the dog's backstory, keeping her was one-hundred-percent nonnegotiable. Maple had informed her adoptive parents of her decision via text and then she'd turned off her mobile phone like a complete and total coward.

But at least she'd done it. She'd made her own decision about her own life, and she was sticking by it. So far, Maple's plan consisted of little more than staying in Bluebonnet for a bit and learning more about her birth father and the place he'd called home all his life...plus working alongside Grover Hayes.

All she needed now was his cooperation.

He plucked the coffee from her hand with a harrumph. "I hope this is decaf."

"Totally," she lied.

Note to self: no more caffeinated beverages for Grumpy McGrumperson. Maybe he needed to rethink that position.

If anyone stood to benefit from a little caffeinated pick-me-up, it was Grover.

He took a gulp from his cup and glared at Maple for what felt like an eternity. Lady Bird started to drift off.

When Grover finally deigned to speak to her again, the dog's head jerked up with a start. "There's a kitten coming in at nine o'clock this morning for a routine checkup and her first round of shots. Do you think you can handle that, Dr. Leighton?"

Dr. Leighton.

He'd called her *Doctor*!

"Absolutely," she said, beaming.

Grover sighed mightily, but Maple couldn't have cared less. She'd take what she could get. At least he was willing to acknowledge her place at the clinic and give her a chance.

"Any questions or problems at all and you come find me. Understood?" He waved his coffee cup at her, and a drop sloshed out of the hole in the plastic lid. Lady Bird licked it up the second it hit the floor.

Grover sighed even harder.

Maple bit back a smile. "Understood."

After a cursory greeting aimed at June, Grover stalked past the reception area, headed for his office.

The instant the door slammed behind him, Maple shifted her gaze shifted toward the receptionist. "You're right. His bark really is worse than his bite, isn't it?"

"Told you," June said with a chuckle.

Maple glanced at the old-timey clock hanging beside the felt letter board that still listed Percy's name alongside Grover's in the reception area. Her feline patient was due in forty-five minutes—just enough time to locate the archaic file and familiarize herself with the kitty's history.

How old was she? Where had the client gotten the cat? Was this their only pet?

But Maple lingered in the lobby, not quite ready to get to work.

"Can I do anything for you, Maple? Is everything okay?" June's forehead creased with concern. "Percy's office is yours now. Don't hesitate to get settled in there. If you need help clearing things out, I'd be happy to assist."

Maple shook her head. She wasn't ready to get rid of Percy's things yet. Not here, and not at home. She wanted to study them first. Who knew what sort of hidden treasures she might find?

"It's not that, but thank you for the offer." Maple cast a curious glance in Grover's wake. "He didn't seem all that surprised to see me here this morning. Come to think of it, neither did you."

At Cherry on Top, Adaline hadn't been fazed. She'd greeted Maple like an old friend, and now Maple had an entire novel to read before the book-club meeting tonight.

June peered at Maple over the top of her reading glasses. "Come on now. You've been in Bluebonnet long enough to know that nothing stays secret here for long."

"But I didn't tell anyone I'd decided to stay," Maple countered. Not even Ford.

Especially not Ford, lest he think that her decision had anything to do with him. Because it didn't.

Not much, anyway.

"You didn't have to, sweetheart. You kissed Ford Bishop right in the middle of the town square yesterday." June tutted, but her lips twitched with amusement. "Did you really think that would go unnoticed in a place like Bluebonnet?"

Maple hadn't been thinking at all. She'd acted with her heart, not her head, which was something that had always terrified her. She knew all too well what happened when people threw caution to the wind and let their feelings go straight to their heads. A year or three later, they ended up sitting in her mom or dad's law office, fighting tooth and nail over everything under the sun. There was an awfully thin line between love and hate. *Razor* thin, honestly. After everything Maple had seen and heard, particularly within the walls of her own childhood home, she preferred to stay as far away from that line as possible. Besides, she liked being in control of her emotions. Things were safer that way…more predictable.

But after Ford told her the story about Percy and Lady Bird, she'd hadn't been able to stop herself.

Who even was she anymore?

All her life she'd been Maple Maribelle Leighton—dog lover, introvert, perpetual good girl and overachiever extraordinaire. Now she was starting to think she might be another person entirely. The trouble was, she had no idea what Maple Maribelle Walker was really like. The more Maple got to know her alter ego, the more dangerous she seemed. This new version of Maple had a penchant for straying far, *far* outside her comfort zone. She did things like purposefully miss flights, defy her family's expectations without thought to the consequences, and willingly throw away a shot at her dream job—not just once, but twice.

Oh, and she also kissed the local Hallmark hunk in the middle of the town square for all the world to see.

"That wasn't a regular kiss," Maple said primly. "That was a thank-you kiss. There's a difference."

"Oh, honey. Not from where I'm standing," June said with a knowing gleam in her eye. "I'm not sure how these things work up in New York, but here in Texas, a kiss is a kiss. Plain and simple."

There was nothing simple about it, though. Quite the opposite, in fact. Maple's feelings for Ford were growing more complicated by the hour, especially considering she shouldn't be having any feelings for him at all.

She blamed Bluebonnet for this entire mess. Everyone here seemed to think Maple was someone that she wasn't, and now she'd jumped right on the bandwagon and begun to believe it herself.

Even worse, she *liked* it.

Maple Maribelle Walker might be dangerous, but she was a heck of a lot of fun.

"Ford!" Oliver's hospital gown dipped off the child's bony shoulder as he struggled to sit up. "You're here! On a Wednesday!"

"I'm here. How's it going, bud?" Ford held up a hand for a high five.

Oliver gave it a weak slap. "Things are great now that you're here. Mom's at work again."

"I heard." Ford nodded.

He'd also heard that the child wasn't feeling well. Ordinarily, that wouldn't have been too much cause for concern. Chemotherapy treatment could be brutal, but according to the call Ford had gotten earlier in the day from Nurse Pam, Oliver had started running a fever after undergoing a bone-marrow biopsy early this morning.

Fever was always a concern for cancer patients. Chemo weakened the immune system, which sometimes led to infections. Oliver's fever had been running right around 100 degrees all day, and as long as it stayed low-grade, things would probably be just fine.

But a constant low-grade fever had also been one of Oliver's first symptoms when he'd been diagnosed with leukemia. His mom had brought him into Ford's office worried he might have an ear infection. Ford had assured her his ears were fine, but looking at the child's pale skin and the smattering of bruises on his extremities had sent a cold chill up and down his spine. He'd known something was wrong—something far worse than a simple childhood ear infection.

He'd been devastated to find out he'd been right.

"I also heard you weren't feeling so great." Ford glanced at the beeping monitor at the head of the bed. The body temperature reading flashed 99.3, and he breathed a little easier.

As soon as they got the bone-marrow biopsy results back, he could relax. Oliver was midway through treatment, and the test had been a routine check to monitor the effectiveness of the chemo. His oncologist expected good news, and Ford had taken the specialist at his word. Oliver was going to live a long and healthy life.

"I'm fine." Oliver's face spread into a hopeful grin. "Fine enough to play a board game."

"You got it." Ford nodded. An evening of board games with his favorite patient sounded great. Maybe it would help get his mind off the fact that Maple had kissed him silly yesterday afternoon.

He'd been busy all day today with back-to-back appointments and a quick lunch at the senior center with Gram. Adaline had called, but he'd ignored her voice mail. Knowing his sister, she'd heard about the kiss and wanted a thorough debrief…with a side of lecture about not letting himself fall for City Mouse.

Ford just wasn't in the mood. What difference did it make, now that Maple had gone back to New York? She'd kissed him, and then she'd fled.

Did she really, though?

He gritted his teeth. Nope, he wasn't going to let his thoughts go down that troublesome road. She'd missed one flight already. The odds weren't great that she'd willingly missed another. Besides, he had more important things to worry about.

Namely, keeping Oliver company.

"What's it going to be?" Ford scanned the collection of games, puzzles, and stuffed animals piled on the shelf below the window overlooking the rolling landscape of the Texas Hill Country. The sun was just beginning to dip below the horizon, spilling liquid amber over the hills and setting the wildflowers aflame. *"Apples to Apples? Candy Land?"*

Oliver groaned. *"Candy Land* is for kids."

"Noted." Ford swallowed a laugh. "My sincerest apologies. How about *Yahtzee?"*

"Yes!" Oliver punched the air.

See? The child is fine.

"*Yahtzee* it is, then." He grinned, feeling just a little bit lighter, a little bit more hopeful as he got the game set up on the bedside tray.

Then Ford noticed a small, greenish bruise on the child's forearm, and a weight settled on his chest.

He frowned at the tender spot on Oliver's arm and wondered where it had come from…how long it had been there. Why hadn't he noticed it before?

It's just a bruise. Kids get them all the time. A bruise doesn't have to mean anything.

Oliver spilled the dice onto the table, and the clatter pulled Ford back into the moment.

"Look, I got three fives already." The boy's eyes lit up as he pointed to the dice. "I'm so lucky. Right, Ford?"

Ford tensed at the choice of words, but he pushed down

his worry and flashed Oliver a smile and a thumbs-up, even as his throat constricted, making a response almost impossible.

"You sure are, kiddo. The luckiest."

Chapter Ten

"Maple!" Adaline held her front door open wide and beckoned Maple inside. "I'm so glad you could make it. Come on in and meet the rest of the girls."

Maple hesitated for a beat. Here she was again, about to dive headlong into an uncomfortable social situation, and this time, Dr. Small Town Charm wasn't there for backup. But the smell of freshly baked pies wafted from the inside of Adaline's house, and Maple had spent every stolen moment today speed-reading her way through the book club's chosen novel. She'd never missed a homework assignment in her life, and she wasn't about to start now. Not even for a recreational reading club.

So in between administering kitten vaccines and removing porcupine quills from an understandably traumatized chocolate Labrador retriever—a task that veterinary school in New York City had in no way prepared her for—she'd snuck into Percy's old office for a few stolen moments and plopped into his chair with her nose in the book. She'd had to resort to speed-reading as the day wore on, but she was here.

And she was ready. Mostly, anyway.

"I hope it's okay that I brought Lady Bird with me," she said as she followed Adaline past the entryway toward the living room, where it sounded like a group of women were talking over one another with happy chatter.

Maple hadn't asked if the dog could tag along, but something told her that if Lady Bird was welcome at Adaline's bakery, her new friend wouldn't have a problem with the golden attending a book-club meeting. Also, the novel was part of a romance series that centered around an animal rescue called Furever Yours. Maple had a feeling she'd stumbled upon a group of pet lovers, which had only made her more excited about tonight. These were her kind of people. Maybe she'd make some genuine friends.

"Are you kidding?" Adaline cast an affectionate glance at the dog. "Lady Bird is practically a local celebrity. Everyone is going to love that you brought her."

Sure enough, the instant they crossed the threshold of the cozy living space, the animated conversation came to an abrupt halt as every head turned toward the dog.

"Lady Bird!" the other two women scattered about the room cried in unison.

A more timid dog probably would've turned tail and hid beneath the closest end table at the effusive greeting. Not Lady Bird. The dog thrived at being the center of attention. Tail swinging, she pranced toward the closest human and sat politely at her feet, waiting to be petted.

Adaline gave Maple a knowing grin. "Told you."

"You must be Maple." A woman with blond hair twisted into an artful bun stood and extended a graceful hand toward Maple. "Hi. I'm Jenna. I own the dance studio on Main Street, just around the corner from the town square."

"It's a pleasure to meet you," Maple said as she shook her hand.

A ballerina, she thought. That made perfect sense. Jenna definitely looked the part.

"We've all heard so much about you. I'm Belle," the

woman sitting beside Jenna on the sofa said with a wave. "I'm the librarian at Bluebonnet Elementary School."

"Wait." Maple blinked. "You're a librarian, and your name is Belle?"

"I know, right? With a name like mine, I guess I didn't have much of a choice." The corners of Belle's mouth turned up. "It's a good thing I love books."

And so it went. The women chatted while Lady Bird shuffled from person to person and wagged her tail with such zeal that she nearly took out the wineglasses scattered atop the coffee table in the center of the room.

"Lady Bird, I would lay down my life for you, but if you knock over my cabernet, we're going to have a serious problem," Belle said with a mock glare in the dog's direction.

"I'm so sorry." Maple attempted to lure the dog back to her side, but she was too busy playing social butterfly to pay attention.

"Don't worry. There's more wine where this came from. I promise." Adaline handed her a glass.

"There's also pie. Adaline makes a new creation for every book-club meeting," Jenna said.

"I like to test out new recipes on our little group before I add them to the bakery menu. I hope you don't mind being a guinea pig." Adaline gave Maple a questioning glance.

"For pie? How is that even a question? Of course, I don't mind."

The conversation grew more boisterous over the next two hours, and the wine flowed while the women discussed the book. It didn't take long for Belle to ask Maple if Lady Bird might have time in her schedule to visit the school library and help struggling readers with their skills. She'd read an article online recently about therapy pets acting as reading education assistance dogs. Jenna piped up to see if Lady Bird could come to the first day of her toddler pre-ballet class in the fall and mentioned that a teacher friend of hers thought that having a therapy dog at Bluebonnet Elementary's back-to-school events would help ease nerves for new students.

Maple loved their enthusiasm, even as it quickly became apparent that she and Lady Bird would never be able to keep up with all the community requests for pet therapy. And so far, all the requests were the result of word of mouth. There was no telling what might happen if Maple put actual effort into building a comprehensive therapy-dog program. The possibilities were endless. Hospitals, nursing homes, schools, airports, courtrooms, crisis response...

During vet school, Maple had read extensively about therapy pets working in all these settings and more. She'd just never imagined she'd have one. There was no question that Lady Bird could help spread love and joy anywhere there were people who needed a little comfort, affection, and support.

But Lady Bird was just one dog. Not to mention the spectacular mess that was Maple's personal life. She didn't know how she was going to keep up with Lady Bird's commitments, as it was.

"Thank you so much for inviting me tonight," Maple said as she helped Adaline get the dessert ready in the kitchen once the book discussion was finished. "Your friends are really great."

"They're your friends now, too." Adaline waggled her eyebrows. "That's how things work around here."

Maple smiled to herself. She had a house, a job, and the best dog on the planet. Now, she even had friends here in Bluebonnet. Somehow, in a matter of days, she'd built more of a life here in this small town than she'd ever had back in New York. If she wasn't careful, she might end up staying for good.

"Don't let them pressure you and Lady Bird, though." Adaline snuck a nibble of piecrust to the dog, who'd been staring intently at the kitchen counter, nose twitching. "You're just getting your footing here, and they know that. But you've also got an amazing dog."

Maple's heart swelled. "I do, don't I?"

"Should I thank her for convincing you to stay, or did that decision have to do with something else?" Adaline's smile faltered ever so slightly as she slid a slice of pie onto a china plate with a pretty rose pattern and handed it to Maple. "Some*one* else, maybe?"

"Oh, you mean Percy?"

"No, not quite." Adaline gave her a sideways glance as she plated another slice of pie. "Here's another fun fact about small towns—there's only one way to stop people from talking about the latest hot gossip. Do you know what it is?"

I wish. Maple shook her head, riveted. As one of the most recent subjects of the Bluebonnet grapevine, this seemed like valuable information. "I don't, but really I'm hoping you're about to tell me."

"You wait it out, because sooner or later something else scandalous will happen, and everyone will start talking about that instead. People have notoriously short attention spans."

"So you're saying eventually everyone will lose interest in my family situation." Maple couldn't wait. Whatever the new scandal might be, she was ready for it.

Adaline's forehead creased. "Oh, honey. Didn't you know? They already have."

"What's the new scandal?" Maple couldn't believe she'd missed it.

Adaline pointed the pie slicer at her. "You kissing my brother in the middle of the town square, obviously."

Oh.

Oh.

Maple's cheeks burned with the heat of a true Texas summer. "That wasn't what it looked like."

Adaline's eyebrows shot clear to her hairline. "So you didn't lock lips with Ford at a picnic table by Smokin' Joes?"

"It was a thank-you kiss," Maple countered.

"That's not a thing," Adaline said flatly.

Why did people keep saying that?

Because it's not, and you know it.

Maple longed for the floor of Adaline's kitchen to open up and swallow her whole. This wasn't a conversation she wanted to have with Ford's sister, of all people.

Of course, Maple found Ford attractive. Very, *very* attractive. And, yes, she might even have feelings for him. But how was she supposed to make sense of those feelings when her entire life had so recently been turned upside down?

"Look, I like you, Maple. A lot. I hope you stay in Bluebonnet forever. Not just because I worry about my brother, but because I want us to be friends. Real friends." Adaline put down the pie cutter and took both of Maple's hands in hers. Lady Bird's furry eyebrows lifted as her gaze darted back and forth between them. "When you live in a town as small as Bluebonnet, new friends aren't very easy to come by. I'm so glad you're here."

"I am, too," Maple said, breathing a little easier. "But can I ask why you're worried about Ford?"

"That was probably an exaggeration. Ford is a grown man, and he can obviously take care of himself. Goodness knows, he takes care of practically everyone else in this town."

"So I've noticed," Maple said. It was one of his most endearing qualities.

Adaline paused, as if weighing her next words carefully. "Did he tell you he left once...just a few years ago?"

"Ford left Bluebonnet?" Maple couldn't wrap her head around it. She couldn't imagine him living anyplace else. He seemed as deeply ingrained in this community as Lady Bird was.

Adaline nodded. "He took a job up in Dallas at a state-of-the-art children's hospital there. I could tell straight away he didn't love it like he loves Bluebonnet, but Ford is very serious about his work. He was excited about the many opportunities to help kids up there. Then he met someone—another doctor, whose father happened to be chief of staff at the hospital. After dating for about six months, Ford asked her to marry him."

Maple's stomach instantly hardened. Spots floated in her vision as a wave of jealousy washed over her so hard and fast that she swayed on her feet.

Ford had been *engaged*?

It shouldn't have come as a surprise. Ford Bishop was clearly the marrying type. He doted on his grandmother, frequented his sister's bakery and devoted his life's work to caring for sick children. If that wasn't the very definition of *family man*, Maple didn't know what was.

Still, the revelation came as a shock. Maple didn't want to think about Ford slipping a diamond on another woman's finger or, heaven forbid, watching someone else walk toward him down the aisle of some cute country church. Someone vastly unlike Maple, obviously. Someone who belonged by his side. Someone gentler, sweeter...kinder.

Someone who'd fit right in someplace like Bluebonnet, Texas.

Then again, maybe not, because Adaline's expression turned decidedly sour as she prepared to finish recounting the story. She took a deep breath and seemed to make an effort to neutralize her expression, but the smile on her face didn't come close to reaching her eyes.

"I was so happy for him. I missed seeing him nearly every day, obviously. Our parents retired and moved to Florida right about the time Ford and I graduated from college, so other than Gram, my brother was all the family I had in Bluebonnet." Adaline blew out a breath. "Then one day Gram had a bad fall. She'd been having some mild memory issues up until then, but the fall changed things. Gram just didn't bounce back. Ford rushed home as soon as it happened. He was only supposed to be here for a few days, but then…"

Adaline's voice drifted off, and Maple could guess what came next.

"He decided to stay, didn't he?" She knew it, because that's the kind of person Ford was. He valued things like family and community and responsibility. He would want to be here with his grandmother when she was at her most vulnerable, no matter how capable Adaline and Gram's caregivers at the senior living center might be.

"He did." Adaline nodded, and her smile turned bittersweet. "I can't say I was disappointed. It was so nice to have him back, and I could tell straightaway that Ford was happy to be home, despite the circumstances. His voice had taken on a certain edge whenever I spoke to him on the phone. Once he came back, he was like his old self again. Even when Charlotte postponed her plans to join him, he seemed unfazed. I don't think it ever crossed his mind that she'd never come here."

Maple swallowed. *Charlotte.* Putting a name to Ford's ex made the woman all the more real, and a fresh stab of envy jabbed Maple right in the heart. Ridiculous, considering they'd very clearly broken up. Somehow, that didn't make her feel any better.

"Never?" Maple asked. "You mean she didn't even give Bluebonnet a chance?"

She wasn't sure why she felt so indignant on behalf of a town she'd first set foot in only a few days ago. It wasn't as if Maple had been thrilled at the prospect of spending one measly year in Bluebonnet.

But here you are, even after getting handed a get-out-of-jail-free card.

"Charlotte kept putting it off, over and over again. Her parents put a lot of pressure on her, especially her dad. Since he was head of the hospital up there, he thought moving to a place like Bluebonnet was akin to career suicide," Adaline said.

Maple shifted her gaze to the countertop as shame settled in the pit of her stomach. She'd had the exact same thought...more than once. How could she not, when there was a prestigious cardiac practice in New York ready and willing to give her a job?

"There's more to life than work, you know?" Adaline said, as if she could see straight inside Maple's head. "Even when your work is something vitally important, like looking after children's physical and emotional health."

That's right. They were talking about Ford's work, not Maple's. Still, she couldn't shake the feeling that this conversation had more to do with her than she wanted to admit.

"Anyway, like I said, I want us to be friends. I really like you, Maple." Adaline handed her the last slice of pie, neatly plated and topped with whipped cream. "But until you're sure that you want to stay in Bluebonnet for good, I hope you'll think twice about giving Ford any more 'thank-you kisses.'"

And there it was.

Adaline was calling her bluff on the entire concept of a thank-you kiss, and Maple didn't blame her one bit. Who was she kidding? She hadn't kissed Ford simply because she'd been grateful. She'd kissed him because the longer she stayed in Bluebonnet, the more she wanted to know what it felt like to press her lips against his... To feel his strong hands cradle her face with a gentleness that made her forget how to breathe... To open her heart just a crack to the possibility of not spending the rest of her life alone...

"You can see why it might get confusing, don't you?" Adaline said with a kindness in her tone that Maple didn't deserve.

"I do." Maple nodded. Boy, did she ever. She'd never been so confused about things in her life.

What happened to the carefully orchestrated plan she'd made for herself? In less than a week, all her dreams had completely fallen by the wayside. Just because she'd discovered she'd been adopted didn't mean she had to change her entire life.

But what if you want to change, a voice whispered in the back of her head. *And what if your dreams change, too? A new life is possible, and so are new dreams.*

Maple blinked hard. She felt like crying all of a sudden, and she absolutely refused to get weepy in Adaline's kitchen over the prospect of something silly like not kissing Ford Bishop again.

It didn't feel silly, though. It felt like another heartbreak, another loss—the loss of yet a different life she'd never experience.

"Don't worry." The effort it took to smile was monumental. "You have my word. It won't happen again."

She wanted to reel the words back in the very second they left her mouth. Maple knew better than to make promises when she was in the midst of an existential crisis. It seemed like she'd completely lost control over rational thought, particularly when she was anywhere in the vicinity of Ford. What made her think she could exert any sort of sensible decision-making where he was concerned?

Because you care about him, and the last thing you want to do is hurt him.

And she wouldn't. *Couldn't*. The next time Maple saw Ford, she'd just turn off her feelings like a light switch. She'd simply have to learn to ignore the way his eyes crinkled in the corners, as if kindness and laughter came naturally to him… The irresistible pull she felt toward him every time he was near… The breathtaking habit he had of seeing past her frosty exterior, all the way down to her tender, aching heart.

That shouldn't be a problem, right? Maple had all sorts of practice at erecting a nice, strong wall around her innermost thoughts and emotions. She'd been doing it her whole life.

But then the back door of Adaline's quaint little kitchen swung open, and there he was—Ford, in the flesh, looking casually heroic in a pair of hospital scrubs that made his eyes sparkle bluer than ever. And the second those eyes homed in on her, they widened in surprise. Maple practically melted into a puddle as he drank in the sight of her, and the corners of his lips curved into a slow and easy grin.

"Well, look who missed her flight." He arched a single, all-too-satisfied eyebrow. "Again."

Chapter Eleven

She's still here. The tension in Ford's body began to ease the instant he spotted Maple. *Not just here in Bluebonnet, but right here in Adaline's kitchen.*

Never had there been such a sight for sore eyes.

Since he hadn't heard a word from her since their kiss the day before, he'd assumed she'd really left this time, as planned. Once he'd checked on Oliver and realized some of his initial symptoms had returned, Ford's singular focus had been on his patient. The fact that he'd missed such an important piece of local gossip was a testament to how distracted he'd been.

"I decided to stay a bit longer." Maple swallowed, clearly caught off guard by the sight of him. She crossed her arms, then uncrossed them, and recrossed then again, as fluttery and nervous as the day they'd met.

Ford tilted his head. "You okay there, Doc?"

"Fine," she said. A lie, if he'd ever heard one before.

What exactly was going on here?

Alas, Ford didn't have a chance to ask because Lady Bird had finally torn her attention away from the pie plate on the kitchen counter and registered his arrival. The dog's paws scrambled for purchase on the slick floor in her haste to get to him. Ford braced for impact as she crashed into his legs and threw herself, belly-up, at his feet.

"Hey there, sweet girl." He crouched down to give her a belly rub. "At least someone's happy to see me."

Maple let out a cough, and Ford winked at her.

"Maple is here for book club. We're finishing up soon." Adaline frowned down at her brother. "What are you doing here? And why are you in scrubs? You already did your shift at the hospital this week."

Ford straightened. "I did, but I wanted to stop by and check on a patient who wasn't feeling well. I ended up staying for a while."

After spending the evening playing *Yahtzee* with Oliver, he hadn't felt like going home to an empty house. Plus he knew that his sister always made fresh pie on book-club nights, so he'd swung by, hoping Adaline would take pity on him and let him crash the festivities. The last person he'd expected to find here was Maple.

Not that he was complaining.

"I hope everything is okay." Concern glowed in Maple's big brown eyes.

A look passed between them. She'd met Oliver and likely had a good idea how special that kid was to Ford.

He wished he could say more, but he couldn't discuss his patients. Ford's face likely said it all, though, as Maple's look of concern only deepened after their eyes met.

He gave his head a small shake, indicating they all needed to move on to a different, safer topic of conversation.

"We have pie." Adaline offered him a plate.

He took it and reached for a fork. "Thanks. I was hoping you might."

Adaline's gaze flitted toward Maple. "Come on in. You can join the rest of the book chat."

"But I haven't read the book."

Adaline shrugged. "It doesn't matter. Right now, everyone is pretty much just gushing over Lady Bird, anyway. If Maple isn't careful, that dog is going to be booked twenty-four-seven with therapy dog visits."

"Grover would love that. I'm not even joking. I think he'd actually prefer it if I was out of his hair and he could handle the pet clinic all on his own," Maple said.

"I doubt that," Ford countered as they headed toward the living room, even though he was fully aware the elder veterinarian could be a little rough around the edges.

Maple knew her stuff, though. Surely, Grover could see that, or maybe Ford just needed her to believe she was welcome at the pet clinic…welcome enough to make her stay in Bluebonnet permanent.

Maple aimed a sideways glance at Ford. "Have you met Grover Hayes?"

"Point taken." Ford laughed, but before he could offer a word of encouragement, Adaline swept between them and steered them toward chairs on opposite ends of the room from each other.

Lady Bird immediately left him in the dust to follow Maple. No big surprise there, but Ford felt lonely all the way on the other side of the living room, despite being surrounded by Adaline's friends. As the evening wore on, his gaze kept straying toward Maple. And once the pie had disappeared and the women had decided on their next book-club read, the night came to its inevitable close.

"Maple, where's your car?" Adaline peered toward the driveway from the front porch, where everyone was saying their goodbyes. "I figured you'd be driving Percy's truck."

Maple shook her head. "We walked."

Adaline's gaze dropped to Maple's feet, once again clad in a pair of strappy high-heeled numbers that looked more appropriate for a beauty pageant than walking a dog. "In *those*?"

"My wardrobe options are limited," Maple said, and Ford could see her blushing even in the silvery moonlight.

"I need to take you shopping," Adaline said.

"Here? I didn't realize Bluebonnet had much in the way of fashion."

Adaline grinned. "Oh, you just wait."

"Meanwhile, I'm happy to give you and Lady Bird a ride home," Ford interjected before someone else could offer.

"Oh." A look of a panic flitted across Maple's face. "That's really not necessary. Lady Bird and I have been walking all over town together. We like it, don't we?"

Lady Bird wagged her tail, which meant nothing whatsoever. The dog would've agreed to anything Maple asked her in that soothing, singsong voice of hers.

"It's late." Without warning, Ford reached for Lady Bird's leash and slipped it out of Maple's hand. "And dark."

And Ford wanted to spend more time with her. Mostly, he wanted to know why she suddenly seemed keen to avoid him. He'd thought those days were over. The last time he'd seen her, she'd leaned over a picnic table in the middle of the town square and given him the most perfect kiss of his life.

"Ford, you know better than anyone that Bluebonnet is perfectly safe. If Maple wants to walk, you should let her," Adaline said with a slight edge to her voice. "She doesn't need your permission."

All at once, Ford knew exactly what was going on.

He turned toward his sister. "Adaline."

"Ford," she said with a tiny quiver in her chin.

Jenna and Belle fled toward their cars, no doubt eager to avoid a sibling squabble. Maple stayed put, and Ford knew good and well it was only because he still had Lady Bird's leash wrapped around his hand.

He knew he shouldn't be angry with Adaline. His sister loved him and didn't want to see him hurt again. She'd already said so at the bakery, but she also needed to mind her own business. He was a grown man, and if he wanted to give Maple a ride or walk her home, there wasn't a pie in the world that could stop him...

Provided Maple let him, of course.

"Maple, may I walk you home?" he asked quietly. He suddenly liked the idea of a nice quiet stroll. It would give them time to talk, which suddenly seemed quite necessary.

Lady Bird's head swiveled toward him, and she let out a booming bark at the word *walk*.

"Your dog seems to love the idea," Ford said. He owed Lady Bird a dog biscuit now...possibly three.

Maple's eyes sparked with amusement. "You truly are impossible, you know that?"

"So you've said." Ford shrugged. "Several times, in fact."

"For the record, I concur. You *are* impossible." Adaline glared at him and then turned toward Maple with an apologetic smile. "Don't let me stop you. I should probably start letting my brother live his own life."

"You really, *really* should," Ford muttered.

"Good night, Maple. I'm really glad you came tonight. I hope to see you at our next book club." Adaline gave Maple a quick hug and, with a wave at Ford, she disappeared inside the house, leaving the two of them alone on the porch.

Ford offered Maple his arm. "Well, what do you say? It's a nice night for a walk, and we wouldn't want to disappoint Lady Bird."

"She might never forgive me, so I should probably say

yes." Maple wrapped gentle fingertips around the crook of his elbow. "For Lady Bird."

"For Lady Bird," Ford echoed and smiled into the velvety darkness as the golden retriever guided them toward home.

"So tell me the truth." Ford gave Maple a sidelong glance that somehow felt as real as a caress, despite the darkness that surrounded them.

A nighttime Texas sky was nothing like the neon lights of New York City. Out here, the darkness was so thick that the stars glittered like diamonds overhead. For the first time ever, she could see the constellations. It made her feel tiny and larger than life, both at the same time.

"The truth about what?" she asked in a whisper. That was another thing about Bluebonnet after hours—the silence. There were no sirens, no honking cabs, no city noises to keep her up at night. Just a casual walk home felt intimate in a way that made goose bumps dance across her skin.

"What's the real reason you're not driving Percy's truck around town?" Ford said with a smile in his voice. "You don't have a driver's license, do you?"

She gasped in mock horror. "I beg your pardon, I certainly do. Just because I'm from Manhattan doesn't mean I don't know to drive."

"And when exactly was the last time you were behind the wheel of an automobile?"

Touché. He had her there.

"The day I got my license." She cleared her throat as Ford chuckled with self-satisfaction. "But I *do* possess one. I know how to drive—at least according to the State of New York."

"I guess I'll have to take your word for it." He gave her

shoulder a little bump with his. "Yours and the State of New York's."

"Do you have any idea how much parking costs in Manhattan? Garage fees are outrageous. Plus, we've got the subway and cabs and Uber. It's just easier to take public transportation."

Ford laughed under his breath again. "Yeah, we don't have much of that here."

"So I've noticed," Maple said. And soon, she'd have the blisters on her feet to prove it.

More than that, she was beginning to worry about the heat. The temperatures were already hovering around ninety degrees at high noon, and it was only the beginning of summer. In a matter of weeks, the pavement would be too hot for Lady Bird's sensitive paws.

At least the evenings were still pleasant. Soft and fragrant with the perfume of wildflowers, almost like walking through a dream.

"I could help you practice," Ford said.

Maple narrowed her gaze at him beside her. "You seriously want to give me *driving lessons*?"

"Not lessons. You already know how to drive, Doc." His grin turned far too sardonic for Maple's liking. "I just thought you might feel more comfortable if you had a little practice. Also, if you started using Percy's truck, you could bring Lady Bird to the hospital more often."

Right. This was about Lady Bird, her therapy-dog work and, by extension, Oliver. No wonder Ford wanted to volunteer as tribute.

Even so, it was a kind offer and one that Maple would probably be wise to accept. It wasn't like she could accidentally let herself kiss him again while she was operating a moving vehicle.

Stop thinking about kissing.

She bit down hard on her bottom lip as punishment, but, of course, her gaze flitted straight toward his mouth.

"I'd like that a lot. Thanks—" she managed to squeak out the last word "—friend."

How awkward could she possibly be?

Ford looked downright puzzled. This was beyond her usual social anxiety. The way she couldn't seem to think straight around him felt like something else entirely.

Something almost like…

Don't you dare think it, Maple! Not even for a second. Love?

She released her hold on his arm, because *whoa.* Being attracted to Ford was one thing, but thinking about the *L* word was more than she could handle. More than she'd *ever* be able to handle. In keeping with the automotive topic at hand, she needed to seriously pump the breaks.

"Maple, I'm not sure what exactly Adaline said to you tonight, but—" Ford began.

"Your sister was nothing but welcoming. Truly. I really like her," Maple said in an effort to cut him off.

She really meant it, too. She liked Adaline, and she'd had a great time meeting her friends. But even though Adaline had backed off somewhat and encouraged Maple to let Ford walk her home when he'd obviously figured out she'd been interfering in his personal life, the warning she'd given Maple still rang true.

Ford had already been hurt once by someone who'd turned her back on Bluebonnet. Maple cared too much about him to risk doing it again.

It would be different if she knew she was staying for good, but Maple couldn't make a promise like that right now…not even to herself. She'd only just recently given herself permission to take things one day at a time. Even that had been a massive leap of faith for someone who'd had an entirely different life mapped out for herself just a few short days ago.

"She told you about Charlotte," Ford said, cutting straight to the chase.

"Yes, but I don't want you to think I was trying to pry. For the record, I don't think that was Adaline's intention, either." This discussion was getting more uncomfortable by the second. How was that even possible?

"I know better than to think you'd try and interject yourself into my business, Maple. Quite the opposite, in fact. For a while there, I wondered if you were actively trying to avoid me." Ford's footsteps slowed. Maple had been so consumed by their conversation and the thoughts spinning in her head that she hadn't realized they'd reached her house until Lady Bird's tail stopped waving in front of them. The dog plopped into a down position at their feet. "Until you kissed me yesterday, that is."

"I shouldn't have done that. It's practically turned into front-page news around here. I keep telling people it was just a thank you kiss, and no one seems to think that's a real thing. Maybe it's not. I don't know. It was kind of a new experience for me. Believe it or not, that was rather out of character."

Maple was babbling. She couldn't seem to stop the stream of nonsense coming out of her mouth, and the more she said, the more tenderly Ford seemed to look at her—so tenderly that she wanted to lose herself in those kind eyes of his. Forget-me-not blue.

As if I could ever forget Ford Bishop, she thought. *Never in a million years*.

"I'm sorry," she blurted, apologizing once and for all for the kiss heard—and more importantly, *seen*—around the world. Or at least Texas, which had begun to feel like the only place on earth.

"I'm not," Ford said in a voice so low and deep that it scraped her insides. Then he took a step closer and gazed into her eyes with such intensity that every sliver of space between them cracked with electricity. "In fact, I want you to do it again."

"You do?" Maple heard herself say. She wasn't sure how, because her heart had never pounded so hard and fast in all her life.

Ford nodded, and tipped her chin upward with a gentle touch of his fingertips until her mouth was positioned just below his. "I do. Right now, in fact."

"Right now," she repeated, as weak and small as a kitten. If she didn't give in, the longing just might kill her. So much for flipping her feelings off like a light.

He wasn't like any man she'd ever known before. He was passionate about his career, just like she was. But when he was with her, he was fully present. He made her feel like there was nowhere he'd rather be than with her. She'd shown him exactly who she was—the messy side of her that she never let anyone else see. And somehow, it only seemed to make him like her more.

How was she supposed to resist that?

She rose up on tiptoe, and just as the yearning became unbearable, her lips met his. And this time, there was no hesitation...no restraint. The warmth of his mouth on hers sent a hum through her body that made her wrap her arms around his neck and pull him closer.

Yes. It was the only semi-coherent thought in her head as his hands slid into her hair. *Oh, my, my, my. Yes, please.*

She felt her soul unfold like the petals on a flower, inviting him in. She needed him even closer—so close that she could feel every beat of his heart crashing against her rib cage. No one had ever kissed her like this before. Like she was special, like she was cherished. Maybe even adored.

Then, without warning, it was over almost as soon as it had begun.

Ford pulled back, and when Maple dragged her eyes open, she found him looking down at her with the strangest expression on his face. He was as still as stone, but his eyes were wild and dark with desire. Maple wished she could press Rewind and live the last two minutes of her life over and over again on constant repeat.

She wanted that so much it scared her a little. "What is it?"

Ford pressed a fingertip to his lips, signaling for her to be quiet.

"I think I just heard something," he whispered.

Maple blinked. *You certainly did. It was every last shred of my resistance crumbling down around me.* "Wh-what did it sound like?"

"A whimper. Or a cry, maybe. Like someone in pain." His head jerked toward the right and he peered over her shoulder. "There. I just heard it again. Did you?"

"Maybe?" She couldn't be sure. Her head was all fuzzy after that kiss, brief as it had been.

But then she glanced down at Lady Bird and snapped back to awareness.

"Ford." Maple's fingers curled around the fabric of his shirt and she balled it into a fist as a shiver coursed through her—and not the good, yummy kind of shiver she'd been experiencing just seconds before. "Look at Lady Bird."

The gentle dog's ears were pricked forward, and her hackles were raised. She'd obviously heard something, too, and whatever it was had her spooked.

"It's okay, girl." Ford rested a hand on Lady Bird's back.

The golden panted and relaxed a bit at his touch, but then a mournful cry pierced the air.

Maple's gaze immediately collided with Ford's.

"That sounds like a hurt animal," she said.

Lady Bird barked and sprang into action. She darted past Ford, dragging her leash behind her before either of them could stop her.

"Lady Bird!" Ford shouted, chasing after the dog.

Maple followed with her heart in her throat. Lady Bird was just a streak of gold in the darkness, dashing sideways across Percy's lawn toward the pet clinic next door.

Now, Maple *really* wished she'd given up on her fashionable stilettos. She could barely keep up. She finally kicked them off and ran barefoot toward the front porch of the pet clinic, where she could scarcely make out the silhouette of Ford's profile in the moonlight.

"It's a dog," he called out, and the tone of his voice alone told her it was bad. *Really* bad. "She needs help!"

Chapter Twelve

Bile rose to the back of Ford's throat as he crouched down next to the small copper-and-white dog. "It's okay, little one. Maple will get you all taken care of."

It didn't take a genius or a medical professional to see that the dog was pregnant and in active labor. Her belly was hard and swollen, but the pup was as a limp as a dishrag, stretched out on the welcome mat to the pet clinic with her eyes closed. She didn't have a collar, tags or any other type of identification. Something wasn't right, and if Ford had to guess, whoever had dumped her here knew it.

How could someone do this? He felt sick just thinking about it.

Lady Bird seemed equally upset as she gently dropped to her belly and curled her body in a protective barrier around the distressed dog. The small pup gave a weak wag of her tail at the contact.

"What is it? What's wrong?" Maple caught up with them, stumbling onto the porch barefoot. She kneeled beside Ford, and her face crumpled as she assessed the situation. "Oh, no. You poor, poor thing."

"The puppies are coming, right?" Ford asked.

"They're trying. We need to get the little mama inside so I can see what's going on, but I'm guessing it's dystocia. She can't push them out." Her hands trembled as she rooted around her purse for her keys.

"Here, let me. I'll get the door." Ford took Maple's bag, found her key ring and unlocked the clinic while she gently scooped the dog into her arms and carried her inside.

The little thing couldn't have weighed more than twenty pounds, even heavily pregnant. Ford thought it best to let Maple handle her, since she was the veterinary professional. He did what he could, turning on lights and making sure Lady Bird didn't get in the way while she carried the dog directly to a table in the clinic's operating room.

Ford winced at the streak of blood on Maple's arm as she set down the pup and slipped into a white coat. Things weren't looking good. The dog could barely keep her eyes open, and she'd started shivering. Maple spoke to her in soothing tones as she did a quick exam, checking the dog's eyes, gums, body temperature and pulse. She scanned the dog for a microchip but couldn't find one.

Then she glanced up at Ford while she gently palpitated the pup's abdomen. "She's a little Cavalier King Charles spaniel. From the looks of it, not even a year old. Dogs really shouldn't have puppies that young. Their bodies aren't mature enough to handle the strain. Plus, Cavaliers have a high incidence of mitral valve disease. No responsible breeder would breed a dog like this until at least two and half years of age, and only then if she's been health-tested and found to be heart-clear, preferably by a veterinary cardiologist."

Ford gritted his teeth. "The very fact that we found her dumped on the welcome mat is a pretty good indication that whoever owns her isn't all that concerned with ethics."

"Owned." Maple's eyes flashed. "No collar, no microchip… Whoever had her before made sure we wouldn't be able to locate them. She belongs here now, and we're going

to do everything we can to save her and her puppies. She likely came from a puppy mill, and when they realized it wasn't going to be an easy delivery, they got rid of her. At least they had the decency to drop her off at a vet clinic."

"I can't believe we found her," Ford said. If they hadn't, she wouldn't have made it until morning. That much was obvious. "What should we do now?"

Maple bit her bottom lip as she studied the dog. "Ordinarily, we'd start with a dose of oxytocin. It enhances uterine contractions. Lots of things can cause dystocia—low calcium, uterine inertia. This dog's small size doesn't help. I doubt she and her puppies have gotten proper nutrition during the pregnancy. She's probably also dehydrated."

"So you don't think the oxytocin would work?"

"It might, but we don't know how long she's been like this. The longer the labor goes on, the more dangerous this situation gets. She needs a C-section." Maple swallowed. "As soon as possible."

"Okay." Ford nodded. They were two medical professionals. They could handle this, couldn't they? "Let's do it. Tell me how I can help."

She glanced up from the dog long enough to flash him a smile. "You seriously want to assist while I do an emergency canine Cesarean section?"

"Of course, I do, but you might need to give me some instructions. We didn't cover this in med school," Ford said as Lady Bird shuffled closer to lean against his leg.

"You know what us veterinarians say, right?" Maple twisted her hair into a bun on the top of her head and miraculously secured it in place with nothing but a pencil from the pocket of her lab coat. "Real doctors treat more than one species."

It was such a Maple thing to say that he couldn't help but laugh, despite the seriousness of their circumstances.

He folded his arms. "Go on, then. Let's make a real doctor out of me."

"I take back what I said." Affection sparkled in her eyes. "You might not be so impossible, after all."

With Ford's help, Maple had the dog—whom she'd christened Ginger, because the sweet thing deserved to be called by a name—prepped for surgery within minutes. Once she'd gotten an IV catheter in place and administered the anesthesia, she got to work shaving Ginger's abdomen while Ford prepared a whelping box for the puppies. He placed a heating pad at the bottom and lined it with blankets for warmth.

With any luck, they'd be able to save Ginger's litter and actually get to use it.

"Ready?" she asked as she positioned the scalpel over the dog's abdomen for a midline incision.

"Ready, Doc." Ford nodded, eyes shining bright over his surgical mask. "You've got this."

She soaked up the much-needed encouragement. Maple had performed C-sections in vet school, but never in an emergency like this. She desperately wanted to save this dog...*and* her puppies. It might seem crazy, but finding a Cavalier in distress like this almost felt like a sign. Like Maple was in the right place at the right time. Like ending up here in Bluebonnet was meant to be, beyond the names that were printed on her birth certificate. A new Cavalier mom and her babies would certainly benefit from having a certified canine cardiologist in town.

But Maple was getting way ahead of herself. She still needed to perform the surgery. Plus, there was the matter of Grover. He was going to flip his lid when he found out about this. He'd demand to know why she hadn't called him before taking matters into her own hands, which was probably a valid question.

Except they didn't have that kind of time. Ginger's pulse was already thready. She couldn't let the dog down.

Maple pushed aside all doubts and got down to business. She held her breath as she made the incision, and then her eyes filled with tears as she caught her first glance at Ginger's moving uterus.

"We've got two puppies, and they're both alive." She pointed toward the squirming pups for Ford to see.

"Well, would you look at that?" he said in an awestruck voice.

"Get ready. I'm going to incise the uterus, and as soon as I remove the first puppy, I'm going to hand it over so you can clear its airway and stimulate breathing."

Ford stood poised with a towel in one hand and a suction bulb in the other.

Everything that happened next seemed to move in fast motion. Maple got the puppies out as quickly as she could. One of them was tiny and delicate, and the other was a downright chunk. The big pup, a boy, had likely been too large for the young mama's birth canal, contributing to her distress. The smaller puppy was a girl, and Maple had a feeling she'd end up looking just like Ginger someday. Mom and her babies all had the chestnut and pearly white markings that the Blenheim variety of Cavalier King Charles spaniels were famous for.

So whoever had unloaded Ginger on the doorstep had definitely been an unscrupulous breeder, angling to crank out a litter of purebred puppies for profit without regard to the health of the mother or her litter. Later, Maple would allow herself to feel properly enraged about that, but right now, all she felt was pure gratitude.

This was why she'd become a veterinarian. Maybe she'd

lost sight of some of the reasons she'd gone to vet school in the first place after she'd become bogged down with exams and all-nighters and the extra effort it took to get a specialty certification. After her disastrous attempt at dating one of her study-group partners, she'd closed herself to other students. She'd always been a driven pupil, but she'd doubled down after Justin had taken advantage of her academic prowess.

She'd once heard her mother tell a client that the best revenge was massive success, and Maple had internalized that message without even realizing it. The one time she'd put her heart on the line, she'd gotten hurt. So somewhere deep down, she'd decided to believe all the things her bitterly unhappy parents had told her—and *shown* her—about love. She'd closed ranks around her heart even stronger than before and decided the only path forward was to be the best. Untouchable in every possible way. In the long run, she could love herself better than anyone else could.

Except for dogs.

Maple had always known they knew how to love better than humans did, which was why she'd chosen this life to begin with. It's why she'd dug her heels in and taken the grant when her mom and dad refused to fund her education. But she didn't need to work in a sleek high-rise building or cater to wealthy Upper West Siders to help animals. She could make a difference right here in Bluebonnet. Maybe that's what Percy's grant and his requirement to work for a year at the clinic had really been about.

It was a humbling thought, and it made Maple's throat close up tight as she clipped the second puppy's umbilical cord. She handed the tiny girl to Ford, and the way he looked at her nearly did her in.

He still didn't get it. They weren't alike at all. She wasn't special. She really wasn't…

But this moment certainly was. And Maple wouldn't have traded it for anything.

"Hey there, welcome to the world," Ford cooed as he massaged the puppy with a soft towel to get her breathing.

Maple couldn't wait to join in and check the new babies out from head to toe, but first she needed to get Ginger stitched up. She wouldn't be able to relax until she knew for a fact that the new mom was out of the woods.

But once Ginger was resting comfortably, Maple finally allowed herself to breathe, take a look around and bask in a happiness so bone-deep that it took her breath away.

Ford was bottle-feeding the girl puppy while the boy slept in the whelping box. Lady Bird couldn't seem to decide whether she should stand guard over the puppies or Ginger, so she alternated between all three, keeping a watchful eye over the whole furry family as best she could. And as crazy as it seemed, Maple could almost sense Percy's presence there, too…or maybe that was just wishful thinking.

One thing she knew for certain: he would've been proud, just like Ford's Gram had tried to tell her the other day at the retirement home.

"You okay, Doc?" Ford looked up from the puppy in his hands, sucking greedily at the bottle. Once Ginger was awake, they'd introduce the puppies to their mama. She'd been through a lot, but it was important for her to try and nurse so she could bond with her babies. Even so, the pups would likely need supplemental bottle-feeding for the next few weeks. "That was a lot."

"It was a lot." Maple laughed and plucked the boy puppy from the whelping box so she could feed him. "But I'm good. I'm more than good, actually. I loved every minute of it. Tonight was…"

She shook her head and held the puppy close to her

heart. "I don't think I have words for what tonight meant to me."

Ford stood, and without missing a beat of bottle-feeding duty, he walked over to Maple and kissed her cheek. "You did it, Doc."

"No." She shook her head and grinned up at him, half-delirious. Maple had no idea what time it was. The past few hours had passed in a blur, but she didn't want to close her eyes. She didn't want to miss a single, solitary second of this magical night. "*We* did it."

The magic ended early the following morning when Maple jerked awake to the sound of Grover's gravelly voice echoing throughout the pet clinic's operating room.

"What in tarnation is going on in here?"

Her eyes snapped open, and for a second, she forgot where she was. What was she doing, sleeping on the floor of the clinic, of all places? And what was *Ford* doing here, too? Other than providing her with a nice, strong shoulder to use as a pillow...

Maple sat up, blinking against the assault of the clinic's fluorescent lighting, convinced this was all a stress-induced nightmare. She'd been feeling so out of sorts lately, not to mention the calls and voice mails from her parents, which she'd been ignoring for days. A nightmare seemed par for the course at this point.

But then her gaze snagged on the whelping box beside Ford, who was just beginning to stir, and the events from the night before came rushing back to her. The abandoned dog... The surgery... Two perfect puppies.

And Ford had been there for all of it.

Magic.

"Good morning, Grover," Maple said. Even Grumpy McGrumperson couldn't spoil her mood today. Although it would be really great if he stopped looking at her like she was a teenager who'd just been caught making out with her boyfriend in a parked car. "I can explain."

Grover glanced around the room, frown deepening as he noticed Ginger resting on a soft dog bed in a kennel piled with blankets. "Please do, because for the life of me, I can't figure out if this is a slumber party or a veterinary emergency."

"Both, actually." Maple laughed. Grover, pointedly, did not.

"Hi, Grover." Ford stood and held out his hand for a shake. He had an adorable case of bed head, which probably would've look ridiculous on anyone else but somehow only made him more attractive. "You should've seen Maple last night. She saved that dog's life."

Grover accepted Ford's handshake, and eyed Maple dubiously.

"I would've called you, but there was no time. Someone abandoned Ginger on the steps of the clinic. She was in the latter stages of labor with obvious dystocia and needed an immediate C-section." She glanced at Ford. "We're lucky we even found her."

Grover regarded Ford, still dressed in the scrubs he'd worn to the hospital yesterday. "You assist with veterinary surgery now, Dr. Bishop?"

"Apparently so." Ford chuckled, and something about the deep timbre of his voice sent Maple straight back to last night and the lump that had lodged in her throat at the sight of him cradling a newborn puppy in his strong grasp. "It was fun. Maybe I can do it again someday."

He snuck a glance at Maple, and a million butterflies took flight in her belly.

I'm really in trouble now, aren't I?

Last night had changed things between them, and now there was no turning back. She knew he felt it, too. Ford held her fragile heart in his hands as surely as he'd held those puppies, and it terrified Maple to her core.

What was she going to do?

"Perhaps we shouldn't make a habit of it." Grover's eyes cut back toward Maple. "You do realize the pups will probably need supplemental bottle-feeding for the first few days, don't you?"

Maple nodded. "Yes, sir. We've already given Peaches and Fuzz two feedings, three hours apart."

"Peaches and Fuzz?" Grover's eyebrows rose. "You named them already?"

"Yes, and the mother, too. I'm calling her Ginger."

Grover's mouth twitched, as if he was trying not to smile. No way. Impossible. "So all these dogs are yours now?"

Overnight, she'd gone from owning one large dog to owning two adult dogs and two newborn puppies. It was going to take a full-size moving van to get her to New York when she finally moved back.

If she moved back.

"It's just temporary," she said, doing her best to avoid Ford's gaze. "For now, they're completely my responsibility."

"Have you introduced the pups to the mother yet?" Grover asked.

"Yes, and it went really well. But she was still drowsy from the anesthesia, and I didn't want her to accidentally roll over the puppies, so I didn't think it was best to leave them all together unsupervised."

"And you're keeping them warm?"

"Yes."

"And you offered Ginger a small amount of food and water a few hours after the birth?"

"Yes." Again, Maple nodded.

The interrogation continued, with Grover barking out

question after question about the surgery, Ginger's post-op treatment, and the care and feeding of her puppies.

Finally, when he'd exhausted his long list of concerns, he waved toward Ginger's kennel, the whelping box and the pile of old blankets Maple had found in the clinic's donation closet and used for a pallet for her and Ford to get some shut-eye in between puppy feedings. "Now clean all of this up, would you? I've got a poodle coming in for a spay this morning."

He stalked out of the operating room before Maple could respond.

She sighed and glanced at Ford. "Well, that went pretty much exactly like I thought it would. That man really needs to reconsider his stance on caffeinated coffee."

Ford grinned and raked a hand through his hair. "Speaking of caffeine, why don't I run over to Cherry on Top and get us a couple of large coffees real quick? I know I could use it before my practice opens in—" he glanced at his watch and winced "—just under an hour."

"I'd *love* one of their hazelnut cream lattes, if you have time. I think Adaline calls that drink Texas Gold. I'll get all of this cleaned up. For today, I think I'll see if June can keep an eye on Ginger and her babies up front in the reception area. I'll take everyone home with me tonight," Maple said.

She started folding one of the blankets and tried not to think about what Ford's sister would say when she found out they'd spent the night together...*again*. Not that medical emergencies should count. But still...

The purely innocent sleepovers seemed to be occurring with alarming frequency.

"Sounds like a plan," Ford said, and just as he swept a lock of hair from her face and Maple thought he might be about to kiss her goodbye, Grover stormed back into the room.

"One more thing," he bellowed.

Maple's heart hammered against her rib cage as she sprang backward away from Ford. "Y-yes?"

Grover jerked his head toward Ginger and the puppies, and his expression morphed into something approximating an actual look of approval. "You did a good job here last night."

She couldn't believe her ears. Grover wasn't Percy, but he'd been his business partner for a long, long time. She'd never get the chance to hear her father utter those words, but having Grover say them was the next best thing.

"Thank you, Grover. That means a lot," she said before he could stomp off again. "Especially coming from you."

"Right. Well." He shifted his weight from one foot to the other, clearly unaccustomed to issuing such effusive praise. "Keep up the good work."

Happiness sparkled inside her, and just this once, she didn't worry about tomorrow. Or the days or weeks that followed. All that mattered was this day. This place.

This *life*.

"I will."

The text came just after Ford dropped off Maple's hazelnut cream latte with June at the front desk of the pet clinic.

He'd gotten a coffee for June as well, and the older woman had gushed about what a fine man he was to help Maple deliver the puppies. Peaches, Fuzz, and Ginger were all snuggled together in a cozy playpen-like contraption behind the reception desk. Maple had already jumped right into an appointment when a walk-in client had shown up with a lethargic hedgehog.

Ford assured June that was just fine. He needed to get going, anyway. But he'd still paused to watch Ginger and her pups for a moment. The mama Cavalier's tail wagged as soon as she caught sight of him, and Ford couldn't help but marvel at the dog's sweet and trusting disposition, after all she'd been through. Joy warmed him from within just looking at the furry little family.

Something had shifted inside Ford the night before. He'd been drawn to Maple since he'd first set eyes on her—that much was undeniable. But even when she'd kissed him— even when he'd challenged her to do it a second time— he'd thought he'd had his emotions under control. He and Maple were nothing alike. She'd been clear about that right up front. She'd never once tried to hide who she was, unlike his former fiancée, who'd never once told him she had reservations about moving to Bluebonnet. In retrospect, he should've known she was lying. The signs were all there. That relationship had always felt too much like work, unlike the time he spent with Maple. With Maple, he could be himself. He could relax. He could breathe easy, because there was no danger of losing his heart. Maple been perfectly honest about the fact that she couldn't wait to put Texas and all it contained in her rearview mirror, Ford included.

But then she'd stayed.

She'd had chance after chance to make good on her word and leave, but she'd never actually gone. And still, somehow it wasn't until Ford helped her save that dog and her puppies that he'd realized he was falling.

In truth, it had been happening all along. He knew that now. How could he not, when he'd watched her spread joy and light on her pet visits with Lady Bird, even when she insisted it didn't come naturally to her at all? Maybe that's why her commitment to it meant more. Or maybe she was more tenderhearted than she wanted to believe. Either way, it had been a sight to behold. Ford couldn't have looked away if he'd tried.

Then it had felt so nice last night when she'd fallen asleep with her head on his shoulder. So *right*. Ford had stroked her hair and stubbornly refused to move, even when his arm fell asleep. He'd told himself he was simply savoring the moment. Holding on to something—some-*one*—whom he'd known from the outset was never meant to be his.

Ford had been doing the right thing his entire life. He'd come back to Bluebonnet to care for Gram. He put his family and his town and his patients first. Always. He'd never once regretted any of it. Just this once, though, he'd wanted to give in to what he really and truly wanted. And he'd never wanted anyone as badly as he wanted Maple.

So he'd let himself believe it was okay to let his guard down…to brush the hair back from her face and caress her cheek and let his fingertips linger on her soft skin while he held her and let himself fall. It might be his only chance to feel this close and connected with the enigmatic woman who'd found her way into his heart when he least expected it.

When morning came, everything had still been okay. Sure, Ford felt like he was walking around with his heart on the outside of his body, but he was good. *They* were good. Even Grover was being decent for a change.

Then Ford's phone chimed with an incoming text.

"See you later, June. Thank you for keeping an eye on the little ones for Maple," he said as he reached inside his pocket for his cell.

He was already outside on the sidewalk soaking up the first rays of the Hill Country sunshine when the message popped up on his screen. He'd half expected it to be from Maple, but instead, the name that popped up above the text bubble was Pam Hudson's from County General Hospital.

Oliver Taylor's bone-marrow biopsy results are in. It's not good news. Thought you'd want to know. I'm sorry.

Chapter Thirteen

Maple had now been in Bluebonnet long enough to expect that word about Ginger and her puppies would spread through town like wildfire. She'd actually been looking forward to it since, according to Adaline's small-town-gossip theory, the next newsworthy event would make everyone forget about the kiss in the town square. If that was the case, bring on the collective amnesia!

What she hadn't expected was the cake. Or the casseroles. Or the pair of giant wooden storks that appeared in her front yard—one pink and the other blue, holding tiny bundles in their beaks labelled Peaches and Fuzz.

Maple peered out her kitchen window at the wooden birds as she handed Adaline a bottle filled with puppy formula. "I don't get it. Can you shed any light on this?"

"You're way overthinking it. They're just yard signs, like the ones people put on their lawns when a new baby is born." Adaline nudged the tip of the bottle into Fuzz's tiny mouth, like Maple had shown her on the first day she'd brought the dogs home to Percy's charming house next door to the clinic.

The puppies had just turned five days old. Ginger was recuperating nicely from her surgery and nursing the babies every day, but because she'd been neglected during her pregnancy, Maple was concerned about her nutrition.

She didn't want to exhaust the little mama, so she'd kept the puppies on a supplemental feeding schedule.

Luckily, there was no shortage of volunteers to help out. Like today, when Maple had found Adaline, Belle and Jenna waiting on her front step after work, ready for dog duty. The book-club girls had been taking shifts since she'd brought the dogs home and were still eager to help.

"We don't have yard signs in Manhattan." Maple laughed. "We don't even have *yards*. I have no idea who put those out there. They just appeared out of nowhere the other day."

Belle held Peaches close while she offered her a bottle. "You did an amazing thing. The town just wants to celebrate you."

And they certainly were. The cake had been from Adaline, naturally—a triple-layer, funfetti-flavored wonder, dotted generously throughout with rainbow sprinkles and *Bluebonnet Thinks You're Pawesome* piped in decadent frosting. Then the casseroles had started appearing, wrapped snugly in tin foil. Thankfully, most of them came with heating instructions since Maple had never cooked a casserole in her life. Yesterday, a teacher from Bluebonnet Elementary School had even stopped by the clinic with a stack of drawings of the puppies her first graders had made for Maple.

It was all so...*kind*.

And nothing at all like her job would've been like at the cardiology practice in New York. Maple knew it wasn't fair to compare, but she couldn't help it. She'd always done her best to keep to herself and fly under the radar. That was impossible in a place like Bluebonnet, and to her surprise, she didn't mind so much anymore. It felt nice.

"Maple, are you doing therapy-dog visits with Lady

Bird, or are you too busy with Ginger and the puppies?" Jenna asked.

Ginger sat in her lap while Jenna ran her hand in long, gentle strokes over the dog's back. Maple had noticed a pattern: while everyone else fawned over the puppies, Jenna seemed more drawn to the mama dog. She was glad. That poor dog needed as much love and affection as she could get.

"Are you kidding? The phone is still ringing off the hook, and it's never for me." Maple glanced at Lady Bird, glued to her legs as usual. "Is it, girl?"

Lady Bird woofed right on cue.

"I'm this dog's glorified assistant. The town might riot if I stopped taking her on visits. Why?" Maple asked.

"I have ballet camp starting at the dance studio in a few days, and I was hoping you could bring Lady Bird in for our first morning? Just to put the littlest ones at ease?" Jenna grinned. "I have a tutu Lady Bird can borrow."

"Then how could I possibly say no? Sure, we'll be there."

The answer flew out of Maple's mouth before she had a chance to feel a twinge of anxiety. Oddly, even after she'd spontaneously agreed, the twinge never came.

She buried her fingertips in the soft fur on Lady Bird's broad chest and gave the golden a good scratch. *You did this, sweet girl.* Social anxiety didn't go away overnight. Maple knew she'd probably have a lifelong struggle feeling confident in social settings. But she had the dog to thank for getting her acclimated to the pet-therapy visits and interacting with strangers—strangers who were becoming friends.

Day by day. Visit by visit.

Maple wasn't the same person she'd been two weeks ago. She'd breezed into town intent on changing things, and instead, the town had changed her.

But it wasn't all Lady Bird's doing. Someone else had been there alongside her every step of the way. And much to Maple's confusion, she hadn't set eyes on him for five straight days.

Ford had returned to the pet clinic and delivered her latte, as promised, on the morning after the pups were born. Since then...nothing.

At first, Maple had chalked up his absence to the fact that they'd both been exhausted. He had a medical practice to run, just like she did it. She figured he was simply getting caught up on things. But then one day had turned into two, two turned into three, and so on. With each passing day, Maple had started to feel more and more like a lost puppy herself.

It's for the best. You were scared to death of your feelings for him, and now you don't have to worry about that anymore.

Maple clung to that thought, just like she'd been clinging to it for the past five days. But the more she repeated the mantra, the less she believed it. Because now that he was gone, she was more terrified than ever.

She'd texted a few times and gotten nothing but short, generic responses. Even when she'd sent photos or videos of the puppies, she'd gotten nothing but a heart emoji in return. If it hadn't been for those brief missives, she would've been worried that he'd had an accident or something. But no. He was simply pulling away, just like Justin had done in college, only this was a gradual withdrawal instead of a clean break. She was beginning to realize that the latter would've been far less agonizing. This felt like death by a thousand paper cuts.

"Adaline, can I talk to you for a second?" Maple tipped her head toward the hallway.

She'd sworn to herself she wouldn't do this. Adaline had never been thrilled about Maple and Ford spending time together. She was probably the last person who'd want to shed light on why he was semi-ghosting her.

But she also knew Ford better than anyone else in Bluebonnet. They were close. So Maple had finally decided to swallow her pride and ask.

"This is about Ford, isn't it?" Adaline said as soon as they were out of earshot of the rest of the group. She didn't even give Maple time to answer before her shoulders sagged with relief. "Thank goodness. I was beginning to worry that you weren't ever going to say anything."

The ache that had taken up residence where Maple's heart used to be burrowed deeper, and deeper still. So she hadn't been imagining things. Ford wasn't just busy. Something had happened to make him stay away.

She wrapped her arms around her middle, bracing herself for whatever was to come. "I know you don't think I'm good for him, and I understand why. I happen to agree with you, but—"

"What? No, Maple." Adaline grabbed onto Maple's arm and gave it a tender squeeze. "I don't think that at all."

"But that night at book club, you told me you didn't think we should be together."

"That's not what I said. I remember distinctly telling you that I didn't think it was a good idea for you to kiss him anymore until you knew for certain you were going to stay in Bluebonnet." Adaline's eyes welled up. "I never thought you weren't good for him. You two are so alike. I think you'd make a great couple."

Maple shook her head. "No, we're really not—"

"Stop. You may seem like total opposites on the surface, but you're alike in the ways that matter most. *That's* why I was worried. My brother is head over heels for you, whether he realizes it or not. I knew if you left, he'd be heartbroken. Because you belong together, not the opposite."

Sorrow closed up Maple's throat. She'd spent the past five days trying to convince herself that she and Ford had never stood a chance, and now his sister was trying to tell her they were soul mates or something.

She wished it was true. She'd never wished for anything so hard in all her life.

"That's not what it's like between us," Maple protested.

But Adaline wasn't listening. "I promised to stay out of his business. I swore. So when I realized he'd been spending all his time at the hospital, I didn't say anything. I thought for sure you knew, and then when I realized you didn't, I knew it wasn't my place to bring it up. I figured he'd come to his senses sooner or later, but clearly he's not."

She was talking in circles, and the more she said, the more Maple realized she should've pushed harder. She should've trusted that Ford wasn't the sort of person who'd vanish from her life without good reason. He'd never given her any reason to believe that.

Maple's past had, though. All her life, she'd been taught that feelings couldn't be trusted and love never stood the test of time. Her own limited experiences with dating had confirmed everything her parents had impressed upon her, either by their words or actions. So she'd kept her heart under lock and key. The less she shared herself with other people—people who would only end up hurting her in the long run—the better. Then Ford had come along and stolen her heart when she wasn't looking. And instead of telling him how she felt, she'd held her breath and waited for the other shoe to drop.

Was it any wonder it had?

"Adaline," Maple snapped. "You're scaring me. What's

going on? Why is Ford spending all his time at the hospital?"

She didn't need to ask, though. She knew, even before Adaline said it.

Oliver.

The child had been on Maple's mind ever since the teacher from the elementary school had given her the colored drawings of Peaches, Fuzz, and Ginger. She'd brought the pictures home and tacked her favorites to Percy's refrigerator with magnets, and every time her gaze landed on the strokes of bold crayon, she thought about Lady Bird's visit with Oliver.

My mom says when I'm better, I can get a dog of my own. When I do, I want one just like Lady Bird.

She could still hear the little boy's voice, so upbeat and happy, despite his circumstances, just like she could still see his tiny form, dwarfed by the hospital bed…the tired shadows beneath his eyes.

He wasn't getting better, was he? And Maple had been so wrapped up in her own messed-up life that she hadn't for a moment considered that Ford might've been experiencing a crisis of his own.

"He's got this patient." Tears shone in Adaline's eyes, and she let out a ragged breath. "Ford is very attached, and let's just say things aren't looking good. He can't tell me much, but I'm worried. My brother is a mess, and I'm not sure there's anything any of us can do to make things better."

Maple just stood there, shell-shocked, until Lady Bird pawed at her foot, pulling her out of her trance. She dragged her gaze toward the dog, eyes blurry with tears. She blinked hard, and her vision cleared a bit…

Just enough for hope to stir as she realized that maybe there was one small thing she could do to help.

* * *

It took longer than Maple would've liked to get ready to go to the hospital. She made an excuse for the book-club girls to leave and then packed things up as quickly as she could, heart pounding all the while.

Lady Bird followed her around the house with her tail hanging low between her legs. Empathy was the dog's strong suit, after all, and she could tell Maple was a jittery jumble of nerves—as evidenced by the way she nearly jumped out of her skin when there was a knock on the front door just as she was almost ready to leave.

Lady Bird, mirroring Maple's disquiet, released a sharp bark. In turn, Ginger let out a low growl in the kitchen. The sweet dog probably thought whoever was at the door must be a threat to her puppies.

"Everyone, let's just calm down," Maple said, as much to herself as to the dogs. "I'm sure that's just Adaline, Jenna, or Belle. One of them probably forgot something."

She swung the front door open without even checking the peephole. Big mistake…

Huge.

"Mom." She gaped at Meredith Leighton, unable to process what she was seeing. Then her gaze shifted to the man standing beside her mother. "And Dad?"

They'd flown clear across the country to Texas and taken a car to Bluebonnet, all the way from Austin? *Together?*

Maybe she was hallucinating. That seemed far more likely.

"Well?" Maple's mother peered past her toward Lady Bird, who'd chosen this most awkward of moments to lose her sense of decorum and bark like she'd never set eyes on a stranger before. Perhaps she'd picked up on the fact that her parents weren't dog people. Either way, it was mortifying. "Can we come in, or will that dog attack us?"

"Lady Bird wouldn't hurt a fly. She just knows I..." Maple shook her head. She couldn't tell her parents she was about to run after a man. They'd probably kidnap her and forcibly drag her out of Texas like she'd joined a cult and needed to be deprogrammed. "Never mind. We were on our way out, that's all."

"Come on in." She waved them inside, then cut her gaze toward Lady Bird. "You're fine. It's all good."

Her mother tiptoed over the threshold, sidestepping Lady Bird as if she was the star of that Stephen King story, *Cujo*.

Dad rolled his eyes at his ex-wife, but once he was inside, he scrunched his nose. "It smells like dog in here."

They still had so much in common, even after decades of trying to tear each other apart. How they couldn't see it was a mystery.

"That's because I rescued a lovely Cavalier King Charles spaniel a few days ago. She was in the late stages of labor when I found her, and I had to perform an emergency C-section. We ended up saving her and her two darling puppies." Maple gestured toward the kitchen. "Would you like to see them?"

Meredith Leighton looked at her like she'd just sprung an extra head and it was wearing a ten-gallon cowboy hat. "No, Maple. We're not here to look at puppies. We're here to take you home."

"What?" Maple shook her head, but somewhere deep inside, she felt like a naughty child who'd done something terribly, terribly wrong. The urge to smooth things over and obey was almost crushing. "If all you wanted was to try and talk me into leaving, you could've just called."

"We've been calling. You never pick up," her father said.

Yes, she'd dodged a few calls. And maybe she'd also deleted a couple voice mails without listening to them. But she knew they'd never understand why she liked it here.

For a second, when she'd first seen them standing there on Percy's doorstep, a sense of profound relief had coursed through her. She'd actually thought that now that they were here, she could show them what made Bluebonnet so special.

The Leightons weren't interested in that, though. Just like they'd never been interested in why she wanted to be a veterinarian instead of going to law school. She knew they loved her, but that love came with strings attached. Too bad they had such an aversion to dogs. Her mom and dad could've learned a thing or two about unconditional love from Lady Bird.

"I'm not going back." Maple took a deep breath and finally let herself say the words out loud that had been on her heart for days. "*Ever.* I'm staying here in Bluebonnet."

Her father's face turned an alarming shade of red.

"You've got to be kidding." Meredith threw her hands up in the air. Lady Bird's head swiveled to and fro, as if she'd just tossed an invisible ball. "You're just going to throw your entire life away for a birth father you never even met? He gave you away, Maple. Maybe let that sink in before you dig in your heels."

Maple reared back as if she'd been slapped.

No wonder she had such a hard time trusting people. She'd been told over and over again she couldn't count on anyone. She might still believe it, if not for Ford.

Ford!

Maple turned away to grab her purse, Lady Bird's leash, and the other items she'd set aside for her trip to County General.

"What are you doing? Where are you going?" Her mother's voice was growing shriller by the second. *"We just got here."*

"I know you did, and I'm sorry. But like I told you, we were just on our way out," Maple said. She'd never spoken to her parents like this before, and she marveled at how calm she sounded.

"Let's all just settle down." Charles Leighton huffed out a sigh. "Maple, sit."

He pointed at the sofa, and even Lady Bird refused to obey.

"No," Maple said as evenly as possible. "I'm leaving now. The two of you can either stay here and wait until I get back, or you can go back to New York. Either way, I won't be going with you. I want to stay here and learn more about my birth father, but that's not the only reason. This town is special. So are its people. They've inspired me in ways that would amaze you."

Her parents exchanged a glance, and Maple could see the fight draining out of them. They were scared, that's all. They were afraid of losing their only daughter.

"I love you both. That hasn't changed, and it never will." Maple beckoned to Lady Bird and the dog sprang to her feet. "Now, like I said, we have to go. We have someplace very important to be, and it really can't wait another second."

Chapter Fourteen

Oliver grinned as he moved a red checker in a zigzag pattern of jumps, ending in the king's row on Ford's side of the playing board. "King me."

Ford then watched as the little boy plucked two more of his black checkers out of play and added them to the sizable stack of Ford's castoffs piled on the hospital bedside tray. This game was going to end just like the others had, and if things kept going at the current pace, he was about to get trounced in record time.

He placed a red checker on top of the one that had just annihilated half of his remaining pieces. "There you go, bud."

"Are you even trying to win?" Oliver cast him an accusatory glance. "You're not letting me beat you just because I'm sick, are you?"

"Absolutely not. I'm genuinely this bad at checkers." Ford made a cross-your-heart motion over the left pocket of his scrubs.

Granted, the fact that that he was preoccupied with keeping an eye on Oliver's vital signs as they flashed on the monitor beside the bed didn't help matters. He was doing his best under the circumstances, though. He could never beat Gram at board games, either—probably because she was a notorious cheat.

"You're even worse at Go Fish." Oliver snickered.

"Careful, there. Or I'll tell your mom you know where she hides the chocolate bars." Ford winked.

He'd never tell. The kid had him wrapped around his little finger. Never in his career had Ford spent every waking moment of his free time at the bedside of one of his young patients. Then again, no other child had touched his heart in the way that Oliver had.

If only he wasn't fighting the same exact disease that had claimed the life of Ford's childhood friend... If only Oliver's most recent bone-marrow test hadn't indicated that this latest round of treatment wasn't working... If only there was something more Ford could do to help...

If only.

"It's your turn again," Oliver prompted.

Ford slid one of his few remaining checkers from one square to another, and Oliver immediately jumped over it with a double-stacked red playing piece. That's right, kings could move in any direction. Ford had forgotten.

He needed sleep. He was so exhausted from trying to keep up with his regular appointments while also monitoring Oliver's progress as closely as possible that he could barely think straight. Was playing games and coloring with the child in the evenings while his mom worked the night shift doing anything to beat Oliver's cancer?

Doubtful. But Ford wasn't about to let that little boy spend his evenings alone when the odds of him beating the disease were suddenly in doubt. He hadn't been there to spend time with Bobby all those years ago. When his friend passed away, the rug had been pulled out from underneath Ford's entire life. He'd never doubted for a minute that Bobby would recover. Kids like them didn't *die*.

That's how naive he'd been back then. That's how idyllic growing up in Bluebonnet had been. Ford knew better now, and he wasn't going to let the rug get yanked out from under him again without a fight.

He hadn't been around when Oliver had his last bone-marrow test. There hadn't been a reason for him to be there since he was only the child's primary care doctor, but that was beside the point. The kid had very little in the way of a support system, hence his deep attachment to Lady Bird, even though pet-therapy visits typically only took place once a week.

The boy needed a friend, especially now, and Ford could be that friend. *That*, he could do. That much he could control.

He'd dropped the ball for a bit, that's all. Rationally speaking, he knew his feelings for Maple had nothing at all to do with Oliver's illness. But the night the puppies had been born had marked a turning point—Ford had finally let loose and given up control. He'd let himself want. He'd let himself yearn. He'd let himself love. And then, when he'd been the happiest he could remember in a long, long time, he'd gotten the text from Oliver's nurse.

It was a gut punch Ford had never seen coming.

The chemo wasn't working. *No change*, the oncologist had said. Ford didn't understand how that was possible. Oliver was handling the treatments like a champ. His spirits were up. His color looked good. Even the nausea was getting better.

The cancer, on the other hand, wasn't.

"Can we play again?" Oliver asked as he leaped over Ford's last checker. "Please?"

"I don't know, bud. It's getting late, and you have another bone-marrow test in the morning." This one would be different. It had to.

Ford scrubbed his face.

When was the last time he'd slept? He wasn't even sure.

Every night when he got home from the hospital, he fell into bed, closed his eyes, and dreamed of Maple. She didn't deserve to be treated like an afterthought. Ford didn't know how to let her in anymore, though. He couldn't wrap his mind—or his heart—around allowing himself to be vulnerable and strong all at once. It was easier—*safer*—to not let himself feel anything at all.

When did you turn into such a caveman?

He wasn't. That was the problem. He couldn't turn it off. No matter how much Ford tried, he couldn't stop thinking about Maple. He had this fantasy that she'd walk through the door of Oliver's hospital room one evening and suddenly, everything would go back to feeling right and good. Ford knew it would never happen. Even if she came, she'd never look at him the same way again. How could she? His actions over the past week had been shameful. Ford knew Maple had trouble trusting people, and in the end, he'd shown her that he was the least trustworthy of them all.

"Lady Bird!" Oliver shouted, fully ignoring Ford's reminder that tomorrow was an important day and he needed to get some rest.

Ford paused from pressing his fingertips against his eyelids to slide his gaze toward the child. He'd known this was going to happen, eventually. Maybe he could get Pam to call Maple and request a visit from the therapy dog, and Ford could make himself scarce before she got there.

No, that would never work. She'd need a ride to the hospital. He'd volunteered the last time, and Pam wouldn't hesitate to ask him again.

"How about one more game of checkers?" Ford offered. "You really need to rest up. Lady Bird can visit another time."

Oliver's face scrunched. "But she's already here."

He pointed toward the door, and Ford's chest grew so tight that he couldn't breathe as he slowly turned to look.

And there she was. Maple, just like in his fantasy—smiling, with Lady Bird wagging happily at her feet. The only difference between his dreams and the impossible reality taking place was the addition of a large wicker basket in Maple arms.

"Hi, there," she said, nodding toward the basket as she lingered in the doorway. "Lady Bird and I brought you a little surprise, Oliver. Is it okay if we come in?"

Her gaze flitted toward Ford, and his dread coiled in his gut as he waited to absorb the full blow of the inevitable hurt in her gaze—hurt that he'd put there. But when their eyes met, the only things he saw in her beautiful expression were affection and understanding and a tenderness so deep that he very nearly wept with relief.

"Yes! Come in!" Oliver demanded, then clamped a hand over his mouth as he remembered his manners. "Please?"

"Come on, Lady Bird." Maple's eyes glittered. "Let's go visit."

Maple's legs wobbled as she entered the hospital room.

She wasn't sure why she was nervous. The look on Ford's face when he'd first spotted her standing in Oliver's doorway had said more than any words of apology ever could. He'd blinked—hard—as if trying to convince himself he wasn't dreaming. And his eyes, the exact shade of blue as Texas twilight, flickered with regret.

Everything is going to be okay, she wanted to tell him. But she couldn't make that kind of promise. Maple wasn't sure exactly what was going on with Oliver, but whatever it was had sent Ford reeling. That was okay…that was *human*. They could figure out the rest later, but the important thing was she wanted to be here for him now, the same way he'd shown up for her—again and again—since the day she'd come home.

Home to Bluebonnet.

"Hi," she said as he rose from the chair beside Oliver's bed and walked toward her.

He looked exhausted to his core—much more so than the morning after they'd stayed up bottle-feeding puppies. That had been a happy sort of exhaustion. This... This was something else. This was a bone-deep weariness that made Maple worry he might break.

"Hi." Ford cleared his throat, and the smile he offered her was the saddest she'd ever seen. "Thank you. I don't how you got here or how you knew how badly Oliver needed this, but thank you. From the bottom of my heart."

"I'm not just here for Oliver," she said as Lady Bird licked Ford's hand in greeting before trotting toward the hospital bed.

Ford looked at her for a long, silent moment until, at last, the smile on his face turned more genuine.

"You could've told me, you know," Maple whispered. "You don't always have to be the strong one—the one holding up the world for everyone else. It's okay to need people. We all do from time to time. That's a lesson I only learned just recently, by the way."

His tired eyes twinkled. "Oh, yeah?"

"Yeah. From someone I've grown quite fond of." *Someone I just might love.* She took a tremulous inhale. Now wasn't the proper time or place to tell him she was in love with him, but she would...soon. "As for how I got here, let's just say there's a pickup truck taking up two spaces in the parking garage downstairs. For the life of me, I couldn't get that thing to squeeze in between the two yellow lines."

Even if she'd heard from him in the past few days, there would've been no time for driving practice. Caring for Ginger and the puppies was practically a full-time job, and Maple was busier than ever at the clinic since Grover had decided she was, in fact, competent. Just this morning, he'd surprised her by adding her name to the felt letter board in the reception area. It was listed right alongside his, where Percy's used to be. *Dr. Percy Walker* was spelled out directly beneath, along with the years of his birth and death.

"You finally drove Percy's truck?" Ford arched a disbelieving eyebrow.

"I had to do it sooner or later." A smile danced on Maple's lips. "I can't live here permanently if I don't drive, can I?"

He gave her a tentative smile that built as the news sank in that she was staying. For good.

Maple had made up her mind even before she'd told the Leightons she wasn't going back to New York with them. She'd decided a few days ago, and she'd been weaving new dreams for her future ever since. There were still a lot of things to figure out, but she was resolute.

"I just told my parents. They're here, if you can believe it." She blew out a breath. "Or they were. I left in a hurry, so I wouldn't be surprised if they're already headed for the airport in Austin."

The look in his eyes turned gentle, as if he knew how hard it was for her to tell the Leightons she wanted to start a new life here in Texas. He probably did. Ford had always seemed to understand her like no one else could.

"I don't know. From what I've seen, your family doesn't have the greatest record when it comes to travel plans. Maybe they'll surprise you and stick around for a while," he said.

"Maybe." She took a deep breath. She might like that, actually. Bluebonnet would probably do them some good.

She'd meant it when she'd told them she loved them,

just like she'd meant it when she'd said she wanted to learn more about her birth family and this town that had embraced her and made her feel like she belonged. Those two things could be true at the same time. The Leightons had loved her as best as they could. It was the only way they knew how.

"I would've been here sooner if they hadn't turned up out the blue. The only other person who knows so far is Grover." Maple shifted the basket in her arms to hide its contents from view until the big reveal. "I didn't want to tell anyone else until we had a chance to talk. I wanted you to hear it from me, not someone else."

"You're just full of surprises tonight, Doc. I haven't slept much in the past few days. If this is a dream, please don't wake me up."

"This isn't a dream." As crazy as it seemed, it was real life. And Maple was finally ready to grab on to it with all her might.

Ford shook his head and grinned like he still couldn't believe it. "So you're really standing here with a basket full of—" He mouthed the next word so Oliver wouldn't hear, although that was doubtful since the child was chattering away to Lady Bird, who'd traveled all the way to the end of her leash to plant her front paws on the edge of the bed. The boy and the dog were in their own little world. "Puppies?"

"Yes and no." At last, she thrust the basket toward him for a closer look. "Peaches and Fuzz are far too young to leave their mom for any length of time, plus they shouldn't get out and about until they're vaccinated. So I brought the next best thing."

Ford's mouth dropped open as he got a good look at the three battery-operated golden-retriever puppies nestled together inside the basket. They were robotic companion animals, just like the one his Gram had. Except these were miniature versions of Lady Bird, Bluebonnet's unofficial town mascot. As soon as Maple had discovered them on the internet, she'd known they were perfect for her new venture. She'd ordered a dozen of them on the spot.

"You're *certain* I'm not dreaming? Because for the life of me, I can't figure out why you'd have these." He shook his head in disbelief.

"I bought them for Comfort Paws." Maple bit her lip. This was the part she couldn't wait to share with him. She hadn't told a soul—the idea had begun as a passing thought at book club, and the more she saw all the good that Lady Bird did in the community, the more it had taken root.

Ford angled closer, lips curving into a slow smile, almost like he already knew. "What's Comfort Paws?"

"It's what I've decided to name the new pet-therapy organization I'm starting. I have a lot to learn, obviously, but Lady Bird has been a pretty great teacher so far. Ginger's puppies will be perfect for this type of work. Cavaliers love people and make great therapy dogs, just like goldens do. Something tells me I know a few dog lovers who'd want to help get a new group up and running." She grinned, thinking of the book-club girls.

"Oh, there's no doubt you're right about that." He looked at her with a combination of wonder and affection that left her breathless.

She could get used to Ford Bishop looking at her like that, and now she had all the time in the world to do just that.

"So you think this is all a good idea?" Maple nodded at the litter of robot companion animals. "Until we get things off the ground, I've bought some of these guys to share with patients like Oliver and your gram."

Ford pressed a hand to his heart, and she wondered if he, too, was thinking about the day they'd met and tussled over Coco and her dead batteries. She'd been so sure she had him figured out, and she'd never been so wrong in her life. She'd never seen love coming, but it had found her, anyway.

That's the way love worked sometimes—it bowled you over when you least expected it. Love could sneak up on you in the form of well-worn bedroom slippers that felt just right, in the steady presence of a dog with a heart of gold…

In the arms of a man who made you believe in yourself again, even when you hadn't fully realized how lost you were to begin with.

"It's a great idea, sweetheart. It's also rather poetic." The warmth in his gaze seemed to reach down into her soul.

"I like it when you call me *sweetheart*. It's a much better nickname than Doc."

"This might be the best dream I've ever had." His eyes crinkled in the corners. "Shall we introduce these guys to Oliver?"

"I thought you'd never ask."

"Hey, bud." Ford turned his smile on his patient. "Wait until you see what Maple and Lady Bird brought for you."

Maple followed him as he walked closer to the bed, and then she set the basket on the edge of the mattress, right next to Lady Bird's front paws. Oliver's mouth formed a perfect *O* as he peered inside. All three puppies wagged their mechanical tails, and when Lady Bird gave one of the puppies a nudge with her nose, it blinked its eyes and yipped.

Oliver gasped and let loose with a stream of giggles. "They're real! I thought they were stuffed animals, but they're *real*."

And just like that, Maple's heart lodged in her throat. It was such a small thing, but to a boy confined to a hospital bed, this trio of tail-wagging, battery-powered companions meant the world. The light in his eyes was unparalleled.

Maple prayed with all her might that he would be okay.

"Not all the way real, but as real we can get for now," Ford said.

The distinction didn't matter to Oliver. He couldn't have been happier.

"They look just like you, Lady Bird." Oliver scooped a puppy out of the basket as gently as if it was a living, breathing animal, and he held it up to Lady Bird's nose for a sniff.

"Good girl, Lady Bird." Maple massaged the golden behind her ears, praising her for playing along.

"I can feel the puppy's heartbeat!" Oliver held the stuffed animal close to his chest. "Can I keep him?"

"Of course, you can. You can keep all these pups, for as long as you want. They're all yours. Lady Bird and I wanted to make sure you had some doggy company when we're not around."

"I love them," the boy said with a yawn. "And they love me, too. I'm going to sleep with all of them in my bed tonight."

"There's no better medicine than a basketful of puppies." Maple tilted her chin up and swallowed the lump in her throat. "At least that's what my dad always used to say."

Ford caught her gaze as he took her hand in his and squeezed it tight. "Your dad was a good man."

"He sure was." Maple smiled.

And hopefully, in time, I'll learn to love the way that he did. I'll keep growing, keep dreaming, keep believing. I'll hold people dear instead of hiding my heart away.

And through it all, I'll become my father's daughter.

Epilogue

The true dog days of summer came in late August, weeks after Oliver Taylor had been found to be in full remission. On the morning the child had been declared cancer-free, Ford called Maple to tell her the good news, and later that night, after they'd celebrated with champagne and cupcakes from Cherry on Top, she'd found him with his arms around Lady Bird's thick neck, weeping quietly into the dog's soft fur.

They'd been happy tears, but they'd also been much more. Ford had told Maple about his childhood friend Bobby shortly after she'd surprised him at the hospital with the basket of puppies for Oliver, and she knew that in so many ways, their friendship had made Ford into the man he was today. Driven, responsible, fiercely protective of the people he loved. But once Oliver was released from the hospital—an occasion marked with a goodbye party, complete with cake and a real, live golden-retriever puppy that Maple had helped his mom adopt from a local rescue group—Ford seemed less wistful when he talked about his old friend. He shared good memories of their years together. Bobby's grandfather sometimes gave them sugar cubes to feed the ponies at the family ranch, and Ford smiled when he told Maple about the feel of the horses' velvety muzzles against his sticky palm. He drove her down a dusty country road to show her the ranch where Bobby's family used to live and whooped with joy when he realized the treehouse where they'd played together still stood among a cluster of live oak trees. The grief was still there and always would be, but it was less sharp than it had been before. Ford could finally let his dear friend rest in peace.

Between the pet clinic and trying to get Comfort Paws off the ground, Maple was as busy as ever—but not too busy to slow-dance in the kitchen whenever Ford's favorite country song came on. Adaline had made good on her promise to take Maple shopping for more practical footwear, but she'd instantly fallen in love with a pair of western booties so bedazzled with rhinestones that they could've doubled for a pair of disco balls. She wore them almost daily, and they glittered like crazy every time Ford spun Maple in a twirl and sang to her with his warm lips pressed against her ear.

Ginger grew healthier by the day and, with Lady Bird as their self-appointed canine Mary Poppins, the puppies had hit all their biggest milestones on the holidays that dotted the summer calendar. On Memorial Day, their bright little eyes opened. By the time Bluebonnet's annual Fourth of July parade marched through the town square, they were eight weeks old and ready to explore the big wide world outside the Sunday house. Peaches and Fuzz loved everyone they encountered, greeting strangers with an adorable wiggle that always transitioned smoothly into a sit position without any prior training. Maple knew without a doubt they'd both make perfect therapy dogs. Both pups displayed the true Cavalier King Charles spaniel temperament—gentle, affectionate and eager to please.

And now, on the Saturday of Labor Day weekend, the time had come for them to go to their new homes. Adaline was adopting Fuzz, whom she'd taken to calling Fuzzy.

Belle had staked her claim on Peaches, and both women were fully invested in completing therapy-dog training. So was Jenna, who couldn't wait to bring Ginger home and give her all the love and spoiling she deserved. Comfort Paws was really happening! On Maple's birthday, her parents had surprised her with a large donation—enough to fund dog training, buy T-shirts with the new Comfort Paws logo, and purchase therapy-dog-in-training vests for the pups scheduled to start class in the fall. Charles and Meredith Leighton hadn't been back to Bluebonnet since their surprise trip a few months ago, and when she'd come home from County General that night, they'd already gone. But slowly and surely, they were coming to accept the fact that Maple had decided how she wanted to live her life and she wouldn't be swayed.

"Ford, what's going on in there? The girls are going to be here any minute," Maple called from the living room, where he'd ordered her to stay put while he got the puppies ready for one last picture with her before they left for their new homes. He'd been holed up with the dogs in the kitchen for several long minutes. She had no idea what they could possibly be doing in there.

"We're just about ready. This is a big day. Peaches and Fuzz are the foundation puppies of Comfort Paws. It seemed like they should dress up for the occasion," Ford yelled from the kitchen.

Dress up? Where had that idea come from? Maple had never once mentioned putting costumes on any of the dogs before. However, Lady Bird was going to make an awfully cute pumpkin when Halloween rolled around.

"Here they come!" Ford announced. Then, in a whisper just loud enough for Maple to overhear, he said, "Wait, Peaches. Come back here. Fuzzy was supposed to go first."

Too late. Peaches came bounding around the corner,

scampering toward the living room in a Tiffany Blue sweater with white lettering that Maple couldn't quite make out.

"He dressed you in a sweater?" Maple squatted and called Peaches toward her. "Does he realize how hot it is outside?"

The little dog's tail wagged so quick and fast that it was nothing but a blur. Her paws skidded on the hard wood floor as she flung herself at Maple before landing in a clumsy sit.

She scooped up the puppy and inspected the sweater. An *M* and an *E* were positioned over the dog's back.

ME? Maple was more confused than ever. "Ford, this is super cute, but I'm not sure I get it."

Fuzz came stumbling into the room next, ears flying as he tripped over his own paws. The sweater stretched over his pudgy little body was identical to the one Peaches had on, with one notable exception.

"What does yours say, Fuzzy?" Maple set Peaches back down on the ground and tucked her hair behind her ears for a closer look.

MARRY.

She glanced back and forth between the two dogs. "Me marry?"

Ford strolled into the room behind the dogs with a sheepish grin on his face, the likes of which she'd never seen before. "Fuzz was supposed to go first."

He reached down to rearrange the puppies. "See?"

MARRY ME.

Maple's heart flew to her throat. She was so stunned that she hadn't realized Ford had dropped to one knee when he'd bent to rearrange the dogs and pulled a small velvet ring box from the pocket of his denim shirt—the same one he'd been wearing on the day they'd met, with the sleeves rolled up to reveal his forearms, just the way she liked.

"Is this a puppy proposal?" she blurted through giddy tears.

"It seemed only appropriate. How else would I propose to a woman like the love of my life? I'm not sure you realize this, but you have a thing for dogs." He flipped open the box to reveal a sparkling emerald-cut solitaire surrounded by a frame of slender baguette diamonds. Maple had never seen another ring like it before.

"I love you, sweetheart. I want to keep building this crazy, unpredictable life with you," he said as the puppies climbed all over him in their delight at having one of their favorite humans down on their level. "Me marry?"

It was the most ridiculous proposal Maple could've imagined—as ridiculous as a man bringing a robot dog into the vet's office with a dead battery and a green bean stuck in its mouth.

And that's precisely what's made it perfect.

"Yes, a thousand times *yes*."

* * * * *

A Small Town Fourth Of July
Janice Carter

MILLS & BOON

Janice Carter has been writing Harlequin romances for a long time, through raising a family, teaching and on into retirement. This is her seventeenth romance and she has plans for many more—along with plenty of personal family time, too.

Visit the Author Profile page
at millsandboon.com.au for more titles.

Dear Reader,

I'm thrilled to introduce you to my new series, Home to Maple Glen, a little community tucked in a deep valley near the Appalachian Long Trail of Vermont.

Maura and Maddie Stuart operate a donkey-riding therapy business on the farm they inherited in the Glen. Their father's death and a promise to take care of his beloved donkeys, Jake and Matilda, have led to a tentative peace between the two previously estranged sisters. That peace is threatened when Maura's adolescent crush, Theo Danby, returns to the Glen.

Recently divorced, Theo has taken a six-week leave from his work as an ER doctor in Maine to reconnect with his preteen son, Luke. The task of selling the farm he inherited from his aunt and uncle is the perfect opportunity for Theo to show his son Maple Glen, the place where Theo spent idyllic summers every year with Maddie and Maura.

The two are aided and abetted in their reunion by a team of unruly donkeys, a reclusive beekeeper and an eccentric fortune teller to finally understand what they really want—each other and a life together in Maple Glen.

I hope you enjoy this book as much as I enjoyed writing it! Stay tuned for book two in the series and more heartwarming characters in Maple Glen.

Janice Carter

DEDICATION

For my feisty family-loving aunt,
Sylvia Marie Dimmel—knitter supreme,
bird watcher and avid romance reader
—with much love.

ACKNOWLEDGMENTS

A big thank-you to my cousin, Nancy Dimmel Row,
for sharing her expertise and experience as a
riding therapist along with anecdotes of her
donkey, Dory, who disliked rain.

Chapter One

*W*here's Jake?

Maura Stuart dropped the pitchfork of hay into the stall trough, muttering at the same time. Stomping down the length of the barn to its opened doors, she stood for a moment, shading her eyes from the early-morning sun. No sign of him anywhere. *Great. Just what I needed today.* And no sign of Maddie, either. Too much to hope that she'd gone looking for Jake—the enticing aroma of coffee was probably just now luring her out of bed. She took a deep breath. Giving in to this constant frustration would gain her nothing, especially if they continued to be business partners. But there were moments—plenty of them—when Maura silently questioned her decision to bring her twin sister on board. Yet there'd be no business at all if she'd had to manage on her own.

She scanned the property, from the two-story farmhouse straight ahead and its adjacent garage, to the shed on the far side of the garage. It was closed up, so no Jake there. She knew the chicken coop behind the barn and the small, fenced riding ring next to it wouldn't be a draw for Jake. Thankfully, he wasn't trotting down the long gravel drive out to the road. Then her gaze drifted east, to their neighbor's fields, overgrown with weeds. No sign of Jake, but she suddenly caught a glimmer of red through the thicket of vegetation separating the two farms.

Maura walked across the drive to the row of cedars along the property line and pushed through them into the adjacent land. She and Maddie used to come this way when they were kids, but the cedars had been newly planted then and only waist-high. Now they were taller than her shoulders.

Stepping onto what was once the Danby homestead felt strange. The elderly owners, Stan and Vera, had passed away several months ago, but the farm had been left derelict since their admission to a nursing home in Rutland two years before. When Maura and Maddie took over their own family farm a year ago, the Danby place was already run-down. The neighboring families had been close when the girls were growing up, but that gradually changed after the sisters left for college.

It was only natural, Maura knew. People aged, withdrew from community and old friends due to health or mobility issues, and lost touch with one another. She and Maddie had experienced a similar loss of contact after being away from Maple Glen for so long. But thankfully, they'd been able to reconnect with former schoolmates and other neighbors since their return.

Maura waded through the field toward the Danby farmhouse, realizing as she got closer that the flash of red was a car—a fancy sports car. When she reached the drive, she could hear the low rumble of a male voice. She paused for a second, debating whether to retreat or continue looking for Jake. The voice pitched nervously as she was rounding the back end of the car to see Jake standing between it and the closed barn door, his stocky frame blocking the object of his interest from Maura's view.

"He won't bite," she said, stifling a laugh as she drew near. "He's just curious."

The man splayed against the barn door grimaced. "Maybe call him off?"

She closed in on Jake, wrapping an arm around his neck and gently pulling him away from his attempt to nuzzle the man. She recognized him then, despite the passage of years and his transformation from teenager to adult.

"Welcome back, Theo." She kept her eyes on him, fighting to ignore the sudden throbbing at her temples, then turned Jake around, slapped him on the rump and ordered, "Home, Jake."

Theo Danby watched the donkey amble off. "Thanks... uh... Maura?"

The fact that he was slow to identify her irked. "Yes," she snapped.

He moved away from the barn door and unzipped his windbreaker. "Warmer than I remember," he mumbled.

So he's going for small talk. "Yeah, climate change and all that. Plus, it's the middle of June." She shifted her attention away from the well-toned chest muscles emerging through his short-sleeved shirt—muscles that the Theo she remembered hadn't had. She felt her cheeks warm up as a trace of a smile crossed his face.

"Are you visiting your folks or...?" he asked.

"No, Mom died about three years ago and my father, last June."

"I'm sorry." His face softened, and she peered down at the ground, hiding unexpected tears.

"We moved back here more than a year ago," she went on.

"We?"

She raised her head, meeting his dark brown eyes again. "Maddie and I."

"Ah."

"So…you're here to…" she continued.

"Have a look at this place before I sell it."

Of course. She'd been expecting that from the day she and Maddie first returned home and had seen that the Danby homestead had been left to ruin. Though she couldn't figure out why it had taken Theo so long to return after his aunt and uncle passed away. She was about to ask him more about his plans when a slamming door and a young voice got her attention.

"Dad?" A boy who looked to be a preteen was standing on the farmhouse veranda, his face wrinkled in disgust. "This place is a dump!" He caught sight of Maura and hesitated before descending the porch steps and walking their way.

Maura shot a glance at Theo. He flushed slightly as he said, "My son."

Maura scolded herself for automatically assuming that Theo might still be single, too. The boy heading their way was a near replica of a young Theo—same thick dark hair and eyes. He sidled up to his father but kept his eyes on Maura.

"Uh, Luke, this is Maura—" The last part of his introduction dropped off, as if he were unsure of her current surname. "Her family owns the place over there." He gestured to his right, though the boy kept his attention on her.

"It's Maura Stuart. Nice to meet you, Luke." She held out her right hand, and after an elbow nudge from Theo, the boy shook it. "My sister and I knew your father years ago, when he used to spend his summer vacations here, with his aunt and uncle."

"Dad told me about that, but he made it sound more interesting than—"

"What you see here?" Maura smiled. She resisted glancing at Theo, but thought she heard a faint sigh.

"Yeah." He looked at Theo and asked, "So now what?"

"Well, uh, I thought after we looked around, we could go into Maple Glen for some lunch and then talk about our plans."

"*Our* plans? It wasn't *my* idea to come here."

Maura took in the disgruntled face and voice. Time to head back to the farm, she decided. "Okay, well, nice to see you again, Theo and Luke... The bakery in the village sells sandwiches and pizzas, but if you want anything substantial, you'll have to drive to Wallingford."

Theo's smile was strained. "Thanks, Maura. I think a bite to eat will help us both. And...uh...is there a place to stay? It's been a while since I was last here."

"Maybe you remember the Watsons? Bernie used to manage the gas station at the junction to Route 7, but he bought the old Harrison place about ten years ago and turned it into a B and B. The Shady Nook. I hear it's quite nice. If you're planning to stay in the area for a few days, of course." When Theo failed to respond, she added, "Unless you'd rather stay somewhere with more to offer, like Rutland or Bennington." Theo was staring, and she realized she'd been babbling. "Okay, well, I better go."

She was about to turn around when he finally spoke. "Thanks, Maura. Um, my plan is to stick around until I can make a decision about my aunt and uncle's place. A few days, anyway—maybe more." He shot Luke a quick look. "Nothing definite yet. But maybe we'll see you around. And Maddie, too, of course. Say hi for me."

"Sure." She managed a smile and headed off, taking the same route across the weed-filled field and through the cedars, feeling two sets of eyes tracking her. Her mind buzzed with random thoughts and questions. *Theo Danby is back. He has a son. Presumably he's married. Or was.*

But the important question was, how long would he be around?

The very thought of Theo spending any amount of time in Maple Glen made Maura's stomach churn. Was it too much to hope that Theo Danby would just drop out of their lives again, as he had twenty years ago, and never discover her secret?

By the time she reached the barn, Jake had instinctively headed for his stall and was munching the hay she'd deposited. She took a moment to inspect the stall door and noticed the hasp was loose enough to give way with a solid push. A small thing to fix, but one more item on the long list of jobs. The other two donkeys, Matilda and Lizzie, were too busy eating to give her more than a half glance, their long ears twitching as she walked by their stalls.

Maura decided that after the encounter with Theo—and his son!—a second cup of coffee was definitely on the day's agenda and headed for the side door of the farmhouse that led through a tiny mudroom into the kitchen. Maddie was sitting at the table eating cereal and skimming through yesterday's Rutland newspaper. She looked up when Maura entered the room.

"What's up?" she immediately asked.

They'd always been good at reading one another, Maura knew. Even though they were nonidentical twins, there was still that inexplicable twin connection. At least, until the summer they'd turned eighteen, when they'd withdrawn from one another and begun new, separate lives.

Maura sighed. There was no point postponing the inevitable. "Jake got out of his stall—it's okay," she quickly put in, seeing Maddie was about to ask how. "I've figured it out. We have to fix the stall gate. Anyway, he'd wandered over to the Danbys', and I followed him." She paused. "Someone was at the house."

Maddie put her spoon down. "Who?"

"Theo."

Their eyes locked for what seemed ages. "He's come to get the place ready to sell," Maura added. "And he has a son who looks to be about eleven or twelve."

Maddie's impassive face revealed nothing. "Okay," she said and resumed eating.

That went well, Maura thought. Clearly her sister was still unhappy with her after last night's disagreement over the ongoing plans for the business, as well as finances. She poured herself a coffee and sat across from Maddie, whose head was still bent over the newspaper. The kitchen filled with the silence that had fallen between the sisters seventeen years ago, and Maura hoped it wouldn't last five years this time around, too. *Not if you do something about it right now*, she told herself.

"Look, Mads, Theo is ancient history. We were all teenagers the last time we were together, and presumably—" she attempted a half laugh "—we're a whole lot smarter now. I got the impression he and his son are here only long enough to sell the farm. Then he'll be gone."

Maddie finally looked at her. "I'm not worried about any of that, Maura. Like you said, that last summer is ancient history. I've moved on, and I hope you have, too."

Maura felt her face heat up under her sister's penetrating gaze. She bit down on her lower lip, quelling an instant rise of hurt. She wasn't going to be drawn into a debate they'd both sworn to put behind them. "Okay," she mumbled. "You're right." She got up from her chair and rinsed her coffee mug, letting the tension seep out. "So, who have we got riding today?"

It *had* to happen. Theo parked the car in front of the Shady Nook B and B and sat, unmoving. He'd known from the start that meeting up with the Stuart sisters—or at least one of them—was a possibility, but he wished fervently that it hadn't happened under such humiliating circumstances. Trapped by a donkey, for heaven's sake! Only to be rescued by one of the sisters. Worst of all, for a second he couldn't recall which was the redhead and which the raven-haired. They weren't identical twins, so it shouldn't have been so difficult. When he was a boy and then a teen, he'd never have made such a mistake.

"Are we going in or what?"

Luke's grumble finally registered. Theo blinked. He was back in Maple Glen. Thirty-six years old, divorced and on leave from his job. With a twelve-year-old son he barely knew who didn't want to be there any more than he did. He sighed. Those few minutes back at the farm with Maura had been a cold-water-shock reminder that time didn't change everything. Her stony expression and clipped voice took him immediately back to his last summer in Maple Glen countless years ago.

"Dad? Jeez!"

"Yeah, yeah. C'mon. We'll leave our stuff here until we know if we can get a room."

"Why don't we go back to the highway? I saw some motels there. Maybe we could get one with a pool, like we did yesterday."

Theo ignored Luke's plaintive tone, which had been incessant since he'd made the decision to take a road trip to Maple Glen and finally deal with his inheritance. Reconnecting with his son was meant to be part of a new, postdivorce direction in Theo's life, but he had a sinking feeling he'd already taken a wrong turn somewhere and now was lost. Like the rookie hikers on the nearby Appalachian Long Trail that the locals used to complain about.

At least the B and B looked like a welcoming place,

with its smoky-blue clapboard siding, white gingerbread-trimmed veranda and wicker chairs and tables. Theo vaguely recalled the original Colonial-style home had been painted white, but any memory of the people who'd lived there—the Harrisons, Maura had said—escaped him. Though come to think of it, had there been a boy roughly his own age?

"Well?" Luke was staring up at him from the bottom porch step.

His expression was a mix of frustration and concern, which made Theo feel a tad guilty. He hadn't been paying full attention to him since leaving Maine. Perhaps their road trip's destination should have been somewhere more exciting than a small place like Maple Glen, Vermont. He reached down and tousled Luke's hair. "C'mon," he said and opened the screen door.

Theo's eyes were adjusting to the cool darkness inside the entryway when a voice called out from somewhere farther inside. "Give me a sec!"

The interior gradually took shape, from the hall table with a vase of flowers and a small display of tourist pamphlets, to the staircase straight ahead. There were rooms to the left and right off the entry, and Theo spotted tables and chairs in one of them. A good sign, he thought. Even if there wasn't a room available, maybe they could get a bite to eat. Breakfast had been early, at a fast-food place on the highway.

Luke was fidgeting beside him, but at least he wasn't complaining. Not yet. Theo was about to reassure him that the next town, Wallingford, was only minutes away and they could always get some lunch there when a large, gray-haired man wearing an apron over baggy pants and a T-shirt emerged from a room at the end of the hall and lumbered toward them.

"Had to pop my bread rolls into the oven," he explained, his big, welcoming smile shooting from Theo to Luke. "What can I do for you folks?"

"We'd like a room, if you have one."

"Aha! That I do. You came at the right time—it's Sunday and I've just had two checkouts, plus the Fourth of July holiday is a couple of weeks away. How many nights are you thinking?" Before Theo could reply, the man headed for one of the rooms leading off the hall and, after a second's hesitation, Theo and Luke followed.

The room still exhibited its early days as a parlor, with a cluster of seating arrangements and an impressive bow-legged table with a Tiffany-style, stained glass lamp in the center of the bay window that looked onto the veranda. The man—Bernie Watson, Theo assumed—was rifling through a drawer in the table. Pulling out a small ledger book and pen, he swung around to say, "Here we go. Have a seat there—" he gestured to a chintz-upholstered wing chair "—and fill in the information I need while I go check on my dinner rolls."

Theo grasped the book and pen that were thrust at him and, casting a quick grin at Luke, sat where he was told. He wrote his name and address on the page headed with the day's date, hesitated over the "length of stay" column before jotting *2-3 nights* and hoped Luke, now standing at his elbow, hadn't noticed. He had yet to tell the boy that his plan was to fix up a couple of rooms in the farmhouse for them until the meeting with the Realtor.

Despite Luke's disparagement of the house as a "dump," the place had been dusted and aired only the week before their arrival by a company from Rutland that Theo had hired. The Stuart sisters obviously hadn't noticed the recent activity there, though the weeds in the fields between the two places could have hidden the cleaning agency's vehicle. Maura's search for her donkey had likely been the only reason for her to discover he was back. A donkey! Theo was pretty certain the Stuarts had never had animals larger than goats.

"Dad? I'm hungry." Luke was pulling on his arm.

Theo roused himself from thoughts that were leading nowhere. He was hungry, too, and the heavy footfalls along the hallway were reassuring. They'd be getting a room and, hopefully, lunch as well.

"Excuse my bad manners," the man was saying as he reentered the room. "I'm Bernie Watson, the owner, general manager as well as cook here."

Theo shook his hand and passed the sign-in book to Bernie, who peered down at it.

"Good heavens," he exclaimed. "Theo Danby!" His beaming grin faltered immediately. "I was sorry to hear about Stan and Vera."

"Thank you," Theo murmured. Luke shuffled impatiently, and he added, "Is it possible to get some lunch?"

"Definitely. Go get your things from your car. It'll be okay parked out front for now. I've got a small lot behind where you can move it later. As for lunch, I don't have any other patrons at the moment, but I can rustle something up for you two." He turned to Luke. "How about a grilled cheese sandwich with fries? I can even manage a chocolate milkshake, if you're up to it."

The smile on Luke's face was the first Theo had seen since the motel with pool they'd stayed at. "I think he's up to it," he said.

Chapter Two

Theo settled his sunglasses onto the bridge of his nose and sneaked a peek at Luke, standing a few feet away on the sidewalk outside Shady Nook B and B. The blissful expression on his son's face as he'd wolfed down waffles and strawberries for breakfast moments ago had morphed to petulance. Theo clenched his jaw, but he wasn't going to give up.

"So, we have a couple of options for this morning, Luke. At some point while we're here, I'm hoping we can do some hiking. There's an easy access route from the village into the Long Trail section of the Appalachian Trail. Remember I told you about my hiking a few times when I used to spend my summers here? Or we can explore the village a bit more before heading back to the farm."

His son looked up and down the street. "Except this is it, isn't it? The whole place?"

Theo could relate to the resignation in his son's voice. He'd had similar feelings his last summer in Maple Glen, when the village boundaries had pressed in. When even the magic of the Stuart sisters—one in particular—failed to raise any enthusiasm for the weeks ahead. But when he'd been Luke's age, the place had still held a promise of adventure and exploration.

Perhaps he ought to have brought Luke here years ago, connected him to Uncle Stan and Aunt Vera, who'd provided the stability his own divorced parents could not. That thought instantly raised the specter of his divorce months ago. Theo sighed. This was his chance to start anew with his son. He couldn't blow it.

"I know it seems like there's not a lot to do here, but once we've settled into the farmhouse and I've organized its sale, we'll have time to explore the parts of this area that are special—the Trail, the parks. *Nature.* That's really what this place is all about. And the people, too. Though we might not be here long enough to meet too many of the residents." He heard Luke mumble something and added, "Pardon?"

"I said, what's the point?" Luke turned to face him. "Why bother meeting anyone when we won't be staying?"

Theo swore silently. He knew he ought to have been more transparent about the trip with Luke than he had been. His ex had asked him to take full custody of their son during his six weeks' leave from his job as head of the hospital emergency department in Augusta so she could finalize plans for a move from Maine with the man she'd left Theo for a year ago. Luke was aware of some of the details, but not all. A decision about where he would eventually end up living—and with whom—was still up in the air.

The timing was perfect, but the reality of having Luke all to himself for more than a month was both gratifying and frightening. Still, the opportunity to bond with his only child was one he couldn't miss, though he probably ought to have told the boy that organizing the farm's sale could take longer than the week he'd mentioned. Plus, he'd have to clear the place out—go through all the possessions, papers and general stuff his aunt and uncle had accumulated over the years. As a teen, Theo had realized the couple were pack rats, and a quick glance inside yesterday had confirmed nothing had been removed from the house, even after their move into the nursing home. Having plenty of time to complete the job was a bonus, but he'd known he'd never get Luke onside with the trip unless he implied a week would be sufficient.

"I could have gone to camp," Luke muttered.

Theo sighed. Camp had been the fallback plan. "I suppose that's always an option for later in the summer."

"Not really. You have to register early if you want a place. Mom told you that." Luke shifted his gaze to his feet.

So camp wasn't a likely possibility now. Maybe he should reassess his plans, but Theo hated to give in too quickly. Luke needed to learn to compromise, or at the very least, to be more open to new experiences. "Maybe later this afternoon we could take a drive into Rutland and watch a movie."

There was a barely audible sigh and then, "Sure."

Theo took a deep breath. "Okay, so let's wander in that direction—" he pointed east toward the distant wooded slopes "—and check out the access to the Trail. If we decide to hike a bit, we could buy you some appropriate footwear when we go into Rutland." He took the lead and after a few seconds heard Luke follow. "I noticed from the sign when we turned off Route 7 that the Glen has a current population of 550. I think that's only an increase of about twenty people since I was here last."

"When was that?" Luke asked.

"My last summer here was when I was sixteen. Twenty years ago." He glanced down at his son, now walking beside him.

"And how old were you when you first came here?"

"Turning nine."

"So for seven years you came every summer."

"Yep."

There was a brief silence, followed by, "I can't imagine spending seven summers in this place."

Theo hid a quick grin. The kid was a real city boy, as Theo himself had been until those summers transformed him. A fragrant aroma distracted him from rambling on, and he stopped in front of a white-framed cottage. A hand-painted sign decorated with gingerbread trim hung above the cottage door—Tasty Delights. An extension attached to the right of the cottage bore a United States Postal Service sign that Theo didn't recall from his summer visits. He was certain that in those days a van delivered mail to the box fronting his uncle's farm.

"This bakery was here then, but not the post office. My aunt gave me a weekly allowance, and I always spent some of it on a doughnut, hot out of the oven." He didn't remember the names of the people who ran the bakery, only that they'd always been friendly, especially to the kids. "Want anything?"

"Dad! I just ate three waffles!"

"Yeah, right." He grinned at Luke's expression.

When his son added, "I bet *you'd* like something, though," Theo laughed.

"Caught me!"

Luke's smile warmed him. Maybe today was going to be all right. They continued walking, then paused in front of the church. "They had fantastic community potluck suppers here every Friday," Theo said. He pointed to the legion hall on the opposite side of the street. "That was a one-room schoolhouse in the 1800s. I think it was turned into a legion after the Second World War, and when I used to come to the Glen, it was often used as a community center."

They stared silently at the A-framed building with its bright coat of blue paint and yellow trim. The sign above the front door lintel read Legion but a smaller sign below, next to the door, added Maple Glen Community Center and Town Hall. "Guess it's multipurpose now," Theo murmured.

"Where do kids go to school?" Luke asked, adding, "If there even *are* any kids here."

"I'm sure there are kids here," Theo said. He hadn't seen any yet, but he hoped so. If they were going to be in the village longer than a week, it'd be nice for Luke to meet some kids his age. The group of kids he recalled from his visits had made those summers extra special. "When I arrived here in late June, it was always fun to meet up with everyone I hadn't seen since the year before. We had a lot of catching up to do, but we quickly got back into the summer vibe."

"*Vibe*, Dad?"

Theo shrugged. "Whatever."

Luke rolled his eyes. "So where did they go to school?"

"Wallingford, by bus, I think. At least, they did back then."

Luke nodded. He could relate to the bus, which was his mode of transport to the pricey private school his mother had insisted on. That was another point of contention to be negotiated. Theo stifled a sigh. This week was meant to be a stress-free adventure. He and his ex, Trish, had even agreed to not text or email unless there was an emergency. Theo welcomed the break.

"Remember when we were driving here yesterday, and I pointed out that range in front of us—the Green Mountains?" Theo asked as they approached the trees at the end of the street and the mountains looming beyond.

Luke nodded.

"Well, that summit is White Rocks Mountain. You can get to it from the part of the Long Trail that exits into Maple Glen."

"The same mountain we saw at the recreation area in Wallingford?"

"The same. I'm hoping we can have a bit of a wander there before we leave."

"Sure." But Luke's voice sounded uncertain.

"It's not a difficult hike, even for newbies like us," Theo hastened to reassure him.

After a minute, Luke added, "Yeah, but I was thinking we might not be here long enough for that."

Okay, Theo thought. Back to square one. "Let's walk up to the bridge anyway and have a closer look." He resumed walking, listening to Luke shuffling behind. A movie later today for sure, he was thinking. As they drew nearer, memories flooded his mind. The bridge was newer, its former wood planks and handrails replaced by metal, though its height and span looked the same.

Stopping in front of it, Theo said, "That's Otter Creek. We used to swim in it."

Luke stepped forward on the crest of the gentle slope leading down to the water. "Is it deep?"

"Not really. Maybe in early spring after the winter snowmelt, but not in the summer, especially when the days were hot and dry. And we didn't go in here, but over there." He pointed left to what he remembered was the McAllister homestead. The place looked exactly the same.

Luke's attention shifted to the imposing house. "It's big. Are the owners rich or something?"

"No, but their ancestors were some of the first people to settle here." He thought about the boy who'd lived there. A bit older, with an unusual name. Started with an *F*, he recalled. He strolled over to the sign by the front gate, but there was only the surname McAllister, painted in faded black letters. Theo wondered if anyone was even still living there until he noticed the main front door on the wraparound veranda was open, revealing an ornately carved screen door.

Just then the screen door flew open and a little girl with blond ponytails, one on either side of her face, stepped onto the porch. She looked at them, and Theo was about to wave when he heard a voice calling out from somewhere among the trees speckling the expansive front lawn. "Kaya? I'm over here."

The child didn't move but continued her silent stare. When she failed to reply, a woman suddenly appeared from the area closest to the creek. She carried a basket and held what looked like a gardening tool. Stopping at the foot of the porch steps, the woman turned around and noticed Theo and Luke.

Theo waved, and she walked toward them. As she got closer, Theo could see wisps of gray hair beneath the straw sun hat she was wearing, and despite her large dark sunglasses, Theo thought he recognized her. "Mrs. McAllister?"

"Yes." She stepped right up to the gate. "Um…"

"Theo Danby," he quickly said, extending his right hand.

"Oh my goodness!" She lowered the basket to the ground and, rising up, shook his hand. "I never would have recognized you." She glanced at Luke. "And this must be…"

"My son, Luke." Theo gave Luke a slight nudge and was proud to see the boy quickly extend his own hand.

"Granny?"

They all looked to the porch, where the little girl was descending the steps. "Come here, sweetie, and meet an old friend of your uncle's."

"Your granddaughter, Mrs. McAllister?"

She smiled. "Indeed! And please, call me Marion. You're clearly not a teenager anymore. Are you here for a while or...?"

"I came back to take care of the farm."

"By 'take care,' do you mean you plan to stay and take it over?"

Theo ignored the audible snort from Luke. "Oh, no. I'm just here to clear everything out before putting it up for sale. You may have heard I inherited it from my aunt and uncle."

"Yes, and I was sorry to hear about Vera and Stan. They were strong community supporters for many years."

Theo nodded and waited a second before asking, "And... uh... Mr. McAllister? How's he?"

Her smile shifted. "Lewis is in a nursing home in Bennington. He has Alzheimer's."

"Oh, I'm so sorry to hear that."

The little girl had reached her grandmother's side. "Kaya, this is Mr. Danby and his son, Luke. Mr. Danby—"

"Theo!" he interjected.

"Theo used to spend his summers here when he was a boy and a teenager," she explained.

The information didn't impress the girl, who continued to stare solemnly at them. Theo smiled at her. "And are you spending your summer holiday here with your grandmother, Kaya?"

"No!"

"Kaya and her mother, Roxanne—maybe you remember her? She was in a younger group than you and Finn. Anyway, they're living with us now...for a bit." She sighed as Kaya ran back to the veranda. "They've just moved in a week ago, so she's still adjusting."

Theo could relate to the child's obvious unhappy mood. "And Finn?" he asked, grateful for the name reminder.

"Finn lives with me now, too. He moved back three and a half years ago to help out when Lewis had to go into care. I had health issues and needed the support." Her face brightened suddenly. "He's on his shift right now, at the Wallingford Fire Department, but I'm sure he'd love to meet up with you before you leave."

Maybe, Theo thought, knowing from personal experience how awkward old friends' reunions could be. The image of Maura Stuart's stunned face yesterday flashed across his mind. "Sure," he said. He felt Luke tug on his shirtsleeve. "Um, guess we ought to be going. It was great to see you again, and please pass on my best to Finn."

"I'll let him know you're back. Are you staying at the farm?"

"We spent last night at the B and B but will be moving into the farm tomorrow or the next day." He heard a loud sigh from Luke and noticed from her quick smile that Marion had, too.

"Wonderful! Maybe we can arrange for you both to come for a meal while you're here."

"That would be great," Theo said, hoping she hadn't noticed the frown on Luke's face.

A quick wave and she was heading toward the veranda, where Kaya was waiting.

"Let's ask Mr. Watson to make us some lunch before heading for Rutland," Theo suggested as Luke stomped ahead. The boy barely slowed down. A movie might just save the day after all, Theo thought.

Maura heaved the last bag of chicken feed into the back of the pickup truck and leaned against the driver side, panting from the exertion. She wiped off the droplets of sweat trickling down her cheek and was about to climb into the truck when a shout stopped her. The cashier at the farm co-op was running her way, waving a sheet of paper.

"A customer has a question about the Fourth of July festival," the woman said between gasping breaths as she drew near. "He wants to know if people will be able to ride the donkeys that day or will they just be looking at them."

Good question and Maura wished she had an answer. She and Maddie were still debating the idea, and since Maddie was the person in charge of the therapy riding, her opinion would decide. Maura had argued that they needed to advertise the program when people from outside the Glen would be attending the fair.

"Um, not sure yet, but we'll definitely have someone on hand to answer any questions."

"Okay, that's fine. He has a young son who might benefit from it. And thanks for the flyers—" she held up the paper "—I'll post them around and pass the rest to some other businesses here."

"Thank you…uh… Wendy," Maura replied, reading the woman's ID tag. "I meant to do that myself but got behind in my chores today."

"How many donkeys do you have now?"

"Three."

Wendy smiled. "I remember when your father got the first one. What was his name again?"

"Jake?" Maura paused her climb into the truck.

"That was it! Your father was so excited. Like a little boy."

Maura smiled. "You knew my dad?"

"Oh, yes, we had lots of chats when he came to the co-op. I was so sorry when he passed last year. I was on maternity leave and couldn't make it to his funeral, but I know others from the co-op went. Everyone here loved Charlie Stuart."

The unexpected lump in Maura's throat made a reply impossible. The two women smiled at one another until Wendy said, "Better get back to my customer. Maybe I'll see you at the fair—I'm bringing my baby, too." She gave a small wave and bustled toward the co-op entrance.

Maura got behind the wheel and turned on the ignition. The encounter was another reminder why she liked living in the Glen. So many people knew one another or had heard of one another, even here in Wallingford. She hadn't appreciated that chain of familiarity when she was a teenager and, like her twin, could hardly wait to escape.

The moment fifteen months ago was so fresh she could still envision the scene—her father slumped in a wheelchair, holding her hand. "Find a way, Maura, to keep the farm and the donkeys," he'd begged. "You won't regret it." And she hadn't, really. Several anxious and sleepless nights didn't add up to regret. The image of a red sports car suddenly flashed across her mind. Not yet, anyway, she thought.

She drove out of the co-op parking lot and turned onto Route 7 toward Maple Glen. It was a beautiful, sunny day and promising to heat up. She ought to have picked up the feed earlier but had spent most of the morning fixing the lock on Jake's stall. The run into Wallingford couldn't be put off, either, as supplies were running low. When the woman—Wendy—had come running out of the store, Maura's first thought was that her credit card had been refused.

The possibility of that happening was frightening, and Maura knew she and Maddie had to have the money talk soon. Maybe after the festival, she thought. She and Maddie were involved with the planning and organization, along with several Glen residents and even a few from Wallingford.

Maura turned off Route 7 onto the county road that changed into Church Street at the village limits and, spotting the Quick Stop gas and convenience store up ahead, glanced at her dashboard. Might as well fill up now, she thought, and made a hard right into the lot, parking at the nearest pump. Minutes later she handed cash to the clerk inside, thinking she shouldn't press her luck by using her card again. Her stomach rumbled, and the clerk—in his late teens, she guessed—looked up and grinned. He nodded to the display of potato chips on a nearby rack. "Lunch?"

Maura shrugged. "Why not?"

After paying, she tore into the bag of chips, shoving a small handful into her mouth. The young man was busy on his cell phone and Maura was noisily crunching, so she didn't register the tinkle of the store's door until she turned to leave. Theo Danby and his son were standing in front of her.

He was grinning as he pushed his sunglasses up onto his brow. "Hi again," he said, his quiet baritone voice distracting the store clerk for a second. Then he noticed the bag in her hand and his grin widened. "Late lunch…or afternoon snack?"

Maura felt all the eyes on her. Her face heated up, its typical giveaway at embarrassment. She was certain there were chip crumbs on her lips, as well as a sprinkle of salt, but opted for silence rather than explanation.

He let her off the hook then, swiftly saying, "Luke and I are on our way to a movie in Rutland and thought we'd pick up some snacks, too."

Maura kept her eyes on Theo but nodded at Luke, who had slipped past her on his way to the junk-food aisle. "Should be cool in the cinema, anyway."

He stood aside as she made for the door. "I thought we might drop by later, after the movie. Or maybe in the morning. Luke wants to see the donkeys." When she hesitated, he added, "If that's okay."

The uncertainty in his voice touched her. Why was she being so prickly? "Sure, though the morning would be better. If you come about nine, you might see a couple of them in action. Giving rides," she explained at his puzzled face.

"Great! Luke will be thrilled."

Would he? She hadn't seen much enthusiasm in the boy so far, though there was a bit of satisfaction on his face as he went up to the cash counter with bags of snacks and a can of soda.

"Okay, tomorrow, then."

"For sure," he said as she opened the door. "And…uh… I see you still like salt and vinegar."

She swung around, frowning.

He nodded at the crumpled chip bag.

She was saved from replying by Luke.

"Dad? Money?"

Back in the truck, Maura shook her head at the pathetic scene. At least Theo's face had reddened, too, after his inane comment about the chips.

Driving off the lot, she glanced at the rearview mirror to see Theo and Luke getting into their car. She blew out a mouthful of vinegar breath. *With any luck, Theo Danby will be on his way back to wherever he's living now, and there'll be no more embarrassing encounters like that one. And so what if I still like salt and vinegar? I can't believe he ever noticed back then…*

Chapter Three

"Seriously?"

The disbelief in Maddie's voice caught Maura off guard. "What's the problem? You give lots of tours to people. Just because it's Theo—"

"He has nothing to do with this. Bernie's niece, Ashley, is coming to help. I told you she'd be volunteering this summer, and I have two clients riding while she's here. We still haven't decided on a plan for the festival—organizing the vendor tables and so on—plus the stables need mucking out."

Maura almost smiled. The stables always needed cleaning. "They're only going to be watching, Mads. It's not a big deal."

Maddie dropped the tea towel she was holding onto the kitchen counter. "Fine, then you can answer any questions they have, because I can't be interrupted." As she headed for the door leading into the mudroom, she tossed back one last comment. "And remember, there's only two weeks left and a lot more to organize."

"I delivered all the flyers yesterday," Maura called as the outside door slammed shut. She couldn't figure out why Maddie was so worked up, unless the stress of hosting the

Glen's annual Fourth of July festival this year was a factor. Usually, it was Maura's anxiety about commitments and deadlines that prevailed while Maddie was blissfully unaware of such mundane matters. But lately it seemed as if the two had switched personalities. She and Mads would definitely have to have a talk. But right then, she had work to do.

She finished stacking the breakfast dishes into the dishwasher and was about to pour the rest of the coffee down the sink when she thought she could offer a cup to Theo. Or even Ashley. She *had* forgotten about her returning this summer to help, along with their two adult volunteers—Nancy and Cathy—who'd been with them almost from the beginning.

The summer holidays would potentially be a busy time for the riding program. At least, Maura prayed the summer would be busy, because they needed the money. She and Maddie had put plans to buy another donkey on hold until they had a clear picture of the summer. Still, Maura was all set to start looking, but Maddie was resisting. "Let's wait and see how the summer pans out revenue wise," she'd said.

Revenue wise? That was a comment right out of *Maura's* playbook. She was the practical, no-nonsense, "let's wait and see" one, not Maddie. The remark had been picking away at her ever since. Maddie had committed to one year with the farm and the business, and the end to that period was looming. In September, she'd know if her sister was going to stay on and become a real partner. Lately, she'd been unusually silent when decisions about the farm and the business arose. The change from her active participation in decision-making to taking a back seat had been gradual, but Maura guessed it may have begun six weeks ago, after their disagreement about applying for a bank loan.

Maura had resisted applying for a loan, but Maddie had argued that they could use the money on property and barn upgrades, along with more advertisement. She'd also suggested the funds might permit hiring an instructor, which disturbed Maura. Did that mean her sister was contemplating leaving? She didn't want to think about that possibility. Besides, a loan application might lead to something worse than a higher interest payment—something like a review of the farm accounts. There was no going back, she told herself. She'd made a decision two months ago not to tell Maddie what she'd found and would stick with it. *For now*.

She headed for the riding ring, where Maddie was prepping Matilda. Maura watched her sister saddle the gentle donkey, whose amiable nature was perfect for training potential volunteers, as well as providing therapy. To her far right, Jake and Lizzie were grazing contentedly in the pasture abutting the Danby farm.

Theo and Luke could arrive any minute, and playing tour guide was the last thing Maura felt like doing after the tiff with her sister. She needed to calm down and put on her business-friendly face, let her frustrations vanish. And what better way to accomplish that than mucking out stables? Half an hour later, she was finishing up when she heard the zoom of an engine.

As she exited the barn, she saw Theo's sports car emerging from a cloud of dust and gravel. The red car came to a stop yards away from the house, and the smile on Theo's face as he spotted her tugged at her heart. For an instant it was that same boyish face, aglow with the promise of a whole summer, when he would greet her and Maddie his first day back in the Glen. But the warmth that flowed through her now as he walked her way felt different.

"I hope this is a good time," Theo began the instant he drew near. "We just checked out of the B and B and were on our way to the farm when we saw the donkeys in the field, and I wondered if we could have our tour now."

That grin is the same, too. A tad sheepish, but confident he could get away with anything—and he always had. She cleared her throat, focusing on the present. "No problem. Um… Maddie's exercising Matilda and is expecting a trainee volunteer later this morning, so—"

"She's busy. Sure. I can catch up with her later." He paused. "Are *you* free now?"

"I can take you to the donkeys out in the pasture, but uh…are you okay with walking through a field? It might be a bit damp or even muddy." She peered down at their city footwear, noting Luke's white sneakers.

Theo turned to Luke, who shrugged. "I think we'll be fine," he said.

"Great. Well, follow me." She heard some whispering behind her as she started toward the pasture.

"Luke was wondering if he'd have a chance to ride one," Theo explained, catching up to her.

"Sure. Let's see how he responds to them close-up. They're small, but they can be a little intimidating. As you know." She couldn't resist adding the slight dig.

"Ah, well, you don't know the whole story," he protested in a light voice. "There's me, on my own land, about to open my garage door when a loud snuffling and hot breath caught me at the back of my neck."

"And?" Maura hid a smile as she unlatched the gate into the pasture.

"I think you know the rest."

She pushed open the gate and looked up at him. "Do I?"

"I think so, but if not, perhaps we can get back to it later on. Tomorrow or the next day." His eyes bored into hers.

"Dad?" Luke had caught up to them.

Maura dropped her gaze and continued walking in the

direction of the donkeys, relieved at the chance to hide her face. How did small talk get so loaded with meaning, or was she imagining his tone? Surely there was a wife somewhere! She was pondering this last point when Jake and Lizzie noticed them and began to trot their way.

"It's okay," she quickly assured Luke and Theo at the sound of scuffling. "They think we've got treats." She turned around to see Luke hiding behind his father.

"Do we have treats?"

Maura smiled at the nervousness in Theo's voice. "Not the apple or carrot they're hoping for, but I do have some turnip in my pocket." She dug into her jeans pockets and pulled out a small plastic bag. "They don't get treats on a daily basis, but I knew you were coming and thought you'd like to feed them."

Luke came out from behind Theo. "Will they bite?"

"Only when feeling threatened or frightened."

"So, uh, is this one of those times?" he asked.

Both Theo and Maura laughed. "No, 'cause I'm here," she said. "And even if you were here with your dad without me, they'd only be curious, not aggressive."

"They're smaller than I thought they'd be," Luke said.

"Jake is five feet tall. Lizzie's a bit shorter."

"They're bigger up close." Luke edged toward Theo as the donkeys were now standing in front of them.

"Hold out your hand and keep it flat." Maura placed four chunks of raw turnip on Luke's palm. Jake wouldn't bite, but she wasn't so certain about Lizzie, whose enthusiasm for treats could result in a nip. "Like this," she demonstrated, offering Lizzie some turnip, which was immediately lapped up.

Jake nudged Maura's arm. "Okay, okay, mister," she said, laughing. "Now your turn, Luke." She saw Theo gently tap Luke's forearm and stand aside as Luke extended his hand. Jake quickly got the message, and his long tongue flicked across Luke's palm, licking up the turnip in one sweep.

"Oooh!" Luke exclaimed. "Wet!"

"Yep!" Maura said.

Theo caught her eye and smiled a thank-you, which sent a rush of warmth through her, and for a moment, Maura couldn't think what to say until Luke asked, "Can I pat him?"

"Of course. The idea is not to startle him. He knows me and my sister well enough, so we can basically touch him anywhere, but he's still a bit wary of you, even after the treat. Start here on his side and work up to his head, then his cheek and then down his nose. Like this."

Luke cautiously followed her movements, lingering slightly on the bridge of Jake's nose. "It's so soft here on his nose, but his fur is thick and rougher than I thought it would be."

"Their coats are different than a horse's. He gets groomed regularly because he'll pick up thistles or seeds from the barley he eats when we move them into the other pasture."

"What do they do all day?"

Maura tried not to smile at a question prompted by his city upbringing. "Eat, mostly. We exercise them, and they also take part in our riding program."

"Riding program? You mean people pay to come and ride them, like horses?"

"Kind of. But some of the people who ride them are doing it for therapy." She noted his frown. "Say you had a lot of stress in your life and needed to chill. You could come here and ride one of them for an hour or so. When you sit on an animal, like a horse or pony or donkey, you get into the rhythm of their movement. You concentrate on the animal itself, how it's moving and where it's going. All of your attention is devoted to what's happening right at that moment, so you might be able to forget about the problems in your mind or in your body for at least that one hour."

Luke nodded. "Yeah, I can see that. My mom told me that's what she liked about going to a spa and getting a massage."

Maura heard Theo's restless shuffle behind her. So, there was a mother and a wife, but not here with them. She was tempted to say something that would lead to an explanation for the mom's absence but sensed that would change the mood, and right now, she liked the easy dynamic between them. "Want to ride one?" she impulsively asked.

"Can I?"

The excitement in his voice made her smile. She looked across at Theo, who now was grinning. "Sure. We'll lead them back to the yard." She gave a low whistle, slapped her thigh and started walking while Jake and Lizzie followed.

"Just like that!" Luke's eyes widened.

Maura and Theo laughed. "Just like that," Maura said.

"Come on, son. I want to see you riding."

She led them toward the yard near the barn, slowing down as she spotted Maddie talking to a woman and a teenage girl—Ashley, she guessed. Maura's mood shifted slightly when she saw the resignation in her sister's face.

There was a time when Theo's arrival at the Stuart farm guaranteed pleasure and excitement for all of them. But yesterday's encounter with Maura at the convenience store had taken him immediately back to his last summer, when the friendship between them changed. Today, he'd seen glimpses of the younger Maura before all the teen melodrama back then and had thought perhaps the next several days would be easier than he'd anticipated—that returning as an adult meant they'd all be able to put the past behind them. But now, catching the frown on Maddie's face, he wasn't so certain.

Surely Maddie—the one Stuart twin with whom he'd had more of a friendship with—would be happy to see him? Maura hadn't been exactly welcoming the day before yesterday, and despite the lurch in his stomach when she'd smiled—even if the smile was at his expense over Jake cornering him—he'd hoped she might have changed enough to be a bit warmer, like Maddie. Yet now it seemed Maddie, too, was aloof. But why?

"Dad? You okay?"

The solicitous tone of his son's voice touched him. He couldn't recall the last time Luke had expressed any concern at all for him, but then, how could he blame the kid? The past year of arguments, tears and recriminations between him and Trish had alienated them all, especially Luke.

"Yes," he replied, "but I just remembered that the company I've hired to pick up stuff from the farmhouse is coming soon and maybe you should take that ride tomorrow." Or maybe never, he silently added. Then he winced at the disappointment in Luke's face.

"Tomorrow could work, too," Maura said, turning his way. "Maddie's busy training someone right now, so we could set a specific time in the morning for Luke."

She'd clearly overheard him. Theo realized there was no way to get out of a second trip to the Stuart farm. "Okay by me. Luke?"

Another maddening shrug, but this time without a scowl. "What time tomorrow?"

Before Maura replied, Theo noticed Maddie walking toward them. Her face lit up as she approached, and for the first time, Theo wondered if the look he'd witnessed earlier had been meant for Maura, not him.

"Maura told me you were coming over, but I had commitments this morning. So nice to see you again, Theo! I'm glad you stuck around. And this must be your son?" Her dazzling smile beamed down at Luke, who responded with one as well.

Theo was relieved to see that Maddie was as warm as she'd always been, though a quick glance at Maura's stony face hinted at some issue between them. *Not your problem,* he reminded himself. *Not anymore.* When he shook hands with her, she held on to his a few seconds longer, her dark brown eyes gleaming. The moment took him back to his confused sixteen-year-old self—a friendship with raven-haired Maddie but a secret crush on Maura, with her flaming red hair. He'd gravitated to Maddie, whose openness drew in everyone. She was easy to talk to. When Theo realized she had a crush on Shawn Harrison, he hadn't really minded. They became buddies, plotting ways to attract Shawn's attention to Maddie.

"Can Luke come back in the morning to ride Jake?" Maura's sharp voice broke the spell.

Theo thought he saw Maddie roll her eyes. "Of course! Does nine work for you?"

She turned her attention back to Theo, who noted the slight twitch at the corner of her mouth. *So it's not me she's angry with, but Maura.* He looked at Luke. "Okay with you?"

"Yes!" The pleasure in Luke's voice cleared the air.

They were all smiling now, and Theo felt his pent-up breath dissipate. As he and Luke headed for the car, he noticed Maura go up to Maddie, touching her arm while speaking to her. They were already deep in conversation by the time Theo was making a U-turn. He glanced into the rearview mirror and watched them move apart. One headed for the house and the other, the barn.

A memory suddenly struck—his uncle, shaking his head one day that last summer and saying, "Those Stuart girls! Something's up with them. Best not get too involved, Theo." At the time, all Theo could think was, *Too late for that, Uncle Stan.*

"Dad?"

Theo shifted his gaze from the windshield to Luke. "Hmm?"

"I asked you if you used to play with Maura and her sister when you came for the summer."

Theo smiled at the word *play*, a reminder that at twelve Luke was still sometimes a kid. "I did, but there were other kids our age here, too. We all played together, and later, when we were about your age, we…uh…kind of just hung out."

"What was there to do *here*?"

Theo smiled again at the disbelief in Luke's voice. "As a city boy, everything in the Glen fascinated me. The woods and the hiking trail, the creek where we swam pretty much every day. My aunt and uncle had a few goats and chickens then, and I helped take care of them. There was always some kind of event happening—a picnic or a barbecue fundraiser at the church, bake sales for various community clubs, potluck suppers. Lots to do."

Luke was silent for a few minutes. "What's a potluck supper?"

"Everyone brings something to eat, and we all sit down and share it."

"Kinda like when we go have dinner with the McNaught family? And Mom always takes a dessert or something?"

Theo felt a twinge of regret for Luke, that those get-togethers would soon only be memories. The fact that Luke had used the present tense, as if the two-family dinners were still happening, made him feel even sadder. "Kind of, but the whole community takes part."

Luke thought a bit longer. "I know what the word *community* means, but I don't really know how it feels."

Distracted by his last image of the Stuart twins, Theo had to ask Luke to repeat what he'd said. He took a few minutes to answer, realizing that his son was articulating the same feeling he himself had his first summer there. "Hopefully someday you will, son. Coming from a big city to a small place like Maple Glen all those summers made me see how different communities could be."

Then he thought, *But could that possibly happen in a week or so? And will it even matter once we've returned home to Augusta and unlikely ever to return to the Glen?*

Chapter Four

Theo watched Luke take his empty cereal bowl to the sink and thought at least the boy's mood had picked up. Once he'd reassured him that, yes, they were going to the Stuart farm so he could ride a donkey, the scowl etched on the boy's face since yesterday disappeared. He knew Luke had been disappointed that the ride hadn't happened, and the afterglow from meeting Jake and Lizzie had completely vanished when Theo had asked for help bringing boxes up from the farmhouse basement that afternoon. "It's gross down there," Luke had protested. "All those spiderwebs, and I think I saw a rat, too."

Theo had wanted to laugh but restrained himself. "No one's been down there for years, hence the spiderwebs. And maybe you saw a mouse, not a rat." He mentally crossed his fingers.

By the time the truck from the disposal company in Bennington had driven away with most of the basement's contents, Luke was barely speaking to him. Even the pizza Theo had picked up from the diner in Wallingford had been wolfed down in silence.

"When are we going?" Luke asked, turning away from the sink.

Theo looked up from skimming over the trucking company's invoice. "Um, anytime, I guess."

"How about right now?"

"Sure—let me finish my coffee first. Why don't you make your bed while I tidy up here?"

"I already made it."

Theo hid his surprise. "Great. Okay, give me a sec." He downed the rest of his coffee and stood up. "I need to confirm my meeting with the real-estate person for tomorrow."

"I'll wait outside," Luke said and left the room.

Theo checked the time. Nine o'clock and Luke had been up for an hour, dressed and had been eating cereal by the time Theo had showered and brewed the coffee. It was an auspicious start to a day that was going to be a long one with yet more clearing out before the meeting with the real-estate agent.

He left a message for the agent, and by the time he closed the screen door behind him, Luke was pacing by the car. "We can walk," Theo said. "You can see the barn roof from here." He pointed right.

Luke shrugged and headed toward the cedars marking the boundary between the farms.

"No, not that way! We'll take the road and avoid all those weeds. I have to organize someone to come and mow this." Another shrug, but Luke turned down the driveway to the road. Yep, Theo thought as he followed him. Definitely excited about riding a donkey.

"Did they have donkeys when you used to come here?" Luke asked as Theo caught up to him.

"Nope. They had chickens and I think maybe a couple of goats. Mostly the farm was used for growing crops. Like this place."

"Why do you think they decided to get donkeys and have that...you know...that riding thing?"

"I don't know how they came to have donkeys, but I remember that Maura was always keen on animals of all kinds." He'd known a lot about the young Maura Stuart yet knew nothing at all about the adult version. Part of him suddenly wanted to fix that, but the thought wasn't rational. He wouldn't be in the Glen long enough.

They paused at the foot of the driveway to read the large sign posted there—Jake & Friends Riding Stables.

"I like that," Luke commented. "'Cause Jake has two friends already but maybe he'll get more. Like another male donkey for company, since Matilda and Lizzie are obviously female."

"Yeah, that would be good, and he wouldn't feel outnumbered." He was suddenly aware of Luke's thoughtful gaze. "What?"

"I was just wondering if you minded hanging out most of the time with...you know...two *girls*."

There was an incredulity in his voice that made Theo want to get the right answer. "When we were young, like nine or so, I never really thought of them as just *girls*. We always liked doing the same things and didn't really need to be around the other kids in the village so much. Know what I mean?"

Luke nodded slowly. "Kinda, though I've never had a best friend who was a girl. What about when you were older? You said you came here until you were about sixteen. Was it the same even then?"

"By then we hung out with the other kids who lived here." He pushed aside a memory that popped up, a sudden flash of jealousy for one of the boys clearly interested in Maura. He elbowed Luke. "Okay, let's go donkey riding! Remember that song? We used to sing it with you when you were really small and fussing. I'd bounce you on my knee and—"

"I'll take your word for it," Luke mumbled and picked up his pace, reaching the end of the drive well before Theo.

Will it always be this way, he wondered, *as both of us grow older? I'll be the one remembering, and he'll be eager to forget?* The weight of parenting felt suddenly intolerable, and for a dark moment Theo wished he could travel back to those years when a simple nursery song brought so much joy. Then he saw Maura, sitting in a wicker chair on the veranda, and everything on his mind disappeared.

Luke, walking ahead, turned around to ask, "Are you coming?"

He'd have been irked by the impatience in Luke's voice but was too distracted by watching Maura slowly get to her feet and head down the steps toward them. He felt the air whoosh out of him. She was wearing white shorts and a pale yellow filmy top that swirled around her as she walked and highlighted the reddish-gold tones of her hair. Today she wore sandals rather than sneakers, and Theo's eyes drifted down to the scarlet nail polish on her toes, a match for the color of her lips. The transformation from yesterday's Maura in torn jeans and mud-splattered boots was breathtaking. He missed what she was saying, hearing only the pounding at his temples, and stared foolishly as she repeated herself.

"Maddie's waiting with Matilda in the north pasture behind the barn. We thought she'd be a better ride for you, Luke. Are you coming with us, Theo?"

"Of course!" he blurted.

"I meant, are you riding, too?" Her hazel eyes teased.

"Um… I think I'll be too big for a donkey."

"They're built to carry very heavy loads."

"Yes, but—"

"C'mon, Dad." Luke was grinning.

Theo knew his face was flushed. "I guess I'd better try, anyway."

Maura's smile widened. "Luke, you go ahead to Maddie and your father can come with me while I saddle up Jake."

Luke dashed ahead.

"That's the fastest I've seen him move since we set out on our road trip," Theo remarked.

"Well, I don't know much about teenagers, other than from my own experience as one, but I'm sure enthusiasm for something is always paired with interest."

"Doesn't that also apply to adults?"

"Of course, but there are more factors involved." She began walking to the barn.

"Like what?" he asked, though he knew what they might be—time, cost, responsibilities—and was curious to hear her reply.

"Way too early in the day for a serious discussion!"

She'd sidestepped that one, he thought, as he followed her into the barn. But she was right. The day was meant for some levity, which he seriously needed after the challenges of the last year. Even if that fun was aimed at him, perched on a donkey.

He watched her remove her sandals and change into a pair of tattered sneakers sitting on the barn floor just inside the entrance and thought the shoe exchange made no difference to the glamour version moments ago. A memory of the teenage Maura and her eccentric fashion sense compared to the other Glen girls back then surfaced. Had her outfit today been meant for him? The idea pleased him, though he couldn't say why.

As she deftly saddled Jake, Theo wondered how and why she came to this stage in her life and career. When they were young, he remembered her saying she wanted to be a veterinarian. Of course, he'd wanted to be an astronaut, so...

"Let's get going," she said as she led Jake toward him. "Maddie will be wondering if we're coming or not. She wasn't sure if you'd be up for a ride, too, but I told her you wouldn't want to be a spoilsport in front of your son."

Ouch. Theo went for a smile. "I hope I can live up to such high expectations," he joked.

"I'm sure you can," she said, her eyes lingering on his face long enough to make him wonder if the remark was a dare. "So do you want to ride him out to the field or wait till we get there?"

"Which will be least humiliating?"

The teasing glint in her eyes disappeared. "You'll be fine, Theo. But maybe get on here, where I can help you without—"

"The mocking face of my son?"

"I was going to say without everyone staring. Don't make too many assumptions about your son. He may live up to *your* expectations yet."

That was an opener he wanted to pursue but not right then. Still, she had a point. Today was supposed to be about Luke, not him. "Sure. Tell me what to do."

She held Jake by the bit in his mouth. "Just like getting on a horse."

"Been a long time for that."

"Okay, mount on this side and put your left foot there in that stirrup. Left hand there, on the horn—" she pointed to a protuberance at the front of the saddle "—and swing up in one smooth movement."

"This saddle, is it big enough for me? It looks small."

"It's a mule or donkey saddle, and it *is* smaller. Donkeys and mules have V-shaped shoulders, so you'll be sitting in a different position than you would on a horse."

He knew overthinking it could lead to trouble, so he took a deep breath and followed through. Jake shifted as Theo settled on his back. "He's moving a bit. Sure I'm not too heavy?"

"You're okay," Maura said. "He's adjusting to your weight. Don't worry—he can handle it. Donkeys have been carrying heavier burdens than you for thousands of years."

"I feel a bit lopsided," he said. She leaned across him to tug on the straps beneath Jake's belly, and his senses were saturated with the flowery warmth of her body, the loose strands from her ponytail brushing against his cheek and her own cheek. He took a deep breath, realizing his teenage self would never have noticed these things.

"That better?" she asked, rising up and away from him in one swoop. He nodded.

"Ready?" She smiled encouragement.

He was a good sport, she had to admit. Donkeys were fun to ride, but their short, stocky frames paled next to the physique of a horse, and a large man perched atop a donkey wasn't exactly an iconic image. But Theo had gone along with it all, letting her lead Jake and him around the pasture while Maddie gave Luke a lesson farther away.

After a couple of short circuits, she began to hear muffled groaning sounds. Not from Jake but from Theo. He was shifting a bit, and she figured he'd had enough. "Want to take a break, get some iced tea up on the porch?"

"Please!"

She bit back a chuckle. "Here, give me your left hand and use your right to hold on to the saddle horn as you swing off."

He did, stumbling a bit as his right foot hit the ground and lurching into her. She grasped his arms to steady him. "You okay?"

His face was near enough to hers that the pocket of warm air coming off it, along with a minty scent of toothpaste, enveloped her, and his breathless reply—"I am now!"—sent shivers down her spine. Did he mean okay to be off the donkey, or that he liked their closeness? There was a fraction of a second when she considered touching his cheek, feeling what the adult Theo's face was like compared to his sixteen-year-old one. That time in the Danbys' barn when she'd almost kissed him.

Thankfully, he broke the spell. "I hate to say it, but my—"

"Butt? A tad tender?"

He matched her grin with a wider one, his eyes locking on hers long enough that Maura, realizing she was holding her breath, exhaled loudly and said, "Help me get this saddle off and we can leave Jake in the pasture."

He easily hefted the saddle off and carried it, along with the bridle, as they headed toward the farmhouse. Maddie noticed them leaving and waved. Luke gave a thumbs-up, and by his beaming face, Maura knew he wouldn't be cutting short his own ride. Theo followed her into the barn, where he set the saddle onto its rail and, while Maura put things in order for the client coming in an hour's time, wandered over to Lizzie, still in her stall.

Maura saw him stroking the donkey's face, along its snout, and hoped Lizzie was in a good mood. She'd been a donation from a hobby farm north of Rutland, her penchant for occasionally nipping at irksome pests—like humans—proving too troublesome for the family who owned her at the time. "Um, careful. She's an unpredictable biter."

Theo's hand jerked away, as if he'd set it on a hot stove. "Is she safe to use for people, then? Your riding program?"

"We usually match her with experienced riders, but she does have a favorite—a young girl with cerebral palsy—

and Lizzie is very calm around her. They've made a connection that's quite amazing, really."

"I've read that some animals sense emotions in humans," he commented as he walked over to where she was setting up the tack for their next rider.

"It's true. We're only beginning to understand how communication works between us and other mammals, as well as with some bird species."

"I remember you were always reading about animals when we were kids and even as teenagers."

The comment pleased her. When they were teens, he'd never seemed to notice anything at all about her. Or so she'd believed at the time. Maura took a deep breath. She had to stop reverting to the past. This Theo Danby wasn't the one she'd thought about far too many years after he'd left the Glen.

"Didn't you once say you wanted to be a veterinarian?"

"Iced tea?" she asked suddenly, moving away from him.

His quick frown appeared and vanished. "You bet!"

He'd realized she hadn't answered his question but didn't press her. Maura was grateful. If she told Theo Danby anything at all about the years since she'd last seen him in Maple Glen, she wanted to decide what and how much of her life she was willing to reveal. Yet for some reason, once they were sitting in the wicker chairs on the veranda and sipping the iced tea she'd made earlier in the morning, Maura felt she *did* want to talk about herself.

"My freshman year at college got off to a rocky start," she began when he asked her what she'd done after high school graduation. "Maddie and I had all these plans. We'd both go to the University of Vermont, where I hoped to get into veterinarian medicine after my science degree and she was interested in occupational therapy. We even talked about setting up some kind of clinic together—much later, of course. But…" She paused, sighing. "…things didn't work out as planned."

"What happened?" Theo leaned forward to set his empty glass on the small table between them.

"She fell in love."

"And…?"

"She wanted to go where *he* was going—Northern Vermont University—while I kept my admission acceptance at the University of Vermont. I could have transferred, too, but didn't want to be a third wheel, as the saying goes." She felt his eyes on her while she swallowed the last of her drink.

"I'm guessing you were disappointed at this change in plans."

Disappointed? *Heartbroken. Betrayed.* Those were better words for how she felt at eighteen, but now, almost seventeen years later, Maura knew her expectations back then hadn't really matched her sister's. Their dreams about college and independence had focused on them being together, not apart. They'd always done everything together, since birth. Until Maddie had found someone to love, whereas Maura had not.

"You could say that," she finally replied.

"Then what happened? With Maddie, I mean," he explained when she shot him a questioning look.

"They broke up partway through first year. The typical cliché of the high school romance and first year of college."

"Oh? Who was he? Someone from around here?"

"Shawn Harrison."

She watched the surprise sweep across his face. A name from the past and Theo's long-ago competition for her sister's attention? A familiar stir of jealousy crept in. *Seriously? Even now, after all these years? Get a grip, Stuart.*

"I often wondered what became of her crush on him." After a minute, he added, "And your veterinary dream?"

"I bombed out my first year—for lots of reasons, none of which had to do with Maddie." *Of course not, because by then we seldom saw each other. By then we'd already unconsciously decided to get on with our own independent lives.* "I transferred over to Vermont State, where I ended up taking their veterinarian technician course. After graduation, I worked in a number of veterinarian clinics, went back to university for some business courses and ended up doing research for a feed-supply company. Then I eased my way into the management side of things, which I found I really enjoyed."

"I get that. You were always the organized Stuart twin."

Maura laughed. "Recently I've been wondering if Maddie and I have changed selves."

"Why's that?"

She hesitated. Perhaps their current state of affairs wasn't a wise conversation topic. "I'm joking, really. But it's true, don't you think, that people change as they get older? Become more like their parents or whatever? Sometimes she seems to be the practical one and I'm verging on the impulsive."

"You? Impulsive?"

She saw that he was teasing and laughed with him. If he only knew!

"I'm curious," he went on, "how all that led to the donkeys and riding therapy."

"Unexpectedly, for sure. I volunteered in a horse-riding therapy program when I was in college and loved it. Very satisfying work. After Dad died, we were left the farm along with Jake and Matilda. I guess you could say I fell in love then, too…only with a couple of donkeys." They both laughed, and for the first time since Theo's arrival, she felt herself relaxing into those past summer days, when everything was still easy and uncomplicated between the three of them.

"How about you? What's your situation? Luke mentioned his mother, but—"

"We're divorced," he said quickly. "Have been for several months now, and when I took leave from the hospital, I decided this trip would be a chance to make up to Luke all he went through during that time. A chance for us to reconnect, in a way, because I don't know what the future will look like for him—or for me."

There was a sadness in his voice that touched Maura, and she wanted to pat his arm, show her sympathy, when a voice stopped her.

"Dad?"

They shifted their attention to the bottom of the veranda stairs, where Luke was standing. Relief washed over her. She'd already said more than she'd intended, but not as much as she might have if Luke hadn't appeared. There was something about Theo Danby's face when he'd talked about his divorce and his desire to spend time with his son that Maura suspected might have led to more revelations from her than the few she'd imparted that day. Like the feelings she'd had for him when she was a teenager— feelings that hadn't changed even after he'd left the Glen. What was the point in revealing so much of herself when his time here was limited?

Chapter Five

Theo walked the agent to the door.

"I'll arrange a survey first," she said, "before listing it. I should warn you, though, that sales in this area have been in a decline over the past couple of years. You mentioned that your aunt and uncle rented out some of their fields to local farmers?"

"Yes, and they also sold some acreage as they grew older. I haven't found any papers yet about the existing property, but I'm gradually sorting through stuff, so I'll give you a call when I find them. I also have an appointment with their lawyer and bank manager on Monday."

"The county registry office should have up-to-date paperwork. Your best bet may be development interest, rather than farming. Satellite communities are cropping up everywhere. You probably noticed that driving here from Maine."

He had, and the sight had made him fearful of what he'd see in Maple Glen, but the housing spread seemed to have ended a bit north of Bennington. An unpleasant image of a large subdivision on the outskirts of the Glen popped into his mind, and for an awful second, he pictured the impact of that on the idyllic place of his childhood.

But he had to do something with the farm. Renting it out and managing it from Augusta wasn't feasible. "I did, and honestly, the thought isn't appealing. This place has managed to escape all that so far but—"

"Maybe not for long," she said, smiling. "There are few options for sellers these days. I'll let you know when the survey will happen." She headed down the porch steps to her car.

Theo closed the screen door and, standing at the bottom of the staircase, shouted, "Are you ready to go shopping, Luke?"

After a moment, he appeared on the top landing. "Maddie said I could go over and help clean out the stables."

Theo fought to keep his jaw from gaping. This from a kid who'd struggled to keep a bedroom tidy only weeks ago. But the invite pleased him. It would be good for his son to participate in some physical labor. Heck, after seeing Maura yesterday, he'd willingly muck out a stable, too. "Um, okay. When will that happen?"

Luke shrugged. "She said anytime before noon."

He hadn't left Luke alone yet, but knew the kid was sensible. "So why don't I drop you off there on my way to get groceries? I'll give you a key, and if I'm not back before you're finished, you can come in and make yourself some lunch. There's salami and cheese in the fridge and bread on the counter."

Luke's eyes lit up, and Theo guessed he'd scored a point. "Sure!"

He didn't need to hurry Luke along and recalled Maura's words yesterday about interest and enthusiasm. Had she been that wise as a teenager? He knew he definitely had not.

When they were buckling up in the car, Luke suddenly

remarked, "Did you know that donkeys are known for their intelligence and good nature?"

Theo pressed the ignition button. "I assumed that, seeing how Maddie and Maura decided to use them for a therapy program."

"A female is called a 'jenny' and a male is called a 'jack,' so Jake's name is kind of appropriate. Maddie said to watch out for Lizzie, though, 'cause she can be—"

"Unpredictable?"

"Yeah. I liked riding Matilda, but my goal is to ride Jake, 'cause he's bigger. And I'm tall for my age, aren't I? That's what people tell me."

It was the longest bit of conversation Luke had spouted on their trip, and given the part about his height, personal. Theo wondered for a minute who the "people" were but thought maybe Trish or her parents. What really stood out was the mention of a "goal." It would be good for Luke to have something to focus his attention on while they were in the Glen. That would give Theo more time to sort things out.

He also thought he'd like to spend some time with Maddie. They'd been such good friends those last couple of summers he was in the Glen. Besides, it would be interesting to get her take on the falling-out between them when Maddie opted to go with Shawn Harrison, rather than with Maura.

"Dad? Are we going or what?"

Theo blinked. The engine was running but they were still sitting in the driveway. "Oh, sorry. I was thinking about what we needed in the way of food."

"Didn't you make a list? Mom always does."

"Yeah, but she usually forgets to take it with her."

Luke snorted. "True! Anyway, can you get some soda

for me? The sugar-free kind is what Mom likes me to have. And maybe some chips?"

Luke's relaxed tone warmed Theo. They were actually referring to Luke's mother without any tension. He shifted into Drive and tapped the accelerator. "Maybe I'll drop into that ice cream store and pick up a tub of— What kind do you like?"

"Cookies 'n' Cream."

"Done." Theo's sense that the day was going to be a good one picked up as he parked and saw Maura standing in the open barn door. The torn jeans, T-shirt and rubber boots were back again, but today her hair was in a single braid that fell between her shoulders. Except for one summer when they'd had short hair, the twins usually had ponytails, pigtails or braids—

Luke flung open the car door and leaped out as Maura walked their way.

"Ready to do some hard work?" she asked him.

Luke must have spotted the twinkle in her eye. He grinned and gave a mock salute. "Aye, aye, Captain."

Theo shrugged as Maura's smile met his.

"Maddie's gone into Wallingford, so you and I will be mucking out today. The donkeys are already out to pasture." Then she raised her eyes to Theo. "We should finish up about noonish. Will you pick him up or…?"

"Oops. Here, Luke." Theo dug into his jeans pocket and handed over the spare key he'd found before they'd left the farm. "Tuck this into your pocket." He waited while Luke stowed it away. "Okay, then. Considering your work this morning, I'm not sure if I should say 'have fun' or 'good luck,' but be sure to follow Maura's instructions, Luke." As soon as those words popped out, Theo knew from the slight shift in Luke's face that he'd goofed up.

"I *am* a tough taskmaster," Maura quickly put in, "but

I have complete confidence in him." She placed a hand on Luke's shoulder, steering him away to the barn.

Neither looked back as Theo left, and he spent the short drive into Wallingford mentally kicking himself for his last comment. By the time he reached the small town, he'd rationalized that he was simply being a typical parent. No harm in that, surely. Except that since he and Trish had split, Theo had consciously worked to be much more—a super parent, in fact. Maybe he should let go of some of the guilt he felt over not spending enough quality time with his son and just try to be himself.

He was exiting Wallingford's only supermarket when he met Maddie on her way in.

"Theo!"

"Hey," he said. "Maura said you were in town."

"Yup. I had a couple of things to organize for the upcoming Fourth of July festival, and now I'm picking up some milk and bread. I guess Luke is helping in the stalls?"

"With almost as much enthusiasm as he had riding Matilda. And thanks so much for that. He was talking about it all night."

"He was great. Listened carefully and followed my instructions. A nice kid, by the way. You and your wife have done a great job."

It was the perfect lead-in, but he chose not to get into the whole sad cliché of a marital breakup while standing on the sidewalk in front of the supermarket. "If you're not in a rush, would you like to go for a coffee when you finish up here?"

"Definitely! There's a coffee place down that way—" she pointed to her left "—called Real Beans and I'll meet you in about ten minutes."

"Great. What can I order for you?"

She grinned. "Large latte, please."

Theo had just placed the order and found a corner table for two when she arrived.

"I wasn't sure if you wanted a pastry or not, so I asked for two Danishes."

"My childhood sweet tooth is still with me. Thanks!"

Her comment suddenly brought back a time when the three of them had baked cookies and eaten them all one rainy afternoon, and he was about to mention it when the barista called out his name.

"It was a surprise to see you turn up in the Glen again after all these years, Theo," she said as he set their order on the table. "But a nice one. Maura said you're intending to sell the farm."

"Pretty difficult to run a farm from miles away. I understand that land sales especially are in a slump now, though, so it may take me longer than I thought."

"We heard you were practicing medicine in Augusta."

"Yes, but in a hospital, not private practice. I guess my aunt and uncle told you at some point that I was a doctor?"

"Probably, but also…you know…the Glen grapevine." She grinned.

He shook his head. "Right. Now you know something about me, what about you? How did *you* end up back in Maple Glen?"

Her grin disappeared. "A long story best told over a glass of wine."

"Coffee works, too."

"I suppose." She shrugged, smiling again. "Where to begin, then?"

He remembered how much easier Maddie was to talk with than Maura. How she never seemed to have secrets like her sister. He broke off pieces of Danish while she spoke, following every word that more or less matched Maura's story. High school graduation, senior prom, where she and Shawn officially became a couple, and, finally, her decision to head to the university he was going to rather than where she and Maura had applied.

"I knew Maura was upset because we'd found a housing unit to share on campus, and she was stuck having to reorganize all that and find somewhere else to live. I also caused an uproar at home, with my parents. They wanted me to stick with the original plan for a year anyway, but... what can I say? I was in love." Her face clouded. "I *thought* I was in love, anyway."

"I remember how you were always trying to get Shawn's attention back when all the gang hung out together."

"You offered a great shoulder to cry on." She frowned. "I sometimes think Maura mistook your intentions, but who knows? She was always so testy as a teenager and kept her feelings to herself."

Theo grinned, thinking of Luke's recent moodiness. That he could relate to! "So you broke up with Shawn?" he asked after a moment.

She nodded and, after a few seconds, said, "But I ended up staying at that university because I got into an occupational therapy program I wanted, and Maura was accepted into a veterinarian tech program at—"

"Vermont State University."

"You already know all this?" Her eyes narrowed.

The past came back in a rush—how the openness of childhood conversations had disappeared with adolescence, and how he'd had to be careful about what he said to which twin. "Maura simply filled me in on what she'd been doing since her graduation."

"Well, except for the standard big holidays at the farm, we didn't see much of each other once we started working on our separate careers. Then Mom got cancer and we spent more time at the farm, but we obviously didn't want to use those days rehashing our falling-out years ago. After Mom passed away, Maura stayed awhile with Dad. She ended up quitting her job and moving back here permanently when he had a stroke, a few months before he died. That brought us together again." She suddenly teared up.

"I always liked your folks," Theo said after a moment. "They were a bit more flexible than my aunt and uncle. Hanging out at your place meant a lot to me."

"Thanks for that." Taking a breath, she asked, "Why did you stop coming back?"

Trust Maddie to ask, rather than Maura. "My folks had divorced around the time I first came to the Glen, and my father moved out of state when I was about to turn sixteen. I wanted to go with him." Not the whole truth, though. He still could have spent his summers in Maple Glen— except by then his teenage self had accepted the hard fact that Maura Stuart wasn't the least bit interested in him. "Everyone kind of drifted apart that summer, didn't they? Getting jobs and so on."

"True."

"What brought you back, then? Seems to me all the gang was eager to leave."

"We were." She gave a light snort. "Though I always suspected Maura had a plan to come back. She never seemed as excited as the rest of us when we were sharing our fantasies about a life beyond the Glen. After Dad died, I wasn't really surprised when she told me she wanted to keep the farm rather than sell. By then most of our acreage had been sold to a farmer in Wallingford who grows commercial crops, leaving the ten we still have." She finished the rest of her latte. "That was yummy. Thanks, Theo."

He was eager to hear more, especially about why Maura wanted to stay. "This was when you set up Jake & Friends?"

"That was her idea, not mine. She had it all planned before she even told me about it." Her tone told him she was still irked at that.

"Luke told me Jake came to the farm first, then Matilda a few months before your father passed away."

"Jake was a rescue donkey that an old friend of Dad's persuaded him to adopt. Then someone dropped off Matilda. Dad never knew who. He just found her tethered in front of the barn one day when he'd been out. Dad loved those donkeys, which was why Maura wanted to keep them. Otherwise..."

She didn't need to fill in the blanks. "I guess Maura's vet tech training led her to the business venture—the riding program?" he probed.

"It did, plus I think she'd had some kind of disappointment...you know...with a love interest and was at loose ends. She'd read about horse therapy and thought—"

"Why not with a donkey?" he interjected, grinning.

Maddie's laugh brought back more memories. He'd always liked her and felt comfortable around her, but there'd never been the spark between them that he'd felt with her twin—the intense yearning for something more than friendship as he coped with adolescent hormones.

"Honestly, the decision to set up a riding therapy stable would have been more characteristic of me than my sister. She told me the other day she thinks we've switched personalities."

Theo still saw a lot of the old Maura—her tendency to keep feelings to herself and the unpredictable shifts in mood. "You haven't said yet what brought *you* back."

She pulled a face, and for a moment, Theo thought she'd dismiss the nudge. But the old Maddie was still there, too.

"What can I say, except that my story is another cliché. I was engaged and...well...it didn't work out. I was at loose ends like my sister, and when she asked me to stay on while she got the business up and running, I promised her a year."

"Then you're here temporarily?" Maura hadn't mentioned that, and Theo wondered how she'd manage running the place on her own.

"That's the idea." She peered down at her plate littered with pastry crumbs. When she raised her head to Theo, she exhaled a sigh. "Frankly, I don't have any long-term plans of my own. But I do know I don't want to be stuck on a farm with donkeys and my sister." She gave a light laugh and added, "I want something more."

Uh-oh. Does Maura know that?

He was about to pursue her comment when she said, "I should get going. It's getting close to lunch, and we've got a client coming at one o'clock." She stood up, reaching for her plastic bag of groceries on the floor.

"Right. Luke must be finished by now, too." He retrieved his own groceries, and they walked out to the sidewalk. "I enjoyed catching up with you, Maddie. A bit like old times."

She smiled. "It was. I probably told you way more than necessary about our lives. I hope I didn't bore you."

"As I said, nice to go back to the past."

Her shrug suggested otherwise. "Maybe. But we have to move on, right? Those days are gone."

Now she *was* sounding like her sister, he thought. "Thanks again for accommodating Luke. He'll have lots of tales for his friends back home."

"He's a nice kid, Theo. Say, we didn't get around to you and what you've been doing all these years! Don't leave the Glen without coming to see us."

Not a chance, he was thinking. He definitely wouldn't leave without seeing Maura at least one more time.

Chapter Six

Maura stepped out the kitchen door and, coffee mug in hand, strolled over to the riding ring, where Maddie was leading Lizzie through the gate. It wasn't quite nine o'clock, but they were expecting their first client of the day—Katie Robinson—in a few minutes. She leaned against the fence and thought how she and her sister had finally mastered a good routine, working together without too much disagreement most of the time. She prayed the arrangement would be permanent.

"Heard from Cathy yet?" she asked. One of their regular volunteers had reported a bad cold last week.

Maddie looked her way and shook her head. "If she can't come, she ought to let us know well in advance. It's only fair."

Maura agreed, but Cathy was a volunteer, not an employee. She and Nancy were invaluable when kids like Katie, who had special requirements, rode. The sound of a car engine got her attention and, shielding her eyes from the bright morning sun, she saw the dust wake of a vehicle coming up the drive. "That might be one of them now. Or maybe Katie and her mother."

She hoped it was one of the volunteers. When Katie was

riding, they needed two helpers, but she could fill in if one of them didn't show. Usually, she or Maddie would lead Lizzie around the ring while the two volunteers walked on either side of the donkey, making sure Katie didn't slide off. Katie's cerebral palsy was pretty much in check, but anything could happen. Fortunately, Lizzie seemed to sense the twelve-year-old's situation, because she was always patient, walking slowly and never balking when Katie rode. And never ever nipping.

The car's engine stopped, and a few seconds later, Theo appeared from around the corner of the barn. Maura frowned. Had they arranged yesterday to get together again? She looked over at Maddie, who shrugged.

"Sorry for the interruption," Theo began as soon as he was close enough. "Luke and I are going into Rutland, but I wanted to let you know that someone's coming in an hour to cut the front section of my land, and I was worried about how the donkeys might react. He'll be using one of those big mowing machines." When she didn't answer right away, he added, "Well, Luke's waiting in the car."

Maddie came up to the fence before Maura had a chance to respond.

"If Luke's not keen on going with you, he can hang around here. We're waiting for our first client of the day, and since our regular volunteers haven't shown up yet, Luke might be a welcome distraction for our rider."

The unexpected invite startled Maura. The other day Maddie had objected to having visitors when clients were riding, and there was no guarantee Luke would be helpful when Katie was on Lizzie. She was about to squelch the idea when Theo said, "He'd love that. Thanks! I'll go get him."

As he headed for the car, Maura turned to her sister. "What're you thinking? We don't know if Luke will be a help."

"You told me yourself he was great working with you in the barn yesterday."

"That's not the same thing at all."

"Katie's mother told me she's been having some problems with a couple of the girls in her class. I'm sure I don't have to spell it out for you. Usually when we take her out, one of us chats with her while she's riding to ease her nervousness. If either Cathy or Nancy fails to turn up, you or I will have to walk alongside, and we won't be able to chitchat with her. That's too much distraction for us. We need to keep aware of how Katie's sitting on the saddle. I just had a thought that Luke might be willing to walk with us and tell Katie something about life in Maine."

It wasn't a bad idea, Maura silently decided, and worth a try. "Okay. I'm going to finish the breakfast dishes while you explain what we want him to do."

As she headed for the kitchen door, she heard Theo driving away. He was becoming almost a fixture at the farm. She had serious qualms about that. Not only because his presence brought back too many memories—good and not-so-good—but because it was better for all of them if he kept out of their lives. Yet every time she saw him, her feelings overruled her common sense.

Nancy had arrived by the time Maura returned and was conferring with Maddie and Luke in the riding ring. "All set?" she asked.

Before anyone could reply, the sound of a car alerted them that Katie and her mother had arrived. Maura reached the driveway as Katie's mother was unloading a wheelchair from the trunk. Katie could walk with the assistance of canes, but her movements were unpredictable, and the uneven ground necessitated a wheelchair.

"Hi, kiddo!" Maura ducked down to greet the twelve-year-old strapped into her special car seat.

"Hi, Maura. Is Lizzie waiting for me?"

"She is, and today we have a new helper. His name is Luke, and he's twelve, too. He's visiting the farm next to us and already loves our donkeys."

Katie laughed, drawing big smiles from her mother and Maura. Together they got the girl into her chair and wheeled her past the barn to the ring behind the farmhouse. Nancy and Maddie led Lizzie to the gate to greet them. Luke hung back, watching as they helped Katie onto Lizzie's back and adjusted her position. She was afraid he might be shy, but seconds later he was heading their way.

"Hi, Katie! I'm Luke."

The big smiles the two kids exchanged told Maura all would be well. He was already chatting as everyone took up their positions. Maddie took Lizzie by the reins while Maura and Nancy walked on either side of the donkey, close enough to intervene should Katie lose her balance.

Luke took up a position just ahead of Maura, even with Lizzie's head, and started talking almost at once. "I haven't ridden Lizzie yet, only Matilda. But my goal is to ride Jake, and if you tell Lizzie not to bite, I might try her sometime, too."

Katie's laugh told Maura the ride today was going to be a success. Luke kept up a steady patter as he walked next to Katie and Lizzie. Maura noticed that the donkey didn't seem to mind his proximity, either. At first, she'd turned her large head toward Luke, curious about him, and Maura worried she might try to nudge him away, but she hadn't.

After a few minutes, Maura moved farther back, closer to Lizzie's haunches. Katie was sitting straight, and her balance was good now, compared to the first sessions months ago. Her success was gratifying and reaffirmed Maura's desire to keep the program running as long as possible. The money situation would be resolved as they got more clients. That had been her reasoning when she'd offered the farm as the site of this year's festival.

She was thinking about the organization of the event when she heard Katie ask, "Will you be here next week when I come?"

For the first time since they'd begun leading Lizzie around, Luke was silent. It was only when Katie prompted him that he finally replied, "Um, maybe. If I am here, I'll definitely come and see you."

"Yay," said Katie.

As they turned for their last lap of the ring, Maura caught sight of a large red machine chugging onto the front expanse of the Danby property. The tractor mower Theo had mentioned. Although it was only partially visible from where they were, she knew once the machine revved up the noise could bother the donkeys. Especially Jake and Matilda, who were grazing in the pasture closest to it.

Sure enough, minutes later a loud roaring sound traveled across the fields. Maddie caught Maura's eye and held up two crossed fingers. But then Maura saw Jake and Matilda raise their heads, their ears twitching, and almost immediately, they began to bray.

There was no cacophony quite like a donkey's bray, as Maura had learned over the past year. By now Lizzie was alerted to the potential danger of a mowing machine and stopped in her tracks, joining her friends. Luke covered his ears, and when he turned to look at Maura, she saw the almost comical but pained expression on his face. When Katie covered her ears, too, letting go of the pommel, Maura knew the ride today should finish. She reached up to hold on to Katie's right leg while Nancy grasped the other one. Maddie stopped and slowly turned Lizzie around, heading for the gate.

Theo must have returned while they were riding and was standing next to Katie's mother at the fence. Maura noticed them both grimacing at the noise. The riding group stopped where Katie's wheelchair was parked, and Maura and Nancy helped Katie down into her chair. By now, everyone was laughing and holding their ears at the same time.

"We'll take Lizzie's saddle off later," Maddie shouted over the din, and as Katie was being wheeled out of the ring, Maddie gave Lizzie a push that sent her trotting toward her friends, still braying.

"Wow, does that happen often?" Theo asked as they moved away from the noise.

"Whenever there's a dangerous predator around," Maura said. "In this case, a big lawn mower."

"Or sometimes they're just annoyed at something. We often don't know," added Maddie.

"But one starts and sets off the others," put in Nancy. "At least we were finishing up, anyway."

"I wouldn't want to be in the barn with them, when that happens," Luke said.

"Yeah," Katie agreed. "Once that did happen, and we all left very quickly." That prompted more laughter and then she looked up at Luke to ask, "Want to walk with me to our car?"

"Sure. I forgot in all that racket to tell you about my favorite video game, and you were going to show me your new cell phone. I want to get one, but my parents say I should wait."

"I know. I had to beg for ages," Katie said.

The adults all smiled, and Katie's mother mouthed a "thank you" that included everyone as she wheeled Katie toward the front yard and the driveway.

"I'm guessing Luke was helpful," Theo said as they disappeared out of sight.

"He was great."

"He's welcome to help out anytime!" Maddie called out to Theo as she and Nancy headed into the barn.

"I was worried he might be shy or something. You know, moody."

"Not at all. In fact, he didn't stop talking the whole time. Katie hardly got a word in." His smile was so pleased she wanted to hug him, to reassure him that his son was a kid to be proud of. "Katie even asked if Luke could come back for her session next week."

"Oh? What did he say?"

"If he was still here, he would." She waited a beat, then asked, "Will you? Be here, I mean?"

"Not sure yet. My plans have altered a bit. The real-estate agent told me a sale might take longer than I thought. I have six weeks off, of course, so there's no hurry, but I'd like to have everything in place before leaving. Plus, there's still a lot more stuff to clear out of the house." At the sound of Katie and her mother driving away, he added, "Guess we should get going, too."

Maura closed the gate and walked with him toward the front yard. She wanted to hear more about his plans, not only because of their potential impact on her own, but also because she liked being with him. If she pushed aside her anxiety about Jake & Friends, she knew she could relax around him and forget about the decision she'd soon have to make—telling him something she'd kept to herself for two months. Something that was bound to affect the sale of his farm, not to mention their rekindled friendship.

Luke was waiting by the car. "She has the latest iPhone, Dad. It's so cool!"

Maura caught Theo's eye and grinned. "Your days are numbered there," she predicted, and his rueful smile made her laugh. The chance to know more about him hinged on how much longer he'd be in Maple Glen, and that realization unexpectedly saddened her.

"Hey, would you and Luke like to come for dinner tonight?" she blurted.

"Yes!" Luke put in before Theo could speak.

Maura and Theo laughed. "There's your answer," Theo murmured, his face close enough to hers that the warmth of his breath made her shiver. "Can I bring anything? Besides a bottle of wine?"

"Um…dessert?" she managed to say.

Maddie was in the kitchen when Maura told her about the impulsive invitation. She turned from the sandwich she was making and asked, "So who's cooking?"

"Uh, well, I haven't nailed down the details yet." Then she saw the grin. "Okay, I will, obviously. I'll drive into Wallingford and pick up a lasagna from the supermarket. We have stuff for a salad. It's no big deal."

Maddie set the knife down on her plate. "Not for me it isn't."

"What's that supposed to mean?"

"Just be careful, Mo. We haven't time-traveled back to those summers."

"What're you getting at?" Though Maura knew.

"I've seen you peeking at him when his attention was elsewhere. You can fool him, but not me. I know how you felt about him back then, and I don't want you to get hurt again. That's all I'm saying," she called out as Maura left the room.

She waited in the hall for Maddie's last words, which she knew would come any second.

"We know each other too well, Mo!"

Maura sighed. That was the one comment she knew for certain was true.

Theo could have been eating anything. Taste took a back seat to his other senses. The vision of Maura wearing an emerald green blouse over white jeans, serving salad and second helpings of lasagna to Luke and then leaning over him, her flowery scent wafting above the food and her breath warm against his ear as she asked, "More salad, Theo?" filled every part of him.

He thought he heard teasing in her voice and wanted to utter a fitting quip, except the words were stuck in his throat. And besides, everyone was looking and listening. He could only shake his head and resume eating, automatically chewing and swallowing, oblivious to everything but Maura, now sitting opposite him at the Stuart kitchen table, where he'd enjoyed many meals long ago. But not a single one like this.

Luke was chattering about the donkeys and the braying while Theo's attention was still fixed on the woman across from him, so he missed part of what Luke was saying.

"Theo?" Maura was smiling at him.

"Um…yes?"

Her smile widened, and he saw the twinkle in her eyes. "Luke was telling us that you two might be staying in the Glen longer than a week after all."

He looked at Luke, who said, "This afternoon when I told you I'd like to walk with Katie at her next lesson if we were still here, you said we probably would be."

"Oh, right." He hoped his face didn't show the embarrassment he was feeling. Tongue-tied at thirty-six wasn't nearly as excusable as it was at sixteen. He cleared his throat. "Well, the real-estate agent has organized a survey of our property, but it won't happen until Monday, and my meeting at my uncle's bank is that same day, too. So yes, we'll be sticking around a bit longer." There was a quick glance between the sisters then that Theo couldn't interpret. He kept his gaze on Maura, but she ducked her head, continuing to eat.

It was Maddie who spoke first. "That's great! Maybe

you'll be around for the Fourth of July, then. The festival's going to be here at our farm this year."

"That sounds cool," Luke said between mouthfuls of lasagna.

"It's a lot of fun. Everyone in the village takes part, and there'll be tables set up with vendors coming from all over the county and beyond."

"Carnival rides, too?"

"Just donkey rides, I'm afraid. But I'm sure some kids' and teens' activities will be organized by community groups here and from Wallingford."

"Dad? Can we stay for it?"

The excitement on his son's face urged him to say, "Of course," but then Maura raised her head. The peculiar expression that flitted across her face was hard to read, though it was definitely not encouragement. His mind searched for the right word. *Apprehension*, he finally decided.

He finished his meal quickly, sensing that the party atmosphere was coming to an end. Maddie began to serve dessert, so Theo resisted dampening Luke's enthusiasm by suggesting an early night. When Maura stood up to clear the table, he said, "I'll help with that."

He noticed Maura's downturned mouth at his offer of help, but decided to ignore it, determined to find out why her mood had changed so abruptly. They weren't teens anymore, and he refused to be put off by her. They stood side by side at the counter, rinsing and stacking dishes into the dishwasher as if they'd been doing that task together all their lives. Theo had an unexpected what-if thought, wondering for a split second how his life might have changed if he'd been more assertive as a teen. *No, don't go down that road, Danby.*

When Maura closed the dishwasher door and pressed the On button, Theo took a chance.

"Let's go outside for a minute, see if that full moon is happening as predicted."

He saw her look at Maddie and Luke, eating ice cream and talking about donkeys, and worried she was about to refuse. But she surprised him, nodding and opening the kitchen door. Theo followed her out into the backyard.

The promised full moon hung in all its splendor, high in the sky. "See? What did I tell you?" he quipped, moving next to her.

She gazed upward, wrapping her arms around herself.

"Are you cold?"

"No, I'm fine, thanks." There was a pause, and then she said, "I'm sorry if I seem a bit—"

"Standoffish?" he teased. He heard a faint snort.

"Yeah, guess that's what you'd call it. It's nothing to do with you, although it might have seemed like that. I just… It's just that I've been worried about the business lately, keeping it running, and the talk about staying in the Glen suddenly reminded me that if Jake & Friends does go under…well…there won't be any reason for us to keep the farm. We couldn't afford it, and we couldn't stay here, either."

He impulsively put his arm across her shoulders, and he almost expected her to shrug it off, as she'd once pulled her hand from his that last summer. But she didn't, and he stood quietly, reveling in the warmth from her body close against his. The urge to do more, to raise her head to his and kiss her, was overwhelming. Instead, he looked up at the perfect moon, its brightness and her nearness lighting up his heart.

But deep inside, he wondered if there was something she wasn't telling him.

Chapter Seven

Maura rolled over and stared up at the ceiling, its crackled plaster and yellowed patches a reminder that her bedroom, as well as her childhood home, was in serious need of repair. Much like her personal life.

Last night's dinner with Theo and Luke had been an impulse she was now questioning. At first it had been like old times. She, Maddie and Theo easily slipping into the teasing banter of their childhood and adolescence as if there'd been no gap at all from then till now. When she'd returned to Maple Glen to care for her father in his last days, she'd found that getting reacquainted with friends from the past had been like putting on a pair of shoes that hadn't been worn for years. The feet eased in, and walking was as smooth as ever. Granted, the shoes might be a tad out of fashion and frayed, but they could be worn, and comfortably.

She sighed. *Where am I going with this metaphor? I need to get my mind under control, not scattered in a hundred directions, all with dead ends.* Swinging her legs out of bed, she sat on the edge a minute longer, her fingers running through her tousled hair as she tried to focus on today—Saturday. Three riders and a break midafternoon when she and Maddie had a festival committee meeting.

Followed by tomorrow, Sunday, when she'd planned to visit Walter Ingram and make sure he knew about the festival, that he and his honey products from his beekeeping business were welcome. The man was a bit of a recluse, and she doubted he'd read the flyers or even heard any of the village talk about the event. Then the day after, Monday, she and Maddie had an appointment with their bank manager in Wallingford.

Maddie had finally persuaded her that a bank loan was necessary to upgrade the barn and stables, citing their hoped-for increase in riders after the Fourth of July festival. Maura had seen her sister's point and reluctantly agreed, mentally crossing her fingers that the inevitable assessment of their finances wouldn't reveal anything unexpected. If that happened, Monday could be a game changer for Jake & Friends.

Standing outside the kitchen door with Theo last night, his arm around her and his solid frame pressing against her with such assurance, she'd allowed herself a brief fantasy of how her life might have been different, if she'd been more receptive to the sixteen-year-old Theo so many years ago.

All water under the bridge, she told herself now. Time to get busy. She showered and dressed and was about to head downstairs when she paused in front of her chest of drawers. Then she grasped hold of the handle on the third drawer from the top and pulled it open. Beneath the socks and T-shirts lay the manila envelope she'd hidden there two months ago. The familiar stomach clench she'd felt back then struck. She stared at the envelope a moment longer, afraid to open it and see those ominous pieces of paper but, at the same time, almost hoping she'd misread them. *Stop kidding yourself, Maura Stuart.* Her fingers fumbled on the clasp as she withdrew the papers.

I, Charles Andrew Stuart, agree to cede to Stanley Danby of Maple Glen, Vermont, four acres of my land abutting the Danby property should I fail to recompense him for the loan of ten thousand dollars, given today...

Maura closed her eyes. She knew the rest, having already memorized the agreement. It was dated four years ago, when her mother was receiving cancer treatment. Those treatments had only delayed the disease, though, and her mother had died a year later. She and Maddie had frequently asked about their parents' medical insurance, but their father had reassured them all was just fine.

She read the second sheet of paper.

I, Stanley Danby of Maple Glen, Vermont, agree to loan Charles Andrew Stuart ten thousand dollars. Should he fail to recompense me, four acres of his land abutting my property will be ceded to me.

The agreement read as though the two men had written it themselves, but it was signed and stamped by a notary public in Rutland, so she assumed it was legally valid. What she'd also discovered subsequently was that a payment of ten thousand dollars had been made to a hospital in Burlington from a bank account in her mother's name—an account that was closed shortly after. There was no indication in her father's accounts that he'd paid back the loan.

She knew she was wrong to keep the document a secret from Maddie, but Jake & Friends had already received some attention and was slowly attracting clients. She and Maddie had worked out a good routine, sharing tasks and chores, the therapy sessions and the costs. But there was never enough money left over. Certainly not enough to cover a loan of ten thousand dollars.

The fact that Theo hadn't mentioned anything about the loan possibly meant that he hadn't found a copy of the agreement. *Yet.* She just needed a bit more time to figure out her next step, and then she'd tell him and her sister. She stowed the envelope back in its hiding place and went downstairs.

Maddie looked up from loading the dishwasher when Maura walked into the kitchen.

"What?" Maura asked, catching her sister's sly grin.

"Nothing. Just that you and Theo must have been enjoying the full moon, 'cause you were out there a long time."

"Give me a break," Maura muttered, pouring coffee into her mug. "We were chatting, like you and Luke."

"Very quietly."

"Maybe you couldn't hear us over your own conversation with Luke." Ignoring her sister's scoff, she popped two slices of bread into the toaster and finished making her peanut butter sandwich. "I see we've got Sammy coming this morning. Have we heard whether Cathy will be here?"

"She will be. Her daughter had a cold yesterday and couldn't go to school."

"Still, she could have let us know," Maura said.

"How it goes. Volunteers, right?"

"Right. Say, what about asking Luke again? He was great with Katie."

"Sammy isn't Katie."

"He doesn't have a meltdown every time he comes," Maura said.

"But we never know. That's why we have one of his parents walking with us, ready to help."

Maura sighed. The nine-year-old needed the riding time, and he enjoyed it once he readjusted to the weekly routine. Problems occurred when anything changed in that well-established pattern. "Worth a try," she said.

"Go for it, then. I'll round up Jake for Heather, who's coming first, and Matilda for Sammy, right after."

"And Janet Hamilton?"

"She wants Jake this time," Maddie said as she headed for the door.

"Okay, well, since she's last, Jake will have a bit of a break when Sammy's riding. I'll text Theo right now to see if Luke is interested." She pulled her phone out of her jeans pocket and sent the message before changing her mind.

Seeing Luke would probably also mean seeing Theo, unless he walked over by himself. He could easily do that now, since the Danby front field had been mowed. She smiled, recalling the braying incident yesterday. It was funny in retrospect, but she knew there was nothing worse than three donkeys going at it all at once.

Theo's reply came almost immediately. Luke would love to and would walk over.

Okay, she thought, just as well. *A bit of space between standing with his arm around me, his body against mine for what seemed like ages, and seeing him again this morning might be a good thing.* She'd lain awake for a long time once she sneaked off to bed, avoiding her sister's watchful gaze. The heat from Theo's embrace had lingered long after he and Luke had left.

"I don't know you," Sammy mumbled when he was introduced to Luke.

"I don't know you, either—not yet, anyway. But we both know Matilda. She's a very friendly donkey, isn't she?"

"I like her better than Lizzie."

"Does *anyone* like Lizzie?" Luke quipped.

Sammy laughed. "Maybe not." After a slight pause, he added, "I feel sorry for her, though. It's not nice when people don't like you."

Maura saw Sammy's mother wince. She was about to change the subject, to steer them toward the ring, where Maddie and Cathy were waiting with Matilda, when Luke said, "Yeah, I know what you mean. But when you get to be my age, which is twelve, you'll realize it doesn't matter if everyone doesn't like you, 'cause by then, you'll have best friends who will always like you. My dad told me that and he was right."

Sammy thought that over. "Are you going to walk beside me today?" he finally asked.

"If you want me to."

"Sure." He started toward the ring, with Luke behind.

Maura let out a whoosh of relief, causing Sammy's mother to say, "I don't know Luke's situation, but can you convince him to come back the next time?"

The ride was as successful as yesterday's, with Katie. As Maura waved goodbye to Sammy and his mother, she looked at Luke standing next to her. "If you're going to be in Maple Glen for a while, would you be interested in doing a bit more volunteering? And anytime you're free to muck out the stables…well…you're pretty good at that, too."

His smile reminded her of Theo's at the same age, and for a second, Maura wondered what it was like to have a child who resembled you in some way. She'd come to terms long ago with the reality that she might not have children. For that, you needed a partner—someone to love and to love you back. There'd been a couple of times in the past when she'd thought that was a possibility, but a reason to end the relationship always seemed to arise.

Luke's question broke into her thoughts. "Do you need me for the other riders today?"

"They don't need extra help, but you're welcome to stay."

"Thanks, but Dad and I are planning a hike tomorrow,

along the Trail. So we're going to get some supplies at the supermarket, like granola bars and other healthy snacks."

Maura smiled at his slightly disparaging emphasis of the word *healthy*.

"No problem, Luke. We're happy to have you whenever you're available." She paused a second. "I guess there's no deadline set for your return to Augusta?" She cringed at her blatant fishing expedition.

He shook his head. "I don't think so. Dad hasn't told me, anyway. It seems like I'm always the last to know."

Spoken like a grown-up, his complaint almost drew a laugh from Maura. Then an idea occurred.

"If you're back before three o'clock, tell him there's a meeting at the community center for anyone interested in helping out at the Fourth of July festival. Maybe you'll still be here for it and either you or your dad would like to volunteer."

Luke's face lit up. "You mentioned that a few days ago, I think. Yeah, that would be cool." Then his excitement lowered. "Except we could be anywhere by then."

She patted his shoulder. "No worries. It's only a thought, and wherever you are, you'll be with your dad, right? That's what matters."

He nodded, but his face expressed some doubt.

"Either way, if you're not doing anything around five o'clock, are you interested in coming over to help groom the donkeys?"

"Definitely!"

Maura watched him work his way through the row of cedars, exactly as she, Maddie and Theo had done years ago. He was a nice kid. Whatever the differences between Theo and his wife, they'd clearly accomplished something good in their marriage.

A stab of envy caused her eyes to well up.

* * *

Looking back, Theo still couldn't explain why his hand shot up when the festival planning committee chairperson—Bernie Watson—asked if there was anyone else who'd like to donate or contribute in some way. It wasn't only Luke's elbow nudge, because he'd already thought of something.

They'd arrived at the meeting shortly after it had begun, missing Bernie's welcome to newcomers and introductory remarks. As he and Luke took two of the last seats in the back row of the hall, he saw Maura wave at him from across the room, closer to the front. Relief washed through him at her smile. He'd been stressed all day about their next encounter after his impulsive embrace last night. He hoped the moment had been special to her, too. As a teen, he'd never been able to predict her reactions.

Bernie gave a big smile at Theo's raised hand. "Theo Danby! Nice to see you here. Folks, for those of you who remember, Theo is the nephew of Vera and Stan Danby, whose farm is located right next to the Stuart place."

Theo flushed as all heads turned his way. He cleared his throat, wishing he'd gone up to Bernie afterward. "Um… I'm happy to have people use my front pasture adjacent to the Stuarts' for extra parking or whatever."

"Terrific!" Bernie's voice boomed across the room. "We can use the extra space, for either parking or vendor tables. Why don't you and the Stuarts get together to discuss how that could work?"

Well, of course he ought to have anticipated that reply. He hoped the Stuarts, one in particular, would be on board with yet more meetings between them. He felt another dig in his side and looked down at Luke, who was grinning. Someone was happy about his impulse, anyway.

The rest of the meeting dealt with reports from various

people, which Theo basically tuned out. The last to speak was Finn McAllister and Theo snapped back to attention. The tall, gangly teen he remembered was now even taller but muscular—someone who worked out regularly or had a job that was very physical. He had a vague memory of Mrs. McAllister mentioning a fire department when he and Luke had met her their first morning back in the Glen. Finn was still as self-assured and poised as he'd been when they were teens, and the way the voices in the room hushed as he spoke was a sign the man held a respected place in the community.

His report was mainly about the safety and emergency measures for the festival, which triggered a memory for Theo. One hot summer day they were swimming in the creek when someone—a girl, Theo thought—seemed to be in trouble. Without hesitation, Finn had jumped into the water and pulled her ashore. She was okay, but he'd instinctively known to turn her onto her side and let the mouthful of water she'd swallowed and choked on drain out.

When Finn referred to his team of volunteers from the Wallingford Fire Department and the local branch of the Long Trail Club, Theo thought how appropriate it was that Finn had a career in rescue work. The meeting broke up half an hour later, and Theo stood to leave until he noticed Finn coming his way and stopped.

"So glad I got a chance to say welcome back, Theo. My mother told me you were here, but she wasn't sure for how long. I've been a bit busy and so haven't made it out to the farm to see you yet."

Theo shook his hand, thinking the man was as welcoming as he'd been as a teen, a gift that made him the natural leader he'd been then and clearly was now. "No problem. I'm glad we had this chance today." He heard Luke fidgeting and said, "This is my son, Luke. Do you remember meeting Mrs. McAllister a few days ago, Luke?"

"Yes, and the little girl, but I can't remember her name."

"Kaya, my niece. She and my sister are staying with us for a bit." He peered down at Luke. "Nice to meet you." He held out his hand, which Luke grasped. "Are you two here to organize a move to the Glen or...?"

"A sale," Theo said. "But there's a lot to clear out and arrange first."

Finn nodded. "I wondered if that might be the case. Well, I'm happy we can see more of you before and during the festival, too."

Theo was about to clarify that he might not still be there for the festival, that it depended on many factors, but kept quiet because now he was hoping his tasks would extend beyond the festival, which would be in ten days' time or so. More opportunities to catch up with some of the old gang, but especially to be with Maura. "I'd like that, Finn. Have many of the gang settled here? I recollect most of them vowing to move away permanently."

Finn laughed. "Yeah, me too. My move back wasn't in my plans, but fate intervened."

His pause gave Theo the chance to say, "I was sorry to hear about your father. How's he doing?"

"As well as can be expected. It's a progressive disease, as you know, but he's in a great nursing home. I heard you became a doctor! Not a surprise, really."

"Oh?"

"You were always one of the more compassionate kids. I remember the time we pulled Sue Webster—well, she's Giordano now—from Otter Creek. She had a panic attack after inhaling some water."

"But it was you who jumped in for her, not me."

Finn shrugged. "Maybe, but you and I both knew what to do."

Theo's memory wasn't as clear. Finn was making more of his part than what actually happened. Still, catching Luke's raised face and proud smile, he appreciated the remark. *Any kudos that elevates me in my son's esteem.*

"At any rate, in answer to your question, there are a few of us who've come back to stay, Sue being one. And I'm not sure if you remember Shawn Harrison? His folks lived where Bernie's B and B is now. He's been gone for years, but I've just heard he's taken a job with the Green Mountain Conservancy in the county and is looking for a place to live here in the valley. Maybe in the Glen itself."

Someone from across the room suddenly called out, "Finn!"

Finn turned around and waved. "Gotta see that guy. Let's get together again, before the festival," he said, patting Theo's upper arm and walking away.

Theo felt his heart rate pick up when he saw Maura approaching. Did she know Shawn Harrison was back in Maple Glen?

Chapter Eight

Inviting Luke to go with her to see Walter Ingram on Sunday was a last-minute idea, but Maura thought maybe he'd be interested in seeing Walter's beehives.

"And I suppose you'll probably see Theo again, when you pick up Luke," Maddie teased.

"Give me a break," Maura mumbled as she rinsed out her cereal bowl.

"Just a reminder that he's here temporarily, Mo. I don't think that facade of cool indifference you mastered as a teen works anymore, despite the efforts I've witnessed this week."

"I don't have a clue what you're talking about." But Maura was thinking, *She knows me too well.*

Maddie snorted. "C'mon. You fooled Theo back then, but not me."

"*Fooled?* What do you mean by that?" Maura turned from the sink to face her sister, who was writing the coming week's riding appointments in the calendar.

"The secret crush that you hid by acting as if you didn't like him. It was a successful ploy with all the kids in the group, but you couldn't fool me." Maddie's grin disappeared. "Though I couldn't understand at the time why you went to such trouble to make him think you didn't like him."

"You remember what things were like that last summer he was in the Glen? How some kids in the group became couples? Sue Webster started dating Finn and that girl whose father was the village reverend at the time was hanging on to every word Shawn Harrison said." Maura kept her eyes on Maddie, watching for any reaction to that name from the past.

"Amy something. But you're evading answering," Maddie said, her face unreadable.

"I didn't like having my feelings out in the open for everyone to see."

"You still don't."

"I'm better than I used to be," Maura pointed out.

"You are, but, sis, when Theo left at the end of the summer and he came over to say goodbye, you disappeared somewhere and didn't reappear until after he'd gone. I'm simply reminding you that he'll be leaving again when the farm is sold, and there'll be no reason for him to come back."

"I know that, Mads. I'm not a teenager anymore."

"You still haven't told me why you went to such trouble to make him think you actually didn't like him, when we both know you did."

"Because I thought *you* liked him! The way you two were always whispering together or casting meaningful looks at one another." There, it was out. The doubts and insecurity she'd carried that whole summer.

"For heaven's sake, Mo! We were friends, and most of our talks were about how I could get Shawn's attention away from that Amy. Because I liked *Shawn*. But nothing really worked until Amy and her family moved away from the Glen partway through senior year."

Maura sighed. "Things really were messed up, weren't they?"

"Well, we were teenagers." Maddie paused, then added, "If only we knew then what we know now. Isn't that how the saying goes?"

Maddie's brief smile held a hint of sadness. Maura wanted to offer some words of comfort, but her sister's hopes and dreams about Shawn Harrison had faded a long time ago.

After a short silence, Maddie muttered, "Not much we can do about the past, but we don't have to make the same mistakes again."

"I'm still going to ask Luke," Maura said.

"Suit yourself." Maddie returned to the riding schedule.

Maura pursed her lips and left the kitchen to get her cell phone. *No, I'm absolutely* not *going to make the same mistakes this time.* Yet a voice inside whispered, *Too late.*

Theo and Luke stood at the top of the drive watching Maura's truck roll up. When it came to a stop, Luke ran forward. "Dad says he'd like to come, too, Maura. Is that okay?"

Theo almost bowed out at her slight hesitation. He'd been foolish to think their connection the other night was something that might thaw her longtime coolness. He'd even allowed himself an occasional thought that they could be more than friends, though that fantasy always ended with his returning to Augusta while Maura stayed in Maple Glen.

After an embarrassingly long minute, she said, "Of course."

Luke's excitement helped smooth over the awkward moment as he scrambled into the back seat of the truck and Theo climbed into the passenger side.

"I barely remember Walter Ingram," Theo said, buckling his seat belt. "Has he been in the beekeeping business for long?"

"I'm not sure when he set up the apiary. Sometime when we were at university, I think." She headed down the drive to the main road and turned toward Route 7.

"But he didn't always live in the Glen, did he?"

"No, and theoretically, he still doesn't. His place is between here and Wallingford but closer to the Glen, so he's always been considered a resident." She glanced at him and asked, "Were you here when the missing children incident happened?"

The question brought back a vague memory. "The case about the kids lost on the Trail? I remember something about it, but I think it happened after I'd returned to Augusta. What did that case have to do with Walter?" He noticed her check the rearview mirror and half turned to see that Luke was more interested in sticking his head out his open window than in the conversation up front.

"At the time Walter was a firefighter in Wallingford and also headed up the local Long Trail search and rescue volunteer team." She paused, looking at Theo again. "He was the one who found the kids. They were in an off-trail section near the Glen's access point."

He let that sink in and would have commented but she added, "Because of the wide interest in the case, a lot of media outlets descended on Wallingford as well as here. Child Protection Services took the kids, and the foster parents were charged with negligence among other things, so Walter became the focus of all the press attention."

"That must have been a challenge for him."

"For sure. Of course, this all happened—" she paused, her forehead wrinkling "—almost twenty-five years ago, so I'd have been ten at the time. My memory is pretty shaky, but I recall being fearful for the kids, 'cause one of them was about my age. Most of what I know came from my parents at the time, and much later, when I read newspaper accounts. Walter's story is a bit sad, though."

"How so?"

"Every year for a few years after, some reporter would show up here or in Wallingford to interview Walter. Then later they came at every milestone anniversary. He basically had to hide. His marriage fell apart, and he became a bit of a recluse."

"Will he mind my coming, then?"

"I think he'll be okay with it. He keeps to himself but sells his honey here and in the county. Plus, I've seen him at the occasional church potluck over the years, and he came to the festival last year, when it was at the community center. He's been getting more involved in life here in the Glen."

Theo thought about how a life could change so drastically, and his interest in Walter Ingram rose as the truck trundled down a long dirt road off Route 7.

"Just to let you know," she said as the house came in sight, "people here are very protective of Walter, despite his tendency to keep to himself, and no one ever asks about that time."

She didn't need to give him the warning. As a doctor who'd treated a broad spectrum of patients and their individual needs, Theo knew all about maintaining respect and consideration of a person's right to privacy.

"Did you text or phone to let him know you're bringing company?"

"I don't know his number or if he even has any kind of phone. But he does have a dog, with a strong sense of territory, appropriately named Magnus because he's very big." She gave a low laugh. "He helps to keep the strangers at bay."

Sure enough, when she pulled up in front of the two-story, somewhat rickety clapboard farmhouse, a large dog careened around the corner toward the truck. Maura turned off the engine and dug into her jeans pocket.

"Do we wait until Walter comes out?" Theo asked, trying not to sound nervous in front of his son, who was now unbuckled and leaning over the front seat to stare at the barking dog near the front bumper.

"We can, but I think this will do the trick." She held up a small plastic bag.

"Salami?" Luke asked from the back seat. "That should work."

"It did the last time I came, though that was a few weeks ago. Wait till I give the word."

She climbed out, leaving her door ajar, and whistled. The dog stopped barking and, tail wagging, padded up to the salami in Maura's fingers. "Yes, you do remember me, don't you, Magnus?"

The dog delicately lifted the meat from her hand and wolfed it down, then begged for more. "That's all for now, pal." She turned her head to Theo and Luke. "I think you can come out now."

Her calm handling of the dog impressed Theo, but she'd always loved animals, and clearly even those that seemed scary. As he and Luke got out, a robust, gray-haired man in his mid to late sixties appeared from around the same corner as the dog had. He raised a palm in greeting to Maura and walked their way. Theo noted the wariness in the man's eyes as he drew near, looking at him and Luke.

"Hi, Walter! Do you remember Stan and Vera Danby? This is their nephew, Theo, and his son, Luke."

The guarded expression in the man's eyes disappeared.

He nodded and offered a hand to Theo. "Sorry for your loss."

"Thank you, sir."

"Walter," he murmured and, turning to Luke, offered his hand to shake.

Theo felt a flush of pride as Luke immediately shook the man's hand.

"I was wondering if Theo and Luke could see some of your hives."

After a few seconds, he nodded. "Why don't we check out the hives right now?" Without waiting for a reply, he turned and headed in the direction from which he'd just come, Magnus at his heels.

Theo glanced at Maura, who shrugged and grinned. They followed Walter around the house, where an expanse of wildflowers and trees spread out before them. Theo paused to take in the scene—the bursts of color among the tall grasses and the blossoms on the rows of trees.

"Pretty, isn't it?" Maura said as she came up next to him.

"I was expecting pasture, but I guess this makes more sense, considering—"

"Beehives?"

"Yeah."

Luke passed them, catching up to Walter and Magnus.

"Fruit trees," Walter announced, stopping at the start of the orchard. "Pear and peach in blossom now, apple coming later this summer." He resumed walking.

"Not a man of many words," Theo whispered to Maura.

She shook her head. "Not until he talks about bees. They're his passion."

Luke seemed undeterred by the man's taciturnity and, along with Magnus, stuck by his side until they reached several rows of white boxes. Theo raised an eyebrow at Maura.

"The hives," she said.

"These are only a few of my hives," Walter was telling Luke as Theo and Maura caught up. "I've got a hundred or so scattered around this part of the county, at various farms and a few commercial orchards. I visit them every second week, see that they're okay. Take off some honey if I need to or deal with any problems that might have cropped up."

"What kinds of problems?" Luke asked.

Walter peered down at Luke. "Good question, son. Could be a queen has decided to leave a hive with her retinue of workers. That's called a swarm. Sometimes I can catch them and bring them back, and sometimes I can't. Other problems happen when a raccoon or some other creature knocks over a super—that's what those individual boxes are called. You can see that every hive has a different number of supers."

"Are they after the honey inside?"

"Yes. All animals like sweet things, don't they? Not just humans."

Luke nodded. Theo was surprised to see him walk from one hive to another, unfazed by the clouds of bees buzzing around the entrances of each hive. "Um…" He began to warn him to be careful when Walter looked his way.

"He'll be fine, long as he doesn't try to get too close. They've got more important things on their minds than stinging a young lad." Then he added, "But he's not allergic, is he?"

Did he even know that? Now he was worried. "I don't think so."

Luke must have overheard. "I'm not, Dad."

Walter's mouth curved up in a half smile. "Seems to be a confident young fellow," he said to Theo, before going up to Luke, who was standing in front of a hive where a cluster of bees circled the small entry hole.

"Put me in my place," Theo muttered to Maura, who was grinning.

As they joined Walter and Luke at the hive, Walter was explaining what the bees were doing. "They've discovered a great source of nectar and are communicating its location."

Luke frowned. "How do they do that?"

"See them moving in those tight circles, with some moving up and down, or to the right and left? That's called a dance, and the way they move tells the worker bees watching exactly how to get to the nectar and how far away it is."

"Cool!" Luke exclaimed. "Like a kind of sign language, but with movement instead?"

"Exactly. And if we waited long enough, we'd be able to see some of those other bees fly off."

"Do they ever make mistakes?"

Walter thought for a minute. "I can't say for sure, but I doubt that happens very often. They're already familiar with what's available to them here—" he gave a sweeping gesture "—and will travel farther, maybe miles away, to feast on other food."

"Food, as in nectar? From plants and flowers, right? I learned that in school."

"That's right. Summer's the best time for nectar, of course."

"What do they eat in the winter?"

"Good question. I leave them lots of honey to eat. They gather around the queen in a big, tight circle, buzzing their wings to keep her and the hive warm."

"Does it work?"

"Pretty much. After a bit, the circle shifts so the bees on the outside move in and the ones closer to the queen move out."

"I think I saw a TV special about some penguins that do that, too, to keep warm in winter."

Theo saw Walter's eyes light up. "You're right. Nature's pretty amazing, isn't it?"

"A lot of work for such small insects," Theo put in.

"Yes, and they have such a short life span."

"They do?" Luke asked.

"About six weeks."

Luke's face fell. "Oh, that's sad."

Maura caught Theo's gaze and smiled. He noticed that Walter himself was smiling for the first time, too, as the man looked down at Luke.

"True, but it's the way of the world, isn't it? The life cycle all us creatures have." After a moment of silence, Walter said, "I guess you'll be wanting some honey, then. Would you like to come to the honey house with me and see how I take the honey off the frames?" he asked Luke.

"You have a *honey house*?"

Maura and Theo laughed at the blend of disbelief and enthusiasm in his voice.

Walter's smile widened. "I do indeed. Follow me."

Theo hung back, watching his son and the big man head for a wood outbuilding closer to the house. "I think Luke might enjoy this on his own. Then he can tell me all about it later."

"You should know that the invitation is a rare one. I can't say when I've seen Walter so…"

"Open?" Theo searched for the right word.

"Friendly," she said. "Luke has clearly made a good impression."

Theo thought about the Luke from a mere week ago, wondering how his son had changed so much in only seven days. *Or maybe I'm only now seeing him for the first time.* He clasped her hand in his and in a slightly shaky voice murmured, "Thanks for this, Maura. Thanks for today." Then he leaned down and kissed her.

He'd intended it as another thank-you, but the instant his lips found hers he found himself sinking into the kind of kiss lovers enjoyed. And this was Maura, whose lips he'd only dreamed of kissing so many years ago, when he'd known nothing of the magic of a first kiss. Even the adult version of that teenage self couldn't have imagined the sweet taste of her lips now, or the way she clung to him, her body swaying against his. The other surprise was that he pulled away first, breathing deeply and wishing they were somewhere else, anywhere but in an open field with his son a few hundred yards away.

Her smile was as wobbly as his felt. "Wrong time and place?" she managed to say.

He heard the tremble in her voice and knew she was as affected by the kiss as he'd been. "Unfortunately" was all he could say.

A hollered "Dad!" brought another smile. Luke was speed-walking their way, clutching a plastic bag. He slowed down as he approached them, and Theo wondered, from the hesitation on his face, if he suspected something was amiss.

Luke said as he drew near, "Mr. Ingram—well, he told me to call him Walter—gave us two jars of honey, and I got to see him spin some off these frames in a big machine. A centri—"

"Centrifuge?" Maura said.

"Yeah, that's what he called it, but it may have another name, too. Anyway, it was supercool how the honey just flew off these frames in that machine. Then it drips into a big bucket, and from there, he pours it into jars."

"Very cool," Theo said.

"This has been the best day ever." Then, remembering

other recent days, he explained, "Not better than riding Matilda or walking with Katie and Sammy, but—"

"In a different way?" Maura helped out.

Luke nodded. "Exactly. And Walter said to come back anytime. Oh, and he told me to tell you that he knows about the festival and is planning to attend."

Maura laughed. "I can see that your father and I didn't need to come on this errand at all. We could have just sent you."

"Anytime." Luke's nonchalant shrug brought more smiles.

Walter waved goodbye from the doorway of the honey shed as they walked back to Maura's truck. Theo's high from the kiss was short-lived. Maura strode ahead, slowing down only when Luke caught up to her. They chatted together as they walked and climbed into the truck without a glance back. Theo had the sense that they could easily drive off without realizing he wasn't with them. He buckled up in the passenger seat and sneaked peeks at Maura, but she kept her focus on her driving.

Now he was regretting the kiss and figured she was as well. When she turned onto the lane leading to his farm, he waited until Luke had exited the truck, carrying his jars of honey and heading to the door. "Maura—"

"What happened back there?" she voiced at the same time.

"I seriously intended it to be a thank-you—"

"I guess we need to talk, Theo. It's about time, don't you think?" She finally looked his way. "Just that we both have our own plans and expectations, and I'm not sure if any of them include…"

"You and me?"

She nodded.

"Okay. You're right, and I'm sorry if I've complicated

things." He swallowed hard over the sudden lump in his throat as he opened the truck door. "We'll talk, sooner than later. Tomorrow is a busy one for me. Maybe Tuesday? I'll text you." He stepped out and added, "Thanks again, for giving Luke the chance to see the hives and meet Walter."

Another nod and she shifted the truck into gear. Theo watched her reverse and head back down the lane. Somehow, he'd have to get his relationship with Maura back on track. Friendship was a more realistic option and probably the best one for them.

Yet, as confused and mixed up as he felt right then, the happiness on his son's face was a sight Theo knew he'd never forget. Long after they'd left Maple Glen, today would still be, in Luke's words, "the best day ever."

Chapter Nine

"What's up with you, sis?" Maddie looked away from the truck windshield to Maura, in the passenger seat.

"Hmm?" Maura shifted her gaze from the scenery on Route 7, heading to Rutland.

"You've been in some kind of other world since yesterday."

Tell me about it, Maura thought.

"Did something happen when you went to Walter's?"

Mads was probing, and Maura refused to get sucked in. "Other than someone getting stung by a bee, what could happen at Walter's place? And by the way, he's bringing honey to sell at the festival."

"Um, okay, I'll put him down for a table. But you're not answering my question. What's going on in that busy mind of yours?"

The memory of Maddie's teenage outburst once, long ago, brought a smile—*Mom and Dad say you're the quiet one, but I know your mind is always busy!* Her sister wouldn't give up until she got a reply. "Just thinking about our loan application," she finally said.

"Fingers crossed." Maddie took her right hand off the steering wheel to demonstrate. "I think we covered everything when we went through it again last night after supper. Though you weren't a hundred percent present."

Maura shrugged. "Worried, I guess. What happens if we don't get as much as we need? Or, worst case, we don't get it at all?"

Maddie's eyes met hers. "Then we'll be making different plans."

And that, Maura thought, was the crux of the problem. Reassessing the plan for Jake & Friends meant a discussion about Maddie's ongoing presence. She'd promised a year, and that deadline was a mere two months away. "I guess," she murmured. Returning her attention to the window again, she let herself drift back to yesterday and Theo's kiss.

Some thank-you, she'd thought in the middle of her restless night. *A thank-you kiss is on the forehead or cheek, not on the lips!* Still, she hadn't averted her face when she'd realized he was aiming for her mouth. She hadn't pushed him away, as she might have when she was fifteen. She hadn't put an end to it, despite the headiness and every nerve in her body wanting more. Theo had.

Theo, the summer friend. Theo, the unexpectedly handsome teenager whose presence caused such fluttering deep inside. Theo, the tall, attractive neighbor—and father— whose time in Maple Glen was limited to days, not weeks.

Maura took a deep breath to calm the anxiety mounting inside. She needed to take up running again. Exercising the donkeys wasn't enough to clear her head and get her mind off all the problems swarming through it. The business, the debts, the loan agreement she'd kept secret from her sister, not to mention the other person directly affected by it—Theo.

When he'd first arrived, she'd hoped his stay would be brief, that he'd sell his farm and leave Maple Glen before learning about the acreage. Then she wouldn't have to face him with what she'd done. Obviously an irrational hope, she told herself. Now old memories and new passions had complicated everything.

"Okay, let's do this!" Maddie announced as she parked in the lot next to their bank.

Maura blinked. They were already here, and she hadn't rehearsed her arguments for the loan once on the drive. Theo vanished from her mind as she followed her sister inside.

An hour later, she climbed behind the steering wheel, taking her turn to drive home.

"It's not all bad," Maddie began. "Half is better than nothing, and he had a point about the slow growth of the business."

The truck engine chugged into life, and Maura waited until it slowed to a rattle. The truck was one more thing to be worried about, she was thinking. But not today. Today was about the business. "He wasn't even listening when I tried to explain how difficult it was to draw more riders when we only have three donkeys. We need at least one more! Plus, we can't depend only on volunteers. You know that from this past week, with Cathy's absence."

"Don't forget Ashley will be starting in a few days," Maddie murmured as she buckled up. "And there's Luke."

"How long will he be around, though?"

"You'd know that better than me."

"What's that supposed to mean?"

Maddie snickered. "C'mon, Mo! For once, drop the 'I don't know what you're talking about' routine, not to mention your ridiculous pretense about Theo Danby. We've already gone over this, and I'm tired of the way you keep skirting around the very obvious fact that the feelings you had for the guy when you were a teen have resurfaced."

Maura bit down hard on her lower lip. "This isn't about me or Theo Danby. This is about Jake & Friends. My…my *dream*." Her voice broke, and as she shifted into gear, the truck surged forward out of the parking lot onto the street.

Maddie didn't speak until they turned off Route 7. "Be kind to yourself, Mo."

If only she could, Maura was thinking. But guilt shadowed her every thought. Now they had a bank loan to pay off on top of the ten thousand dollars from Stan Danby. Now she had mere days to tell Theo, as his stay in the Glen was certainly coming to an end. And then there was Maddie, her twin and best friend, who deserved to know the truth. Soon, she silently vowed. *Soon.*

Theo waited in the car while Luke was choosing snacks in the convenience store for their afternoon hike on the Trail, which had been postponed from yesterday due to the spontaneous trip to Walter Ingram's place—the meadow, the hives alive with buzzing under the hot sun, and Maura Stuart, in his arms. *Kissing her.* Several times in the night he'd had to tell himself all of that had actually happened. The sweetness of her lips on his and the way she'd fit so perfectly against him. She'd wanted the moment to go on as much as he had, until he'd heard nearby voices as Luke was leaving the honey shed. Then Theo had remembered where they were. And what they were doing.

The kiss had been at the forefront of his mind all the way to Bennington and through part of the bank manager's opening remarks. Then the woman had said, "I didn't know your uncle well, having transferred here only half a year before he died, but reviewing his file, I see that except for one anomaly, he and your aunt were very conservative and predictable with regard to their savings and expenses. That frugality, along with the blue-chip investments they made years ago, account for the substantial nest egg you've inherited." She looked up from the computer and smiled at Theo.

The amount of his inheritance had been the surprise that shifted his thoughts from the kiss yesterday to the present. "This is news to me because I couldn't get a clear picture of their assets from the scattered bookkeeping system Uncle Stan used." *Maybe now I can simply throw all those papers into the old oil drum in Uncle Stan's barn and have a bonfire.* Then he'd focused on the first part of her remarks. "What kind of anomaly?"

She'd scrolled through the computer again. "Let me see… About four years ago your uncle withdrew a large sum of money." She frowned as she read. "Ten thousand dollars, to be exact."

Theo had blinked. That was a large amount for a man who'd saved every elastic band and plastic food container through the years. He almost missed what she'd said next.

"It was actually a cashier's check. Made out to a Charles Stuart. Do you know him?"

Do I know him? "Uh…yes. He was a neighbor of my uncle's. Is there any mention of why that payment was made?"

"No, we don't collect that kind of information."

"Right, of course not. And…uh…any other payments made to Charles Stuart since?"

"No, just that one."

Theo had intended to close the account at the meeting but changed his mind, deciding to wait and see what more he could find out about the mysterious payment. Had his uncle owed the money to Charles Stuart or purchased something from him? The matter of the money occupied him until they got back to the farm, when Theo decided he should bring it up with Maura.

He quickly texted her a suggestion to meet at the Glen

bakery tomorrow afternoon. The place did take-out coffee and maybe they could talk while walking around the village. A neutral and public place, where they could focus on discussion, rather than their physical proximity. Luke climbed back into the car as Theo pressed Send.

"Everything okay?" Luke asked, looking at the cell phone in Theo's hand.

"Hmm? Oh, sure… Let's get a move on. The Trail awaits us!"

Luke rolled his eyes. "Sheesh."

Theo smiled, shifted into gear, and they rolled away from the convenience store. Half an hour later, after a quick lunch, he helped Luke adjust the small daypack they'd bought in Bennington, and he slung his slightly larger one over a shoulder. He started to walk past the car when a thought occurred. He opened the door and bent down to retrieve the small first aid kit he always carried in the glove compartment. When he closed the door, Luke whined, "Aren't we driving to the place?"

"It's only a mile into the village, and the walk will be a good warm-up." He ignored Luke's pout, an expression he hadn't seen for several days. The county road turned into Church Street at the village's Welcome to Maple Glen! sign, and Theo was just beginning to hit his stride when a car approaching from behind slowed down. He turned quickly, checking to see if Luke was safely on the gravel shoulder, then stopped as the car's window rolled down.

Finn McAllister was behind the wheel and nodded at Theo. "Hiking?"

Theo walked over to the passenger side. "Thought I'd show Luke some of the Trail."

"Great idea. Do me a favor? Someone told me a couple of the signs had been either pulled off or fallen in that windstorm we had a week or so ago. The blue blazes. You remember them, right?"

"They mark the off-trail sections?"

"Yep. How far you planning to go?"

"It depends on my son." He tilted his head to indicate Luke, taking his time catching up to them.

Finn chuckled. "Maybe a short one the first time? I'd appreciate your checking the signs, and also, if you see anything unusual, let me know."

"What do you mean by unusual? It's been many years since I've been in this area, Finn."

"Maybe some branches fallen on the trail, from that storm. Any evidence of camping, litter, that sort of thing. The Glen section is off-limits for camping, but some people still do it."

"Okay, and if you don't hear from me, you'll know all was good." He thought for a second. "I'm guessing there's no cell phone coverage?"

Finn grinned. "Not much. Maybe at the start, but once you get into the woods or deeper into the valley, nothing. But you won't be going that far, right?"

"Not planning to, and realistically—" he glanced at Luke, scuffing the gravel as he approached the back end of the car "—not likely to."

"Okay. Thanks again. Saves me a short walkabout today."

"How often do you and your volunteer team do an inspection?"

"In summer, once a week due to the increased numbers of hikers. Less so in early spring and late fall. In winter, maybe once every two or three weeks." He stared at Theo for a long minute. "We could use someone like you on the team. Athletic and with a medical background."

"I haven't worn hiking boots in years, and my walking

has been basically limited to hospital corridors, but thanks for the vote of confidence."

"If you plan on staying here for any length of time, would be great to have you. Okay, then, take care!" He rolled up the window, and Theo stepped back onto the shoulder as the car continued into the village.

"Wasn't that man offering us a ride?"

Theo stifled a laugh. The disappointment in his son's voice was confirmation that the hike would probably be a short one. "No, that was Finn McAllister. He's a fire-fighter in Wallingford but heads up a team of volunteers who check the Trail and act as a search and rescue group if necessary."

Luke stared at the car a moment longer, lost in thought. "Can we get something to eat at that bakery before we get into the woods? In case our snacks aren't enough."

"Definitely." He patted Luke's shoulder, and they re-sumed walking.

Twenty minutes later they were standing at the foot of the pedestrian bridge spanning Otter Creek. Theo strapped his backpack on properly, cinching its waist belt. There was water, the bakery purchases, the snacks and the first aid kit, which he hoped they wouldn't need.

"Remember what I told you last night? About the blue and white blaze signs on the trees? They mark the path, and basically, we just have to follow them. I'm thinking we might only go as far as the junction where the Glen's off trail meets up with the main one. When we see our first white blaze, we'll stop, have a look around and re-turn. Okay?"

"How far is that?"

"Honestly, I can't remember the last time I hiked here."

"Your last summer in the Glen?"

Theo smiled at his son's use of the shortened name, spoken like a real local. "Yeah, probably. All set? We can walk side by side most of the time, but if the trail narrows, stay close, don't wander off. And if you want to rest or if you see anything interesting, speak up. Okay?"

"Okay."

Theo sensed the mumbled response was trepidation, not reluctance. "Let's do this, then!"

Luke snorted, which made Theo smile. They crossed the bridge and stepped out of the blazing sun into the cool, dark woods. A hush descended on them, and Theo stopped, held a finger to his lips and pointed to an ear.

"Listen…the sound of the forest."

Luke pulled a face but after a second whispered, "It's so quiet. It's not even this quiet at night, back home."

"True, but it is here in the Glen."

"I haven't noticed 'cause I'm asleep."

"Which proves my point." He nudged his son and said, "Let's walk."

He led the way past the first blue blaze, still intact, on a tree a few yards beyond the footbridge. Occasionally, he craned round to see Luke, glancing right and left as he kept pace. A good sign, he thought.

They'd just passed the second and third blaze markers when Luke whispered loudly, "Dad! I can hear something rustling over there."

Theo looked where Luke was pointing. A bevy of birds flew up into the air from the underbrush, startled either by them or by some unseen predator. "Lots of small mammals and birds around, and as quiet as we are, we're still disturbing them. It's important to keep one ear attuned, but even more important to watch the ground beneath your feet. See that root sticking up there? If it were dead center on the path, someone could trip over it if they weren't paying attention."

Luke nodded solemnly. "But can we talk once in a while? I have some questions."

Theo's laugh echoed through the woods. "Yeah, let's take a rest and ask away."

"First of all, where are we going?"

They'd been through some of this the night before, but Theo figured Luke hadn't taken it all in. "Well, all of this—" his arm swept a broad arc "—is part of the White Rocks National Recreation Area. Remember I pointed out the parking lot and entrance when we drove through Wallingford, our first day coming to the Glen?"

"Will we see any white rocks?"

"They're on the side of White Rocks Mountain. If you look up, you can see its summit above the tree canopy." He gestured upward.

"Does this path take us there?"

"No, this is the off trail, but it'll connect to the main one, which would take us to the summit. It also would take us down, to the ice beds below the summit."

"Ice beds? Cool."

"Literally."

"Are we going up or down, then?"

He was relieved that Luke was interested enough to try either route but knew going up meant tackling a steep climb and going down, the jumble of icy rocks that, even in summer, could be treacherous. "Maybe for the first time, we'll walk to the fork, where this path meets the main trail. By then we'll be ready to turn around, hike back to the village and maybe visit the bakery again. I noticed some homemade pizzas."

"Sure." Luke smiled. "I might want two. They looked a bit small."

"You're right. Okay, let's get on with it." Theo resumed walking but had to stop a few feet beyond to pick up a large branch across the path. He tossed it into the bush, causing birdcall alarms from the trees.

The next blue blaze sign they encountered was dangling from a nail, partially protruding from a tree trunk. "I'll see if I can fix this," he said, peering around for a stone to hammer in the nail more securely.

"Here." Luke bent over to pick up a large stone, which he handed to Theo.

The sign was quickly fixed, and they continued upward. Later, Theo figured they'd been walking another fifteen minutes when he heard a low sound, unlike any bird or small mammal. His heart rate shot up, and fearing it was a very large animal—like a bear—he held up his hand, motioning for Luke to stop and to be silent.

There it was again. But this time, he recognized it. Low moaning, from a human.

"That sounds like a person." Luke's voice trembled.

Theo stared ahead. The path rose sharply and then took a hard turn at its crest. "Stay here." When Luke was about to protest, he added, "I'm going up to have a look. It could be anything. Don't worry. I'll give you a shout when it's okay to follow me." He kept his eyes on Luke's face. "Got it?"

"Okay."

He kept his backpack with the first aid kit on and topped the hill in seconds. There was no one in sight, but the moaning was louder. Making the sharp turn, he hoped whoever was in trouble was on or near the path and not lying somewhere in the brush. "I'm on the way," he hollered. "Stay wherever you are." Despite his long strides, time seemed to slow down. A trailing vine slapped against his cheek, and he thought he heard Luke calling from below, but Theo pushed on until he rounded another bend in the path and saw a man slumped against the base of a tree ahead.

Slipping out of his pack, he lowered it to the ground and sank onto his knees in front of the man, whose moaning ceased immediately. The man's color wasn't good, but at least he was conscious.

"What's the problem, sir? Have you fallen? Hurt yourself anywhere?" He skimmed over the man's body but didn't see any obvious injuries. His ashen face and the way he held a hand over his chest led Theo to suspect a heart condition. He placed two fingers at the base of the man's neck to feel his pulse. It was racing and erratic.

"Nitroglycerin?" Theo asked.

The man nodded.

"Where?"

The man turned slightly to his left, where Theo noticed a small daypack. He pulled it toward him, unzipped it and rummaged through it. Finding the small vial of pills in an inside pocket, he shook one out. Then he clasped hold of the man's chin again, using a finger to open his mouth, and slipped the pill under his tongue.

"It won't be long now. Try to relax. You're going to be all right."

The sound of footsteps caught his attention, and he swung around, getting up onto his feet at the same time. Luke was standing, wide-eyed, behind him.

Now wasn't the time for reminders about following instructions. "He's all right, son. In a few minutes, when his chest pains have subsided, we're going to help him get to the house at the footbridge. The McAllister place."

An hour later, the man was carried off in an ambulance. Finn drove Theo and Luke back to the farmhouse. Luke still hadn't uttered a word. Theo was reheating dinner from the night before, while Luke sat silently at the kitchen table, watching his every move. Theo guessed the boy would soon speak but was taking his time processing what had happened.

Finally, Luke said, "You saved that man's life, Dad. You're a hero."

Theo took in the dampness in Luke's eyes. "No, I'm not a hero, son. That man might have been able to eventually get to his medication."

"But we don't know for sure."

"It was good timing for him, our being on the scene when he needed help. That's all."

As he moved past Luke to get to the microwave, his son grabbed hold of his forearm. "*I* think you're a hero, Dad."

Theo felt his eyes well up. He bent down to kiss the top of Luke's head. "Thank you, son. Now, let's eat." He opened the microwave door and pulled out the bowl of spaghetti. "Sorry it's not that pizza we saw."

"Tomorrow night, Dad."

And they began to eat.

Chapter Ten

Maddie came into the kitchen while Maura was listening to a voice mail from Walter Ingram.

Are you and Maddie interested in another donkey? I just got a message from a friend about a farm foreclosure, and the fellow needs to find a home for his donkey. No home means bad news for it. I can truck it to your place this morning. Say ten? Let me know.

"I'm going to order another delivery of hay," she was saying before she noticed Maura's concentration. "What's up?" She moved toward Maura, who was sitting at the table where the bank loan agreement was strewn.

Maura handed her the phone. "Two things. One, Walter definitely has a cell phone, and two—this." She watched as a frown appeared on Maddie's face while she listened to the message. "It's free," she put in as Maddie set the phone on the table.

"We still have to feed it, have it checked by a vet, take care of it!"

"But the whole point of the loan was to expand the business, even if in a small way. This is what we need to do that."

"More riders are what we need."

"They go together, Mads. You can't have one without the other."

After a long minute, her sister yielded, but with a caveat. "Fine. You're right. As long as another animal doesn't end up costing us too much. We could also wait till the end of the summer."

When you might not be here? Maura was tempted to ask. *No, you've made your point, so don't raise another issue.* She picked up her phone and texted YES before her sister could change her mind. She managed to keep the excitement from her face as she asked, "What do we need to prepare?"

"I'll change the hay order if we're getting another animal, and I guess you'll be prepping another stall. Right now, they're all out in the northwest pasture."

"Any riders today?"

Maddie pursed her lips. "No" was all she said as she left the room.

Maura sat a moment longer, until the brief euphoria of winning an argument passed. The new donkey would have to earn its keep. She'd been so eager to let Walter know they were willing, she hadn't thought to ask for any details. She slipped into her rubber boots in the mudroom and headed for the barn. It was another bright, sunny day, though she could see clouds building in the south. They could use the rain, but she hoped it would hold off until the new donkey was inside getting used to the stall, not to mention the other donkeys.

Maura had always loved entering the barn early in the morning, with its warm, earthy odors. When their father was a boy, his family had horses and pigs, but when she and Maddie were young, there'd only been chickens and a few goats using the same stalls that the donkeys now called home. Gradually, the goats were sold off, leaving the chickens. Maura knew selling the goats, along with most of the farm's acreage, had been necessary after their mother's cancer diagnosis and her ongoing care. Though she'd been unaware of the entire cost of that treatment until she'd found the loan papers. *The loan.*

Her long sigh rebounded around the empty barn. She and Theo were supposedly going to talk about the unexpected shift from friends to…what? Something new and exciting but, she had to admit, scary, too. Maddie's warning about getting too involved had resonated even more after the other day at Walter's. Even now she couldn't explain why she'd responded as she had to his lips on hers. Only that she hadn't wanted the kiss to end.

When she'd received Theo's text about meeting somewhere in the village, she'd snorted at his comment about a neutral, public place. Clearly, he'd forgotten village life, with its hidden eyes and ears, not to mention tongues. No, she figured they could pick up treats and walk back to his place. She had to have Theo all to herself because today she was determined to find out if he knew about the loan agreement.

Half an hour later, the stall was clean with fresh hay and water in its troughs, and Maura was about to go inside to shower when she heard the rumble of a truck. She pulled her phone out of her jeans pocket to check the time. Walter was early. She opened the back door and hollered, "Mads, Walter's here," then walked around to meet him. The instant she saw his face, Maura knew something was amiss.

Instead of unlocking the horse trailer, he strode toward her. "Something I have to confess, Maura, and feel free to change your mind about taking Roger. If you do, I've got someone else who might take him."

So the new donkey—Roger—was a male and company for Jake, she was thinking as Walter went on to say, "I didn't give you all the details because I kinda hope you'll fall in love the minute you see him." He tried for a smile but pursed his lips instead. "The fact is, Roger isn't a young fellow and may need some extra attention."

Maura was about to reassure him that age probably wouldn't be a factor, as a mature donkey would be best for a new rider, when the kitchen door slammed shut and Maddie joined them in time to hear Walter add, "He contracted some kind of infection when he was young and eventually lost the sight in his left eye."

Maura saw her sister frown and preempted any questions by asking, "Is he trained, though? Is his vision good enough that we can use him as a riding animal?"

"Yes, he's trained. He's slow, but calm and patient. A gentle giant compared to your other donkeys. I think you'll be charmed."

"Then I'm sure we'll be fine, won't we, Maddie?" Her sister didn't look as optimistic as Maura was feeling.

"That's great. I'll bring him out, then." Walter went back to the trailer and unhitched the rear door.

Maura stretched her neck over Walter's shoulder to see four sturdy legs. Walter grasped the donkey's lead rope, and Roger ambled nonchalantly down the trailer ramp. His large head slowly swiveled left and right, and he came to a halt a few feet from Maura, raising his head and sniffing the air. He was taller and bulkier than Jake, a good option for adult riders. Maura noticed his left eye was opaque and cloudy, while the other absorbed everything within its range. She slowly moved close enough to stroke his large forehead. He reared his head slightly at her touch, but she didn't withdraw her hand, reassuring him with steady, firm strokes. Then he bared his lips and snickered, making a strange clicking sound, and half turned his head to the right, his good side.

Maura was about to ask what Roger was doing when Walter quickly said, "There's one more thing."

A black-and-white, long-haired dog trotted down the ramp and stood next to Roger. Maura blinked and heard her sister mutter, "Whaaat?"

Walter sighed and raised his shoulders apologetically. "This is Shep. He and Roger are not only best buddies but soulmates. Least, that's my opinion. When Roger lost his sight, the family had just gotten Shep as a puppy, so they trained him as a kind of Seeing Eye dog. The two have been together ever since, ten years now." His eyes shifted from Maura to Maddie and back to Maura again. "Like I said, there's someone else south of Bennington who might take them. But they're a couple. Roger and Shep. A package deal."

Maura peered down at Shep, sitting on his haunches and gazing up at her, every feature on his face begging to be accepted. Roger gave a loud snort, bent his head and gently nuzzled Shep.

"We'll take them," she announced.

Theo finished his phone call with the land surveyor when he heard Luke thumping down the stairs. The surveyor had to change his arrival time to late afternoon, which meant that Theo would also have to change his meeting with Maura, and it was already noon. The timing would be tight, but he didn't want to rush his talk with Maura. Nor did he want to put it off any longer. They needed to sort out how they felt about one another if there was any chance of an ongoing relationship, which, after a tormented night's sleep, he was hoping for. Luke would be fine on his own for lunch, and after maybe he could help out at the farm.

"Dad," Luke began as he dashed into the living room, where Theo was sitting at his uncle's old rolltop desk. "Can you text Maura to see if I can go to the farm and see the donkeys, instead of being here on my own this afternoon?"

Theo grinned. Great minds… Now, if only Maura was available. He fired off a text, adding his own message about their meeting. His phone pinged almost at once, and he skimmed her reply, noting her suggestion about getting lunch at a diner in Wallingford instead. Then he saw a reference to the arrival of a new donkey.

"You're in luck, kiddo. Maura says they just got a new donkey and asked if you'd like to meet him and his sidekick." Theo checked the text again. "Hmm, not sure what she means by that. Maura and I are going to get some lunch in Wallingford, so why don't you make yourself a sandwich before we head over?"

"Oh?" Luke hesitated. "Um, sure, but Maddie will be there, right?"

Theo checked his son's puzzled face. He hadn't told him about the plan to meet Maura, thinking he could do that later. "Yes, Maddie will be there. But remember I told you about my offer to help with the festival? Maura and I need to organize something. We'd planned to do that later this afternoon, except now I have to meet with a land surveyor here. The timing has changed a bit, but you still get to go see the donkeys."

Luke thought for a moment. "Okay." On his way to the kitchen, he suddenly stopped to say, "Then I guess we'll be here for the festival?"

"Is that all right with you?"

"Definitely!" He held up a thumb and ran into the kitchen.

Theo silently blessed the donkeys for the umpteenth time, realizing how problematic the stay in the Glen might have been without that distraction for Luke. He replied to Maura's text and went upstairs to change. Fifteen minutes later, he and Luke were walking up the lane to the Stuart farmhouse. The place was quiet until a sudden outburst of barking sounded from the barn.

He caught Luke's eye and shrugged.

"A *dog*?" Luke asked, his eyebrows raised.

"Guess so." They headed for the barn and were greeted at the door by Maddie, followed by a midsize black-and-white dog.

"Hi, guys, this is Shep. He's hungry, which is why he was barking. He figures Roger's being fed and he should be, too."

"Um, two dogs or...?"

Maddie smiled. "Nope. Roger is the new donkey, and Shep here is his best friend. Come on in. Maura's bringing something to eat for Shep... We don't have any dog food 'cause we didn't know Roger came with a dog. Long story," she added.

When Shep whined, Luke walked up to him and extended his hand, palm side up. Shep sniffed it, wagged his tail and licked the hand. Luke laughed. "I think he smells peanut butter." He stroked the dog's back, which brought more tail wagging. "Can I go see Roger?"

"Sure, but don't go into his stall. He's very calm but is still getting used to his new home and us. Oh, and one thing. Roger can't see out of his left eye, so if you want to pat his nose, approach him from the right, so as not to alarm him."

Luke nodded. "Come on, Shep," he said and headed into the barn, the dog at his heels.

Theo grinned at Maddie. "I'm not sure if Luke will ever want to leave Maple Glen now."

His light remark was met with a serious expression. "I heard you're probably staying for the festival, though," she said.

"It's looking that way." He hesitated, then asked, "Why?"

She glanced to the kitchen door across from the barn. "Mo said you two were going to discuss the plans for it. In Wallingford."

"Uh, yes." Was that *all* Maura had told her, and where was Maddie going with this?

"I've noticed that you both have made some kind of connection over the past few days."

Theo's face heated up. He was about to make light of the matter when she added, "It's okay. Maura told me. She'll hate me mentioning this, but—"

Now Theo was annoyed. "We're both adults, Maddie. We can figure something out. Don't worry about Maura… or my intentions." He managed a half smile, trying to lighten his tone.

Her face relaxed and a telltale blush rose up her neck. "I know, Theo. I trust you, believe me, but keep in mind that Maura will never leave this farm or Maple Glen."

The closing kitchen door got their attention. Maura headed toward them, holding a stainless steel bowl. "I don't see Luke, so I'm guessing he's inside getting acquainted with Roger and Shep?"

Her eyes sparkled, but not as much as her smile. She was wearing a sundress the color of spring lilacs—a perfect match for the fiery red hues of her hair, falling onto her shoulders. She was always beautiful, he was thinking, even in torn jeans and muddy boots. But this…*this* Maura was a vision he never could have imagined. Definitely not as a teen, and not even as a man.

It was Maddie who spoke up, saving Theo from stammering. "Luke's already made a friend of Shep and is meeting Roger. I warned him about the eye," she added as Maura was about to speak.

"I knew he and Shep would like one another." Maura looked at Theo. "Do you want to go meet Roger now? Or later?"

He cleared his throat. "Maybe later?"

"Sure. Here, Mads, I found some leftover roast chicken in the freezer and added some mashed potatoes from the other night. I'll pick up some dog food in Wallingford." She handed Maddie the bowl, then turned to Theo. "Ready?"

He could only nod, as tongue-tied as he'd been as a teen.

"I'll drive." She headed for the Ford Fiesta parked next to the pickup.

Theo caught Maddie's expression. "Don't worry. Everything will be fine." He meant to set her mind at ease, but as he followed Maura, he wished the confident reassurance in his words matched his feelings.

Chapter Eleven

"How do you think the other donkeys will respond to Roger?" Theo asked.

Maura was checking out the menu. She guessed he was avoiding getting around to the conversation they'd agreed to have. The kiss—what it meant, what were the next steps and how were they going to make it work.

She hid a smile. If Maddie could read her mind right now, she'd quip, *Getting down to business, Mo, with an agenda that hasn't any items of fun on it?*

No, Maura thought. *Today I'm going to break the pattern.* "He's a male," she answered, raising her head to meet his dark-eyed gaze, a shiver racing down her spine. "So they'll be wary—especially Jake, who might feel he's losing his place in the hierarchy."

"Is that a thing with donkeys?"

"As with all animals," she said. "That's why we gave Roger the stall farthest away. They'll see him and smell him, but he won't be too close. The real problem for the next few days is Shep."

"How so?"

"The others will view the dog as a predator. They don't know Shep and won't want him around them. Walter said

Shep is used to sleeping in a stall with Roger, but I think we might have to have him in the house with us until the others are accustomed to him. It'll be a gradual introduction, but I'm hoping all will work out." She pulled a face. "It better, or I'm in big trouble."

"Maddie?"

"How'd you guess?"

"I couldn't help but notice her expression."

"Yeah. She's just worried about...you know...how we can take care of another animal, given our financial situation." She noted his instant frown and regretted mentioning finances, which she knew could lead to a topic she wanted to defer as long as possible. Despite her vow yesterday to tell him about the loan, she knew that money and romance weren't a good combination. *One issue at a time, Maura.* She stared at the menu again, its offerings blurring as her eyes welled up. The server came to take their order, and Maura chose the daily special, whatever that was.

Theo immediately said, "I'll have the same." He toyed with the spoon in his mug of coffee for a second. "I told Luke we were meeting to discuss how I can assist with the planning for the festival, so..."

"We better get around to that. I told Maddie basically the same thing."

"Uh-huh?"

Maura saw a flicker of doubt on his face and recalled how he'd lingered behind, chatting to her sister. "Did she say something to you? About us?" When he hesitated, she said, "C'mon, Theo. Out with it. There's no point having an honest discussion about what's happening between us if we can't be open with one another." She ignored the instant pang of guilt.

"Yeah, you're right. I think she's worried about us getting into something that will probably be temporary and not good for either of us."

Maura pursed her lips. "She gave me the same speech."

"And?"

She noted the combination of hope and dread in his eyes. "I think... I *know* that's a concern for me. I have a lot of serious issues to deal with at the moment, and frankly, a romance will only complicate things." His face fell in disappointment. "But," she quickly put in, "at the same time, I know I need some levity in my life."

"Levity? Sadly, I'm not known for my sense of humor or wit."

"You know what I mean. My family always referred to me as the 'serious' twin, and I think I bought into that label, especially as a teenager, so I basically—"

"Lived up to it?"

"What can I say?" She sighed, dramatically.

He reached across the table to clasp her hand. "I definitely saw that side of you the last summer I was here, but now..."

"Now?" she prompted.

"Now I see that aloofness as reticence or—" his brow wrinkled in thought "—caution." He pressed her hand. "I think you were afraid of your own feelings back then. We all were! Teenagers and hormones. Not a great situation." He shook his head. "What I'm trying to say is that you shouldn't beat yourself up about how we behaved when we were that young."

"I know all that, but my current worries are adult ones, and totally realistic."

He reached for her other hand, wrapped around her coffee mug. "Here's my idea. Why not take this new situation between us as far as it will go over the next week or so? Let's simply get to know one another as adults. You can't deny that there's already a great dynamic happening, with Maddie, Luke, the donkeys…"

Her laugh raised a few heads in the busy diner.

"So, let's go along with it. Have some fun. Enjoy each other's company. When it's time to leave, you and I can talk. Maybe work something out."

She wanted to believe all that he said, but as she nodded, part of her mind centered on one word: *maybe*. Still, he had a point. Some fun in her life—*and a little romance*—sounded like a good antidote to stress. "You're right. One day at a time kind of thing, then?"

"One day at a time and no analyzing or predicting as we go along."

"I see you already know things about me," she quipped.

"*Some* things, but my goal is everything."

She felt that shiver again and ducked her head from the intensity in his gaze. There was a rustling at her side as the server placed their order in front of them. Maura stared at the food. "What is this?"

"The daily special," said the server, in a weary tone. "Liver with onion gravy and mashed potatoes."

Catching Theo's expression as the woman walked away, Maura grinned. "Guess I skimmed over exactly what the special was."

He gave a forlorn nod. "The potatoes and gravy look good."

"Maybe leftovers for Shep?"

"Sounds like a plan."

Fifteen minutes later they waited while their server packaged up the remaining food. "Well, there's no other diner here in Wallingford, or even a fast-food outlet, so—"

"Ice cream to finish off?"

"Reading my mind."

They collected their container and headed for the ice

cream parlor a block away. "This is one of Luke's new favorite places in the area," Theo said as they entered the busy shop and got in line.

"And the others?"

"One other—your farm with the donkeys." They moved forward a few inches, and then he added, "I'll be eternally grateful to you and Maddie for giving him the chance to help out."

"He's been great, otherwise we wouldn't have been so willing. We're getting a high school student for the summer. She helped out a bit in the early fall, when we were just starting up. The daughter of an old school friend and Bernie Watson's niece. And Ashley, that's her name, is also a second cousin of Sue Giordano, the owner of the bakery. She used to be a Webster."

Theo shook his head. "I'd forgotten—or maybe hadn't realized—all the intertwining of people in the Glen when I summered there. I do remember Sue, but only because Finn McAllister mentioned her when we met up at the festival planning committee. Luke and I've been into the bakery a couple of times but haven't met her in person yet."

"Do you remember the time she fell into Otter Creek and inhaled some water and was choking? You and Finn pulled her out."

"Right."

"See, you were destined for a career in helping people and saving lives." She was teasing but noted his red face.

"That was mostly Finn. I just followed his instructions. Not surprising that he went into search and rescue work. And speaking of that…"

He suddenly stopped.

"What? Speaking of what?"

"He told me that Shawn Harrison was moving back."

"To the Glen?"

"Or someplace nearby. He works for the Green Mountain Conservancy and is taking over the management of the county's section of the Trail."

Maura was speechless, mainly because the way word spread in the village guaranteed rapid public knowledge of every morsel of news or gossip. Did Maddie know? She was about to probe for more information when it was their turn to order, and all thoughts were immediately devoted to eating ice cream.

They were almost at the cutoff on Route 7 when Maura realized the clouds darkening to the south were now hovering directly over the Glen and the farm.

"Looks like rain," Theo remarked, peering out the windshield.

Maura pressed down on the accelerator.

"Is that a problem?" he asked, shifting his attention.

"It may well be. We wanted the donkeys to stay out for a couple of days, until Roger and Shep are used to the barn and our routines."

"I've seen animals outside in rain."

"Sure, it's not a problem unless there's lightning and thunder. The problem is Matilda. She hates rain."

"Say again?" he asked, laughing.

"Seriously. If she's inside and it starts to rain, she won't go out. We've had to physically push and pull to get her out the barn door."

"Well, what will she do? She can't get out of the pasture and into the barn on her own."

"No, but she'll start braying, which will set off Jake and Lizzie. Then they'll charge toward the gate and press on it. Maddie won't be able to handle them on her own, and Luke isn't big or strong enough to be much help."

"Hmm, I get the picture. Maybe it'll hold off until we get

there." He'd only finished the sentence when large drops splattered onto the windshield.

Maura gave the car a bit more gas, and they were driving up the lane when the rain fell faster, with more intensity. She parked, leaped out of the car while Theo was still unbuckling his seat belt and dashed past the barn toward the pasture. She could hear the earsplitting brays above the gusting wind and reached the fence in time to see Maddie struggling to grab hold of Matilda's halter while Luke stood behind the opened gate. Jake and Lizzie were pacing behind Matilda, and Maura's first troubled thought was that, in a panic, they might charge the gate, which Luke was holding.

"Get Lizzie," Maddie shouted when she saw her.

Maura guessed the plan. Lizzie and Jake could be left in the pasture, but unless Matilda was removed, they'd keep pushing at the gate until they, too, were out. She took in Luke's pale face as she squeezed past Matilda and grabbed hold of Lizzie's halter.

Maddie pulled Matilda through the opened gate just as Theo arrived. "Can you close the gate?" she hollered.

Maura saw both Luke and Theo struggling against the wind to push the gate. She let go of Lizzie, slapping her on the rump to encourage her to move away, and managed to slip out just before the gate clicked shut. Jake and Lizzie were still braying and pacing in circles on the other side of the fence. Maura pointed to Maddie and Matilda, heading for the barn.

"We need to go help," she shouted. "Roger and Shep are going to get caught up in all this racket."

The din continued into the barn, where Roger, in his stall, had joined in and Shep started barking. Despite being out of the rain, Matilda kept braying and snorting, now alarmed by the presence of a strange donkey and a potential predator—a dog. Maura rushed to Roger's stall, easing open the door so that Shep, leaping against it from the other side, wouldn't escape and cause even more panic for Matilda. She forced herself to keep calm, making shushing noises to let Roger and Shep know everything was okay. She cautiously approached Roger from his good side, keeping as clear of his legs as possible. Getting kicked by a frightened donkey wasn't how she wanted the day to end.

By now Maddie had secured Matilda in her stall, trying to calm her as well. Maura figured the two animals would quiet down eventually, but she knew some factor in the noise equation would have to change. Theo and Luke, covering their ears, entered the barn. Maura scanned the scene around her—two noisy donkeys, a barking dog, three adults and a boy all holding hands against their ears. It reminded her of a Christmas carol, and she smiled at the random thought.

Luke reached the stall as Maura, stroking Roger's head, grabbed hold of his halter. The kid seemed to know intuitively what to do, she later thought, as he stooped over the closed stall door and beckoned to Shep. "Here, Shep!"

Maura watched the dog trot over to Luke, who held out his hands. Did he have a treat of some kind? Then she remembered the incident earlier, when Shep had smelled peanut butter on Luke's fingers. Sure enough, Shep began to lick them again, wagging his tail. Seconds after Shep stopped barking, Roger stopped braying. Maura exhaled. She let go of Roger's halter and worked her way around him and out of the stall. She saw that Maddie had managed to soothe Matilda and was now latching that stall door.

Except for Matilda's chomping on some hay in her trough, Shep whining for more attention from Luke, and Roger shuffling nervously in his stall, the barn was quiet. After a few seconds, Maura said, "Tea, anyone? Coffee?"

"Something stronger?" Theo suggested.

Maura and Maddie laughed at the pitch in his question. "Some caffeine, I think," Maura said. "Luke, can you try to get Shep to come into the house with you? I want Matilda to get accustomed to Roger first, then Jake and Lizzie tomorrow. After that, we'll see how Shep fits in."

"But he will, won't he? I mean, this is his home now."

The combination of anxiety and optimism in Luke's voice touched Maura. She'd have replied, "I hope so," but knew he was looking for reassurance. "It may take a few days, or even a week, but he will," she said.

Maddie looked out through the large, open barn door. "The rain is tapering off. I'm going to check on Jake and Lizzie. And I'll have tea, not coffee," she said over her shoulder as she left the barn.

"Want me to get the liver from the car?" Theo asked.

"Liver?" Luke's jaw dropped.

"We'll explain over coffee, or tea," Theo said, grinning at Maura.

She watched him walking to the car, thinking about the agreement they'd struck at the diner. His broad-shouldered back and long stride reflected the confident, strong man Theo Danby had become. She could hardly wait to learn more about him—his view of the world, his private thoughts and even his secrets. But was there time for all of that? *Maybe I'll have to content myself with the taste of his lips or the warmth of his hand in mine. Perhaps that will be enough.*

"Maura?" Luke's voice broke into her thoughts. "Will you help me get Shep out of the stall?"

They returned to Roger's stall and Maura slowly opened the door, keeping herself between it and Roger. "Call him, Luke. But quietly."

Luke extended his hands in a beckoning gesture. "Here, Shep. Come."

The dog scanned the stall, his dark brown eyes lingering a minute on Roger, and then walked out to Luke. Maura closed the door. Roger was either unaware of the dog leaving or unbothered. A good omen, she thought, as she followed Luke and Shep.

Theo was waiting by the kitchen door. He held up the Styrofoam container of liver. "Lunch for Shep. And maybe a snack for us humans?"

"I'm starving!" Luke exclaimed.

"Not to worry," Maura said. She smiled at Luke, tousling his hair. "Plenty of food for us, too."

She led the way into the mudroom, where everyone slipped out of their wet shoes while Shep trotted nonchalantly into the kitchen, as if he'd been living there all his life. A sense of contentment washed through Maura. This felt like…*like a family.*

Chapter Twelve

Theo sat, phone in hand, for a long moment. He had the kitchen to himself, and his sigh was loud in the quiet room. Thank goodness Luke was still asleep, another sign of his soon-to-be teens. The news he'd received from Trish didn't bode well for Theo's improving connection with his son.

When she'd asked him to take Luke for the summer, Theo had suspected she was making plans that involved a move and, possibly, a remarriage. None of that was a surprise for Theo. The affair with a colleague of hers had been revealed a year ago, and after a few months' separation, she and Theo had gotten a divorce—uncontested and polite. Not because he didn't care for her, but by then he'd realized the marriage had begun to dissolve long before.

Everything had moved at a dizzying pace, and Theo, struggling with the stress of running the emergency department along with the unexpected death of a patient he'd come to like and admire, hadn't had the stomach to contest any of her conditions. For Luke's sake, he'd refused to drag the whole sad story into court. She could continue to live in their home in Augusta, Maine, with Luke, whose school was nearby, but when Luke started high school, they'd sell the family home, split the money and discuss with whom

Luke would live. They'd been frank with Luke, explaining their plans and assuring him he'd share both parents. But now...

He'd tried to negotiate more time in the half-hour phone call, but she was adamant. The couple were moving out of state next month, and Luke would have to go with them or stay with Theo. There were so many problems with that scenario that Theo couldn't think straight. When she'd hung up, asking him to discuss it with Luke and make a decision as soon as possible, Theo had sat, staring blankly at the run-down kitchen, as if he could find an answer in its cracked walls and worn floor tiles. If his own situation were uncomplicated, he'd reorganize his life and his work. But right now, there were no other career opportunities at his hospital. He'd been granted the six weeks' leave for some much-needed rest and a chance to "clear his head," as the administrative chief had recommended. Ha! If only.

The decision to return to Vermont to take care of his inheritance and show his son Maple Glen, where he'd spent his summers, had certainly improved his sleep and appetite, and taken his mind off the twenty-four-hours-a-day demands of the emergency department. Except the return had also raised an unexpected glitch. *Maura Stuart.*

Last night had been fun. They'd impulsively ordered pizzas that Maddie had picked up, leaving Theo, Maura and Luke to get the animals settled. They'd brought Jake into the barn, after realizing that Matilda had accepted Roger's presence. Lizzie, Maura asserted, would have to wait. By the time the pizzas were consumed, Jake had ceased stamping his hooves on the stall floor and snickering warnings to Roger. Introducing the donkeys to Shep, who'd be staying in the house, could wait a day or so.

The night was quiet when Theo and Luke finally headed home, pushing through the cedar hedges and pausing to gaze up at the sky littered with thousands of twinkling stars. Theo had scarcely listened to Luke's ongoing recount of the day, his mind dwelling on the possibility of some kind of relationship with the person he'd been smitten with years before. He'd been filled with such comforting hopes—even dreams—of the future that his sleep had been deep and restful, a record for him.

Now he went through all the potential reactions from Luke about this new development. Of course, their stay in the Glen had always been finite. In fact, his original plan had been to clear out, sell and leave all in a week, ten days max. That goal had passed without event yesterday, and he was no closer to selling than he had been his first day back. The crux of the problem was that he was no longer in a hurry. He still had four weeks left, and since his talk with Maura, he planned to make full use of every minute of that time. Maple Glen wasn't that far from Augusta. Seeing one another would be complicated, given his work schedule and her responsibilities with Jake & Friends, but not impossible.

The reality that Luke might not be part of that scenario, assuming his son would choose to live with his mother, altered everything. The converse, that Luke would want to live with Theo, was equally problematic. Theo's hospital job meant Luke would be alone a lot—too much, Theo figured, for a young teenager with divorced parents. He could relate, because his own parents had divorced when he was nine, the first summer he came to stay with his aunt and uncle. And how lucky he was to have the couple and their farm as a refuge against the loneliness and insecurity of those early postdivorce years. Who would Luke have, with his mother many miles away and his father rotating through long shifts?

He got up and poured himself a third cup of coffee.

When he heard the slam of the bathroom door upstairs, he popped some bread into the toaster and took the peanut butter and jam out of the fridge. Luke's fussiness over food was gradually shifting into teen territory, with a bigger appetite and more willingness to experiment, but PBJ remained a staple. He was spreading those condiments on the toast when Luke came into the kitchen, his hair still damp from a shower. Another milestone of sorts, Theo thought with a smile. No reminding necessary.

Luke snatched a piece of toast and started munching as he opened the fridge to take out the milk. "Are you going to sit for breakfast, or eat on the run?" Theo asked.

"I'll sit but only for a few minutes, Dad. The new volunteer is coming in this morning, and Maddie said I could work with her. She's in ninth grade and worked with the donkeys last fall. Her name is Ashley Watson and guess what? She's related to the man who owns the B and B where we stayed our first night here."

That explained the shower. "You didn't mention you'd be working with her."

"Maddie said it was a possibility, so I decided to—"

"Err on the side of safety by taking a shower anyway, 'cause Ashley is a girl?" he teased.

"C'mon, Dad. Gross." But his blush was telling. "Anyway, can you check your messages and see if Maddie let you know?" He heaved a loud sigh. "If I had my own phone, we wouldn't have to do this!"

Theo peered down at his phone, grinning as he logged in. But the realization that Luke would definitely need a phone in the fall, if he was on his own with him in Augusta, hit hard. His vision blurred as he scrolled to his messages, finding an unread one sent while he was on the phone with Trish. He cleared his throat and waited a second longer. "Yeah, Maddie says come over anytime."

Luke fist-pumped the air. "Yes!" He got up, swallowed some milk, grabbed the other piece of toast and headed for the door.

"Hey, hold on a second. What's the plan, then? Are you there all morning or…?"

"I don't know. Does it matter? When I finish there, I'll just come home."

Home. Theo had no idea when exactly that word first applied to the decrepit farmhouse as far as Luke was concerned, but his son's casual use of the term brought another lump in his throat.

"What about you, Dad? What's happening with you today?"

The grown-up question, coming from the son who could barely utter a whole sentence to him the first week of their road trip, was overwhelming. He couldn't speak until Luke got to the kitchen door. "Um, not sure. Maura asked me to go with her to a planning meeting for the festival this afternoon. And the real-estate agent is coming by this morning with the surveyor's report." He added the last part as a gentle reminder that their stay at the farm was temporary, something he had to keep in mind himself.

Luke didn't turn around, but mumbled something that Theo couldn't decipher, which he figured was just as well. Perhaps his son had the same conflicting feelings about leaving Maple Glen as he had. Theo rubbed his forehead, going back to the early-morning phone call about Luke's future, and felt the energy he'd awakened with that morning draining out of him.

The Realtor arrived an hour later to report that the survey was all in order, as Theo had anticipated. She brought a For Sale sign that she hammered into the lawn near the road. After she left, Theo's outlook on the day took a nosedive. Weeks ago, he'd expected to celebrate this moment—

the final resolution of his inheritance. Instead, his whole body seemed to sag under the weight of regret and nostalgia. He thought back to his persuasive message to Maura at the diner in Wallingford. *Let's just enjoy our time together—get to know one another. Have fun.*

If only life—and love—were that simple.

Maddie noticed the sign first because she was driving, and the Danby farm was on her side. She turned sharply to Maura. "Did you see that?"

Maura craned her neck as they sped by. She was so startled she couldn't speak. Of course, she ought to have remembered that the sign and all it represented was inevitable, like Theo's leaving the Glen. But a big part of her mind, and heart, had resisted accepting that hard fact. *He might have told me*, she was thinking.

"I guess this was inevitable," Maddie murmured, eerily echoing Maura's thoughts. After a brief silence, she added, "Life goes on, doesn't it?"

Maura felt a rise of annoyance. "For heaven's sake, Mads. Cut the corny philosophizing." She averted her head and stared bleakly out the passenger-side window until they reached the community center. The small parking lot was packed with vehicles, so Maddie pulled onto the adjacent side street and parked.

Before Maura could get out, Maddie grabbed her forearm. "I'm sorry, Mo. That was silly. I didn't intend to trivialize what you must be feeling about Theo leaving. Forgive me?"

Maura didn't smile, but she nodded. "If my twin can't bring me down to earth, no one can."

"Thanks, and I'll try not to puncture your balloon of happiness any more than I have to."

This time Maura smiled. "Likewise, sis." Then she recalled Theo's news yesterday about Shawn Harrison. The whole brouhaha with the donkeys had erased that bit of information from her mind. She was about to mention it when a tap sounded at Maddie's window. It was Sue Giordano. Maddie rolled down her window.

"Hey, ladies! Haven't seen you gals in ages. What's up? Not eating carbs these days?"

"You're kidding, of course," Maddie said.

"We've been too busy feeding donkeys," Maura said, leaning forward. She finished unbuckling and got out of the truck.

"I brought some treats with me for the volunteers, so you'll get your fill." Sue held up two canvas bags.

"Can't wait," Maddie said as she followed Maura out.

"I heard Theo Danby's been back in the Glen for more than a week, and I still haven't seen him."

Maura resisted glancing at her sister. "I know he's been into the bakery. His son, Luke, is already a big fan, Sue."

"A son? No kidding. Is there a wife, too?"

Maura kept her eyes on the open front door of the community center, but heard Maddie say, "They're divorced. Sue, are you setting up a table of your bestsellers on the Fourth of July? Because I haven't received your registration form yet."

"You bet! I've even persuaded my niece to help sell. I'll get the form to you right away. How many tables have you got registered now?"

Maddie reached into her handbag and pulled out a small notebook. "Let me see." She flipped through some pages. "About thirty-five so far, and I'm hoping to sign up more at the meeting. Plus, a woman from the co-op in Wallingford told me a few people there have filled out the forms and paid her the fee."

Sue screwed up her face in thought. "So thirty-five tables for sure, times the twenty-five-dollar fee... That's a good start on our goal of a thousand or more for the community center's new roof. Oh, there's Barb," she said, spotting a friend entering the building. "Okay, see you ladies inside."

Maura watched her greet the friend—not a Glen resident, she thought—and turned to Maddie. "By the way, Theo told me—"

"What did I tell you?"

Maura swung around as Theo came up beside her. "Oh...uh...that...you know...you were going to section off the whole side of your frontage for vehicle parking." Theo's arched eyebrow and Maddie's frown caused more hesitation. "And...um...is Luke here? Did he tell you he and Ashley really hit it off this morning?"

"He did and he also said she's going to introduce him to some other kids here. Apparently, there's some kind of youth club every Friday evening, so he's excited about going with her this Friday. Right now, he's just hanging out at the farm. I left my phone with him so he could play some games."

"Uh-oh," said Maura "The slippery slope..."

"Yep. A matter of time, I think."

"Ashley lives on the next street over from this one." Maura pointed to her left and was about to relate some family history when Maddie interrupted.

"Maura, I already knew about Theo's offer of land for parking. I was at that meeting, too, remember?"

"Oh, right. Anyway, we better get inside and grab a good seat." She hustled toward the center door, aware that she'd left Theo and her sister with the impression that she was really losing it. And she was, she told herself. Why would she want to blurt out the news about Shawn Harrison right before a community meeting?

By the time the three of them found seats, Bernie was calling the meeting to order. Maura tuned out while people stood to give their updated reports, followed by an occasional round of questions. At last, Maddie stood to give her report—an update on the number of tables, a plea for more registrations, and an announcement that the final numbers had to be in by the coming weekend.

"Maura and I will create a map so people will know where their tables will be located, and we're asking that everyone with tables arrive at the farm by nine that morning, which should give everyone plenty of time, as I think we decided the official start would be eleven. Right?" She directed this last word to Bernie, at the front of the room.

"Yes, Maddie. Folks, try to get your table organized well before that time, though. And you'll have a map of the whole festival area for them, as well, is that right, Maddie?"

"Yes, Bernie. We'll have the layout on a large board, and to be clear, the table area will be our entire front lawn, with spillover onto the northwest pasture. The donkeys will be in the riding ring, for petting and… We haven't decided yet about giving rides. However, some of the shady areas on the front lawn and maybe the veranda will be allocated to parents with small children or seniors needing some quiet time."

"Hey! We seniors are just as hardy as everyone else," someone called out, and the room erupted with chuckles.

Maura caught Maddie's eye and grinned. Then she whispered, "The first aid station?"

"Oh, I almost forgot." Maddie raised her voice, stilling the buzz of chatter. "The first aid station will also be located on the front lawn." A hand shot up from the first row.

Maura couldn't see who wanted to speak until Finn McAllister stood up.

"Guess I might as well step into this conversation now,

Maddie, if you're finished?" When Maddie nodded and sat down, he went on to say, "I've got everything organized for our station, with a rotating team of volunteers from the fire department. Oh, and two of my men are bringing our main engine for kids to see and maybe even sit on, so I'll have to confer with the Stuarts and Theo Danby about the best place to park it."

The room broke into more chatter until Finn held up a hand. "One more thing—and this is nice news for us long-time Glen residents. I've enlisted another volunteer who's not only well qualified but will soon be the administrator of the county's Green Mountain Conservancy search and rescue department." Finn motioned to a man sitting at his side.

A swell of dread surged up from the pit of Maura's stomach. She glanced at her sister—calm, impassive and unsuspecting.

"Let's give a hand for a guy some of us remember as a nerdy teenager—Shawn Harrison." There was some applause, a sharp whistle from the back of the room and more talk as a few people stood to see over the heads in front of them.

Maura kept her eyes on Maddie, whose face was now the color of new-fallen snow. She clasped her sister's hand in hers, squeezing gently, as a ruggedly handsome man got to his feet and turned around to wave at the crowd. Maddie's grip on Maura's hand tightened. "It's okay, Mo. I'm fine," she whispered.

But as soon as Shawn sat back down, Maddie got up and began pushing her way across the row of chairs. Maura was about to follow when Theo, sitting next to her, grabbed her elbow. "Better to leave her. She won't want to have any further attention focused on her."

He was right.

The meeting broke up shortly after Maddie left, and when Maura exited the hall, she couldn't see her sister anywhere, nor could she see their truck. Stifling a curse, she went back to look for Theo, somewhere in the crowd of people mingling outside. She could easily walk home, but a ride with Theo meant another chance to be alone with him, and maybe tell him about the loan.

He was in the last group leaving the center, and as Maura wound her way through the small clusters of people, she spotted him talking with Shawn. She hesitated for a minute, then told herself she was not only being silly, but unrealistic. From what Finn had said, Shawn would be living in the area, perhaps permanently.

As for Maddie…she decided not to think about the possibility that her sister's commitment to staying may now be hinged on Shawn's move. When Theo caught sight of her and beckoned, Maura took a deep breath and walked over to say hello to the man her twin had been madly in love with years ago, and deeply hurt by.

"Welcome back to the Glen, Shawn," she said as she joined them, hanging back just far enough that a handshake or a hug would be awkward.

"Good to see you again, Maura. It's been a long time." His smile was warm, which eased some of her tension.

"Seems like some of the Glen gang have moved back, despite our vows not to."

"You never know the opportunities life will throw at you," he said. "Finn told me that you and Maddie have donkeys and are running a riding therapy program at your parents' farm now. That's pretty awesome."

"Well, it's a business venture and we enjoy it. And congratulations to you on this new job of yours. Have you been in search and rescue long?"

"I got into it when I was in the army, and after my discharge, I took some courses. Started with the Conservancy a few years ago. The chance to head up things here was irresistible."

"And your parents?"

"Enjoying retirement in Florida."

There was a lull after this, and Maura was about to ask Theo for a ride home when she realized she'd also have to mention Maddie leaving with the truck.

As if reading her mind, Theo asked, "Want a lift back to the farm?"

"Yes, thanks." She was about to add that she'd wait for him at his car when Shawn spoke up.

"How's Maddie? I heard her report but couldn't see her from where I was sitting at the front. Is she still here?" He quickly scanned the remaining people.

"Uh, no. She had to get back to the farm for the animals."

Another long pause until Theo said, "Good to see you again, Shawn. Drop by the farm sometime."

"Thanks, Theo. I'm currently staying in a rental unit in Bennington, where my office is located, but I'm hoping to find a place closer to Maple Glen. The lure of nature... plus the Trail. Have you been out on it yet?"

"I have once, with my son, and will try to get some more hiking in before we leave."

"I'm looking forward to a combination of work and hiking. Finn and I are going out for an inspection tomorrow. You and your son are free to join us, if you like."

"That sounds good, though I'll have to check with Luke. Lately, he's begun to make his own social plans."

Shawn chuckled. "Okay, well, now that we've exchanged phone numbers, text and let me know by eight in the morning," he said.

Maura felt Theo glancing her way but kept her eyes

focused on Shawn. His nerdy teenage self had morphed into an attractive man—burlier than, but not as tall as, Theo. His hair was military-style short, and she thought she saw some silvery strands in it, but the thick, horn-rimmed glasses of his adolescence had been replaced by trendier frames.

"Will do. Uh, Maura," Theo said, breaking into her thoughts, "are you ready to leave now, or…?"

"Oh, yes. Thanks, Theo. And nice to see you, Shawn."

As she and Theo began to walk away, Shawn called out, "Say hi to Maddie for me."

She didn't reply, but kept pace with Theo. When they reached his car parked farther up the side street where her own truck had been, Theo said, "Don't get ahead of yourself, Maura."

"What do you mean by that?"

"Just that once Maddie is used to the idea of Shawn being around, there won't be a problem. I'm sure there'll be some tension between them at first. That's only to be expected. But they've both gone on with their lives."

Maybe so, she was thinking as she stopped to get into Theo's car. As for his advice not to get ahead of herself, she already had dozens of questions demanding answers, and she knew Maddie would be grilling her with even more once she was home.

But there was one above all that she needed to know right away. "Is he married?"

Theo was starting the car and shrugged. "I don't know."

Maura sighed. Trust a man not to find out the most important bit of information.

Chapter Thirteen

Maura pitched the last forkful of hay into Roger's trough and listened to the other donkeys munching contentedly on her way out of the barn. She'd awakened at daybreak after a restless night and, noting the gray clouds to the east, decided to bring the donkeys in from the field. This way, she and Maddie wouldn't need to corral a panicked Matilda. She couldn't remember the riders booked for today, but if the clouds became a full-out storm, she and Maddie would call them to reschedule.

When Theo had dropped her off at the farm after the meeting yesterday, he'd given her one more piece of advice that she'd heeded. *Let Maddie be the one to start talking about Shawn.*

She'd been grateful for that, because she knew she tended to push people, especially her sister. It wasn't until after a mostly silent supper that Maddie got around to talking, and for the first time Maura heard the full story of the sudden breakup that had blindsided her sister in her freshman year.

"I never got a clear reason from him. I swear there was no sign at all, except he was moody and very distant for a couple of weeks before," she'd told Maura. "I heard through mutual friends that he left university before the end of the year with no explanation even to them." She'd paused to collect herself. "He never wrote or got in touch with me."

She'd stopped then and, after a moment, Maura told her own story—how she'd always measured any potential partners against her teenage memory of Theo. "I know I passed up a couple of chances to have something special with someone, but I knew I'd be making comparisons. How ridiculous is that, right? Clinging to a memory from years before! Now I have this unexpected second chance with him, and there are so many obstacles to the possibility of anything developing that I... I can't even—"

"Don't." Maddie had placed her hand on Maura's arm. "Just let it all play out. Worry about things when...when his farm is sold." Maura had nodded, but she was thinking, *By then it will be too late.*

"I hope you'll take that advice, too, Mads. With Shawn."

"I'll have to, won't I? If he's going to be living here. Unless..."

Maura hadn't wanted to hear what her sister had left unsaid and, yawning, had used fatigue as a pretext to head to bed.

Now Maddie was making coffee when Maura entered the kitchen from the mudroom. "I put the donkeys into the barn because it looks like rain, coming from the east."

Her sister peered out the window over the kitchen sink. "Hmm, good idea. Didn't you say last night that Shawn had invited Theo and Luke to walk the Trail with him and Finn?"

Maura marveled that Maddie could utter Shawn's name with such ease. A good omen. "Yeah. But who knows— the weather could make a sharp right turn and head north to Montpelier."

Maddie laughed. "Oh, I've missed that great line of

Dad's, Mo. I remember how he always had some reason for us not to stay home from school, no matter how hard we tried to convince him and Mom that a storm was brewing, and the buses would surely be canceled."

Speaking of Dad, this was a good time. "Did you ever wonder how Dad managed to cover Mom's medical expenses?"

At that precise moment, Maddie turned on the coffee bean grinder. When she finished dumping the ground coffee into the filter, she looked across the room and said, "Sorry, you were saying?"

"Um, just thinking of Mom and Dad, and how they must have struggled to pay for Mom's health care."

"I assume they had some kind of insurance, didn't they?"

"Maybe."

"Well, we just saw his bank manager and there were no outstanding debts from when he was alive, so…"

"True, but it was odd that he withdrew fifty dollars a month like clockwork, always the day he got his pension money. I mean, such a regular amount, and it wasn't for living expenses, because those were obvious in his bank statements," Maura said, wending a circuitous path to her revelation.

Maddie flipped the On button of the coffee maker. She reached into the cupboard for mugs and turned to ask, "Are you having toast this morning or cereal?"

"Cereal," she said. The moment was passing, Maura realized, and she felt some relief as she let it go, rationalizing later that it was Maddie's next comment that got her attention.

"I can't believe Shawn enlisted in the army. Did that happen before or after he graduated?"

"He didn't say. Why? Do you think it's peculiar that he

did?" Maura poured milk over her granola and sat down at the table to eat.

"He never seemed the army type, and he's an only child, so he'd have left his parents on their own, which must have been difficult."

"Maybe he just wanted to get away. I don't know where he was deployed, but it could have been Afghanistan. He did mention it was the army that led into his search and rescue work." When Maddie didn't respond, Maura went on to say, "How do you feel about bumping into him, either before or at the festival?"

"It won't be a problem. I'm fine." Her eyes locked on Maura's. "Seriously, Mo, I'm not so fragile. Not anymore. Besides, I may not be around too much longer myself." She finished her coffee and took her breakfast dishes to the sink. "I don't think that storm is going to make a right turn. It's coming our way."

"Guess we should start making phone calls," Maura automatically said, though a large part of her brain was still processing the dropped information she'd feared.

"We had four riders set for today, and one is a newbie. Let's hope we can rebook them all."

"Why don't you do that while I call our volunteers?" Maura waited until Maddie left the room, then got up to take her cereal bowl and coffee mug to the sink. Her hand shook as she rinsed them, and she silently wished Shawn Harrison had never returned to Maple Glen.

The rain started shortly after Maura finished her phone calls. She debated texting Theo to advise Luke that there wouldn't be any riders today but remembered that he might be hiking, too, unless their plans changed due to the weather.

She was restless, hemmed in not only by the rain but by circumstance. She couldn't spontaneously visit Theo to discuss their future, if any, because Luke would be there, and she didn't know what Theo might have told him about their relationship. Merely thinking that word caused Maura to pull a face. It was such a generic term and could mean anything. Or worse, nothing at all.

Still, it wasn't likely that Theo would talk to Luke about her…*them*…considering their time in the Glen was now coming to an end. They'd be staying for the festival, but what would be the point in lingering afterward? Theo didn't have to wait until the farm was sold. If time was running out for Theo, it certainly was for Maura, too.

She heard Maddie on the phone upstairs in her bedroom and went into the den and her father's desk, where she'd found the envelope with the loan agreement. By the time she'd searched through every drawer, looking for any piece of paper or bank statement confirming the loan repayment, Maddie was coming downstairs.

"What're you doing?" she asked, seeing Maura leaving the den.

"I… I was just looking for…" she stammered, thinking of an excuse. But looking at her sister's face, both puzzled and a tad concerned, Maura knew this was the time. "Mads, let's go sit in the living room. I have something to tell you."

When Maura finished speaking, silence fell over the room. Maddie had averted her face partway through, staring bleakly out the bay window at the rain. After what seemed like ages, she rubbed her hands across her face, took a long breath and asked, "Have you told Theo?"

Maura shook her head.

"Do it. Right away." Then she stood up and left the room.

Maura blinked back unexpected tears. She'd never seen her sister with such a grim, unyielding expression. *What did you expect? If you'd told her in the beginning, you both could have dealt with the problem.* She knew Maddie would forgive her, hopefully in a matter of days. As for Theo…the odds of their newfound relationship continuing up to the festival and beyond weren't looking great.

"Have you got rain gear?" Finn asked.

"Nothing good enough." Cell phone in hand, Theo walked over to the kitchen window. The rain was still hammering down. "I'd be up for it, but I wouldn't want Luke to come. He's only been out with me once and—"

"Yeah, not a good idea. I'd cancel myself but Shawn is still keen. We'll probably only walk to the junction."

Where the off trail joined up with the main one, Theo was thinking. "I could leave Luke here on his own, but it's a rainy day and he'd probably get antsy." There was the option of Luke helping out in some way at the Stuarts', but he figured there'd be no riders that day, and it wasn't fair to expect Maura and Maddie to be supervising his son. The other problem, an inescapable one, was that Trish had texted first thing that morning to ask if he'd had the discussion yet about Luke's coming school year.

"Honestly, I think Luke and I should bow out today, Finn. Another time?"

"Can't say I blame you. For sure, another time. Talk to you later," he said, hanging up.

Luke appeared at the kitchen door as Theo was setting his phone onto the table. "Are we still going today or what?" he asked.

"Finn and Shawn are, but I decided it wasn't a good idea for us to go." He saw the disappointed frown and added, "Maybe we could check out another movie in Rutland."

"Sure." He didn't sound enthusiastic.

"Got any other ideas?"

"What if I went next door to see if I can help with anything?"

"I doubt there'll be any riders today, Luke." Theo gestured to the kitchen window.

"Still, there's other work to be done, you know. Mucking out, or grooming, or whatever."

Theo couldn't help but smile. None of those terms would have been familiar, much less of interest, to his son before coming to the Glen. "Maura and her sister might be busy. I know they still have some organizing for the festival, and it's only a week away now."

"Can you text them and find out?"

Theo sighed. Clearly his son wasn't getting his hint about infringing on the Stuarts' hospitality. "I suppose." But when he went to text Maura, the earlier one from his ex popped up in the thread of messages. Perhaps right now, he thought, and the promised movie could help soften the inevitable blow when he told him his mother's news.

"Tomorrow's Friday, and won't you be riding with Katie again?"

"Oh, right. Yeah."

"So maybe wait to visit the farm until tomorrow morning?"

His shrug was half-hearted, but Theo figured he'd be fine with a movie. "Okay, so a movie for sure, after lunch. I'll check what's playing…but first, um… I have something to pass by you. Have a seat."

He'd barely begun when the first interruption came. "She's getting *married*? To *Joel*?"

"I'm sure you suspected that would happen, didn't you?" Theo was a bit worried by the look of horror on Luke's face but kept his voice level. "And, uh, do you have a problem with Joel?"

"He's okay, I guess," Luke mumbled. "But he's really boring, and he talks a *lot*!"

Boring was okay, Theo decided, hiding a smile. He went on to explain Trish's options: move with them to Washington State in early August or live with Theo. After a year, they could renegotiate.

"So if I went there, I'd have to switch schools?"

Theo tried to find something to counter the growing unease on his son's face. "It would only be a year and—"

"I'd be leaving all my friends, that I've known forever!" He leaped to his feet. "And…and if I live with you, that means I'll be alone while you're at the hospital! Like last year, when you had to cancel a lot of my weekends with you because you had to work."

This was the dilemma Theo had struggled with since getting Trish's ultimatum. His position in Emergency meant long, unpredictable hours. Luke was twelve, going on thirteen, but would still need some kind of supervision and, especially, companionship. "I'm hoping to figure that out, Luke."

He cringed at the pessimistic tone of his voice and took a deep breath, about to aim for a more positive note when Luke shouted, "No way for any of this! It's not fair!" He ran out of the room and thumped upstairs to his bedroom.

Theo decided to let Luke have some time to himself and was about to make sandwiches for lunch when his phone pinged. It was the real-estate agent.

"I have an interested party," she told him when he answered. "It's a property development firm in Burlington. They want to know if they can send a couple of people out to have a look at your place. Probably an engineer of some kind and an architect. I'm not sure. Is there a day early next week when they could come?"

"I think so. Hang on." Theo checked his phone calendar, noting only the festival on the Thursday, which was a holiday anyway. "Any day but obviously not the Fourth."

"Great. I'll get back to you as soon as I know."

After she hung up, Theo sat for a while, thinking that despite living in the idyllic bubble of Maple Glen, events in the outside world were ticking along at normal speed. He'd simply forgotten that, although Trish's news should have been a reminder. He closed his eyes, his mind suddenly going back to Luke's last words—*"It's not fair!"*— as he left the kitchen. *My sentiments exactly, my boy*. It didn't seem fair that his return here should raise so many conflicting emotions, the strongest being a desire to stay.

There was no way around the problem, he knew. Leaving the Glen was inevitable, and it was time he and Luke accepted that reality. He picked up his phone again and, wandering into the living room, browsed movie options and times. There were a couple that might appease Luke.

When he returned to the kitchen to make lunch, he noticed the back door was ajar. Frowning, he peered out to the yard before closing the door. Then a gut instinct led him to the bottom of the staircase. "Luke? You ready for lunch?"

No answer. He took the stairs two at a time and strode down the hall to Luke's room, which was empty. Swearing under his breath, he phoned Maura. The call went to voice mail, and he left a brief message asking her to let him know if Luke had gone over to their place.

Almost ten minutes later, she called. "Hi, Theo. Sorry I didn't get back to you sooner, but I was charging my phone, and yes, he's here. Is everything okay? He seems a bit out of sorts."

"He's upset about some news I had to share with him. Um, I'll come over and get him, okay?"

"Sure, but he's fine. He and Maddie are grooming the donkeys. Do you want him home?"

Theo figured that donkey grooming would work better than a movie. "No, no, it's okay. We'd talked about a movie but obviously he'd rather be there."

There was a brief pause. Then she said, "You're welcome to come by, too. An extra hand with grooming and all."

Her light laugh sounded a bit strained. Perhaps he ought to go over, make sure Luke hadn't arrived there at an awkward time. He recalled Maddie rushing out of the meeting yesterday after Shawn's introduction. Perhaps there was some emotional aftermath she was dealing with. He'd check out the situation and bring Luke home if necessary. Besides, looking ahead to the future, there would be fewer opportunities to spend time with Maura.

"Sure, okay. Thanks."

He wrapped up the sandwiches he'd made and was about to head for the car, but noting the rain was still teeming down, he ran upstairs to get a change of clothes for Luke. The fact that the boy had run off like that worried him. It might be no big deal here, because other than the Stuart farm, there were few places for him to go. But in Augusta…one more issue to deal with, he figured, as he drove next door.

Despite his instant apology to Maura when she opened the kitchen back door, Theo saw that something was troubling her. Perhaps Luke had told them about the plans for the coming year.

"Come on in," she said. "I told Luke you were coming over but…"

"Was he unhappy about that?"

"Not exactly, and it seemed he was expecting you to show up."

"We had a bit of a…not an argument, more like a tiff."

"Oh? Do you want to talk about it?" She motioned to a kitchen chair and sat opposite.

He set the bag of sandwiches on the table and slumped onto the chair. "It had to do with an ultimatum from my ex—Trish." He saw the gleam of interest in her eyes. "She's getting married and moving out of state. What she wants is for Luke to either decide to go with her for a year or stay with me."

"Ouch. That's a tough one for a twelve-year-old."

"Tell me about it. I've heard his arguments. Anyway, I'm sure he'll get used to the idea eventually, and at least there's the festival next week. We're definitely staying for that, now I've committed my land for parking."

"That's great, Theo. I was hoping…you know…that you'd be around a bit longer."

"I was, too, Maura." He reached across the table for her hand. "I think staying for the festival has always been in the cards after our…you know…our decision to get to know one another more. To enjoy being together."

She squeezed his hand before withdrawing hers. "Yes," she murmured.

Her lack of enthusiasm was puzzling, but Theo guessed she might be thinking about the For Sale sign at the front of his property. "And you'll let me know if there's anything Luke and I can do to help you and Maddie—for next week, I mean."

"For sure." She got up and went over to the counter, staring out the window over the sink.

Theo wondered if she and Maddie had had a difficult conversation about Shawn, after the meeting yesterday. That could explain the flat response to his offer of help. This obviously wasn't a good time for entertaining unexpected visitors.

"Say, you know what? I'll take these sandwiches out to

Luke and give him and Maddie a hand with the grooming. Then we'll head out, as there's a movie we might see in Rutland."

That seemed to rouse more energy from her. "Sure, okay. It's just that Mads and I still have to assign people to tables and map out where they'll go."

"No problem." He stood to leave, but some impulse made him add, "I have some work cut out for me, too. There's a potential buyer coming early next week, and I have yet to finish going through everything in Uncle Stan's office. Okay, well…see you tomorrow?"

He waited a few seconds before she finally murmured, "Sure."

Theo decided that was all he was going to get from her and headed to the barn. Something was definitely amiss with the woman he cared for, and the dark cloud hanging over him since Luke's outburst was just getting bigger and bigger.

Chapter Fourteen

"I understand why you didn't tell him yesterday," Maddie said, "but don't leave it any longer. Especially if people are coming to look at the property. They have a right to know about the possibility that the acreage will be different."

"I know that, Mads, but first I think you and I need to go through every bit of paper left in the house to find out if Dad repaid the loan." Maura slipped her boots on and followed her sister out the door to the barn.

"We've seen his accounts and there's no record of any payment."

"What about the fifty-dollar withdrawals every month, right up to Dad's stroke? He could have been giving that money to Stan and Vera."

Maddie snorted. "It would have barely made a dent in the total amount."

"Still…"

"Which is why you need to tell Theo, so he can search for any papers, too," Maddie said as she headed for Jake's stall.

Maura scanned the barn, looking for Shep. She'd let him out of the house earlier and figured he'd go to the barn, where he usually parked outside Roger's stall. Both Shep and Roger had adjusted to the change in their routine at the farm. Shep spent the day with Roger, either in the barn or wandering the fields. Nights he slept in the kitchen and was always ready and waiting at the door every morning, just past daybreak. She and Maddie were now used to having a dog around and had talked about getting another one. That idea would have to be on hold, though, given recent developments. *Like Shawn Harrison living in the Glen. Like Maddie deciding to stay...or not. Like if our business keeps going.*

She whistled, and seconds later Shep came running into the barn. His feet were covered with mud. "Uh-oh," Maura said. "Have you checked the riding ring this morning?" she called across the barn to Maddie. "It might be too muddy."

"What next!" Maddie muttered as she closed Jake's stall door and stomped outside.

Maura knew she wasn't off the hook for keeping the loan a secret, and Shawn's return was the other curveball thrown Maddie's way. She'd have to make amends somehow—for her part, at least. If only her sister and Shawn could strike some kind of friendly rapport, something like the one she and Theo had agreed to. *Though the connection between us is more than friendly. Our kiss when we were at Walter Ingram's place was hardly platonic, and now...*

Maddie returned seconds later. "It's muddy, but not overly. I think we can go ahead." She went to Jake's stall and led him out of the barn.

Maura knew what was on her sister's mind. They couldn't afford to lose bookings two days in a row. Of course, the regulars canceled yesterday had rebooked, but not the new client.

She got Roger ready, and she and Shep led him out to the field. They hadn't used Roger for riding yet because she and Maddie had decided one of them needed to ride him first, to see how he handled their weight. Walter had said Roger was used to working, and his previous owner had ridden him. But considering his vision problems, she and Maddie wanted him to get used to carrying one of them.

She met her sister leading Lizzie into the ring. "What time did you ask Ashley to come?"

"About nine thirty. Katie's due at ten, but I figured Ashley could spend that time with Lizzie, so the two can get used to one another."

"How is she working out?"

"Fine. She walked with Matilda on Wednesday."

"And Luke, too?" Maura grinned.

"Yeah. They definitely hit it off. Speaking of Luke, didn't he promise Katie he'd be here today?"

"I'm sure he'll show up." Maura thought back to the dark mood the boy was in yesterday and hoped he and Theo had worked something out. "Who else is coming? Cathy or Nancy?"

"I thought we'd manage on our own today with Ashley and, hopefully, Luke. I'll lead Lizzie and you can monitor the two kids from behind."

Maura knew Cathy had mentioned changing or even canceling her volunteer hours because of the summer holidays and having to arrange childcare. She and Maddie had discussed hiring one of the volunteers part-time, figuring wages might be more incentive. But that was another option that would have to be put aside until they worked out a loan repayment to Theo.

"Plus, Luke won't be around for the whole summer, right? And come September, Ashley will only be available on weekends. Then we'll need Nancy and Cathy during the week, assuming both will be able to help," Maddie said.

One more complication to deal with, Maura thought.

At least her sister didn't mention the possibility that she might no longer be involved then.

The sound of a vehicle coming up the drive diverted them from more serious talk about the future of the business, something Maura was happy to shelve for another day. She left Maddie and walked around to the front, where Ashley's father, Ed, was dropping her off. He was backing up his pickup when he stopped at Maura's approach and rolled down his window.

"Hey, Maura! Just want to tell you that Betty hasn't signed up for a table yet, but she wants one. Can you set one aside for her? She's bringing along some of her art."

"Of course. I'll phone her with details since I don't have her email."

Ed and Betty Watson were a few years older than her and Maddie, and their group's teen exploits in the Glen had provided inspiration for Finn and the gang—like the annual summer bonfire at the end of August and stealing jack-o'-lanterns at Halloween.

As she watched Ed reverse and drive away, she couldn't help but think how the Glen was such a unique place with its lore and traditions continuing through the generations. She was grateful to be part of that cycle and she wished Maddie could stay permanently and be a part of it, too.

Ashley headed for the riding ring, where Maddie was waiting with Lizzie. Minutes later, another car turned onto the driveway. It was Katie and her mother, a bit earlier than planned. Fortunately, at that moment, Luke pushed his way through the cedar trees.

Luke gave her a quick nod but greeted Katie with a big smile, so Maura figured the ride should be okay.

Ashley returned to greet Katie and pushed Katie's wheelchair, the three chatting all the way to the riding ring, oblivious to the adults trailing behind. As soon as the group reached the gate, Shep spotted them from the adjacent field and ran to greet them.

Katie squealed with pleasure as the dog leaped up to lick her face. "When did you get a dog?"

"It's a long story," Maddie began. "See that donkey in the far field? His name is Roger, and he and Shep here are best friends."

"Walter Ingram brought them because their owner had to sell his farm and couldn't keep them," Luke added. "And Roger can only see out of one eye, so Shep is like his Seeing Eye dog."

Katie mulled this over. "I think I'm going to like Shep and Roger."

Katie's mother smiled at Maura and whispered, "Another happy experience for Katie, and thank you. Is it okay with you if I make a quick run to the bakery here? My hubby loves their cinnamon rolls."

Maura nodded and watched her dash off as soon as they'd helped Katie up onto the saddle. It was a good sign that Katie's mother had the confidence to leave her daughter with them, even for a brief period. She noted Luke, Katie and Ashley were deep in conversation about something and was about to say, "All set?" when a loud barking ensued, and she swung around from her position feet away from Lizzie's hindquarters to see Shep pacing on the other side of the riding ring. Then she noticed the gate was slightly ajar. Shep was as observant as Maura, and he slipped through the gap into the ring, running eagerly toward them.

"Maddie!" Maura called out to her sister, who turned around and immediately tightened her grip on Lizzie's bridle.

The three kids had been pleased at Shep's arrival, but not Lizzie, who reared her head up and snorted a warning.

Shep appeared oblivious to this and trotted up to Luke, eager for a pat or a treat. Maura tensed, watching Luke casually reach down to run his hand over Shep's head and then grasp the dog by the collar and slowly lead him away from Lizzie.

Maura felt herself relax. Luke was taking Shep out of the ring, but Lizzie wasn't appeased. She snorted again, pawing at the ground with her front right foot. She was making a point, Maura figured, and was about to tell Maddie that perhaps they ought to get Katie down before Lizzie's mood worsened.

But it was Katie who solved the problem, as she began stroking Lizzie's neck and mane, murmuring soothing sounds and whispering words that only she and Lizzie could hear. The gate closed, leaving Shep whining on the other side of it. Luke returned to his position, and Maddie raised an eyebrow at Maura, who nodded. *Don't underestimate the power of kids*, she thought.

Then Maddie said, "Let's walk, people."

The rest of the ride was uneventful, and Maura even had a chance to mentally replay yesterday's talk with Theo in the kitchen. Her instinct to cheer him up and reassure him came automatically. For a few seconds she could forget about her promise to Maddie and the sickening possibility that telling him about the loan would threaten any hope of a future together. She'd be facing that hurdle soon enough, though, because Katie was the only rider that day, and there'd be no excuse to procrastinate further.

Theo couldn't remember the last time he'd seen Luke so animated.

"And Ashley said this youth club is kinda divided into age groups. Like twelve to fifteen forming one group, but the older teens—sixteen and seventeen—mostly doing their own thing." He shrugged. "Whatever that is."

Theo looked down at the sandwich on his plate, hiding his smile. "And you're going to check it out today, at the community center?"

"Do you mind? The meeting starts at four, and then after the talking and so on there's pizza and a movie. Ashley said she and her dad will pick me up and bring me back here."

Do I mind? It was sweet of Luke to think of his father, maybe sad and alone on a Friday evening, but plans were forming in Theo's mind. "That's great, son. I'm glad you'll get a chance to meet some of the Glen youngsters."

Luke frowned. "Preteens and teenagers aren't youngsters, Dad!"

"Oh, no, of course not. Did I sound like an old fogy there?"

"Definitely. Anyway, do you want me to help you bring up the rest of the boxes from the basement before I go?"

Theo was feeling as if he and Luke had stumbled into some alternate universe—a metaverse or whatever it was called, and he planned to take full advantage of the unexpected opportunity. When Luke went downstairs for the first load of boxes, Theo texted Maura and invited her for dinner. A home-cooked meal, he wrote, but nothing gourmet. He was about to go help Luke when she replied, Sure, thanks. What time?

He puzzled over this apparent lack of enthusiasm, but reasoned text messages could be misleading. Though she had seemed out of sorts yesterday. *No, don't make assumptions about people's moods, Theo. You've been led down that path too often. Especially when you were just a few years older than Luke, and decided the girl you dreamed about nightly wasn't at all interested in you.*

"Dad? There's a big one I need help with," Luke hollered from the foot of the basement stairs.

"Coming." He set his phone on the table and went downstairs.

"That was delicious," Maura said as she set her fork down on her plate. "But seriously, too much for me."

Theo eyed her leftover steak and salad. The meat wouldn't go to waste, anyway, not with a growing preteen in the house. Still, something wasn't right… She'd arrived fifteen minutes late, with no excuse or apology, and had turned down his offer of a predinner glass of wine. An early start in the morning, she'd claimed.

"How about coffee?"

"Okay, thanks." She peered around the kitchen. "I haven't been inside this place since… I don't know… I think when your aunt and uncle celebrated an anniversary, maybe, when I was on break from college."

"It hasn't changed since I used to come for the summer," he said, getting up to start the coffee.

"I suppose whoever buys it will want to renovate— maybe even gut it and start over. What do you think?"

Theo thought about the people from a development company coming on Monday and figured a teardown was more likely. But that was in the future and not a topic he wanted to raise with a kid-free evening ahead.

"I guess. Luke and I are gradually getting things cleared out. We brought up the last of the boxes from the basement today, and all that's left down there are some rusting tools and general stuff that can go to a dump or wherever people take things in the area." When she failed to reply, he turned away from setting up the coffee maker. She was staring blankly at the basement door, as if expecting someone—

Luke?—to pop up any second with another box. Theo shook his head. *You're making too much out of this, pal.*

He switched on the machine. "Let's have it in the living room—or the parlor, as Aunt Vera used to say." He reached for her hand as she got to her feet. A waft of some unknown but heady fragrance rose up with her, and he put his arms around her, drawing her against his chest. She tucked her face into the crook of his shoulder and time stood still, until the coffee maker beeped, and she slowly pulled away. Regretfully? he wondered, noting an unreadable expression on her face.

"The coffee smells good," she said.

Small talk? What's going on? He stifled his impatience. This was the teenage Maura he remembered—unaccountably shifting from one mood to another. "Why don't you go into the living room while I get the coffee, and there are cookies from Sue's bakery."

"No sugar in my coffee."

"Hey, do you think I'd forget?"

Her smile was the most genuine of the evening, and Theo thought maybe the dinner date wasn't going to be a bust after all. Not if she was remembering the same rainy day he was.

"How old were we?" she asked.

"Twelve. Luke's age."

"And how come the three of us were alone?" Her brow wrinkled in thought.

"Your parents had to go pick up something at the co-op in Wallingford."

"But why did we make coffee? That's so random."

"We didn't. It was in the machine, left from breakfast."

"No wonder it was so awful."

"Yeah, and all the sugar we dumped in to make it taste better—"

"Didn't work." She laughed with him. "I swore I'd never drink coffee again."

"Yet here we are."

"Yes, Theo. And here we are."

Her soft voice and wistful look filled his heart with a longing he hadn't had in so many years he could barely identify it. *Love?* He pulled her close again, kissing her gently at first and then urgently. Forget the mystery moods and the memories of an unreachable teen. This was adult Maura—beautiful, tender, compassionate.

This time he broke away, lifted by the hope that the night was still salvageable. That whatever was on her mind would be resolved. "Living room," he murmured, letting her go.

His hands trembled as he poured coffee. But by the time he was taking the two mugs with a well-balanced plate of cookies into the living room, he was calm and steady—except for an increased heart rate.

She was standing in the center of the room, looking thoughtfully at the papers strewn on the side table next to the sofa and the pile of boxes stacked against one wall.

"Oh, sorry about this," he said. "I decided to keep everything on the ground floor, to simplify hauling it away once I've gone through it all."

He was shoving aside papers to set down the coffee when she said, "Theo, I have something to tell you."

Her face told him two things: more romance that night was not going to happen, and he wasn't going to like whatever she had to say.

Chapter Fifteen

Processing it all was a challenge for him, and Maura's anxiety was shifting to impatience. He finally believed her when she handed him her phone with the photos of the loan agreement. She paced the room, her hands curled into tight fists, while he read.

Then he looked up from where he was sitting on the sofa. "This explains the cashier's check. When I went to see the bank manager about Stan and Vera's accounts, I found out my uncle had withdrawn ten thousand in a cashier's check, made out to your father."

"Why didn't you say something?"

"It was only a few days ago. I figured your father had sold Uncle Stan something, or that the debt was the other way around and my uncle was repaying your father. I've been searching for a record of it." He handed her the phone. "How long have *you* known about this?" His eyes fixed on hers.

She averted her face, uncomfortable under his cool appraisal. "A couple of months before you arrived. I suppose I was hoping all of this was just a mistake or—"

"A bad dream?"

He smiled for the first time since she'd blurted her secret minutes ago. But it was a sad smile, Maura thought. "It's just that we don't have the money to pay back the loan, Theo."

"I assume Maddie knows?"

She nodded but refrained from telling him her sister had been in the dark until yesterday.

"I'm not too worried about the money, Maura, but there's another problem. From what I can see in those pictures, the agreement was signed by a notary, making it a legal document. There's probably a record somewhere, which means that if I'm going to sell this property—"

"Our pastures would be included in your tract." She'd figured that out herself, when she first found the papers, but her focus had been on how to repay the loan.

"I'll need to get another survey done to include the land in question, and also let my Realtor know. I have a prospective buyer coming after the weekend."

Maura watched him rub his forehead, stress obviously mounting inside him. She wished she could turn back time to the decision she'd made weeks ago. For now, she was grateful that he wasn't angry.

"This may complicate our timeline here. Luke and I planned a road trip after leaving the Glen, but that wouldn't be until after the festival anyway, so…"

So his plans would be delayed but not changed. That reality hurt. "Maybe there's something we can do, before you contact your Realtor." She suddenly thought of the monthly withdrawals from her father's account. "My dad might have paid back the loan or was in the process of doing so. Your uncle must have a record, too. Why don't we start looking?"

"Worth a try. Let's each take a box."

She heard him sigh as he slowly got up from the sofa. He seemed drained of energy, and she felt another pang of guilt. "I'm sorry, Theo. I knew I'd have to deal with this, but I suppose I unconsciously chose to forget about the whole mess until you came back."

"I've been back almost two weeks, Maura."

There was no good response to that, other than to tell him his return had raised feelings she hadn't had for many years. She'd been content to drift along with the possibilities of what his presence in the Glen could mean for her, without considering the impact of her secret.

Rather than reply to this, she lifted a box from the pile and took it into the kitchen, where she set it on the table. Seconds later he joined her, and they worked silently, wary—or so Maura thought—of continuing the discussion about why she hadn't told him sooner. When she finished with the first box, she returned it to the living room, placing it against the opposite wall.

Four boxes later, with no luck, she asked, "Can you think of any place your uncle might have stored valuable papers? You told me he was a pack rat, but there must be someplace in the house where he kept important things."

"Seriously, I don't really know. When they went into the nursing home, I hired a company from Rutland to check on the place every couple of weeks."

A horrifying thought occurred to her. "Haven't you already had boxes hauled away?"

He held up his hands, as if in surrender. "Yes, and I've been thinking these last few minutes that what we're looking for may already have been sent to recycling."

Maura blew out a mouthful of sour breath. "We may as well finish going through what's here, just in case." She left the kitchen and returned with another box.

"This isn't turning out to be the night I'd anticipated," he joked.

His faint smile brought one from her, though she refrained from saying that the night *she'd* envisioned after deciding to confess could have been so much worse. She stopped counting the number of boxes they rummaged through, but each time she went back for another, she noticed the piles were shifting from one side of the living room to the other. Her hope of finding any mention of the loan was fading fast. She was about to suggest they call it a night when the kitchen door flew open and Luke rushed into the room.

"What's going on?" he asked, looking from Theo to Maura, then at the boxes and papers scattered across the table.

"We're searching for some important papers that my uncle might have had," Theo explained. "Uh… Maura was here for dinner and I…uh…asked her to help me."

"What kind of papers?"

"Relating to a legal document Uncle Stan signed, years ago. So how was the youth group?"

"Great, Dad. And guess who the speaker was tonight? Finn McAllister!"

Maura exchanged grins with Theo.

"You mean *Mr.* McAllister?" Theo teased.

"He told us to call him Finn. Anyways, he was telling us some cool stories about rescuing people on the Trail and how he got into it. Did you know he and his father went hiking on it when he was really young? Like eight or nine."

"No, I didn't know that, but I went with him a few times, when we were teens. Sounds like you had a good time."

"I did, but the pizza wasn't as good as the one we got from Wallingford." He was staring at the boxes on the table and asked, "Do you want some help with that?"

Maura smiled at the half-hearted question. "We're good, Luke," she said. "I'll be going in a few minutes anyway."

Luke nodded and was about to leave the room when he

turned to say, "Oh, and by the way, Finn told me to ask you if you and I want to go walking with him tomorrow, to make up for yesterday when we had to cancel because of the rain."

"Uh, sure, if you want to."

"I do because he told us about some interesting things to look for when we hike on the part leading out from the Glen."

"Okay, I'll text him before I go to bed."

"And he said that another guy… Shawn?…might come, too." He paused a second before saying, "I'm going to bed now. I'm beat. G'night, Dad. 'Night, Maura."

"Wonder of wonders," Theo murmured after Luke left. "If we were in Augusta, I'd be lucky to get him off the recliner and away from his PlayStation console to come for a meal."

"The miracle of Maple Glen." Maura met his gaze for a second and then turned her attention to the table. "And… um… I'm beat myself, Theo. Can we continue this tomorrow after your hike?"

"Sure. I'll let you know when we're back."

She plucked her cardigan from the back of a kitchen chair and headed for the door.

"Wait," he said, as she opened it. He crossed the room in three strides. "Look, don't worry too much about all of this. We'll deal with whatever happens when…well… when it happens." After a minute, he added with a wry grin, "Worst-case scenario, I just forgive the loan." He placed his hands on her shoulders, and she felt her tension give way as he drew her close against him, his arms a refuge from the turmoil of questions and self-doubt. But her certainty that he was going to kiss her faded as he gently pulled back. "I'll call you tomorrow," he whispered.

When he closed the door behind her, she stood in the

yard a moment longer to collect her thoughts and calm the surge of longing. The night hadn't been as awful as she'd expected and there was a plan to meet again. But he hadn't kissed her when he could have.

"Dad? Dad!"

That voice has no place in my dream about Maura. Theo opened his eyes, squinting against the sunlight streaming from the bedroom window, then turned over to see Luke hovering in the doorway.

"It's late," his son was saying, "and we slept in. You have to hurry." Then he vanished, his footsteps thudding downstairs.

Have my son and I traded places, he wondered, *as in some old movie?* He swung his legs out of bed and sat on its edge, rubbing his eyes. He hadn't slept well. After Maura left, he'd gone through a few more boxes until fatigue and despair forced him to stop. For a couple of hours in the night, he'd made a mental tour through the farmhouse, thinking of possible hiding places. Then he'd segued to Maura, her pale face and trembling lips as she'd told him about the loan, her weak answer when he'd pressed her about keeping the information from him.

And always, lurking in the shadows of his mind, was the question *why didn't she trust me enough to tell me sooner?* Okay, maybe not the first few days he'd been back, but surely after that pact they'd made to enjoy one another's company, to renew a kind of friendship and see where it might lead. Which begged the question, could that lead anywhere now? Could he trust her to be transparent with him in the future, if there even *was* a future with her?

He dressed quickly, shying away from that last question, and hurried into the kitchen as Luke was swallowing the end of a piece of toast and peanut butter. Crunching loudly, Luke pointed to another slice of toast on the counter.

Another first, Theo thought. The wake-up, and now breakfast. *We* have *traded places!*

"We better take the car," Luke said after he gulped down a mouthful of milk.

"Right. I packed some sandwiches last night before I went to bed. They're—"

"I put them in your pack." Luke pointed to the small backpack on a kitchen chair.

"Great, thanks. Where's yours?"

"In the car. And there's your fob. I took it from the hallway table. To save some time."

Theo had no idea how long this version of his twelve-year-old son would last, but he intended to enjoy every minute. "Okay, well, let's go!"

He was turning onto the county road when Luke spoke again. "So…uh…is Maura like…your *girlfriend*?"

Theo kept his eyes on the road ahead, giving himself some time to find an answer. "Well, she's not a girl anymore, but—"

"Dad, c'mon."

"We…we're getting to know one another again. It's been a long time, so we like being with each other and…well, we'll see what happens."

"What about Maddie?"

Theo turned to look at his son. "What do you mean, what about Maddie?"

"You told me the three of you always hung out together. Is it different now? 'Cause you seem to be around Maura more than Maddie."

Theo stopped the car at the crosswalk before the church. The McAllister place, where they'd agreed to meet Finn and Shawn, was several yards ahead, but Theo figured he needed to wrap up this discussion now. "I like Maddie very much, as a good friend. What I feel for Maura is a bit stronger, more special."

"Like what you used to feel for Mom?"

Theo winced. It was a loaded question and one he'd prefer to discuss anywhere else but in the car minutes before hiking with friends. "Luke, I think we need to talk about this later, all right? When we have more time."

"Sure," Luke mumbled and stared out the window.

Theo took his foot off the brake and continued along the street, feeling the silence pressing in. He hoped the day's hike wasn't going to be ruined. He pulled up in front of Finn's place where the two men were standing by the gate and turned off the engine. Luke waved, then glanced with a quick smile at Theo before jumping out the door. Theo's mood rose a notch. Everything was going to be okay.

Finn spent a few minutes going over some rules with Luke. Basically, the same ones Theo had mentioned days ago, on their own walk. He noted that Shawn was quiet, smiling at Luke's chatter with Finn about last night's youth club meeting. But once they crossed the bridge into the woods, Luke fell silent. Theo was proud of his son's intuitive sense that small talk could wait until their guides indicated otherwise. When they reached the first blue blaze, Finn stopped and held up a finger.

"Hear that? A mockingbird, you think, Shawn?"

"Could be. If Walter Ingram was here, he'd know for sure. Right now, I'm seeing some tracks." Shawn pointed to the side of the path. "Deer. And see that?" His finger moved beyond, off the path to his right. "Deer scat," he added at Luke's frown.

Luke moved closer to the cluster of almond-shaped droppings nestled among some mossy plants. "Oooh, weird."

The men laughed. "Not much for such a big creature," Shawn agreed.

"Will we see a bear?"

"I hope not." Shawn's grin took the edge off his answer. "Okay, let's keep going." He led the way up the first sharp incline, which Theo recalled would bring them closer to the junction of the off trail and the Long Trail itself.

For a long time, there were no other sounds in the forest but their breathing and the crunch of boots on vegetation. When they reached the first white blaze, indicating the main trail, Shawn stopped and, looking at both Finn and Theo, asked, "Up or down?"

"What's your preference?" Theo asked.

Shawn glanced quickly at Luke. "Maybe up and avoid the ice beds. The White Rocks cliffs trail?"

It was the right call, Theo knew, given the presence of two inexperienced hikers—he and his son.

"I know a good lookout where we can rest and have lunch. Maybe decide there to go on or go back," Finn said.

By now Luke was at the end of the group. Theo slowed down and waited for him to catch up. When he did, he patted him on the shoulder and murmured, "You're doing great." Then he fell into place behind Luke. If his son needed to quit before the lookout Finn had mentioned, they would.

There were a few more stops along the way, as Finn and Shawn indicated types of flowers or trees. Once a coyote fled from the path ahead, and they watched silently until it disappeared into the brush. Theo was beginning to question his own ability to reach the lookout, wherever it was, when Finn rounded a curve in the path ahead and suddenly halted. He was taking his backpack off and Shawn was gazing through binoculars as Theo and Luke caught up to them.

Theo remembered the view at once, though he'd only seen it a couple of times as a teenager. White Rocks Mountain, across the shallow valley, its namesake white rocks sprawling down its northwest side as if some mythical titan had scattered them in a game. Or in a rage, Theo thought, for their appearance was both awesome and frightening. No one spoke for a long time, until Finn said, "Lunch?"

Then packs were opened, and the sounds of containers popping open or sandwiches being unwrapped echoed in the quiet. Theo sat next to Shawn, enjoying the sight of Luke wolfing down his lunch while keeping his eyes on the scene across from them. Theo ate half his sandwich before taking a break to ask Shawn if he'd found a place to live.

"I gave up my place in Bennington, since it was a bit too far away. For now, I'm staying at Bernie's B and B."

That seemed appropriate, Theo thought. "Is it a bit like going home for you?"

"Not really. Bernie's changed it around so much, but I guessed which room used to be mine when we lived there, and it was available, so that was pretty cool."

Theo noticed Luke turn their way, listening to the talk. He was about to mention that his farmhouse was for sale, but Shawn would know that already from the posted sign. Besides, the proximity to the Stuart place might be problematic for Maddie.

As if on the same wavelength, Shawn suddenly said, "I still haven't seen Maddie around. I was sorry I missed her at the festival meeting."

"Had to leave early to feed the donkeys, I think," Theo said.

"Donkeys!" Shawn smiled and shook his head. "Who'd have thought?"

"Yeah, right," Theo murmured. He saw Luke edge closer to them.

"That was Maura's idea, wasn't it?" Finn put in. "When Maddie came home after Mr. Stuart died, Maura convinced her to help out with the riding therapy program she'd set up."

"Oh?" was all Shawn said.

Then Finn added, "Maddie promised to stay for a year at any rate, and that'll be coming up by the end of the summer, I think."

Theo was taken aback by what Finn knew, but then he thought of the Glen grapevine. He opted to keep eating.

After a moment, Shawn asked, his voice husky, "How *is* Maddie?"

"She's great!" Luke suddenly interjected.

The three men exchanged smiles, and a few minutes later, Shawn stood. "Keep going or head back?"

Finn said, "Maybe head back? I'm on dinner duty tonight and have some shopping yet."

Theo wasn't about to argue. He and Luke gathered up their lunch remains, and as Luke was slinging his small backpack on, Theo bent down to say, "Good job today, son. Pizza again tonight or…?"

Luke grinned up at him. "Yeah, but from the bakery. And, Dad, why don't we invite Maddie and Maura?"

Why not? Theo asked himself. He smiled, elated by good exercise, the beauty of nature and his son, who never ceased to surprise him.

Chapter Sixteen

Maura sat back in her chair, her gaze drifting from Shep, curled up in front of the kitchen door, to Luke, midway through his account of the hike that afternoon, then to Maddie's smile as Luke described the deer scat they'd found, and last of all, to Theo. His face shone with love and pride as his son spoke, and for the first time in her life, Maura wondered what that unconditional love of a parent for a child would feel like. Would she ever have the chance to experience it? She closed her eyes against the question, not liking what the answer might be.

"Mo?"

She blinked and sat upright to see her sister smiling at her from across the table. "Hmm?" Maura's face heated up as she realized everyone had not only finished their ice cream but also their stories of the day. Theo's grin was irksome. Almost indulgent, like parent to child. Or maybe he was thinking back to last night, the two of them in this very kitchen, rummaging through boxes.

"I asked if you and Theo could clear up while Luke and I go check the donkeys. They're still out in the field, but Roger's with them, so I figured if everything's okay we can leave them all out for the night. Weather looks good.

No rain to spook Matilda." As soon as Maddie uttered Roger's name, Shep leaped to his feet and began whining.

"He knows you're talking about Roger!" Luke exclaimed.

Now Shep was barking.

Maura grinned at Maddie and Luke. "I think you're committed to checking on Roger and the others now. And I guess you'll be taking Shep, too."

More barking and whining from Shep, standing at the door with a somewhat impatient expression on his face.

"Okay. Well, Luke, we better get going, and I'll walk you back when we're done," Maddie said, getting to her feet.

"I can find my own way," Luke protested.

Theo frowned and was about to say something when Maura interjected, "Maddie can text when you're finished over there, and I'll meet you at the break in the cedar trees. You know the one, Mads." She saw that Luke was about to protest further and added, "I'm sure I'll be ready to leave by then anyway. Maybe we should consider making a bigger gap between the two properties before the festival. That would enable people who'll be parking on Theo's land to pass through rather than walking along the road to us." She knew it was a good idea, but Theo took his time replying.

"Let's discuss that after my meeting with my Realtor. For now, I think Maddie's plan to walk Luke partway is a good one," Theo said with a tone of finality.

Back to reality, Maura was thinking. Of course, Theo was reluctant to change things on his property, which even a temporary path linking the two farms might do.

The prospect of a sale and permanent move fell over the room, and for a moment, no one moved. Then Maddie prompted, "Luke? Let's see how Roger's doing." When she and Luke stood up, Shep began leaping at the closed door. "Hold your horses, Shep!" she cried.

"Or maybe hold your donkeys," Luke suggested, and they all laughed.

The scene was almost like family but not quite, Maura was thinking. A new and different version of family, and she was struck by a desire to hold on to this moment for as long as she could. But the door closed behind them, and the room fell silent.

"What are your plans for Roger and Shep?"

Theo's unexpected question startled her. Did he have to ask? Or was he thinking they might not be able to keep them, given the possibility of Maddie leaving when her year was up?

"We're hoping to attract more riders like teens and adults, not necessarily for therapy, but for fun," she said, "and Roger is our largest animal, so he's the best candidate. Jake can handle bigger people, too, but he's younger than Roger and not as docile."

"I can attest to that." Theo grinned.

She had to smile at the image of Theo trapped between Jake and the barn door, the day he first arrived back in the Glen. Was it only a couple of weeks or so ago? How everything had changed since that day, when she'd feared her whole world was toppling down on her with the possibility of having to repay a huge loan. Not to mention the emotional equivalent of a tidal wave—meeting up again with Theo Danby, her teenage crush.

As Theo started clearing dishes, Maura felt the line of tension between them tighten. Something was bugging him, and she knew her confession last night was the reason. She got up to remove the rest of the plates and carried them over to the sink. "Do you want to talk, Theo?"

He looked up from rinsing. "We need to, Maura, but

maybe we should hold off on making decisions about the loan and the land until after I meet with the agent on Monday. Does that make sense to you?"

Was he having second thoughts about their pact to enjoy one another's company, she wondered, or worse, regretting that he'd even come back to Maple Glen? "I guess so," she finally said. She set the stack of plates and cutlery onto the counter and was turning back to the table when he grasped her arm and pulled her close.

"We'll figure something out, Maura. Try not to worry too much. I have a lot of things to work out as well."

She rested her head in the dip between his shoulder and neck, closing her eyes and trying not to imagine how this moment could go if...

Theo's cell phone chimed from the table. "Luke's probably ready to come back." He began to pull away but suddenly stopped, clutching her tighter for a second before kissing her forehead. "We *will* continue this discussion tomorrow or Monday, okay?"

"Okay."

He picked up his phone and replied to the text, then turned to Maura. "Luke's ready to come back, and I'll go with you to meet him at the cedars." Then, tucking his phone into his jeans pocket, he reached for her hand and clasped it in his as they went out the door into the quiet night. They walked quickly across the front lawn to the gap Jake had forged almost two weeks ago. "I remember doing this when we were teens. Sneaking into our mutual homes after curfew," he said in a low voice.

"Yes, though it was always the three of us."

"True, but I tried my best that last summer to have you to myself."

His light chuckle warmed her, despite a fleeting wish that she'd been more responsive back then, when she was fifteen and feared revealing her feelings to the sixteen-year-old boy next door. When she saw a flashlight's beacon bobbing their way, she dropped her hand from his.

Maddie waited on the other side of the cedars as Luke crossed through. "They're all okay," he announced, "but Shep wouldn't go inside, so we left him in the field, too." He turned briefly to Theo to say, "Maddie asked me to help out tomorrow morning 'cause the rider I helped with before—Sammy—wants to come for another session."

This was a new development, Maura thought, as Sammy had been riding every two weeks. Whatever the reason, the change was good for him and for business.

"That's great, Luke, and I have more clearing out to do." He shifted his gaze to Maura. "Talk tomorrow, then, when you're finished with your rider?"

"Okay." She pushed through the weeds around the cedars and joined Maddie, waiting with flashlight in hand.

"That was a nice evening," Maddie said as they walked across the lawn.

Maura knew her sister was fishing for an update on the status between her and Theo, but she refused to be drawn in. She wasn't ready to talk about the situation without giving in to emotion. And emotion wasn't going to help solve the problem. She glanced to the field on their right and the silhouettes of grazing donkeys. "Think we should leave Shep out for the night?"

"Worth a try. He absolutely refused to go inside when I walked Luke back."

"So this is a new development," Maura said, changing the subject. "Sammy wanting another ride after his session last week."

"Yeah, his mother phoned when Luke and I were checking on the donkeys. She said he had such a great time he didn't want to wait another week. She thinks a weekly ride will be better through the summer, to give him a break from the day camps she's enrolled him in. She also said he asked if 'that boy' who was here last time was going to help again."

"Aw, that's sweet and so nice for Luke."

"He literally swelled with pride when I repeated that to him."

Maura thought how much Luke had changed in the short time she'd known him and hoped the inevitable parting wouldn't be too hard on him, or on all of them. She'd miss him.

Once inside and on the way up to their bedrooms, Maura suddenly hugged her sister. "Thanks for being so patient and understanding with me, Mads, about keeping the loan a secret and…well…basically everything." She closed her eyes. They hadn't hugged like this since their father died, and Maura had forgotten how wonderful it was to have someone who'd understand and forgive, no matter the transgression. Or so she wanted to believe.

Maple Glen without Theo and Luke would be painful, but the village without her sister—her twin—would be devastating. She decided to do everything she could to ensure that never happened.

Theo was at loose ends. He had the place to himself and had been plugging away at sorting the rest of the stuff in the basement while Luke was next door, but now his energy, as well as his resolve, was flagging. What was the point of all this work, when he could easily hire one of those companies that swooped in, gathered everything for a flat fee and took it away? He doubted there was hidden treasure in any of the boxes, cabinets, drawers or cupboards in the entire farmhouse—unless you wanted to count a piece of paper regarding a loan made five years or so ago.

Ten thousand dollars! It wasn't a fortune but definitely not to be dismissed, as he'd so blithely done when Maura had confessed. He couldn't explain that blurted reassurance, except that she'd looked so darn sad and forlorn. And forgiving the loan was obviously a solution to the problem but, realistically, not one he could afford. He'd be paying child support—if Luke decided to move and live with his mother—until the boy was eighteen and even after that because Theo wanted his son to be able to go on to whatever postsecondary education he wished. He also had a mortgage on his condo in Augusta and a few more car payments on the impulsive purchase he'd made right after Trish left their home, and the sports car was definitely not going to stay in the family, either.

Family. Last night had felt so natural, so good. Better than any family experience he'd had since Luke's early years when he and Trish were still in love. After Maddie and Luke left to check on the donkeys, he'd been half hoping the illusion of family might continue. But then Maura had suggested they talk, and Theo'd had a bad feeling where that would lead. What he'd really wanted at that moment was to keep her in his arms and fantasize about keeping her in his life.

Long after Luke had gone to bed, he'd sat in the dark living room and mentally played through possible scenarios: forgive the loan, which meant shrugging off money he knew he himself could use, or ask the sisters to pay him back in installments, which obviously would have an impact on their business.

If he sold his property to that developer—his agent had implied a big-name company—he wouldn't have any financial problems for a long time. The only win-win solution was to forgive the loan, contingent on selling his land. He knew Maddie and Maura would be grateful. He might even be a hero in their minds. But right then, he wanted none of that. He didn't want to be that kind of hero and he didn't want gratitude, especially from Maura. The money—repaid or forgiven—would inevitably be a wedge between him and the sisters.

The best immediate course of action would be to check county records for the notarized loan agreement, and he could do that after the prospective buyers came tomorrow morning. Then he'd sit down with Maura and Maddie to discuss next steps. He scanned the room, littered with boxes. Tomorrow he'd hire a company to collect and dispense with everything.

Maybe Luke would be interested in keeping some of Uncle Stan's mementos. There was a small box of medals garnered during his uncle's military service and photograph albums meticulously collated and captioned by his aunt during Theo's summers in the Glen. Skimming through it, he'd grasped how important his visits had been to the childless couple. Most people didn't keep actual photo albums anymore, but perhaps when Luke was an adult, he'd want to share memories of Maple Glen—both his and his father's—with a child of his own.

Theo groaned. This kind of sentimental thinking wasn't like him. He'd always been a "calm under pressure" kind of person, which fit with his career. A bit like the adult Maura he was beginning to know better. For some reason she'd kept her emotions in check at a young age, though, which had resulted in the Glen gang of kids thinking she was cold. He hadn't understood her when he was a kid himself, but as an adult he figured her behavior was a defense mechanism against being hurt. Perhaps if he'd been able to realize that about her when they were teens, he might not have been deterred by her aloofness.

Back then, the dynamics of the group had seemed so complex, but in hindsight, the drama of those last two summers was plain silly.

He got up from the sofa and went into the kitchen and poured a glass of water, which he drank standing at the sink and staring out the window overlooking the rear of the property. Although he'd gone through just about everything in the basement and bedrooms, there was still the barn and tool shed. He groaned again. He checked the time, thinking that Luke might be finished helping with today's rider, the young boy Maddie had mentioned last night.

He marveled at the connections Luke had already made in the village, in a mere two weeks. Either he'd been misjudging his son or hadn't seen his potential, and the thought saddened him. Long hours at the hospital and the missed teacher interviews and school events had exacted a heavy toll on his marriage, but also on his bond with his son. That wasn't going to happen anymore, he decided, clanging his empty glass onto the kitchen counter.

The sound of a vehicle's horn pulled him back to the moment. He went out the kitchen door and rounded the corner to the front, where Walter Ingram was getting out of his pickup.

"Theo." The older man's gravelly voice broke the silence of a Sunday morning. "Came to see if Luke would like to come and help me extract some honey today for the festival."

Theo was touched by the man's thoughtfulness. "I'm sure he'd want to help, but he's at the Stuart place right now."

"Okay. I'm heading over there anyway to talk to them about the tables for the festival."

As Walter was about to get back into his truck, Theo impulsively blurted, "I'll come with you. I'm finished cleaning up here for now and feel like I need a break."

"Climb aboard," Walter said. "Guess sorting through your aunt and uncle's things has been challenging."

"No kidding," Theo agreed as he sat in the passenger seat. "My aunt and uncle were complete pack rats."

Walter chuckled. "Yep. I sometimes offered to help them remove anything they didn't want or need, but their answer was always that they were saving it all for their great-nephew." He shifted the truck into gear, made a sharp U-turn and headed back down the drive to the county road.

Theo moaned. "What I figured. Say, do you know of any local trucking companies that I could hire to haul stuff away? It needs to be sorted for recycling or donating to any charities. And then there are some things that simply need discarding somewhere, I guess."

"Sure thing. I'll contact a guy I know in Wallingford." After a slight pause, he turned Theo's way and asked, "Any word on the property sale?"

"My agent is bringing some people tomorrow to have a look at it." He decided that was enough information to pass along at the moment.

Walter nodded. "Hopefully good people who'll fit into the community."

Theo kept his thoughts about that to himself. He doubted a development company would be interested in preserving the tone of a small village. That thought nagged until they were parking alongside a car in front of the Stuart farmhouse. He was about to head toward the riding ring behind the barn when he noticed Walter getting something from the back of the truck.

He was carrying a bright green ball about the size of a large beach ball as he walked toward Theo. Up close, Theo saw that the ball was made of heavy-duty rubber.

Walter grinned as he held it aloft. "Thought it'd be good for us all to have some fun today."

Some fun would definitely be a good thing, Theo mused, as he followed Walter.

Chapter Seventeen

Maura's heart skipped a beat when she saw Theo walking her way. She and today's volunteer, Nancy, were helping Sammy down from Matilda while Luke and Maddie, with Shep's assistance, herded the other donkeys into the northeast pasture. When Sammy was safely on the ground and heading for his mother at the riding ring fence, Maura took a few minutes to remove the saddle and bridle from Matilda, setting them on top of the riding ring fence. She looked toward the barn again and this time saw Walter Ingram behind Theo. Right. He had phoned yesterday to say he'd pop around to discuss the setup for the tables on festival day.

She was a bit relieved that Theo wasn't alone, not yet ready for the talk he'd mentioned last night—the loan and what the three of them could do about it. When the men reached the riding ring, Walter spoke briefly to Sammy and his mother. Then all four headed toward her and Nancy, who was holding on to Matilda's halter. Sammy's face was lit with excitement, and Maura soon found out why.

Walter was carrying a very large green ball. As he drew near, Maura noticed Nancy tighten her grasp on Matilda's halter. She, too, had noticed the ball.

"Thought a bit of fun was in order before getting down to work this beautiful morning," Walter said.

Sammy's whoop sounded all the way to the pasture, catching the attention of not only Luke and Maddie, but the other donkeys.

"Roger and Shep played with a ball like this at their old home, so they'll get into the idea right away," Walter said. He led the way to the pasture, followed by the procession of Maura, Nancy, Matilda, Theo, Sammy and his mother. By now Maddie and Luke were waiting at the pasture gate, their faces creased with curiosity.

Maura nudged Matilda through the gate and was about to close it when Shep ran out to greet them.

"Best leave Shep with us for now," Walter advised. "He might get kicked inside there."

When everyone was lined up at the fence, Walter hurled the ball into the center of the field. It was Roger who trotted after it, braying raucously. The other donkeys watched, suspicious of this strange green object that now was flying through the air after Roger's kick. Jake got the hang of it quicker than Matilda and Lizzie, running after the ball and flicking it with a deft hoof.

"They're playing soccer!" Luke exclaimed.

"How did they learn that?" Sammy wanted to know.

"I met Roger's former owners while shopping in Wallingford the other day and they told me about this game he used to enjoy. So I went and bought a ball right away. Thought it'd be fun for the others and us." He was staring at the other donkeys when the ball suddenly landed at Lizzie's feet. "Will she get into the game or is she too ornery?" he asked.

"I'm betting she'll want to," Luke said, joined at once by Sammy's "Me too."

Everyone waited. Maura caught Theo's eye and grinned.

As if sensing the audience was expecting something from her, Lizzie slowly lowered her head to the ball, sniffed it, poked at it with one hoof and then, with a bray that must have carried all the way to the Glen, kicked it to the far side of the pasture. Roger quickly galloped after the ball, flinging it up into the air with a hoof, but when Jake tried to intervene before the next kick, Roger pivoted to nip at him.

"Uh-oh," Walter said, chuckling. "Maybe it'll take a while for them to play fair."

"They have to learn to share," Sammy affirmed.

The adults and Luke smiled at his solemn tone.

"Who's going to be brave enough to go in and retrieve the ball when they're finished with it?" Theo asked.

"They'll tire of it eventually," Walter said.

"Maybe donkeys have a short attention span, too. Right, Mom?" Sammy peered up at his mother.

"I think so," his mother said, smiling.

"We'll take away their new toy later, when the excitement has died down," Maura said and began walking toward the barn.

Theo caught up to her as the others lagged behind. "I didn't plan on coming over this early, but Walter showed up at my place to see if Luke was available to collect honey, and then he mentioned something about a fun event, and I was all set for that."

Fun. Maura could hardly recall enjoying some of that the past year, yet despite her initial misgivings about Theo and Luke's arrival in the Glen, there'd been fun times and, underlying those lighter gatherings, a sense of contentment.

"I thought maybe we could discuss the loan after lunch, if Luke goes to Walter's place."

So much for the fun part of today, she was thinking. "Sure. I'll let Maddie know. Our chat with Walter about the tables will probably be brief, so call or text after lunch."

"It's a deal," Theo murmured.

His pat on her shoulder was warm and reassuring, and Maura watched him move away, joining up with Luke and Sammy. His tall, straight physique was so familiar now she could barely remember her response to the adult Theo Danby when he'd first arrived days ago. She'd grown accustomed to the man he'd become since those summers. His strength, his purposeful walk, his quick decision-making, even his unexpected silences and hard-to-read expressions. If she'd mentally carried the teenage Theo around for so many years, how long would it take to shake the memory of this man when he eventually left for good?

The morning's fun disappeared at that thought. Maura stopped to take a long, deep breath. One day at a time, she reminded herself.

The goodbyes at the front of the house took some time, with Luke promising Sammy he'd look for him at the festival and the boy's happy face eliciting more smiles. Nancy reminded Maura that she, too, would be on hand to assist with rides on festival day. And watching her drive away, Maura thought again how lucky she and Maddie were to have volunteers. It was a situation that could change with a substantial increase in clients, as volunteer hours were always finite. *Another potential financial complication.* Okay, Maura told herself, no more thoughts like that. Not today. She joined the others standing by Walter's pickup.

"Walter and a friend will deliver the tables on Tuesday," Maddie said at her approach, "so I suggested we plot locations and match table to vendor on Wednesday, mainly because you and I have yet to figure out where everything will go."

"I can help with that, too," Theo put in. "Maybe when I drop by later this afternoon?"

"Theo's coming over to discuss…you know…" Maura said quickly at the question on her sister's face.

Fortunately, Maddie got the hint. "Oh, right. Sure."

There was an awkward lull until Walter said, "Okay, then. Luke is keen to help with honey and maybe Theo can drop him off after lunch."

"What about the ball?" Luke asked.

Walter chuckled. "I've a feeling they're more interested in grazing right now. I'm sure Maura and Maddie will extract it at a convenient time."

"That was so much fun today! Thanks for bringing it, Walter."

They all smiled at Luke's grown-up voice.

After Walter's pickup chugged down the drive, Theo said, "I'm ready for lunch. How about you, Luke?"

Luke nodded. "It was a good morning, but now I'm starving."

When they were out of sight, Maddie asked, "What's this talk Theo mentioned?"

Maura caught the sharp tone of the question and felt her face heat up. "Last night he said the three of us should discuss—"

"The loan?"

Maura nodded. Her sister's expression was daunting. "Sorry, I meant to tell you last night but—"

"You were busy apologizing again for keeping it a secret."

Maura expelled a loud sigh. "Seems my go-to state of being these days. Apologizing."

Maddie allowed a brief smile. "Better than keeping everything to yourself, Mo."

Relief surged through her. She was forgiven—again.

Then Maddie went on to say, "Remember that after the

festival, when real life takes over again." She turned away and headed for the kitchen door.

Maura stood awhile longer, her thoughts forging ahead to the day after all the hoopla, when, as Maddie warned, real life would take over once more.

The fun part of the day was over, Theo thought when he tapped on the door and entered the Stuart kitchen. Maddie was sitting at the table where a handful of papers lay among leftover lunch plates, glasses and cutlery. Maura was brewing coffee and turned around as he came in.

"Coffee?" she asked. "I can make instant decaf, too, if you prefer."

He figured he'd need all his senses to be alert. "Regular, please. I brought some cookies." He held up a paper bag. "Made a pit stop at Tasty Delights because Luke wanted to pick up a couple of their specialty doughnuts for him and Walter."

"He was excited about helping with the honey," Maura said as she clicked on the coffee maker and began to clear away the lunch dishes.

Theo sat down on the chair nearest the door, opposite Maddie. "Yeah. He told me they might be working late because Walter had hundreds of jars to fill. 'Don't hold supper for me,' he said." Theo laughed. "As if."

"Hopefully he's as enthusiastic after pouring fifty jars, let alone 'hundreds,'" Maura said.

"I can't remember the last time he hauled out his video game console. Certainly not since our second night here. He hasn't even asked to use my phone to contact some of his friends." Theo shook his head, frowning. "I worry a bit about that. Not keeping in touch with his school friends."

"Did you, when you were here all those summers?"

"Well, no cell phone but—"

"Stan or Vera had a landline."

He thought for a minute. "Funny, but I never thought about contacting my school buddies. Maybe because I knew we'd all be together again in the fall."

"Or maybe because you were here, cemented in the community of Maple Glen, and that other world was too far away," Maura suggested.

"Yeah, I think you may be right. This place is a bit—"

"Otherworldly?" quipped Maddie.

Maura snorted a laugh as she brought the coffee to the table and sat on Theo's right. "Anyway," she said, "it's great that Luke will have so many different memories of this place—and all good ones."

"Amen to that," Theo murmured as he sipped the dark brew. He hoped that his son's memories would carry him through the inevitable emotional tumult of a possible move at the end of summer.

"Okay," Maura announced, setting her mug down on the table with a decisiveness that put him on guard. "Here are the hard copies of the loan agreement, plus statements from the bank account in our mother's name where Dad deposited the money. Have a look." She gathered the papers in the middle of the table and pushed them his way.

Reading the actual documents rather than skimming the photos on Maura's phone made everything real. The language might be prosaic, but there was the notary's signature and stamp. "Have you found out anything about this person? The notary?"

"I googled him," Maddie said. "He's the town clerk at city hall in Rutland."

"After my meeting with my Realtor tomorrow, I'll go there just to confirm this is on file. As I see this, we have a couple—maybe three—courses of action." He paused, wanting to get his message right. "One, I forgive the loan entirely and find out how I go about doing that." He waited, but neither sister glanced up from her coffee mug. He felt a stir of impatience. Did the Stuarts always have to be so hard to read?

"Two, we work out a repayment schedule. If I sell my property for a good price, I'll have enough equity not to have to worry about getting the money back all at once. The payment schedule could be spread out in small amounts to accommodate your business plans." Now Maddie was looking at him from the other end of the table. Her face was pale, but she was nodding. Maura, on the other hand, seemed engrossed in some breadcrumbs scattered around her coffee mug. Theo bit down on his lower lip.

After a long minute, she looked up and asked, "And three?"

Ha, he thought. *She's already dismissed the two most likely possibilities and is going for a third.* The problem was, he actually didn't have something specific in mind for number three. He swigged some more coffee, his head now buzzing more from what to say than the caffeine because a lightning-strike thought had just occurred. What if he didn't sell the land after all but kept the place as a holiday getaway for him and Luke?

His surge of optimism dropped almost immediately. The idea was preposterous. Luke would have summers off, but he wouldn't. Luke might not even be living with him after the fall. Could he even afford the luxury of a summer home? Wouldn't he have to hire someone to care for the place? Or maybe the sisters could extend their business onto his land. Random thoughts and questions scattered across his mind like playing pieces in a board game.

"Number three?" Maura repeated, her eyes steady on his, bringing him back to the moment.

"Um, well…" He cursed his stammering, but the intensity in her expression was unsettling. If Maddie hadn't been present, he'd have sprung to his feet and wrapped Maura in his arms and told her...*what exactly?* Nothing about the loan because the issue here wasn't really the loan. The issue was that he was desperate for a way to have it all—her land, his land, *their* land—and her.

But none of that was going to happen. He had important work in Augusta, a son who might be wrenched from his childhood home and shipped off to a new school, bills to be paid and now a piece of land to be dealt with.

He took a deep breath. "I'm not sure yet about number three. It's a work in progress." He added a light laugh that fell flat. He saw the immediate disappointment on Maura's face and wished he'd never raised some bogus third option.

"Okay." Maddie's voice broke the mood. "Those two options are doable, but Maura and I need to discuss them alone because, frankly, Theo, it isn't fair to expect you to forgive this loan. We're not talking a few hundred dollars here!" She got up from the table. "I'm going to retrieve that ball now before it's destroyed by the gang out there."

When the door closed behind her, Maura said, "She's right, Theo. You deserve to have that money or the land, whichever you prefer." She stood up to carry coffee mugs to the sink.

Theo rose to help, but when they nearly collided at the sink, he grasped hold of her forearms and drew her close. "I'm sorry we even have to consider a solution here. My choice is to wait and see. If I get an offer on the land, well, then we'll have to decide. If not, we can—"

"Wait and see some more?" she asked, pulling apart from him. Her brow was raised teasingly, but her face was serious.

He shook his head and groaned. "I'm cursing my uncle's disorganization this very minute."

"His money gave my mother another year. That's pretty special, and… I'll be forever grateful to Stan and Vera for that chance. I'm sure Dad was."

Theo thumbed away the tears spilling onto her cheeks, stroked down and onto her lips, which were trembling now. "Maura, I… I…" The words were stuck in his throat. She brought her hands up to his face and gently lowered his head to hers, setting her mouth on his in a long, slow kiss.

What seemed an eternity later, the shrill blare of a truck horn ended the moment. Maura gave a breathless sigh as they separated, and Theo was about to jokingly ask if she felt like she'd been running a marathon because he definitely did when she peered through the kitchen window and quietly swore.

Theo ducked his head to see a pickup parked in front of the house. Finn McAllister stepped out of it, followed almost at once by Shawn Harrison.

He caught Maura's eye. "Expecting them?"

She shook her head. "Can you greet them while I sneak out to warn Maddie? Just give her a heads-up. You know?"

Theo ran his palm down the side of her cheek. "I do know, Maura. Not to worry."

Her mouth twisted in a half smile. "My dad used to say that, and though I chafed at it as a teenager, I knew deep inside I wouldn't really have to worry."

"You *don't* have to worry."

"Thanks, Theo," she whispered.

Then she was out the door, running toward the barn, before he could say another word.

Chapter Eighteen

Maddie was stowing the rubber ball in the empty stall where they kept the riding tack when Maura rushed into the barn.

"What's up, Mo? Has Theo left already?"

"No, he's still here. But…um…did you hear that horn?"

"Nope, but I've just come from the pasture and Shep was barking about something. Maybe that was it." She paused, frowning. "Come to think of it, Roger started braying at the same time. Weird, eh?"

"Maybe we have a guard donkey as well as a guard dog now," Maura quipped, prolonging the inevitable.

"So who's here?"

"Finn McAllister…and Shawn's with him."

Maddie was rooted by the stall door, her hand on the gate. "Were we expecting them?"

"No, but I'm assuming they're here about the festival. Do you want me to give you an excuse? You could sneak into the kitchen while Theo and I talk to them."

Maddie shook her head. "No, that's silly, Mo. Maple Glen is too small to go on avoiding someone, but thanks for the warning. Just…um…give me a minute, okay?"

What Maura wanted to do was to give her sister a big

hug, but she feared that might result in tears for both of them. Besides, Maddie was right. Shawn had moved back to the area and encountering him was inevitable.

"Okay, see you out there." She hesitated a second. "By the way, there's a smudge on your left cheek and a strand of straw in your hair...right there, by your ear."

Maddie laughed as she pulled a tissue from her jeans pocket and rubbed at her cheek. "Okay?"

"Gone. Here, let me." Maura moved closer to brush off the straw. "Once a farm girl, always a farm girl. Isn't that what Dad used to say?"

"I think that was Mom, out of frustration."

"Makes sense. She did her best to get us into frilly clothes occasionally."

"At least they weren't matching outfits."

"Only that one time, those dresses Grandma sent one Christmas."

"Ugh! There's a photo of us somewhere."

"Yeah, with our scowling faces." Her sister's laugh was reassuring. "Okay, see you outside," Maura said.

Theo and the other two men were standing by Finn's truck as Maura headed over to them.

"We've come to check out a site for the first aid tent," Finn said. He scanned the large front lawn extending from the house to the road. "Have you allocated any places, yet? I believe you and Maddie were organizing that."

"Yeah, we are. I mean, we're working on it." She avoided Theo's amused gaze. "But right now, the area is pretty much free. What about over there, by that oak tree?" She pointed to the giant old oak centered in a cluster of other trees at the far west side of the property.

"Won't you want that shade for some vendors' tables?" Finn asked. "We have a tent, so it doesn't matter too much where we go. Just someplace visible."

Maura bit her lip. She wasn't presenting a credible image as one of the festival's organizers.

Theo rescued her by saying, "How about there, closer to the front veranda? That way anyone with a minor issue—dehydration, heat or whatever—can be treated under the tent and then move up onto the veranda to sit a bit longer if necessary. That would free up spaces in the tent."

Finn and Shawn looked at one another before Shawn said, "That'll work." He turned to Maura. "We've also booked a table to display pamphlets from the Green Mountain Conservancy, and Finn has some about Wallingford Fire Department's new search and rescue initiative."

"Do you want the table for the flyers to be near the tent?" Maura asked, finally getting her thoughts focused.

"If there's room, that would be the logical place," Finn answered. "And I haven't organized a volunteer to man it yet, so whoever's on duty in the tent can replenish the stock." He hesitated a moment, then turned to Theo. "I hate to ask because I know you're on holiday, but would you be able to relieve our first aid volunteers if necessary? I've got a lineup of people from the fire department, but you know how these things play out with volunteers. Stuff happens and they have to cancel. It would just be on a 'needs must' basis."

"Of course. But I don't have any supplies with me," Theo said.

Finn waved a dismissive hand. "We're well equipped, and thanks, Theo—that's great. All right, then, that's about it for now, isn't it, Shawn?"

Maura was intrigued by Shawn's shrug. He hadn't spoken much, but she'd noticed his attention shifting now and then to the house. *Wondering where Maddie is?*

As if on cue, the slamming kitchen door answered the question. Maddie must have sneaked inside to change from jeans and T-shirt to slim-fitting capris and a floral top. There was an air of breathlessness about her as she strode their way, and Maura guessed that she'd taken a few seconds to summon her courage. She sneaked a peek at Shawn and saw he was captivated by the image breezing toward them.

"I thought I heard people talking out here," Maddie called as she approached.

Yeah, right, Maura thought. She turned slightly and caught a quick wink from Theo.

"Hi, Maddie," Finn said. "We came to have a look at where we can set up our tent on Thursday." He gestured to Shawn. "I don't think you two have met up yet. Shawn was at the community meeting last week."

"I had to leave early, so no, didn't get a chance to say hello." She shifted slightly to look directly at Shawn. "Welcome back to the Glen, Shawn."

"Thanks, Maddie." He cleared his throat. "Good to see you again…and Maura, too."

Maura didn't dare look at Theo, guessing he'd be grinning at the awkward afterthought. She admired her sister's composure, though the split between Maddie and Shawn had happened so many years ago surely painful emotions were long gone. But then she remembered her own gut reaction to Theo's return. Was there an expiry date on a broken heart?

"I saw your sign out front, Jake & Friends," Shawn was now saying, "and Finn's told me you and Maura are running a riding therapy program but with donkeys instead of horses. How did that come about?"

"It's a bit of a long story," Maddie answered.

"I'd love to hear it sometime," Shawn said, his eyes glued on Maddie.

"Sure, whenever you like."

It was Theo who broke the moment. "Think it's almost time to pick up Luke from Walter's place."

Everyone stirred into action then.

"Let us know if you need any more help before the big day," Finn said as he got into the pickup.

Theo began walking to the cedar hedge to get his car while Maura stood still, transfixed by the tableau of Maddie and Shawn reconnecting.

"Maura?" Theo beckoned from the hedge.

Reluctantly, she moved toward him, keeping her sister and Shawn at the edge of her vision.

"You're both funny and obvious," he murmured when she reached him.

"Huh?"

"That." He nodded toward Maddie and Shawn. When Maura pivoted, she saw that they were now saying goodbye.

"I don't know what you mean," she blustered, aware of heat rising up her neck into her face.

"It's good that they're talking. What happens next is beyond your control, so…"

"Are you saying that I'm meddling in my sister's affairs?" She saw his wince and backtracked. "Sorry, I didn't mean that to sound so blunt. I'm just—"

"Looking out for your twin sister. I get that. But she's an adult now, and so is Shawn. They'll work something out between them." He set his palm against her cheek. Reassuring her. Telling her he was on her side.

He was right, Maura knew. She leaned against his hand for a moment longer, then drew back.

"I'll call you tomorrow when all my business is dealt with." Then he pushed through the hedge and disappeared.

Maura turned around to see Finn driving out to the road. Maddie was still standing where she'd said goodbye. She glanced over at Maura, her eyes shining. With tears, Maura wondered, or happiness?

Then she smiled. "It's all right, Mo. I'm fine. The first awkward meeting has come and gone, and you know what? It wasn't nearly as bad as I'd expected." She started toward the house but stopped to add, "He's coming over Wednesday morning to help set up tables." Steps away from the side door she shouted, "I'm changing my clothes and then we have to feed the donkeys." The kitchen door closed behind her.

Wonder of wonders, Maura was thinking. Theo's words from the other day resurfaced. *Don't get ahead of yourself.* She needed to keep that in mind. But if the problem that broke apart Maddie and Shawn could be resolved or at least mitigated, that could be a game changer. Her sister might decide to stay in Maple Glen—and Maura would do whatever she could to make that happen.

Theo watched the flashy black SUV and his Realtor's compact car drive away. The interested buyer, a statewide construction company, had sent a team that included three engineers, an architect, a surveyor and a lawyer. He'd spent their two-hour inspection of the entire property tucked inside the house—the one area they weren't interested in. He'd found the visit stressful but couldn't explain why. The farm had to be sold, and although he figured it shouldn't matter to him who the buyer was, the fact was it did.

His Realtor had informed him that the company spokesperson liked the location, and his acreage, though not as big as they'd envisioned, would suffice. When she added that she'd indicated the adjacent farmland might also be available, Theo's anxiety rose. "They have no plans to sell," he quickly asserted.

She'd shrugged. "You never know. People make surprising decisions sometimes."

When the vehicles hit the county road, Theo went back inside. The place was a shambles because he'd spent the nerve-racking hours before the team's arrival conducting another search for any documents, memos or Post-it notes regarding the loan.

Luke, on his way to help clean out stables, had scarcely noticed the mess. After downing breakfast, he'd lingered long enough to tell Theo that he and Ashley Watson plus two other kids from the youth club had planned a short hike on the off trail leading out of the village that afternoon.

This news had buzzed around Theo's mind like a confused hornet. When and how were these plans made? he'd asked.

"Ashley and her mom came when I was finishing up working with Walter yesterday. Her mother is a pretty good artist, and she'd made some labels for Walter's honey jars. So all of us wiped the jars clean and then stuck the labels on. We didn't finish, though, 'cause there were too many jars and not enough labels."

"Okay, but the hike thing?" Theo had prompted.

"That's when Ashley said I could go with them if I wanted to, and I said yes."

So much for seeking parental permission, Theo thought. He'd have pointed out that Luke might have mentioned this last night but decided not to make an issue out of it. Besides, Luke's absence would give him some alone time with Maura and Maddie to report whatever he found at Rutland Town Hall.

Luke returned from stable cleaning just as Theo finished making his lunch. "Can I take that with me?" he asked, eyeing the sandwich.

"Sure, but I thought you were hiking after lunch."

"Ashley texted Maura to tell me that they're meeting at the bakery earlier 'cause one of the kids wants to buy his lunch there."

"That sounds like a complicated network… Ashley sending messages to you via Maura."

"What happens when I don't have a phone of my own."

Theo would have laughed if he hadn't been struck by the realization that this kind of interchange would only increase as Luke went from preteen to actual teen. "True. Maybe we can negotiate a phone in the fall, if you're with me in Augusta."

"Seriously?"

Theo pursed his lips. The instant perk in his son's expression was both charming and unsettling. Would the kid choose which parent to live with based on the availability of a cell phone? That saddened him because he knew Trish would allow Luke to have a phone.

"Sure," he mumbled, accepting defeat.

"Cool. I'm going up to change. My clothes kind of reek from you-know-what."

"Good idea. Maybe some deodorant, too?"

"Jeez, Dad."

Theo grinned as he packed a lunch. There would certainly be adjustments for both of them in the months ahead. Trish needed a decision by the end of July, and Theo knew he and Luke would have to make plans that could potentially affect his long-term relationship with his son. But not until after the festival, he told himself.

When Luke returned in clean shorts and a T-shirt and carrying his small daypack, Theo handed him the paper bag lunch. "How far you guys going?" he asked as Luke sat in a chair to put on his hiking shoes.

"To where the blue blazes meet with the white ones. Where you and I were heading the day we found that man."

"Right. Good. And I take it someone will have a cell phone, just in case."

"Of course. They probably all will!"

Luke's head was bent as he tied his shoes, but Theo guessed he was scowling. "And just a reminder that cell phone access in the woods is—"

"Unpredictable. Ashley told me. But they're taking theirs anyway." He stood up and reached for the daypack.

"Water bottle?" Theo asked.

"Oh. Right."

Theo hid a grin while he reached for the bottle on the counter and passed it over. As Luke was stowing it in the pack, Theo said, "Have a good time, son, and get one of the kids to text me when you're back in the village, so I'll know everything worked out okay."

"You'd know right away if I could text you myself."

Theo ignored the gibe. Best to send him off without any more conflict. A car's engine ended the matter.

"That's Ashley," Luke said. "Her mom's giving us a ride to the bakery."

The information just kept trickling in, Theo was thinking, as he watched his son head out to the car. This was going to be life with a teenager. Everything on a need-to-know basis, which actually meant the teen decided who needed to know, how much and when. Theo sighed. Was he really up for this, on his own, given the long, unpredictable hours in urgent care? Yet if he didn't try to make it work, he'd lose the opportunity to be a real part of his only child's life. And that was something he couldn't stomach.

The best-and worst-case scenarios for the end of the month's decision filled Theo's mind as he drove to Rutland an hour later. Getting what he wanted at the town hall was relatively easy, and soon he was on his way to the Stuart farm to tell them that the loan transaction was indeed on record and therefore would have an impact on any sale of his property.

His Realtor had told him the company needed the rest of the week to come up with an offer, as there were other properties they were considering. This was the first indication she'd given that his land wasn't the only choice for the company, and surprisingly, the news was almost a relief. He might have time to look at other options than selling. He wasn't sure what those might be, but maybe he could ask Maura to be part of the brainstorming. And Luke, too.

By the time he reached the outskirts of Maple Glen, the weather was changing. The sunny day that had been promised by local forecasts was shifting as dark, ominous clouds formed over White Rocks Mountain. Theo glanced up at the sky through the windshield, then checked the time on the car dashboard. Luke had been gone for a couple of hours and hopefully would now be back.

He exited Route 7 onto the county road and impulsively turned into the Stuart driveway. As soon as he parked the car, he checked his cell phone for any messages and, finding none, let out a frustrated groan. He was heading for the kitchen door when Maura emerged from the barn.

"Hey, Theo, are you returning from Rutland? What did you find out?"

Theo smiled. Getting right down to business, as Maura was wont to do. "Yes, I am, and all of us should discuss it. Is now a good time?"

She nodded. "Mads and I've been bringing in the donkeys, and she's getting Roger right now. There's going to be a storm."

"Yeah." He peered anxiously up at the sky.

"Problem?"

"Luke's gone hiking on the trail with some kids from the youth club."

"How long ago? When are you expecting him back? Did they take cell phones?"

Her questions flew at him, like the ones he'd peppered Luke with hours ago—a shift that might have been amusing if a sudden lightning bolt and crack of thunder hadn't made them both jump.

"Inside maybe?" Maura said.

"I should check on Luke. Do you have Ashley's mother's number?" The question was followed by another crack of thunder, and rather than a reply, they dashed for the kitchen. The rain pelted down the instant they closed the door.

"That was close," Maura gasped. "I hope Maddie made it into the barn. Do you want me to contact Ashley's mother, see if the kids are back yet?"

"Please." But his phone rang as soon as he spoke—it was Luke, using Ashley's phone.

"Hi, Dad, we just got back, and we're waiting out the storm inside Mrs. McAllister's house."

"Oh, great. I was worried. Do you want me to pick you up?"

"No, Dad, please. Mrs. McAllister's making us hot chocolate, and she baked cookies today. Ashley said her mom will drop me off later, after the storm."

Theo was chuckling as he hung up.

"All's well?" Maura asked, smiling.

Theo nodded. "I've had some interesting parenting situations today."

"Good ones?" She turned to look at him as she went to the counter.

"Learning ones."

"Hmm, maybe the best kind. I'm making coffee, by the way. For our talk."

No backtracking now, Theo told himself. Though what

he'd really like to do was to brush back the tendril of hair that was clinging to her damp cheek, which would mean he'd have to take her into his arms and then…

Maddie rushed into the kitchen, the door blowing shut behind her. "Just made it. They're all safe and sound." Her attention shifted from Maura to Theo. "What's up?"

"I went to Rutland Town Hall and confirmed the notarized record of the loan."

Minutes later the three of them were sitting at the table, drinking the hot brew and still postponing the talk. Finally, Theo said, "This is what I think. We don't need to worry about the loan until I know for sure I'll be selling the property. My agent tells me the interested party will likely wait until after the weekend, considering the holiday this Thursday. If the offer is a good one, and I'm compelled to take it, we still have options."

"You forgive the loan on paper, for the records, and we repay you in installments every month until it's finished," Maura preempted.

She and Maddie had clearly been discussing this, and Theo figured that course was the best one for all of them. "Looks like we have a decision, then."

The silence in the room spoke volumes. Maura and Maddie nodded, stone-faced.

Theo wished he could tell them to forget about the money completely because he knew how money could drive a wedge between people. He and Trish had spent several months hassling over money, and unnecessary acrimony had resulted.

Now they had a plan—something to act on—but he had a bad feeling this was a risky situation when it came to a future with Maura.

Chapter Nineteen

The blare of a horn shook Maura from a deep sleep. She shot up, rubbing her eyes, and saw that it was eight o'clock. Walter was here with the tables. If she was lucky, Maddie was already up and had breakfast on the go. They'd stayed up late, making a huge map of the festival grounds and assigning spots to all the registered vendors.

Last night they'd both skirted around the money talk with Theo until Maddie had commented, as they headed upstairs, "We're lucky we owe the money to Theo, and not some stranger."

Maura had to concur, though she'd lain sleepless for a long time, thinking that owing money to someone you cared for deeply, someone you wanted to have some kind of future with, might not be such a good thing. Would it always be between them, a deterrent to open and transparent conversation? Plus, he'd implied there were other options but hadn't specified what they might be, instead agreeing at once to their payback plan. Of course, they were obliged to repay, but what were the other options he'd hinted at? She had no answers by morning.

As she got into shorts and a T-shirt, she peered through her bedroom window to see Walter and another man chatting with Maddie. *Saved by my sister, and not for the first time*, she thought as she finished dressing and ran downstairs. Coffee was brewing in the machine, and Maura smiled at the loaf of bread, with jars of jam, peanut butter and honey on the table. Entertaining Maple Glen–style.

The three glanced up as Maura exited the side door.

"Maura." Walter nodded. "This here is Bill Moyer, from Wallingford. He's helping transport tables with me today and can come tomorrow, too, if need be."

Bill, a man approximately the same age as Walter, shook hands and then said, "Nice place you've got here. I was just telling your sister that my granddaughter would love to ride one of your donkeys, so I'm bringing her on Thursday."

"That's great," Maura said, "and thanks for helping." She turned to Walter. "Maddie and I've put together a site map, which we've mounted on a plywood board, so feel free to help yourself to breakfast in the kitchen while we get it from the barn."

"Maybe we should do some unloading first, but thank you," Walter said. "How about if we lean the tables against the barn for now? Or were you thinking of arranging them in their assigned spots for folks?"

"We thought we'd place them today or tomorrow. We've asked people to come as early as possible on Thursday to find their table and set up. The official starting time isn't until eleven."

Walter nodded. "Sounds good. When we finish with this lot, we'll pick up the tables from the church, and then we can help organize them where they're supposed to go, if you like." He and Bill began lifting the folding tables out of the back of the truck and carrying them to the side of the barn.

Maura signaled Maddie and went to get the plywood

board. "Thanks for letting me sleep in a bit, Mads, and also for organizing breakfast."

"I figured you had a late night. Your light was still on when I turned mine out. Personally, I slept very well," Maddie said.

Maura smiled. No anxious thoughts about Shawn Harrison, then, she figured. A good omen.

"By the way," Maddie added as they were lifting the heavy board. "Ashley and Luke are coming over sometime today or maybe tomorrow to braid red, white and blue ribbons in the donkeys' tails, and also to help decorate the riding ring."

"What a good idea!"

"It was Ashley's, and her mother is providing the ribbon. I'm thinking just do Jake and Matilda, Lizzie if she's in a good mood, but maybe not Roger."

"I guess we should bring them into their stalls, then, make it easier for the kids."

"That's what I thought."

Maura grasped one end of the plywood board and Maddie, the other. "Ugh, this thing seems heavier than it was yesterday," she grunted as they lifted the board up, carrying it out to the front yard. On the way they passed Walter, who was adding another table to the stack leaning on one side of the barn door.

"Want us to help with that?" he asked.

"We're good, thanks, Walter."

They'd already decided to prop the board up on the veranda where vendors could check it on the day, and the board would be out of the way of children dashing about. After they lugged it up onto the veranda and leaned it safely against the house, they surveyed the map.

"Still a few empty places," Maura pointed out, "which means we can accommodate last-minute vendors." She watched Walter and Bill, who didn't even live in the Glen, finish unloading. "The Fourth of July Festival has been happening in the Glen ever since we can remember, right? Did you ever think about all the people in the village and even beyond who worked to make it happen?"

Maddie shook her head. "Nope, as kids and teens we just enjoyed it. We're lucky, though, to have such community spirit in the Glen."

"Let's hope it never changes." Maura instantly thought about the sale of the Danby land. "And let's hope whoever buys Theo's property gets involved in our community, too." She noticed Maddie's frown. "What? Do you think that couldn't happen?"

"I was in the northeast pasture yesterday when some people came to inspect it. There was a bunch of them, and they all looked like professionals. Not regular people. I watched for a while and not a single person went into the house."

"Which means—"

"They weren't interested in the house."

"Why didn't you bring this up when Theo was here to discuss the loan? We could have asked him about this potential buyer."

"Wasn't the loan repayment enough of an issue?" Maddie huffed.

True, but Maura found this information disturbing. Although their land would still be theirs thanks to the loan repayment plan, the future of Jake & Friends could be affected by whoever bought Theo's place. Maura held up two crossed fingers. "Wishing for a nice, friendly family."

"Same here but…" Maddie pivoted at the sound of an engine chugging up the drive. "Guess we've got company."

Walter was closing the rear end of the pickup as an old-model Volkswagen camper van rolled to a stop yards away.

Maddie glanced at Maura and quipped, "That looks like something from the sixties."

The multicolored van bore a single large blue eye on the side door behind the driver. An array of calligraphic words spread across and around the van's panels. Near the roof, a painted black sign read Clair Voyant, Palm and Tarot Card Reader.

Maura noticed Walter and Bill exchange smiles, and she grinned at Maddie. "Cute!"

When the engine shut down, the driver door creaked open, and a petite woman with short, gray-streaked dark hair and wearing a pair of faded jeans topped by a tie-dyed T-shirt stepped out. "Morning, folks. I'm Rita Moretti, and I'm hoping it's not too late for me to sign up for a spot for your festival."

It was Maddie who moved first, smiling broadly. "Great! I'm Maddie Stuart. My sister and I—" she gestured to Maura "—are hosting the festival this year."

Rita nodded at Maura as Maddie went on to introduce the two men.

"How did you hear about the festival?" Maura asked, thinking of all the flyers they'd delivered and posted throughout the area.

"The internet. Isn't that how everyone gets information nowadays?"

Maura heard Walter chuckle. "I guess someone on our planning committee posted it," she quickly said.

"There are dozens of websites devoted to local and state events, as I'm sure you know, and they're a great guide. I spend most of the year traveling from one place to another to participate in celebrations of all kinds. That's my work." A smile lit up Rita's face.

"Well, we do have places available," Maddie said. "Will you be doing...um...readings from the van or a table?"

"Normally I use the van, parked in an accessible spot." She peered around. "But it looks like this area is going to be for tables only?" She looked at the last pair of tables leaning against the bumper of Walter's pickup.

"Right. People who arrive in vehicles will be parking them on the property adjacent to ours," Maura said, pointing to Theo's place.

"Okay. I'm happy to use a table if there's one available, and I guess I can park my van over there, too." She scanned the area once more and said, "You've got donkeys. I noticed the sign driving up. I'd love to see them."

"Sure. My sister can find you a place on our map while I show you the donkeys," Maura said.

"Anywhere suits me," Rita told Maddie. Then she turned to the men and said, "Nice to meet you two," and followed Maura.

As they approached the side door, Maura heard Shep barking inside the kitchen. They'd left him there while the men were unloading, to keep him from getting in the way. "Hang on," she said to Rita, pausing to open the door.

Shep bounded out, jumping up on Maura and then turning his attention to Rita. The dog's love of attention could be overwhelming, Maura had learned, but Rita didn't mind his eagerness to please as she leaned down, stroking his head and back, while Shep lavished love on her.

"Lovely dog," she said, standing up. "I used to have one, but after he passed away, I didn't replace him. Nomadic life and constant contact with strangers aren't always the best things for a pet. I miss him," she added, her face clouding over.

Shep ran ahead as they rounded the corner of the barn, and Rita stopped when the pasture came in sight. "Donkeys can be pets, too, right?"

"For sure." Maura liked the woman already.

They walked to the fence where Shep paced, whining at the gate. Maura opened it, and he raced inside, heading straight for Roger. Matilda and Jake wandered over to greet the humans, while Lizzie stood motionless in a far corner of the field. Shep was now running circles around Roger, greeting him as he did every morning when he was first released into the field.

"They're gentle creatures and very intelligent," Rita commented as she stroked Matilda's long face and snout. Jake was vying for attention, too, and Rita chuckled as she rubbed his head and neck at the same time. "Have you had them long?"

Maura briefly recapped how Jake and Matilda ended up at the farm and her decision to set up the riding program. She liked the fact that Rita listened quietly, without asking questions or tossing off a comment. Instead, the woman simply kept administering affection to Jake and Matilda as Maura spoke.

When Maura mentioned Lizzie's aloofness and penchant for nipping, Rita said, "She was ill-treated, but I bet there's someone she can connect with."

Maura thought of Katie and her almost magical bond with the unpredictable Lizzie. She was about to tell Rita this when the woman said, "I can see that Shep and the big donkey out there—Roger, you said?—are best friends." After a moment longer of watching them, she turned to Maura. "Thanks for letting me have a sneak peek at them, and I'm looking forward to maybe riding one before the festival's over." She paused to survey the field and the donkeys. "I've a feeling this is going to be a new and wonderful experience for me."

Shep ran up to the gate, and Maura let him out. They followed the dog around to the front, where Maddie was saying goodbye to Walter and Bill.

Rita made for her van, but paused to ask, "Is there a campground close by?"

"Um, I don't think so. What about Wallingford?" Maura looked at Walter, who was leaning out the driver-side window of his truck.

He shook his head. "Closest one I can think of is to the south of here, toward Bennington. A bit far for a commute, though."

Rita was frowning, and Maura was about to offer her some space at the farm when Walter suddenly said, "I've got lots of property and an electrical outlet as well as a water supply in my honey shed. You're welcome to camp there, if you like."

"A honey shed? You keep bees?" Rita was beaming.

"I do. But the hives aren't anywhere near the shed, so if you're worried about getting stung—"

"Not at all. And thank you, that would be wonderful. I'm happy to recompense you."

"My pleasure. Be nice to have another human around for a couple of days."

"Perhaps I can repay you in kind," she said, gesturing to her van. "A reading?"

Maura hid a grin at Walter's expression but admired his discretion as he merely shrugged.

"Bill and I are going to pick up the rest of the tables, and I'll meet you back here in about twenty minutes or so." With that, he turned on the ignition and reversed to make his turn before heading back to the village.

Maura glanced at her sister, thinking she might be having the same idea right then. "Would you like some breakfast, Rita, while you're waiting?"

"Lovely, my dear."

They trooped into the kitchen accompanied by Shep, who dashed for his food bowl next to the door. As they ate,

Maura and Maddie told Rita more about their decision to establish Jake & Friends and gave her a snapshot summary of growing up in Maple Glen. It seemed like only moments had passed before Walter's truck horn sounded.

Waving goodbye, she thought how quickly Walter, notoriously private, had offered Rita space on his property. He'd been actively helping with this year's festival, something he hadn't done previously. She also realized that despite the ease she and Maddie had felt talking about themselves and the locals, they'd heard almost nothing about Rita Moretti herself.

Theo had intended to pop next door and help with the tables but was interrupted by a series of texts from his Realtor fielding queries from the company about the property's water and sewage mains, as well as gas and electricity lines. They were simply confirming details the team must have already investigated, but Theo's irritation notched up at each message. He rationalized that was probably the reason for his abrupt reply when, later that day, Luke asked him about the people who'd come to see the farm.

"We were in the pasture with the donkeys when we saw some people wandering around here. They had clipboards and stuff and didn't look like ordinary people," Luke reported.

"They work for a company that's interested in buying this place."

Luke's eyes widened. "What kind of company?"

Theo sighed. Hadn't they discussed this already? Or maybe they hadn't. "It's a development company. You know, building."

"Like condos and apartment buildings?"

"Or houses."

Luke frowned. "So not like a family that's going to buy the farm and renovate or something."

"No." He could see the distaste in his son's expression and felt impatience rising. "My Realtor hasn't had a single inquiry from anyone wanting a farm."

"But wouldn't a lot of buildings and people change Maple Glen? It wouldn't be a village anymore."

There was nothing Theo could say because Luke was absolutely right.

"You can't sell this place to just anyone. That's…that's a horrible thing to do." He stomped out of the kitchen and up to his room.

Theo was anticipating negative reactions to a possible sale to the company, especially from Maura and Maddie, whose land would be most affected by development, but he hadn't considered such a strong response from Luke. He'd seen his son's growing attachment to the Glen but figured their stay would eventually fade into a vague memory once life in Augusta resumed.

Of course, he'd been in denial about the consequences of selling the land to a company, or even a family. Once it was gone, what would draw him back? He knew the answer at once. *Maura.* But would she want him if he sold out to big business?

Chapter Twenty

Maura was up at daybreak. She'd had a good sleep, likely because she'd been exhausted when she'd finally collapsed into bed. After Walter and Bill had moved the rest of the tables from the church, all four of them had set up the tables on their assigned sites and numbered them to correspond to the map.

During all this, her mind had been fixed on Theo's absence. Why hadn't he come to help as he'd promised? Even Luke had failed to turn up in the afternoon, a break in his daily routine of hanging out with the donkeys and helping with chores. Something was off, and she wondered if it might be connected to the people who'd inspected the Danby property. Business types, Maddie had said.

It was her turn to make breakfast, and the coffee was ready when Maddie came into the kitchen and slumped onto a chair. "I'm beat already," she said, "and today is going to be a marathon of work."

"True, but thanks to Walter and Bill, we don't have to set up tables."

"What else do we have to do?"

"Clean the stables, feed and groom the donkeys. Let's see if Luke and Ashley can help with that, as well as braid their tails. Plus, we've got streamers to decorate the fence around the riding ring, remember? They're in a box in the barn. Nancy said she was available today and Cathy texted to say she could help with riders on the day itself." Maura sat down and poured cereal into a bowl. "It's funny that neither Luke nor Theo came by yesterday, though," she added seconds later. "In fact, I didn't notice any activity there at all."

Maddie laughed, sputtering coffee onto her cereal bowl. "Are you the Glen's neighborhood watch now?"

Maura felt her face heat up. "No, but the place is pretty visible from the northeast pasture, so…"

"Maybe we should look for Dad's binoculars, to help you with this new job of yours."

"Ha ha." Not a bad idea, she was thinking.

They ate in silence for the next few minutes until Maddie asked, "What are your thoughts on the days after the festival, when Theo and Luke will be making plans to leave, assuming he sells the property?"

Maura kept her eyes on her cereal bowl. "Today and tomorrow will be far too busy to think about anything beyond the festival."

"I know you too well, Mo. Hedge all you want—I'm sure you've been playing all kinds of scenarios in your head about what happens after Thursday."

"What about you? In two months, your promised year working with me will be up. Surely, you've been considering your options, too."

"I guess we're both on the same page regarding our futures, then."

"As always. We're twins, right? We don't look alike, and we don't always think alike, but deep down, we're bound by something…indefinable." She managed a smile despite the unexpected threat of tears. "And can we agree to preserve that bond, no matter what?" She stretched her arm across the table, setting her hand on top of Maddie's.

"Yes." Maddie's smile was wobbly, too, as she turned over her hand to clasp Maura's. "For us and for Mom and Dad, because they'd want us to stick together…no matter what."

Maura took a deep breath. "And we won't let any…" She searched for an appropriate word. "…entanglements with men come between us."

"Entanglements?" Maddie grinned.

"You know what I mean."

"And these unnamed men?"

"You know who they are. Deal?"

Maddie gave a mock salute. "Deal."

"Pinkie swear?"

Maddie's laugh startled Shep, who was dozing by the kitchen door. He gave an obligatory bark and settled back down onto his piece of carpet. "I think that's one childhood tradition we can forget."

"All right, then," Maura said, standing up. "Let's get to work." But as she began to clear dishes, another question stopped her.

"Are you in love with Theo, Mo?"

Maura was afraid to turn around, to reveal the anxiety on her face. She stared bleakly out the kitchen window. "I think I am."

"Have you told him?"

"No. What's the point? He has an important job in Augusta and a twelve-year-old son to support. There's nothing in Maple Glen for him, except a decrepit farmhouse and acreage that he can't do anything with other than sell."

"*You're* here."

"No kidding."

"But you don't have to be. We've never discussed the

possibility, but we can always sell the donkeys or give them to a shelter and get rid of the farm."

Maura swung around. "Is that what *you* want?"

"We're talking about you, not me."

Maddie's shrug irked her. Hadn't they just had an emotional moment between them, a pledge of solidarity? Now her sister was suggesting an extremely unpalatable idea. "I… I absolutely couldn't do that," she blustered. "I've put so much into this business, and I love those animals, Mads! They're a part of my life."

"I know that, Mo. But would you sacrifice a chance for a future with Theo and even Luke, out of… I don't know… some kind of fixation on this place?"

"How about you? What are *your* current feelings for Shawn, and would *you* sacrifice a second chance with him because you feel restless here?" She regretted the retort at the pained expression on Maddie's face, but the question was as valid as the one Maddie had hurled at her.

They stared at one another until Shep's whine and pawing at the door distracted them. Maddie got up to let him out and, turning back to Maura, said, "We're doing what we swore we wouldn't do."

"What?"

"Letting two men come between us."

Maura gave a sharp laugh. "True." Her phone pinged just then, and when she picked it up from the table, she noted a text from Theo.

"Speaking of men…"

Maddie raised a querying eyebrow.

"Theo and Luke are heading over after Finn and Shawn arrive with the fire engine."

"So it begins," Maddie murmured, getting up from her chair. She carried more dishes to the kitchen counter, and as she stood next to Maura, she added, "Let's not allow these men to get in our way today. We can deal with them tomorrow."

Maura's smile felt tentative. "Agreed. Let's have some fun." She threw her arms around her sister in a tight hug.

Theo made a full breakfast for Luke, knowing a normal lunch might not happen, as the day before the festival promised to be busy. In the middle of the rough patch yesterday with his son, Theo had realized going next door to help with tables might not be a good idea. He'd managed to strike a truce with Luke over the two main problems that had precipitated the blowup between them: the potential sale of the land to a development company, which could ruin the tone of Maple Glen, and the looming deadline regarding where and with whom Luke would live next year. Theo had promised to discuss these two issues with Luke right after the festival.

He'd even managed to extract a wan smile from Luke when he told him they'd shop for a cell phone when they left the Glen and had added that they both needed to try harder to communicate their feelings in an appropriate way. The irony of such a pact wasn't lost on Theo. He was the adult, after all, and there'd be many more conflicts when Luke was a teen, but at least the current situation was stabilized.

When he heard Luke coming out of the bathroom, he went to the foot of the staircase and hollered, "Pancakes and bacon are ready!"

By the time he was plating the food, Luke was sitting down, fork in hand. "Juice?" he asked.

Theo rolled his eyes. *Yeah, he's a preteen all right.* "You know where it is."

After pouring himself a glass of orange juice, Luke stood in front of the open fridge door a second longer.

"What're you looking for?" Theo asked, dishing out his own pancakes.

"Is the syrup all gone?"

"I don't know. You're the syrup fan here." He sat down to tackle his breakfast, adding, "It was only a small bottle, so yes, maybe so." There was a trace of a pout as Luke plunked down onto his chair. "Look in the pantry—that narrow closet next to the fridge. There might be some kind of substitute, like jam or sugar."

Luke pulled a face but got up to check. Seconds later, he was bringing a large porcelain canister labeled SUGAR. "Better than nothing," he muttered and unsnapped the lid. He peered inside and frowned.

"Well, is it sugar?" Theo teased.

"Nope." He stuck a hand in and pulled out a plastic bag, which he dropped next to his pancakes.

Theo stared at the bag, not really understanding what he was seeing, until Luke untied its knot and dumped elastic-bound rolls of bills onto the table. "Money," Luke whispered. "And a lot of it."

Theo gawked at the small pile and knew instinctively what this was. The regular monthly withdrawals Maura had mentioned, missing from her father's account. The bills were fifties, and he counted as he spread them out across the table.

"How much is there?" Luke asked, wide-eyed.

"I think about twenty-five hundred dollars."

"That's a fortune!" Luke exclaimed.

Not compared to ten thousand, Theo was thinking, but it would help Maura and Maddie.

"There's something else," Luke said. He pulled out a scrap of paper and flattened it on the table.

Theo recognized his uncle's handwriting and skimmed

the note. *From Charlie Stuart, for the loan. He's struggling. I'll forget about the repayment.*

Theo looked at the date, realizing it had been written only months before his uncle, newly diagnosed with dementia, went into the nursing home. Aunt Vera had followed soon after, and their mutual decline had accelerated. Neither had had the chance to follow through with this, much less tell Theo about it. At least now there was evidence of intent to forgive the loan, and Theo hoped Maura and Maddie would no longer feel indebted to him. Perhaps the awkward shift in their relationship that he'd felt since suggesting a payback scheme would disappear with this find.

"What's this all about, Dad?" Luke asked after reading the note.

"It's a long story, Luke, and I'll for sure get around to it later. For now, we're due next door and..." He paused, hearing a roar of engines. "I think that might be Finn, parking his department's fire engine for the big day tomorrow."

Luke dashed for the door, his interest in the money already fading. Theo scooped up the bills and replaced them in the canister, a hiding place that had proved to be a good one. He stacked the unwashed plates and cutlery in the sink and went out to join Finn and Shawn standing next to the fire engine.

The day had begun, and it was already an auspicious one.

Chapter Twenty-One

Maura figured some mischief-maker had messaged the Glen's residents to arrive at the same time on festival day, because as soon as she and Maddie closed the kitchen door behind them, leaving Shep whining inside, she saw a stream of people walking along the road from Theo's place, toting baskets, bins and large bags.

As she approached the gap in the cedar hedge, she saw that Theo's entire front lawn was almost filled with cars already, at eight in the morning. Then she spotted Theo and Luke heading her way and felt a burst of happiness.

Luke rushed ahead. "Is Ashley here?"

"Honestly, Luke, I've no idea. When we came outside after breakfast, people were already checking the site map and looking for their tables. Maddie has gone to bring the donkeys into the barn because we decided braiding their tails in their stalls was the least distractible place. Why don't you…?" But he was already racing toward the barn. She grinned at Theo. "Someone's super excited."

"Yep. Listen, Maura, I want to say, first of all, that I love you. And also, that—"

"Theo, I love you, too, and—"

He laughed with her. And she was about to tell him that

she hoped for some kind of future with him when someone spoke from behind. She swung around to see Sue Giordano from the bakery, her husband and their teenage son, holding baskets and trays of baked goods.

"Maura? We can't find our table."

Maura caught Theo's wink and mouthed a silent "later" as she led them to their table. Knowing they'd be selling baked goods, she'd purposely given them a shady location in a place suitable for a lineup of buyers. When Maura returned, Theo had vanished into the growing crowd.

On her way to help Maddie with the donkeys, she was held up several times by people with questions and requests—some wanted a better site for their table, while others wanted to trade places. By the time she reached the barn, she was ready to run and hide in one of the stalls. She peeked inside to see Ashley standing next to Jake as she braided his tail, while Luke was with Matilda in the next stall.

"Are they being good?" she asked as she got closer.

"Matilda is," Luke said, "but Jake wasn't into it at first."

"He's okay now," Ashley added. "But I had to relax him with some pieces of turnip."

Maura laughed. "That'll do the trick. You might need some for Roger. He's still a bit wary of people."

"We think Roger's upset at all the commotion and also missing Shep—he was braying," Luke told her.

"Where's Maddie?"

"She's bringing Roger inside anyway, and Lizzie's going to stay in the pasture today," Ashley replied.

"All good," said Maura. She pivoted round at the clatter of hooves as Maddie led Roger into the barn. His nostrils were flared, and his eyes seemed to be rolling around in his head. Maura saw that Maddie was having trouble holding on as he kept jerking at his halter. She ran over to help, grabbing hold of the lead rope along with her sister.

"He'll settle down now that he's inside," Maddie gasped. Together they steered him into his stall and Maura kept her distance as Maddie unclipped the rope. She had no idea what to expect from Roger. He hadn't been with them long enough for her or Maddie to predict or understand his moods, though she bet Shep could.

"I'll get Shep," Maura said. "Maybe he'll help settle Roger. Keep talking quietly to soothe him but stay out of kicking range." She waited until Maddie backed away from Roger. Then Maura sidled along the stall's partition and out its gate. Seconds later she was tugging at the kitchen door, but as soon as she flung it open, Shep bounded out.

Confused by the people milling about in the yard, he ran away from the barn and toward the front of the house and the driveway. Maura chased after him, hoping he wouldn't make it to the road. She ignored the voices calling out to her for assistance or tossing questions at her as she jogged around people, trying to keep Shep in sight. When she finally spotted him, he was yards away from the end of the drive. There was no point in shouting his name, for the place was echoing with all the noise people generated. Heart in mouth, Maura picked up her pace, dodging a couple hauling goods in a wagon, and hoping someone would stop a runaway dog. Thankfully, someone did.

Rita Moretti was on her knees, patting and stroking Shep, when Maura finally caught up to him. Once her breathing was under control, she thanked Rita.

"He must be wondering what's going on, poor thing," Rita murmured. Shep whined as if he understood exactly what the woman had said.

The multitude of bracelets, along with strings of love beads around Rita's neck, jangled and swayed as she stood up. She was wearing a long floral skirt and a filmy batik-style blouse over a camisole. A scarf matching the skirt was wrapped around her head, its ends dangling down Rita's back. She looked exotic and a tad out of place compared to what others were wearing, but Maura figured the outfit was exactly what her customers would expect.

"Were you able to park your van over there? The space is filling up pretty quickly." Maura pointed to Theo's place.

"Yes, thanks. I found a great spot. So, lead me to my table!" She hoisted a large cloth tote bag farther up on her shoulder and gave a low sharp whistle that caused Shep's ears to perk up. The dog trotted behind as they walked up the drive to the front lawn, where people were organizing their table displays.

"I've put you over there," Maura said, pointing to the same shady area where Sue Giordano and her family were arranging tablecloths and signs.

"Hmm, so if people want treats, they can consult with me either before or after they've indulged. That'll work. I need at least one folding chair for clients to sit while I perform my magic." She beamed another smile.

"Okay, I'll see about that chair. I think we might have some in the basement. Oh, and I should take Shep with me." She peered around and noticed Shep curled up under Rita's table.

"He's fine here with me. If he gets restless, I'll bring him to the house or put him with Roger."

Maura thought that might be too much responsibility and was about to insist on taking the dog now when Rita said, "Shep seems to be the kind of dog who likes to stick with his own people. There's Roger, and you and your sister. I think I'm on the list now, too." She gave a light laugh. "You have lots to do today, so off you go."

Maura had lots to think about, especially the one task that she was determined to make happen that day—the talk with Theo. "Okay, thanks."

As she began to walk away, Rita called out, "Come for a reading—on the house!"

Maura waved, thinking she already had an idea of what her future might look like, and it wasn't great.

Theo stood gaping at what seemed like pandemonium. When he'd attended the Fourth of July Festival all those summers as a kid and teen, he'd never witnessed the prelude to the actual festival. Although it appeared that people were moving about in random patterns and bumping into one another, he began to see that they were simply carrying out their individual tasks of finding and arranging their tables.

He'd agreed to meet Finn and Shawn to help put together the first aid station and was heading in that direction when he spotted Maura talking to a small woman dressed in flowing, multicolored clothes. Walter intercepted him before he could reach them.

"Theo," he said, "I heard some interested buyers were looking at your land the other day, and rumor has it they didn't seem to be the type to work a farm."

Theo stifled a groan. *The Glen grapevine.* "Just a visit to see what's what, Walter, nothing serious."

Walter pursed his lips and frowned, too polite to push the matter. "Okay. Hate to have this place go the way of far too many other small villages these days."

Theo figured Walter's remark was only the start of negative reactions from the Glen's residents, should he sell to the company. But everything was still up in the air, and there had yet to be an offer. There might not be one at all, he rationalized, recalling his agent's comment about another possible site. No need to rush the explanations.

"Hey."

Theo flinched as someone tapped him on the shoulder but rallied a big smile when he found Maura standing behind him.

"I've been looking for you."

Her smile erased all the doubts and confusion plaguing him the last couple of days. He'd have taken her into his arms right away but for the passersby. "Same here. This scene is…"

"Chaotic?"

"Maybe not that but extremely busy. Have you seen Finn? I'm supposed to meet him where his tent is going to be erected."

"Um, no, I haven't." She looked in the direction of the first aid site.

Rather than follow her gaze, Theo kept his eyes on her. She seemed remarkably relaxed for someone who was hosting the festival, but her pale face and the light blue pouches beneath her eyes told him otherwise. They seriously needed to talk, and he had news to pass on about the cash Luke had found.

Reading his mind, she said, "Maybe we can find some time today to discuss…you know…what's going to happen with us."

He reached down to clasp her hand. "It's a deal."

"Later, then," she murmured, loosening her hand from his.

As he watched her walk away, Theo was overcome with a kind of despair. Sure, they could talk, but to what avail? How would talking change anything? He had an albatross of acreage on his shoulders, a stressful job to return to and a child custody arrangement to settle. Not one of those factors would be easily resolved.

A sharp whistle got his attention. He swung round to see Finn and Shawn, loaded with equipment, heading his way.

"Give us a hand?" Finn asked as they approached. A long canvas bag hanging over his shoulder had begun to slip, and Theo quickly intercepted its fall, grunting at its unexpected weight.

"The tent," Finn explained as he rotated his shoulder, wincing. "There's a lot more in my truck over there, so I'm very happy we found you in this crowd."

The next hour had Theo realizing that although his hospital work frequently involved physical activity, he wasn't as fit as Finn and Shawn. By the time they'd erected the tent and transported the portable stretcher, gurney, two crates of bottled water, a large folding table and a couple of plastic bins that held an array of medical utensils, bandages, cotton swabs, tissues, latex gloves—all the paraphernalia necessary for first aid treatment—he was exhausted.

"I think we're good to go!" Finn announced, wiping his brow with the cuff of his shirt. He pulled out his cell phone from his back pocket. "Gates are open at eleven and it's almost that now. Shawn and I are taking the first two hours. Want to come about one to relieve us for lunch, Theo?"

"Perfect. I'm going to find Maura to see what else I can help with," Theo said, "but if you need me sooner, give me a buzz on my phone." He was about to leave the tent when Finn stopped him.

"I know you'll be heading back to Augusta soon and your life there, but I feel I have to tell you this. There's going to be a medical clinic in Wallingford. All the permits have been approved and funding granted, but it'll be a year before it's up and running. I'm on the citizens' planning committee, and we'll be hiring staff in about five or six months' time. The hope is that our medical teams will consist of local professionals." He shot Theo a meaningful look. "People like you."

Theo was flattered. "Well, I do have—"

"Commitments. Right. Just giving you a heads-up, that's all. Folks here in the Glen would love to have you."

Theo saw Shawn nodding agreement. The unexpected offer threw him. Of course, as Finn said, the timeline was a long one, and Theo had many obligations ahead. "I appreciate your thinking of me," he said, "and will for sure consider it." He was about to ask when they'd need an answer when one side of the tent's flap lifted, and Maddie came in.

"Hi," she said, her face flushing as the three men stared at her. "Can I help with anything?"

"Um, I'm just leaving," Theo said and was partway out the door when he heard Shawn reply, "Sure. That'd be great, Maddie."

They'd already finished the work, Theo was thinking, but the smiles of pleasure on both Shawn's and Maddie's faces made him happy.

He found Maura minutes later, helping Luke, Ashley and a younger boy Theo didn't know decorate the fence around the riding ring with red, white and blue streamers.

"Can I help?"

Maura's face lit up, and Theo felt a surge of pleasure. He also felt Luke's eyes on him and immediately turned his attention to the kids, complimenting them on their handiwork.

"I think we're good here," Maura said. "But Walter and Bill are trying to string up some LED fairy lights around some of the trees to make the area look pretty after dusk. Maybe they could use an extra hand. Oh, and by the way, I've invited the few people who might still be around after it's all over for hot dogs and burgers."

Theo figured he and Luke would definitely be assisting with some cleanup, and that could be a good time for their talk. He nodded and waved goodbye, off to find Walter.

Much later, when the crowds had thinned and Theo, Walter and Bill had finished stringing lights and were taking a break on the veranda steps, the woman he'd seen chatting with Maura a while earlier approached. As Walter made the introductions, Theo realized that the two had only met the day before.

When he shook hands with Rita Moretti, she seemed to

hold on to his a fraction of a second longer. She told him she'd already met his son and what a fine boy he was. He thanked her, filled with parental pride.

"Come to my table," she said, "and I'll give you a reading."

His frown prompted Walter to explain. "Rita is also known as Clair Voyant, palm and tarot card reader."

It took Theo a few seconds. The others, including Rita, chuckled when he exclaimed, "Aha!" Then he added, "Thank you, and, um...maybe I will."

She smiled before saying to Walter, "And don't *you* forget to come for your reading, either."

Theo saw the spark in her eyes at Walter's harrumph, along with the rise of color in his neck.

"Well, I should get back to my table. Nice to meet you, Theo," Rita said and walked away.

An interesting woman, Theo thought, but even more intriguing was how Walter's need for privacy had eased enough to offer such hospitality to a stranger.

"Looks like the crowds are arriving," Walter said, standing to peer down the driveway.

"Guess I'd better look for my daughter and her family," Bill announced. "They're coming soon, and here's hoping they get a parking space."

"I've put up a sign indicating overflow spots in my north pasture," Theo said. "A couple of Bernie Watson's nephews came first thing this morning to direct people and assist with any parking issues."

"I'll go over and see if they can use more help, or even a break." Walter hesitated a second, adding, "It's great to have you and your son for this, after all these years. I'm hoping it won't be your last Fourth of July here." He gave a brisk nod and walked off with Bill.

The lump in Theo's throat caught him off guard. Years of medical training had instilled in him the ability to hide

certain emotions in difficult situations, yet it suddenly occurred to him that some of that training seemed to have
vanished since his return to the Glen. What that meant, he
had no idea. Except he felt there was a new and different
Theo Danby emerging from his former self and suspected
that a return to the Glen was only part of the answer. The
other, larger part? *Maura Stuart.*

He decided to look for Luke, and perhaps if he was
lucky, he'd find Maura, too.

"Hey, Dad, come see the donkeys!" Luke cried when
Theo reached the barn. He grasped Theo's hand and led
him inside. "We brought them into their stalls to give them
some quiet time before the rides start."

All of the donkeys, except Lizzie, were munching quietly in their stalls, their swiveling ears following Theo's
and Luke's footsteps.

"At first we weren't sure about braiding Roger's tail,"
Luke chattered away, "but Ashley had treats and we figured we could try. And guess what? He was just fine with
it. In fact, he stood still better than Jake did."

Luke's animation tickled Theo, and he wondered if he'd
see more of this Luke after they left Maple Glen. "If you
need help giving people rides later, come and find me.
I'm on duty in the first aid tent at one o'clock, for at least
a couple of hours."

"Okay. We're starting the rides about noon, Maddie
said, but Nancy and Cathy will be helping, too." Suddenly
he threw his arms around Theo. "I'm glad you're helping
in the first aid tent."

Theo closed his eyes for a second, reveling in a rare
hug from his son. Then he pulled away, patted him on the
shoulder and left before Luke noticed his damp eyes.

Chapter Twenty-Two

Maura stood at the top of the veranda stairs, shielding her eyes against the sun as she surveyed her land. Well, her and Maddie's land, she silently amended. It was almost midday, and the festival had yet to reach its peak, judging by the steady stream of people from Theo's place to hers. The county road itself was lined on both sides with parked vehicles, though many people were still driving onto Theo's far pasture.

Despite the stress and work of hosting the festival, she felt proud that she and Maddie had pulled it off. Their parents, longtime community supporters in Maple Glen, would be proud, too, and for a split second her eyes filled with tears. She swiped them away. Today wasn't for nostalgia but new beginnings. That was her hope when she finally had Theo to herself, to tell him how her feelings for him had changed—deepened—the last two weeks.

She'd also promised herself some free time to explore the festival as a regular attendee and not an organizer. It would be an opportunity to determine the success of the event for future planning committees. Not that she wanted to actively participate again, she thought, her mouth turning down at the idea, though she might feel differently in a year's time. A year… So much could happen by the next Fourth of July. *Best not to go there, Maura. One day at a time, as Theo would say.*

The first aid tent was straight ahead, and she could see one of Finn's paramedic volunteers talking to an elderly man sitting in a chair. Luke had told her Theo would be working in the tent, news that had raised an improbable scenario in her mind—Theo discovering the benefits of country medicine and moving to the Glen permanently. She'd have laughed at the highly unlikely fantasy if, deep inside, she wasn't yearning for some version of it to come true and change her life. *Not today, though, and maybe not even tomorrow.* She sighed and rounded the corner of the veranda to see what was happening at the riding ring.

Maddie had set up a small table with a shoebox for cash, and Katie was handing change to a young woman at the front of the short line of would-be donkey riders. Katie's mother, sitting next to her, was supervising, but Maura saw right away that the twelve-year-old was managing just fine. She waved, marveling at the growth in Katie's self-confidence since beginning the riding program last fall.

The ring was festooned with red, white and blue streamers, tightly wound so as not to alarm the donkeys, and someone had stuck colorful plastic flowers into the streamer knots. Nancy, Maddie and Ashley were leading Jake, Matilda and Roger slowly around the ring. The riders included two teens, aiming for a casual look, and a gray-haired woman whose gleeful face suggested she might be a future customer.

Luke was standing at the gate next to another small table on which sat a motley collection of helmets—some borrowed, some belonging to her and Maddie—and speaking to a boy his own age who was waiting a turn. She gave Luke a thumbs-up and his instant smile warmed her. What a change from the slumped shoulders and scowl that first day she'd met him and Theo!

Turning to leave, she noticed a younger boy marching around the far side of the ring's fence, fastening the plastic flowers onto the fence. Maura squinted in disbelief. Sammy, focused and actively participating. Another surprise. She scanned the area for the boy's parents, but he seemed to be on his own. Perhaps they were enjoying some of the festival for a few minutes on their own, reassured by the presence of Sammy's riding team. Passing the queue again, Maura couldn't help thinking that maybe all the work she and her sister had devoted to Jake & Friends— her dream!—was finally paying off. The people lining up to ride a donkey were potential clients and customers that would grow the business. Casting a last glance at Katie and Sammy, Maura was filled with pride. However things turned out with the program, she and Maddie already had two success stories.

As she passed the side kitchen door, she heard Shep whimpering inside and had a pang of guilt. The last time she'd seen him he was dozing under Rita's table, and Rita had mentioned she'd return him to the house if he got restless. She went into the kitchen and was almost knocked over by a very excited dog. His water bowl was full, and the kibble she'd left on the counter earlier sat on the floor beside it. Maura picked up his leash, draped over the door handle. "So sorry, fella, but it's all good now. Let's go for a walk."

Shep pulled her out the door and headed straight for the barn, where he thought Roger might be. "Oh, no, not yet, and he's busy now anyway," she told him. She tugged on the leash, forcing him in the opposite direction, toward the tables where buyers and browsers were clustered. It was her first opportunity to check out the variety of goods being sold, and though she'd attended many past festivals, she was still in awe of the talents and initiatives of the Glen residents, as well as the many vendors who'd come from Wallingford and beyond.

Ashley's mother's table featured a variety of handmade cards and miniature, framed watercolor scenes of Maple Glen. Maura bought one of the small paintings of the Otter Creek bridge leading into the woods and the Long Trail. She'd give it to Theo as a memento, though she still clung to the irrational hope that he might not leave. The cloying, sugary fragrance of cotton candy from a cart nearby reminded her that breakfast had been consumed hours before, and judging by the sun, beaming directly onto her, she figured it was noon. Time for lunch. Then perhaps a drop-in visit to the first aid tent, where Theo might be on duty. She veered away from the drive toward the trees on the far west side of the front lawn.

The line in front of the bakery table was long, but Maura decided the wait would be worthwhile. She'd only been standing at the end a few minutes when she noticed Rita waving to her from her table yards away. The woman gestured to the empty chair at her table, and Maura thought, *Why not?*

"By the time I read your cards, that bakery line will be much shorter," Rita told her, smiling, as Maura sat down. "And I'm happy to see you enjoying today as well."

"The festival's been a real memory trip," Maura told her. "My father passed away just before last year's festival, so I only made a very brief visit. Otherwise, this is the first Fourth of July I've attended in years."

"Compared to many fairs and festivals, Maple Glen's is smaller and more low-key. I like its strong community involvement and especially the lack of outside businesses with their mass-market products."

"We do have a strong community here," Maura agreed. "As teenagers, though, my sister and I yearned to escape its closeness, if you know what I mean."

"I do, and I commend you for recognizing its value now. Many people leave their happy places and never return."

Maura thought instantly of Theo and how lucky he was to have had a chance to come back, even if temporarily.

"All right," Rita said, placing a deck of cards in front of Maura. "You shuffle."

After she shuffled, Rita fanned out the cards face down across the table.

"Before I start," she said, her voice now solemn, "I want to remind you, in case you don't know, that tarot cards don't reveal your future. Instead, the cards you choose may tell you something about yourself or indicate something that's been on your mind. Something you may want—or not want—to explore."

"Okay." Now Maura was curious.

"Please pull any two cards from this spread and move them aside but keep them face down."

Maura hesitated, then slipped one card from the end of the fan and another from the center.

Rita gathered the rest of the deck and pushed it aside. She stared at Maura's choices for a moment, then deftly turned one card over. "Hmm," she murmured. "This card is called the Wheel of Fortune."

Maura stared at the stylistic drawing of dragons and other mythical creatures surrounding what resembled a compass, but without any cardinal points.

Rita looked at Maura. "Does it connect with you in any way?"

"Well, I wish I had one," she quipped. "A fortune, I mean."

Rita smiled. "A natural thing to wish, though I've found that people often misunderstand what a fortune can mean."

"As in *good* fortune," Maura asked, "rather than money?"

Rita nodded. "I think that over the next few weeks—or even days—you will decide which fortune has significance for you." Then she turned the other card over.

Maura stared at the title above the man and woman, dressed in what looked like medieval clothing, their arms intertwined and their heads together. *Lovers*. She glanced up at Rita and felt heat rising into her face.

"Maybe this card has special meaning for you, as it has for many people." Her smile was tender. She picked up the two cards and set them atop the deck. "You have much to think about, Maura."

What Maura was actually thinking was, *This is it?* But she merely smiled. "Thanks for this, Rita, and..." She looked in vain for a sign listing the reading fee next to the glass fishbowl at the end of the table.

"On the house, Maura! But if you want to make a donation..."

Maura dug into the pocket of her capris and pulled out a five-dollar bill, which she added to the collection of coins and bills in the bowl. "Thanks, Rita. This was very...interesting."

"It was indeed, for both of us. Have a great day, Maura, and good luck with your decision."

My decision? Maura wondered as she walked away. *Which one?*

It was late afternoon by the time Theo was free to leave the first aid station. He was tired, but in a good way. There'd been a variety of conditions, mostly minor ones: dehydration, dizziness, headaches, a stubbed toe and a

couple of superficial cuts. They'd been easy to handle—
water, food, acetaminophen, bandages and rest. The idea
of using the shady veranda as an auxiliary site for the tent
had been a good one.

He left when Finn and one of his fire department colleagues relieved him. "Thanks again, Theo, and please
give some thought to what we were discussing earlier,"
Finn said on parting.

The Wallingford medical clinic and a potential job. All
up in the air for now, Theo figured. Still, the option of
staying in the Glen was, as far-fetched as it seemed right
then, compelling. He'd liked the novelty of quietly chatting with patients as he treated them, no rushing about
to insert IV lines or run for a defibrillator. The pace had
been refreshing.

Finn's proposal stuck with him as he went to check on
Luke. If he was lucky, he'd find Maura, too. Maybe he'd
have a chance to tell her what Finn had said, see her reaction. Or maybe not, he quickly decided, realizing there
were far too many factors to consider before a decision
about his future—and Luke's—could be made.

That sobering reality was at the forefront of his mind as
he made his way around the tables, so he didn't at first hear
his name being called. He stopped, scanning the crowd,
and noticed a woman beckoning from a table. Rita, he
remembered, though the name on the large sign leaning
against the table read Clair Voyant. A couple were walking away from her table, and Theo was tempted to do
the same, but something in the woman's welcoming smile
drew him to her.

Despite his intention to make an excuse, he found himself sitting down and watching her spread cards across
the table as she spoke. Her patter barely registered, as
Theo's mind shifted back to Maura again and, inexplica-

bly, the company interested in his property. He needed to tell Maura about that before she heard it through the Glen grapevine.

When Rita told him to draw two cards from the semi-circle in front of him, he did so without much deliberation, impatient to get through the reading as quickly as possible. Theo only caught a quick glimpse of their colorful illustrations, but Rita studied them for what seemed a long time.

Finally, she pointed to one and said, "This is called The Juggler. Also known as The Magician. An interesting choice, Theo."

Curious now, he wanted her to say more but remembered her words at the start of the session. This wasn't about his future but about his connections. Whatever that meant, he thought. "Well, I'm constantly juggling priorities, as well as my time, when I'm working," he said, offering an explanation.

She nodded. "Perhaps decisions, too. And working some magic, I'm guessing."

Maybe, he thought.

She upturned the second card, and Theo leaned forward to stare at it. *Lovers.* Definitely an easier one to figure out than a juggler.

"Most people like this card," Rita said, studying his face.

Theo's indifferent shrug didn't seem to bother her as she added, "But it's a card not too many people draw, in my limited experience. Only one other today."

He waited for further explanation, but when none came, he felt a tad disappointed. Okay, he thought. Definitely not a fortune-telling, as she'd asserted at the beginning. He stuffed a bill into the fishbowl and stood to leave.

"Thanks, Rita. That was…well…interesting."

Later he thought her expression had been slightly

amused by his comment. But what dominated his thoughts much longer were her last words.

"Don't be afraid of the *M* word, Theo. And good luck with your juggling!"

The *M* word. Did she mean Maura? Because that was the first *M* word that came to mind. Except it wasn't a word, really, but a name. An alternative suddenly popped into his head—*money*—a word that had consumed his thoughts recently. The loan and the potential sale of his land. Another interpretation occurred—one that stopped him in his tracks as he went looking for Luke.

Marriage? He shoved aside that connection right away. His life was already far too complicated. What else had Rita, or Clair Voyant, said when he was leaving? Something about juggling and decisions. Those were two words he could relate to because they were constants in his working life in Emergency. But of course, the card and her reference to decisions were simply coincidental.

Theo knew coincidences were random events that people wanted to attach meaning to, and he was no exception when it came to accounting for the random things that had happened since his return to Maple Glen: the discovery of a mystery loan that jeopardized a possible future with Maura, Shawn's unexpected return just when Maddie was faced with a decision to stay or leave the Glen, the offer of a potential job in a new clinic, and the hard fact that the only possible buyer for his land was a development company that could ruin the Glen. He was at a loss to explain any of it. He headed for the riding ring, where he hoped to find Luke and maybe Maura.

When Maura saw him and waved, her smile almost had Theo changing his mind. Walking from Rita's table to here, he'd concluded that he must tell Maura about the potential buyers now, rather than wait until after he heard back from them. But as he drew near, he realized why Maura had been smiling. Luke was in the ring, riding Jake.

Theo stood beside Maura, his heart bursting as he watched his son ride Jake around the ring. When he spotted Theo, Luke waved, and Theo's eyes welled up at the proud grin on the boy's face.

"He told me after his first donkey ride that his goal was to ride Jake," Theo said to Maura. "And he did it."

"He did, and you're obviously as proud as he is." She smiled and reached for his hand, squeezing it. Then she added, "You're finished in the first aid tent?"

"Yep. Fortunately, it wasn't very busy. Um…" He peered around. "Do you have a minute?"

"We're shutting down the riding ring shortly. The donkeys need a break and so do we! How about you? Do you need a break, too?"

The question, posed with arched eyebrows and a coy smile, was flirtatious, and he wanted to fold her into his arms and bury his face in the crook of her neck. But no. He'd made a decision and had to proceed.

Pulling her off to the far side of the ring, he said, "I need to tell you a couple of important things."

Her smile faded at the tone of his voice.

He kept his eyes on hers. "First of all, Luke and I found a hidden stash of money at the farm. Rolls of fifty-dollar bills and a note from Uncle Stan saying he was going to forgive the loan to your father. I think that he forgot, or maybe all this happened just before he and my aunt went into the nursing home. I'm not sure."

Maura's eyes widened. "That explains the monthly withdrawals from Dad's account." She paused, clearly processing what this meant to her and the business. "And you also said?" she finally asked.

He was happy at the relief on her face, but knew he had

to go on to the next part that might not be so welcome. "The potential buyer for my property is a company. A big one, known for commercial and residential construction."

The words seemed to take a long time to sink in. Her light frown gradually deepened as her lips moved without speech, as if she were underwater. "I'm not sure I understand," she finally began to say, "but when you say *potential* buyer, do you mean there are others or…what, exactly?"

"*Potential* because they haven't made an offer. But so far, the company is the only interested buyer."

She took another long moment.

"And your thoughts?"

He tried to ignore the tremor in her voice but couldn't. Instead, he looked toward the ring, where Maddie and the other women were now leading the donkeys out and to the barn.

"Theo?" she prompted.

He sighed and faced her. "As I said, they're the only interested party."

"And?"

He swore silently. She was pushing him to say it. "I may not have a choice."

"People who say that almost always do have choices, Theo. Are you seriously telling me that you'd consider selling your land—right next to ours—to a construction company that will be building on it? Houses? Condos? In Maple Glen?" Her voice pitched in disbelief.

"I don't know, Maura. I… I have decisions to make and—"

"You're not the only one with decisions to make, Theo. I just hope you'll make the right ones."

At that she spun around and marched away, faster than Theo could catch his breath.

Chapter Twenty-Three

The rest of the day was a blur for Maura. She scarcely remembered later how she endured it, pasting a fake smile on her face while inside she was seething. She knew Maddie suspected something because her sister kept flashing concerned sidelong glances her way, but there was no opportunity to tell her what she'd just learned. But she'd recalled Maddie's remark the other day about spotting people walking around Theo's land. "Not regular people," Maddie had said, and Maura wished now that she'd followed up on that with Theo at the time. Perhaps she could have confronted him right away, instead of having today ruined. That was what it felt like.

Were they always going to fall into this cycle of keeping something from one another? What did that mean for the chance of a future together? The specter of her tarot card rose up—Lovers. Ha! Perhaps she should see Rita for another reading.

"Maura? Got a minute?"

She swung around, only then realizing that she was standing near the kitchen door staring blankly at the festival crowd, now in various stages of leaving.

Walter smiled. "You were so deep in thought I hesitated to disturb you. Is there a problem? Anything I can help you with?"

Her mood lightened a tiny bit at his kind face. "No, but thanks, Walter. I'm just wishing all this would end soon."

"You must be tired, but I'd say the festival's been a great success and a tribute to the hard work you and Maddie devoted to it."

"All of us, Walter. The committee. The people of Maple Glen."

"True. Anyway, I was about to say that many folks have had enough and are packing up. I know our volunteers will be here in full force early tomorrow, but I'm happy to get a start at some of the cleanup now. Collecting trash or recycling that didn't make it into our bins, for example. You don't want to draw any animals in the night."

Her thoughts, still fixated on Theo's bombshell, hadn't gotten as far as cleanup. Did Walter know about the possible sale? "Thanks, Walter, a good idea. And…um…have you heard that a potential buyer for Theo's property is a big construction company?"

Walter's face creased and he shook his head. "No, though I heard the people who inspected it were definitely not farmers, or even hobby farmers."

"He told me an offer hasn't been made yet."

"Hmm, makes sense he'd want to keep that close to his chest, then, rather than upset everyone for no reason."

"But they're the only interested buyers so far." She felt tears well up and looked away.

"I guess he'll have some tough decisions to make." He patted her shoulder. "Let's wait and see what happens."

She nodded, grateful for the advice, though she knew following it would be a challenge.

"You and Maddie will appreciate a relaxing evening

later on, unless you're planning to go to Wallingford for the fireworks."

Years ago, the Fourth of July organizers had decided not to host fireworks at the end of the day. The fireworks in Wallingford and beyond drew most of the Glen's residents anyway, and the village wouldn't have to spend more money or to compete with those other displays. That had been a factor in Maura and Maddie's offer to host, knowing their donkeys wouldn't panic at the sounds and flashing lights.

"No, I think I'll be ready to sit and put my feet up. How about you?"

He chuckled. "Same here. And thanks for the supper invite. Maddie mentioned it when Bill and I were stringing the fairy lights. He can't stay, but I'd love to."

The plan for a simple barbecue with a few friends at the end of the day had been concocted at breakfast that morning. She'd almost forgotten, though she knew she'd invited Theo and Luke. Maddie had said she'd like to ask Finn and Shawn because they'd have to stay longer to dismantle the first aid station, and Maura had given her a knowing grin that had her sister blushing.

Maura took a deep breath. She had to rally the energy to get through the rest of the day, help host a barbecue and then deal with this new, unwelcome situation with Theo. "That's great, Walter, and thanks for staying on to help. If you see Rita, pass on the invitation to her."

His smile shifted. "I would, but I think she's already left." He must have seen Maura's expression. "Likely she has another fair or some other small-town event to head for and figured she'd beat the inevitable traffic jam of folks leaving the parking area at Theo's."

"Oh, I'm sorry I didn't get a chance to say goodbye."

"I think she wanted it that way," Walter said. "Goodbyes

aren't such a big deal when you're always making them. I guess that might be her philosophy, as a nomad."

Maura thought back to Walter's words throughout the rest of the day. The goodbyes in her life had been a mix of pain, relief and, occasionally, pleasure. They definitely had never been easy. The stark image of a goodbye to Theo and Luke hit her in the pit of her stomach. She knew that one wouldn't be the "see you later" kind of goodbye.

As the last stragglers trudged down the drive, Maura headed into the kitchen, where she'd seen Maddie disappear minutes ago. She let out a long and loud sigh of relief when the kitchen screen door closed behind her.

Maddie looked up from the salad she was preparing and smiled. "Same here. I think this will be enough with the burgers and hot dogs, won't it?"

"We have potato chips, too."

"That's a yes, then. By the way, Luke asked if Ashley could stay, too, and her parents said it was okay. Finn offered to drop her home on his way, afterward."

"Shawn staying?"

Maddie grabbed a tomato from the bowl on the table and began chopping it up.

"That's a yes, then?" Maura teased, mimicking her sister. She'd have pushed a bit more to see how far the color rising up into Maddie's neck would go, but this was the best time—maybe the only time—to tell her what Theo had revealed.

Maddie set the knife onto the cutting board and listened, the color draining out of her face. "I don't like the sound of that. I...well... It's difficult to process the impact on our business. I mean, the donkeys are skittish enough when that farmer from Wallingford who rents Theo's back acreage comes with his combine."

Another factor Maura hadn't considered—she'd been

so focused on Theo keeping the information to himself. "Maybe *he* could buy the land." At her sister's frown, she added, "The farmer, I mean."

Maddie dismissed the glib suggestion with a shrug. "I'm sure other options will come up when we know for sure what's going to happen. In the meantime, let's end today on a positive note, okay? We've got good friends coming for supper and hopefully an early night for both of us."

Maura wanted to pursue those options, but Maddie was right. She needed to collect her thoughts and present as a calm, rational person when the others—especially Theo— came for supper. "Want help with prepping?" she finally asked.

"I think I can handle this. Luke and Ashley are setting up the veranda, where I thought we'd eat. Theo's getting the barbecue ready out by the barn. Shawn and Finn, as you may have seen, are packing up the first aid tent."

"Okay. Walter and Bill are collecting trash and any- thing perishable left behind on tables. And Bill can't stay, but Walter will."

"What about Rita? Did we invite her?" Maddie asked as she scooped the tomatoes into the salad bowl.

"She left early."

"Hmm. I suppose that makes sense. She probably has other places to travel to. I liked her, but there was some- thing about her..." She thought for a minute, then shook her head. "Can't say what, exactly." She raised her eyes to Maura. "Did she read your cards?"

"Yep."

"And?"

Maura grinned. "I'll never tell." And she knew she defi- nitely would not, especially now. "How about you?"

Maddie nodded and began slicing a cucumber. "C'mon. I asked first."

Maura chose the easy way out. "She hinted I'd be making a decision."

"Only *one*?" Maddie teased. "Given what we've been discussing, I imagine there'll be *many* decisions in your future, Maura Stuart."

If only it were a future I'd want, Maura thought. "I think any options informing my decision now will be seriously limited."

Maddie pursed her lips. "Let's not jump ahead, Maura. We don't know anything about Theo's plans, much less what's going through his mind."

Trust Mads to think of the other guy. She'd been the peacemaker as a kid and teen, the one who wanted to mend situations, whereas Maura always wanted to leave, walk out the door and forget everything. "I hope whatever Rita helped you to see involves happiness," she said in a low voice.

Maddie ducked her head, but finally replied, "I drew this card called Strength, or Fortitude. My first thought was how ironic because I've never considered myself a strong person, you know? But then she put a spin on it, saying how we perceive ourselves isn't necessarily how others do. I mean, that's obvious, right? But later I began to think of another way of looking at it. What if my real strength was *giving* courage rather than having it?"

Maura could only nod around the swelling in her throat.

"So what I'm telling you right now, dear twin, is that I know you will find the way to tell Theo what's really on your mind. That you will focus on the long term and not the short. That you will search inside yourself for an answer to the question 'how much would I give up to have Theo?' And last, but this is the most important one, Maura, you will tell him exactly how much he means to you—without reservation."

Maura brushed a finger across her damp cheek. "I love you, Mads." She hugged her sister.

Theo muttered and cursed as he wrestled with the barbecue as if it were a living creature. It certainly had lots of life inside, as he discovered when he opened the lid and strands of cobwebs and scattering spiders made him jump back in alarm. He was glad Luke wasn't around at the moment. Tasks like this weren't really his thing, but Maura had asked and...well...he'd do anything for Maura.

That thought made him pause. Anything? Like turn down a mega offer on his land, should it arise? Days ago, he'd have laughed at the absurd idea. Now he was more confused than ever. What was it that Rita had said as he'd been about to leave? "Don't be afraid of the *M* word"? He realized he could add "magician" to the list of *M* words he'd already compiled, because he knew it would take some magic—or a lot of it—to get Maura to forgive his lapse in judgment about keeping the buyer's identity to himself. That was all it had been, really—a poor decision—and he knew her reaction hadn't been about that miscall, but the unthinkable impact a large building site would have on her riding program.

He found a broom inside the barn to sweep out the interior of the barbecue, and with each hard brushstroke, he cursed himself for all the missed chances to tell Maura exactly how he felt about her, the sale of his land, even Maple Glen itself.

"Dad?"

Startled, Theo looked up to see Luke standing in front of him, holding a large, clear plastic bag of recycling in one hand.

"What's happening?"

Theo pointed to the barbecue. "Just cleaning it up a bit. Why?"

Luke shrugged. "You had a funny look on your face, that's all. But now that I see you, and we're alone, I've got something to tell you."

That sounded ominous. Theo set the broom across the top of the barbecue. "Okay. Go ahead."

"Today was so much fun and...well... I want to come back next year for it. Even if our farm and land are gone, we could stay at Mr. Watson's B and B or in Wallingford, but I will always want to be here on the Fourth of July."

Theo felt his heart constrict. Not only at the solemn earnestness in his son's expression, but his phrase "our farm and land." *Our.* A connection to his birthright, an inheritance, and the Danby family. He nodded, too overcome to speak.

"The other thing is, I've decided I want to stay with you in the fall. I can see Mom in the holidays, and since I'll have my own cell phone, I can keep in contact with you when you're working. Okay?"

Theo could only nod his answer. He drew his son close in a long, tight hug until Luke said, "I've got to finish helping tidy up. See you at supper." And he disappeared into the barn, towing the bag of recycling.

Thoughts and ideas were flitting across Theo's mind. Decisions were already being made without his input. He had to get moving and start making some of his own. When a voice broke through his mental confusion, he looked up to see Walter standing where Luke had been minutes ago.

"Want a hand with that?" His tone was amused, his eyes twinkling.

"Please," Theo murmured. He handed Walter the broom, and then he went to find a private place to make a phone call before looking for Maura.

She was in the kitchen chatting to Maddie, and they both raised surprised faces when he walked in.

"We have to talk," he said quickly, before he could be sidetracked. He held out his hand and was relieved when Maura reached for it, no questions asked. As he led her out the door, he caught Maddie's encouraging smile.

They walked silently together, Theo heading for the gap in the cedar hedge—their old escape route—and out onto his front lawn, now an empty expanse of churned-up dirt ruts and tire marks. He grasped her hand a bit tighter, giving himself courage, and told her what Luke had expressed moments ago. She didn't say anything, but he saw her eyes glistening.

"After he told me that," Theo went on, "I felt a bit guilty, that a twelve-year-old could make a life-changing decision quicker than I could."

Maura's mouth lifted in a light smile, so he pushed on. "This land—" he gestured in a broad arc "—is more than money in the bank. It's a legacy—the Danby legacy—from my loving aunt and uncle who nurtured me here all those summers. I... I'm sorry it's taken me so long to accept that importance. That my son and you, Maddie and even Walter saw what I couldn't." He dropped his hand from hers and forked it through his hair, giving himself time to find the right words. "The irreparable damage to the very soul of Maple Glen that selling this to...to that outfit...would bring."

He inhaled. "That's one thing I have to say. And, for the record, I've just made a phone call to remove the property from the market." He ignored her gasp and went on. "The second thing is that Finn told me about the approval of a medical clinic in Wallingford. He's the community representative for the project, and they're looking for doctors. He said he'd support my application if I was interested."

He paused, taking another deep breath. "The thing is, I *am* interested, Maura. And I'm more than ready to make a career change from emergency medicine. I liked the low-key approach with people and patients while I worked at the first aid tent and the connection I made with them. Finally, the most important thing I need to say is that I have decisions to make about the future, but I want you to be part of that. I want—with all my heart, Maura—for you to be in my future and Luke's."

She brought her hands up to the back of his neck and drew his face to hers. "Theo," she whispered, her voice husky, "I'm in your future right now and for always."

Maura leaned back in her chair, surveying the group sitting around the table they'd set up on the veranda. Walter, Finn, Shawn, Theo, Luke, Ashley and Maddie. Not exactly a family, she thought, but perhaps the closest she and her sister might come to have.

Walter left first, followed by Finn, who was driving Ashley home.

Theo took her aside. "Got a minute—or two?"

She caught the glint of a tease in his eyes and eagerly followed him onto the dark front lawn, lit by the sparkling fairy lights strung through the trees. He took her hand in his and led her past the barn to the pasture where they stood gazing up at the moon.

The silence and scents raised childhood memories of hot summer nights when she and her sister sat out on the veranda with their parents, absorbing the sounds of the country—crickets, owls, nighthawks, and frogs singing from some pond miles away. *How could I ever leave this?* she asked herself.

Yet right after Theo's news earlier, she'd blurted that if she had to sell the business and move to Augusta, she would. He'd smiled and held her closer. "I won't hold you to that, Maura," he'd assured her before kissing her again.

Now she leaned against the pasture fence, soaking up the balmy night air while Theo stood behind her, his warm arms compensating for the sweater she'd left on the veranda.

"Can we make it work, Theo? A future together?" she asked, her voice wobbly at the seemingly impossible obstacles ahead. "There'd be some commuting while you organize the change in jobs, whenever that can happen. And at some point Luke would have to change schools if you move back to the Glen. How does he feel about that?"

"I discussed it with him briefly before supper, and he surprised me by interrupting to say he'd give up graduating from eighth grade in Augusta for the chance to live in Maple Glen."

"Wow! That's quite a concession for a twelve-year-old."

"I think he made that decision before our talk. Today's celebration was simply the icing on the cake, so to speak."

Maura's mind was already buzzing with plans. She smiled, thinking how Maddie would tease her later on, when she recounted all of this to her sister. They'd agreed to talk about the future of Jake & Friends, as well as the farm. Although Maddie hadn't revealed the reason for her smiles and glances Shawn's way during supper, Maura was guessing a future in Maple Glen for Maddie might be possible. She certainly hoped so. She was about to tell Theo how much she loved him when a loud explosion sounded from the west. They spun around to see bursts of color striking the dark sky. "The Wallingford fireworks," Theo said. "Luke will be watching with Shawn and Maddie from your veranda."

"Shall we join them?"

"In a minute," he murmured, tilting her chin ever so slightly and lowering his mouth to hers.

It was a long kiss, one that made up for all the missed kisses since they were teenagers, Maura figured. They broke apart only when another firework hit the sky, followed immediately by eruptions from the barn. Donkeys braying.

Theo laughed. "Good thing you left them inside for the night. What were you saying about this coming fall?"

"Can we make it all work?"

He brought her back into his arms. "I love you and you love me. We'll find a way to make it work, Maura."

And she knew they would.

* * * * *

Special EDITION

Believe in love. Overcome obstacles. Find happiness.

Available Next Month

A Beach House Beginning RaeAnne Thayne
A Beauty In The Beast Michelle Lindo-Rice

....

The Bachelor's Matchmaker Marie Ferrarella
Her Fake Boyfriend Heatherly Bell

Keep reading for an excerpt of a new title
from the Medical series,
HER FORBIDDEN FIREFIGHTER by Traci Douglass

CHAPTER ONE

"I'M NOT LOST," Luna Norton said to the chipmunk watching her from across the wooded path. "I've been down this trail a million times. But I don't suppose you know which way to go?"

His nose twitched, then the chipmunk turned tail and vanished into the underbrush.

Well, that's what she got for asking for directions from a wild animal.

Luna stood there another moment trying to get her bearings, with the hazy winter sun seeping through the evergreen branches, her phone in one hand and her sketch pad in the other. The forest around her was a profusion of greens, thick with the remnants of the latest snowstorm a week ago. Even with the chilly mid-January temperatures, the place was abuzz with activity, and she constantly had to leap away when birds and squirrels chattered at her. Luna was used to life in the tiny town of Wyckford, Massachusetts—quaint shops, cozy diners and people constantly around. Coming out here to the wilderness, which she did at least a couple of times a month, was her escape. From stress, from work, from basically everything she didn't want to deal with. At thirty-five, she supposed she ought to have better coping skills than running away, but hey. If it wasn't broken, don't fix it, right?

She yawned and turned in a circle, searching for the trail out, which was easier said than done given all the snow on the ground. She'd been up since before dawn that morning, first working a full shift as a physical therapist at Wyckford General before driving out here to the trails this afternoon, and she was still on her feet, if a little unsure about which direction to go.

With a sigh, Luna tried the GPS on her phone again, but it was still out of service. Great.

She hiked for what felt like forever, going in the direction she was pretty sure was right, searching for more bars. The terrain looked so much different in January than it did in the summer, but Luna was usually spot-on when it came to the trails. And she'd come prepared for the cold in her winter gear, as well. She wasn't one of those dumb tourists who got stuck out here at least once a week. She knew what she was doing. Or at least she thought she did. Luna wasn't exactly a wait-and-see kind of girl. Never had been. Patience wasn't a virtue she possessed. At least that's what her parents always told her growing up anyway.

She'd always been more of a mess-around-and-find-out kind of person. Or she had been until life had other ideas.

Ugh. Life.

She'd spent her whole life in Wyckford, and she had what most people would consider success—a good job, a nice apartment, loving family, great friends. And while she was beyond grateful for those things, recently she'd noticed an inconvenient yearning for something more. Probably because her two best friends—Cassie Murphy and Madi Scott—had found their forever person over the last year, and their happiness had suddenly made Luna uncomfortably aware of what was lacking in her own life. And it was inconvenient because with all their love in the air and in her face, she felt a bit left out, even if she didn't really believe in happily-ever-after.

As she continued walking, Luna dodged obstacles like rocks, jutting tree roots and, in two cases, downed trees with trunks bigger around than her car. But Luna knew a thing or two about taking detours and getting back on the right path. So she kept moving, amid sky-high evergreens she couldn't even see the tops of, feeling small and insignificant.

And awed.

She just needed to find a new direction, a goal. Some peace would be good, too. And love? Well, she didn't care so much about that. Love, of the romantic kind anyway, was scary and dangerous and best avoided, in her opinion. Her past run-ins with romance had included a bunch of one-nighters and a few relationships that had lasted a few months even, but nothing beyond that, which was fine. Luna preferred her freedom and her safety over "till death do us part" anyway. Especially the death part.

When she finally stopped to check her GPS again—still out of service—she took a break and opened her backpack, going directly for the emergency brownie she'd packed earlier. Luna sat on a large rock and sighed from the pleasure of resting for a moment.

Then a bird dive-bombed her with the precision of a kamikaze pilot, and Luna jumped up and eyed her fallen brownie, lying forlorn in the dirt. With a sigh, she checked her smartwatch and saw it was 4:30 p.m. It would start getting dark soon, and Luna figured she had maybe another half hour to find her way out of here before nightfall. She slung her backpack over her shoulders and decided to retrace her steps back to where she'd started when an odd rustling sound had her swiveling fast as the hairs on the back of her neck prickled. "Hello?"

The rustling stopped and she caught a quick flash of blue in the bushes. A hoodie, maybe?

"Hello?" she called again, her heart racing and throat dry. "Who's there?"

No answer.

Luna reached into the pocket of her parka for the pocketknife she kept there just in case.

Another slight rustle, then a glimpse of *something*—

"Hey," she yelled, louder than necessary, but she *hated* being startled.

Sudden stillness fell, telling her she was alone again.

Blood still jackhammering in her ears, Luna turned around. Then around again.

She walked back along the path for a minute, but nothing seemed familiar, so she did a one-eighty and tried again. Feeling like she'd gone down the rabbit hole, Luna tried her cell phone again, but still no service.

Don't panic.

Luna never panicked until her back was up against the wall. Eyeing an opening in the ever-greens, she headed toward it. Maybe if she could get into a clearing, she could get better reception. But she emerged through the trees to find herself standing at the edge of a steep embankment down to a frozen creek bed, sharp, jagged pieces of ice jutting up like knives waiting for a hapless victim.

The ground beneath her feet was slick, and somewhere behind her, Luna heard rustling again.

She inched back from the edge of the embankment as the scent of pine made her nose itch, looking around and wondering what sort of animals were nearby, hunting for their next meal. She'd read online there were bobcats in the state, but primarily in the central and western parts. Also, black bears. In fact, there had been more recent reports of them coming closer to town because of the food. She should have brought bear repellent.

Why didn't I bring bear repellent?

With the sun rapidly setting, she needed to get a move on before the temperatures dropped below zero that night. She resettled the comforting weight of her knife in her palm and wished for another brownie.

As she headed back into the forest, the noises started up again. Birds. A mournful howl echoed in the distance, and goose bumps rose over her entire body. Luna nearly got whiplash from checking them all out. But as she'd learned long ago, maintaining a high level of tension for an extended time was exhausting. Eventually, she heard footsteps coming up the path from the opposite direction she *thought* she'd come from. They weren't loud, but Luna was a master at hearing someone approach. She could do it in her sleep. Her heart kicked hard as old memories resurfaced, heavy, drunken footsteps heading down the hall to her bedroom…

"You owe me, Luna."

The footsteps got closer, sounded heavier. A man, who was apparently not making any attempt to hide his approach. Luna squeezed the knife in her palm, just in case. Then, from around the edge of a towering evergreen, he appeared. Tall, built, gorgeous and, best of all, *familiar*!

She knew him. Mark Bates. A local firefighter. They saw each other around Wyckford General regularly, and from when Luna taught stretching classes at the fire station to help the guys reduce occupational injuries. All the ladies of Wyckford fawned over Mark, which Luna attributed to the electrifying mix of testosterone and his uniform. Women loved a man in uniform.

Well, women except Luna. She'd learned long ago not to trust appearances.

He stood near an evergreen, wearing a black down jacket with a reflective Wyckford Fire Department logo on the front and a red knit hat covering his blond hair. Dark sunglasses hung around his neck, his light blue gaze missing nothing in the gathering dusk. Those sharp eyes were in complete contrast with his lazy smile, all laid-back and easygoing, but Luna suspected Mark was trouble with a capital T, *mainly because he was just so darn attractive*, and she'd given up trouble a long time ago.

Dammit. Out of all the people in town, he would have to be the one to find her.

She was still and silent, but Mark's attention tracked straight to her with no effort at all. "Kind of late to be out here on your own, isn't it?"

If he wanted to hear Luna admit she was lost, he'd turn to a block of ice first.

When she didn't answer, Mark's smile grew.

Childish and immature? Yeah, probably. But Luna didn't like the way her pulse tripped and her skin heated when he was around. It scared her, and she refused to be afraid again. Or ask for his help. Even if he did look like he knew exactly how to get her out of this forest.

"You need help getting back to your car?" he asked after a while. "I'm pretty familiar with the territory since the fire department trains out here a lot."

Luna squared her shoulders, hoping she looked more capable than she felt. "I'm fine. I know these woods, too. I wouldn't have come out here if I didn't."

He smiled, his teeth even and white in the growing darkness. "Great, then."

"Great." For some reason, his smug grin annoyed the crap out of her. Like he knew she was lying. Which was impossible, because if there was one thing Luna knew how to do, it was hide her secrets. Whatever. She didn't have time to stand around chatting with him. Luna waved her hand dismissively as she passed him. "See you around. I'm sure you have kittens to rescue or something."

"Kitten rescues *do* actually take up a lot of my time," he agreed good-naturedly. "But if you're heading out, maybe I'll just tag along, then. For the company."

His voice always did funny things to Luna's stomach. And lower, too, but she ignored those things because it was safer that way. And all that unwanted tingling only made her more determined to get away from him. Injecting as much sarcastic venom as she could into her words, she gave him a saccharine smile. "I don't need company."

"Okay." Mark shrugged, looking completely unbothered as they continued walking side by side. "You might not know this, but on top of all the kitten wrangling I do, rescuing fair maidens is also part of my job description."

"I don't need rescuing—" Outraged, Luna turned and prepared to let him have it, but something screeched loud directly above her, and she crouched instead, covering her head, and ruining her tough-girl cred.

"Owl." A hint of amusement edged Mark's tone now. "They're getting ready to hunt."

Luna straightened as another animal howled

in the distance. She pointed in the direction of the noise. "What about that? *That* was no owl."

"Coyote," he agreed. "Lots of predators in these woods."

"I know that." The words squeaked out of Luna's suddenly constricted throat before she cleared it and turned away. "I'm usually just gone when they come out. I need to get home."

Mark shrugged, looking completely unperturbed as he followed beside her. "I'm sure you've heard about the recent bear sightings and—"

Luna kept her attention focused straight ahead, not answering. With his charming, "I'm here to help you" facade, he was everything she didn't trust. She'd fallen prey to that once before and had the internal scars from her attacker to prove it. Easy smile, easy nature, easy ways—it all had to be an act, no matter how sexy the packaging.

Mark loved his job. Having come from first the military, then Chicago FD, the current shortage of high-rise blazes, tenement fires and Jaws of Life rescues in his workweek was a big bonus. But his day at the Wyckford Fire Department had started at the ass crack of dawn this morning, when two of his fellow firefighters—there were only five of them total—had called in sick, forcing Mark to give up his much-needed day off, a chore that ranked right up there with having a root canal.

After spending a long day stocking supplies at the station and cleaning the fire truck inside and out, he'd then helped on a couple of EMT runs in town. Nothing major—suspected heart attack, allergic reaction to shellfish, Viagra mishap at the town's local retirement home. Then he'd gone back to the station to handle some dreaded paperwork, until he'd been ordered out here to check the fire gates on the trails.

Finding Luna Norton had been an unexpected bonus, standing there with her mile-long legs encased in faded jeans beneath her big puffy parka, winter boots and her stormy gray eyes that gave nothing away except her mistrust.

As usual when he saw her, Mark felt a punch of awareness hit him in the solar plexus.

Man, she was so beautiful. And so very much radiating serious "keep away" vibes.

He couldn't help wondering why, even though it was none of his business.

Besides, she wasn't even his usual type. Still, something about Luna drew him in like a bug to a zapper. Ever since he'd moved to Wyckford, he'd had his eye on her, though not much else since she seemed to go out of her way to avoid him whenever they were in the same vicinity. Which was a real feat given that they seemed to run into each other a lot, between the hospital and the fire station and the Buzzy Bird diner, which her parents owned in town. And in the two years he'd been here, he'd never once seen Luna date anyone.

Another thing that intrigued him.

Not that he was exactly a Casanova himself. Nope. He was done with relationships, after his marriage had blown up back in Chicago. Once the divorce was final, he'd said sayonara to love and was happy being on his own. No commitments. No complications. No problem. He'd stayed away from dating since he'd been in Wyckford and was perfectly happy about it.

And maybe the nights did get long and cold, especially this time of year.

He was fine on his own. Just fine and dandy.

They continued walking, in the exact opposite direction of the parking lot, but far be it from him to correct a woman who was obviously on the warpath. If she wanted to continue to be bafflingly stubborn and adorable, so be it. He hazarded a side-glance at her in the quickly fading light. Took in her short black hair spiked around her face from beneath her pink knit hat, her pink lips glistening slightly from the balm she used, her ever-present tough expression and the proud tilt to her chin, not giving an inch.

He tried a different tack. "You hike out here a lot in the winter, huh?"

She glanced out at the last rays of the setting sun, then back to him with a tight smile. "Yep."

Not for the first time, Mark wondered what it would be like to see her smile with both her eyes and her mouth at the same time. He also noticed the tightness at the corners of her mouth and eyes. Luna was scared, which stirred not only his protective nature but also his natural curiosity and suspicion—good for the firefighter in him, dangerous for a man no longer interested in romance.

"That's good," he said agreeably. "Because you know we're going the wrong way."

She stopped short and faced him, hands on hips, lips compressed. "You could've said that half a mile ago."

"I could, but I value my life." He leaned back against a tree, enjoying the flash of annoyance on her face. It'd been a hell of a long day, and it was shaping up to be a longer night. There wasn't enough caffeine in the world to get him through it, but this was a nice distraction. How someone who'd been here before could get so completely turned around was a puzzle he suddenly wanted to solve.

Luna sighed, then stalked off in the opposite direction, which was also wrong.

"Need help?" Mark called from behind her.

She slowly turned to face him; her teeth clenched. He still leaned against that evergreen, arms crossed over his broad chest, his shoulders looking sturdy enough to carry all her burdens. Which only made her angrier. He watched her like he had all the time in the world and no concerns.

Maybe he didn't. *He* wasn't lost.

The air between them crackled, and it had nothing to do with the wildlife.

It'd been a long time since Luna had allowed herself to experience this kind of tension with a man and she wasn't sure how to react, so she went with her default. Anger. Because men were dangerous, in more ways than one, and she knew beneath their chosen veneer, whatever it may be— nice guy, funny guy, sexy guy, whatever—their true colors lurked, lying in wait.

In his defense, she'd seen Mark around for two years now, and he was always just… *Mark*. Amused, tense, tired, regardless he remained cool, calm, even-keeled. Nothing seemed to get to him. Luna had to admit she was confused. *He* confused her.

She crossed her arms. "No."

He arched a brow, his expression filled with polite doubt.

Admitting defeat sucked, but the sun was nearly gone now, and the temperatures were dropping fast. "Please just point me in the right direction."

He did.

Right. Luna stalked off in the correct direction.

"Watch out for bears," Mark called after her. "Three o'clock."

She froze and glanced sideways to see a huge, hulking shadow. A bear. A *big* bear. Enjoying the last of rays of the day and scratching his back against the trunk of an evergreen, his huge paws in the air, confident he sat at the top of the food chain.

Luna held her breath as every bear mauling she'd ever seen on TV flashed in her mind. It had been a while since her last trip out here to the forest and now it might be her last because she'd not prepared properly. Great.

Definitely bringing bear repellent next time. And an old-fashioned compass.

Slowly, she backed up a step, then another, and another, until she bumped into Mark and nearly screamed.

"Just a black bear," he whispered near her ear, his warm breath on his skin nearly as unsettling as the wild animal in front of her as he gently rubbed his big hands up and down her arms. "You're okay."

Okay? That bear was the size of a bus as he wriggled around, letting out audible groans of ecstasy, latent power in his every move. Luna swallowed hard. "Does he even see us?"

The bear tipped his big, furry head toward them, studying her and Mark.

Guess that's a yes.

Reacting instinctively, Luna turned fast and burrowed her face into Mark's chest as his strong arms closed around her, warning him, "If you tell anyone about his, I'll kill you."

For once, he didn't even smile, his blue eyes unreadable as she looked up at him. "No worries. And anyway, I'm hard to kill."

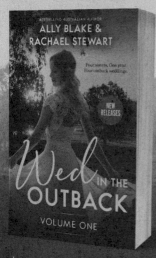 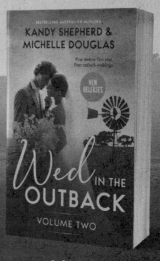

...ribe and ... in love with a Mills & Boon series today!

You'll be among the first to read stories delivered to your door monthly and enjoy great savings.